T0245281

Praise for *Seven Dials*

"One of the best [novels] that Perry has written . . . The sights, sounds, and smells of Alexandria are intensely communicated by Perry and transport us to that exotic locale."

—*The Historical Novels Review*

"Mesmerizing . . . another fascinating Victorian mystery."

—*Midwest Review of Books*

"*Seven Dials* is loaded with buried secrets. . . . Once you start [reading], you might as well plan on spending a day or two in bed—or on the couch—with Detective Pitt and his associates."

—Montreal *Gazette*

"Perry has an undeniable knack for suspense. . . . Her re-creation of the Victorian era is engrossing."

—*Omaha World-Herald*

"No matter which series she's writing about, Perry is really exploring issues of guilt and redemption, widening her scope to a global scale that gives her much more than just nineteenth-century London to worry about."

—*The Boston Globe*

"The intricacies of the plot are sustained by the well-developed supporting characters, from the unflappable Lady Vespasia, to the low-born but tenacious Gracie, the Pitts' maid."

—*Romantic Times* (Top Pick)

"Perry once again delivers a complex and satisfying tale that fans of the series will devour."

—*Publishers Weekly*

"[A] blend of Victorian social history, political intrigue, and exemplary detective work . . . As usual with Perry, the mystery ripples out in complications and new dangers."

—*Booklist*

BY ANNE PERRY

Featuring Charlotte and Thomas Pitt

The Cater Street Hangman
Callander Square
Paragon Walk
Resurrection Row
Bluegate Fields
Rutland Place
Death in the Devil's Acre
Cardington Crescent
Silence in Hanover Close
Bethlehem Road
Highgate Rise
Belgrave Square
Farriers' Lane
The Hyde Park Headsman
Traitors Gate
Pentecost Alley
Ashworth Hall
Brunswick Gardens
Bedford Square
Half Moon Street
The Whitechapel Conspiracy
Southampton Row
Seven Dials
Long Spoon Lane
Buckingham Palace Gardens
Treason at Lisson Grove
Dorchester Terrace
Midnight at Marble Arch
Death on Blackheath
The Angel Court Affair
Treachery at Lancaster Gate
Murder on the Serpentine

Featuring Daniel Pitt

Twenty-one Days

Featuring William Monk

The Face of a Stranger
A Dangerous Mourning
Defend and Betray
A Sudden, Fearful Death
The Sins of the Wolf
Cain His Brother
Weighed in the Balance
The Silent Cry
A Breach of Promise
The Twisted Root
Slaves of Obsession
Funeral in Blue
Death of a Stranger
The Shifting Tide
Dark Assassin
Execution Dock
Acceptable Loss
A Sunless Sea
Blind Justice
Blood on the Water
Corridors of the Night
Revenge in a Cold River
An Echo of Murder

ANNE PERRY

SEVEN DIALS

A CHARLOTTE AND THOMAS PITT NOVEL

Ballantine Books Trade Paperbacks
New York

Seven Dials is a work of fiction. Names, characters, places, and incidents are the products of the author's imagination or are used fictitiously. Any resemblance to actual events, locales, or persons, living or dead, is entirely coincidental.

2011 Ballantine Books Trade Paperback Edition

Published in the United States by Ballantine Books, an imprint of The Random House Publishing Group, a division of Random House, Inc., New York.

Originally published in hardcover in the United States by Ballantine Books, an imprint of The Random House Publishing Group, a division of Random House, Inc., in 2003.

Library of Congress Cataloging-in-Publication Data
Perry, Anne.
Seven dials / Anne Perry.
p. cm.
ISBN 978-0-345-52371-6
eBook ISBN 978-0-345-46352-4
1. Pitt, Charlotte (Fictitious character)—Fiction. 2. Women detectives—England—London—Fiction. 3. Pitt, Thomas (Fictitious character)—Fiction. 4. Police—England—London—Fiction. 5. London (England)—Fiction. 6. Police spouses—Fiction. I. Title.
PR6066.E693 S48 2003
823'.914—dc21 2002035605

www.ballantinebooks.com

Book design by Jaime Putorti

147028622

To Doris S. Platt in friendship

CHAPTER ONE

PITT OPENED HIS EYES but the thumping did not stop. The first gray of mid-September daylight showed through the curtains. It was not yet six, and there was someone at the front door.

Beside him, Charlotte stirred a little in her sleep. In a moment the knocking would waken her too.

He slid out of bed and moved quickly across the floor and onto the landing. He ran down the stairs in his bare feet, snatched his coat off the rack in the hall, and with one arm through the sleeve, unbolted the front door.

"Good morning, sir," Jesmond said apologetically, his hand still in the air to knock again. He was about twenty-four, seconded from one of the local London police stations to Special Branch, and he considered it to be a great promotion. "Sorry, sir," he went on. "But Mr. Narraway wants you, straightaway, like."

Pitt saw the waiting hansom just beyond him, the horse fidgeting a little, its breath hanging vapor in the air. "All right," he said with irritation. It was not a particularly interesting case he was on, but he had it nearly solved; only one or two small pieces remained. He did not want a distraction now. "Come in." He gestured behind him towards the passage to the kitchen. "If you know how, you can riddle the stove and put the kettle on."

"No time, sir, beggin' your pardon," Jesmond said grimly. "Can't tell you wot it's about, but Mr. Narraway said ter come right away." He stood firmly on the pavement as if remaining rooted to the spot would make Pitt leave with him even sooner.

Pitt sighed and went back in, closing the door to keep the damp air out. He climbed the stairs, doffing his coat, and by the time he was in the bedroom, pouring water out of the ewer into the basin, Charlotte was sitting up in bed pushing her heavy hair out of her eyes.

"What is it?" she asked, although after more than ten years of marriage to him, first when he was in the police, now the last few months in the Special Branch, she knew. She started to get out of bed.

"Don't," he said quickly. "There's no point."

"I'll get you a cup of tea, at least," she replied, ignoring him and standing on the rug beside the bed. "And some hot water to shave. It'll only take twenty minutes or so."

He put down the ewer and went over to her, touching her gently. "I'd have had the constable do it, if there were time. There isn't. You might as well go back to sleep . . . and keep warm." He slid his arms around her, holding her close to him. He kissed her, and then again. Then he stepped back and returned to the basin of cold water and began to wash and dress, ready to report to Victor Narraway, as far as he knew, the head of the Secret Service in Queen Victoria's vast empire. If there was anybody above him, Pitt did not know of it.

Outside, the streets were barely stirring. It was too early for cooks and parlor maids, but tweenies, bootboys, and footmen were about, carrying in fresh coal, taking deliveries of fish, vegetables, fruit, and poultry. Areaway doors were open and sculleries were brightly lit in the shadows of the widening dawn.

It was not very far from Keppel Street, where Pitt lived in a modest but very respectable part of Bloomsbury, to the discreet house where Narraway currently had his offices, but it was already daylight when Pitt went in and up the stairs. Jesmond remained below. He had apparently finished his task.

Narraway was sitting in the big armchair he seemed to take with him from one house to another. He was slender, wiry, and at least three inches shorter than Pitt. He had thick, dark hair, touched with gray at the temples, and eyes so dark they seemed black. He did not apologize for getting Pitt out of bed, as Cornwallis, Pitt's superior in the police, would have done.

"There's been a murder at Eden Lodge," he said quietly. His voice was low and very precise, his diction perfect. "This would be of no concern to us, except that the dead man is a junior diplomat, of no particular distinction, but he was shot in the garden of the Egyptian mistress of a senior cabinet minister, and it seems the minister was unfortunately present at the time." He stared levelly at Pitt.

Pitt took a deep breath. "Who shot him?" he asked.

Narraway's eyes did not blink. "That is what I wish you to find out, but so far it unfortunately looks as if Mr. Ryerson is involved, since the police do not seem to have found anyone else on the premises, apart from the usual domestic servants, who were in bed. And rather worse than that, the police arrived to find the woman actually attempting to dispose of the body."

"Very embarrassing," Pitt agreed dryly. "But I don't see what we can do about it. If the Egyptian woman shot him, diplomatic immunity doesn't stretch to cover murder, does it? Either way, we cannot affect it."

Pitt would have liked to add that he had no desire or intention of covering the fact that a cabinet minister had been present, but he very much feared that that was exactly what Narraway was going to ask him to do, for some perceived greater good of the government or the safety of some diplomatic negotiation. There were aspects of being in Special Branch that he disliked intensely, but ever since the business in Whitechapel he had had little choice. He had been dismissed from his position as head of the Bow Street station, and had accepted secondment to Special Branch as protection for himself from the persecution that had followed his exposure of the Inner Circle's power and its crimes. His new assignment was the only avenue open to him in which he could use his skills to earn a living for himself and his family.

Narraway gave a slight smile, no more than an acknowledgment of a certain irony.

"Just go and find out, Pitt. She's been taken to the Edgware Road police station. The house is on Connaught Square, apparently. Somebody is spending a good deal of money on it."

Pitt gritted his teeth. "Mr. Ryerson, I presume, if she is his mistress. I suppose you are not saying that loosely?"

Narraway sighed. "Go and find out, Pitt. We need the truth before we can do anything about it. Stop weighing it and judging, and go and do your job."

"Yes, sir," Pitt said tartly, standing a little straighter for an instant before turning on his heel and going out, thrusting his hands into his jacket pockets and pushing the entire garment out of shape.

He set out along the street westward towards Hyde Park and the Edgware Road, intending to pick up a hansom as soon as he saw one.

There were more people around now, more traffic in the streets. He passed a newsboy with the earliest edition, headlining the threat of strikes in the cotton mills of Manchester. This problem had been grumbling on for a while, and looked like it was getting worse. Processing cotton was the biggest industry in the whole of the West Midlands, and tens of thousands of people made their living from it, one way or another. The raw cotton was imported from Egypt and woven, dyed and manufactured into goods there, then sold again all over the world. The damage of a strike would spread wide and deep.

There was a woman on the corner of the street selling hot coffee. The sky was calm and still, shredded with ragged clouds, but he was chilled enough to find the prospect of a hot drink welcome. There could well be no time for breakfast. He stopped.

"Mornin', sir," she said cheerfully, grinning to show two missing teeth. "Lovely day, sir. But a nip in the air, eh? 'Ow abaht an 'ot cup ter start the mornin'?"

"Yes, please."

"That'll be tuppence, sir." She held out a gnarled hand, fingers dark with the stain of the beans.

He gave her the money, and accepted the steaming coffee in return. He stood on the pavement, drinking slowly and thinking how he could approach the police when he reached the Edgware Road station. They would resent his interference, even if the case threatened to be so ugly they would be glad to pass the blame on to someone else. He knew how he had felt when he was in charge of Bow Street. Good or bad, he wanted to handle cases himself, not have his judgment overridden by senior officers who knew less of the area, of the details of the evidence, and who had not even met the people concerned, let alone questioned them, seen where they lived, who they cared for, loved, feared, or hated.

The cases he had handled so far in Special Branch were largely preventative: matters of finding men likely to incite violence and stir up the cold, hungry, and impoverished into riot. Occasionally he had been involved in the search for an anarchist or potential bomber. The Special Branch had been formed originally to combat the Irish Problem, and had had a certain degree of success, at least in keeping violence under control. Now its remit was against any threat to the security of the country, so possibly the fall of a major government figure could be scraped into that category.

He finished the coffee and handed the mug back to the woman, thanking her and continuing along the pavement. He took the last few yards at a run as he saw an empty hansom stop at the intersection, and he hailed the driver.

At the Edgware Road station an Inspector Talbot was in

charge of the case and received Pitt in his office with barely concealed impatience. He was a man of middle height, lean as a whippet, with sad, slightly faded blue eyes. He stood behind his desk, piled with neatly handwritten reports, and stared at Pitt, waiting for him to speak.

"Thomas Pitt from Special Branch," Pitt introduced himself, offering his card to prove his identity.

Talbot's face tightened, but he waved a hand for Pitt to sit down in one of the rigid, hard-backed chairs. "It's a clean case," Talbot said flatly. "The evidence is pretty hard to misunderstand. The woman was found with the body, trying to move it. It was her gun that shot him, and it was in the barrow beside the body. Thanks to someone's quick thought, we got her in the act." The expression in his face was a challenge, daring Pitt to contradict such blatant facts.

"Whose honesty?" Pitt asked, but his stomach knotted up with foreknowledge of a kind of hopelessness already. This was going to be simple, ordinary and ugly, and as Talbot said, there was no way of evading it.

"Don't know," Talbot replied. "Someone raised the alarm. Heard the shots, they said."

"Raised the alarm how?" Pitt asked, a tiny prickle of curiosity awakened in him.

"Telephone," Talbot answered, catching Pitt's meaning instantly. "Narrows it down a bit, doesn't it? Before you ask, we don't know who. Wouldn't give a name, and apart from that, the caller was so alarmed the voice was hoarse—and so up and down the operator couldn't even say for sure whether it was a man or a woman."

"So the caller was close enough to be certain it was shots," Pitt concluded immediately. "How many houses have telephones within a hundred yards of Eden Lodge?"

Talbot pulled his mouth into a grimace. "Quite a few. Within a hundred and fifty yards, then, probably fifteen or twenty. It's a very nice area, lot of money. We'll try asking, of course, but the fact the caller didn't give a name means he or she wants to keep well out of it." He shrugged. "Pity. Might have seen something, but I suppose more likely they didn't. Body was found in the garden, well concealed by shrubbery, all leaves still on the trees, barely beginning to turn color. Laurels and stuff on the ground, evergreens."

"But you found it straightaway," Pitt pointed out.

"Could hardly miss it," Talbot said ruefully. "She was standing there in a long white dress, with the dead man draped over a wheelbarrow in front of her, like she'd just dropped the handles when she heard the constable coming."

Pitt tried to picture it in his imagination, the dense blackness of the garden in the middle of the night, the crowding leaves, the damp earth, a woman in an evening gown with a corpse in a wheelbarrow.

"There's nothing for you to do," Talbot interrupted.

"Possibly." Pitt refused to be dismissed. "You said there was a gun?"

"Yes. She admitted it was her gun. Had more sense than to try and deny it. Handsome thing, engraved handle. Still warm, and smelled of powder. There's no doubt it was what killed him."

"Could it have been an accident?" Pitt asked without any real hope.

Talbot gave a little grunt. "At twenty yards, possibly, but he was shot within a few feet. And what would a woman like that be doing out in the garden with a gun at three in the morning, except on purpose?"

"Was he shot outside?" Pitt asked quickly. Was Talbot making assumptions, possibly wrong?

Talbot smiled very slightly, only a twitch of the lips. "Either that or he was left lying outside for some time afterwards; there was blood on the ground. And none inside, by the way." His expression tightened, his eyes bright and pale. "Takes a lot of explaining, doesn't it?"

Pitt said nothing. What on earth did Narraway expect him to

do? If Ryerson's mistress had shot this man, there was no reason why Special Branch should even think of protecting her, much less lie to do it.

"Who was he?" he said aloud.

Talbot leaned back against the wall. "I was wondering when you'd ask that. Edwin Lovat, ex–army officer and minor diplomat with an apparently good record behind him, and until last night, a promising future ahead. Good family, no enemies that we've found so far, no debts that we know of yet." He stopped, waiting for Pitt to ask the next question.

Pitt concealed his irritation. "So why should this Egyptian woman shoot him, in or out of her house? I assume there was no question of his trying to break in?"

Talbot's eyebrows shot up, wrinkling his forehead. "Why on earth should he do that?"

"I've no idea," Pitt replied tersely. "Why should she be outside in the garden with a gun? None of it makes any sense!"

"Oh, yes it does!" Talbot retorted fiercely, sitting forward and putting his elbows on the desk. "He served with the army in Egypt. Alexandria, to be precise. Which is where she comes from. Who knows what goes on in the minds of women there? They're not like white women, you know. But she's definitely moved up a bit now. She's the mistress of a cabinet minister, Member of Parliament for a Manchester constituency, where all the trouble is over cotton at the moment. She's not got time for the likes of an ex-soldier who's only on the bottom rung of the diplomatic ladder. I daresay he was less keen in taking no for an answer, and she didn't want him interfering in her new affair and upsetting Mr. Ryerson with tales of her past."

"Any evidence of that?" Pitt asked. He was angry, and he wanted to prove Talbot prejudiced and inaccurate, but he could not dislike him totally; in fact, he could not seriously dislike him at all. The man was faced with a task in which he could not satisfy his superiors and still keep any kind of honor. Neither would he keep the confidence of the men he commanded, and with whom he would have to work for months and years after this affair was over. What would Pitt have done in the same circumstances? He honestly did not know. He would have been angry as well, casting around for answers, his thoughts leaping ahead of facts.

"Of course there isn't!" Talbot responded. "But I'll lay you a pound to a penny that if Special Branch, or someone like them, doesn't charge in and prevent me, I will have such evidence in a day or two. The crime's only four hours old!"

Pitt knew he was being unfair.

"How did you identify him?" he asked.

"He had cards on him," Talbot said simply, sitting back upright again. "She was going to dispose of the body. She hadn't even bothered to remove them."

"Is that what she said?"

"For God's sake, man!" Talbot exploded. "She was caught in the garden with his body in a wheelbarrow! What else was she going to do with him? She wasn't taking him to a doctor. He was already dead. She didn't call the police, as an innocent woman would have done; she fetched the gardener's barrow, heaved him into it, and started to wheel him away."

"To go where?" Pitt asked, trying to imagine what had been in the woman's mind, apart from hysteria.

Talbot looked slightly discomfited. "She won't say," he replied.

Pitt raised his eyebrows. "And what about Mr. Ryerson?"

"I haven't asked!" Talbot snapped. "And I don't want to know! He wasn't on the scene when the police got there. He arrived a few moments afterwards."

"What?" Pitt said incredulously.

Talbot colored. "He arrived a few moments afterwards," he repeated stubbornly.

"He just happened to be passing at three in the morning, saw the light of the constable's bull's-eye shining on a woman with a corpse in a wheelbarrow, so he stopped to see if he could help?"

Pitt said with heavy sarcasm. "He did arrive in a carriage, from the street, I assume? He didn't by any chance come out of the house—in his nightshirt!"

"No, he did not!" Talbot retorted hotly, his thin face flushing. "He was fully dressed, and he walked over from the direction of the street."

"Where his carriage was waiting, no doubt?"

"He said he came by hansom," Talbot answered.

"Intending to call on the lady, only to find her conspicuously unprepared!" Pitt observed waspishly. "And you believe him?"

"What choice do I have?" Talbot raised his voice for the first time, his desperation ragged through his rapidly slipping composure. "It's idiotic, I know that! Of course he was there. He was actually coming from the mews, where I imagine he'd gone to harness up a horse and hitch it to a trap, or whatever she has, to take the body somewhere and get rid of it. They're only a stone's throw from Hyde Park. That would do. It would be found, of course, but there would be nothing to connect it with either of them. But we got there too soon. We didn't see him with her, and she isn't saying anything."

"And you don't ask him because you don't want to know," Pitt finished for him.

"Something like that," Talbot admitted, his eyes hot and wretched. "But if you want to, then Special Branch is very welcome. Have it! Have it all! Go and ask him. He lives in Paulton Square, Chelsea. I don't know the number, but you can ask. There can't be many cabinet ministers there."

"I'll see the Egyptian woman first. What is her name?"

"Ayesha Zakhari," Talbot replied. "But you can't see her. That's my orders from the top, and Special Branch or not, I'm not letting you in. She hasn't implicated Mr. Ryerson, so you've no brief here. If her embassy says anything it'll be a matter for the Foreign Office, or the Lord Chancellor, or whoever. But so far they haven't. She's just an ordinary woman arrested for the murder of an old lover, and there's no reasonable doubt that she did it. That's how it is, sir—and that's how it's staying, as far as I'm concerned. If you want to make it different, you'll have to do it somewhere else, 'cos you're not doing it here."

Pitt pushed his hands into his trouser pockets, finding a small piece of string, half a dozen coins, a bull's-eye sweet wrapped in paper, two odd lumps of sealing wax, a penknife, and three safety pins. In the other were a notebook, a stub end of pencil, and two handkerchiefs. It flicked through his mind that that was too much.

Talbot stared at him. For the first time Pitt saw in his face that he was frightened. He had cause to be. If he were wrong, either for Ryerson or against him, not a matter of fact but of judgment, he would be ruined. He would take the blame, possibly for others' mistakes, men of greater power and with more to lose.

"So Mr. Ryerson is at home?" Pitt asked.

"As far as I know," Talbot said. "He certainly isn't here. We asked him if he could help us, and he said he couldn't. He said he thought Miss Zakhari was innocent. He didn't believe she would have killed anyone, unless they were threatening her life, in which case it wouldn't be a crime." He shrugged. "I could have written it all down without bothering to ask him. He said the only thing he could—he doesn't know anything about it, he only just arrived—to protect her honor, and all that. Decent men don't say a woman's a whore, even if she is and we all know it. He said she wouldn't have killed anyone without a reason, but then he wouldn't say she had, would he? Apart from anything else, it would make him look like he was betraying her—and that his mistress, which we all know that she is, was a likely murderess and he knew it. And as I said, she didn't deny the gun was hers. We asked the manservant she has, and he admitted it as well. He kept it clean and oiled, and so on."

"Why did she have a gun?"

Talbot spread his hands. "God knows! She did, that's all that matters. Look, sir—Constable Black found her in the garden with the murdered body of an old lover of hers stuck in a wheelbarrow. What more do you want of us?"

"Nothing," Pitt conceded. "Thank you for your patience, Inspector Talbot. If there's anything further I'll come back." He hesitated a moment, then smiled. "Good luck."

Talbot rolled his eyes, but his expression softened for a moment. "Thank you," he said with a touch of sarcasm. "I wish I could walk away from it so easily."

Pitt grinned, and went to the door with a feeling of overwhelming relief. Talbot, poor man, was welcome to what was almost certainly no more than a domestic tragedy after all, cabinet minister notwithstanding.

All the same, Pitt decided that he would walk past Eden Lodge and look at it before going back to report to Narraway. Connaught Square was less than ten minutes away and it was now a very pleasant early morning. More deliverymen were out and the clip of horses' hooves was sharp in the air. In the areaway of one large house a between-stairs maid of about fourteen was whacking a red-and-blue rug with enthusiasm and sending a fine cloud of dust up into the sunlight. He wondered if it was just exuberance or if the rug stood in for someone she disliked.

He crossed the road, cobbles still gleaming in the dew, and threw a penny to one of the small boys who swept away the manure when the need arose. It was too early for the boy to have much to do yet, and he leaned on his broom, his flat cap a couple of sizes too big for him, and resting on his ears.

"Ta, mister!" he called back with a grin.

Eden Lodge was an imposing house facing the open space of Connaught Square, and with a further wide view of St. George's Burial Ground behind it, beyond the mews. It might be interesting to find out whether Miss Zakhari owned it or rented it, and if the latter, from whom? Or possibly they had not bothered to be so discreet, and it was simply owned by Ryerson in the first place.

But of more importance now was to see the garden where Miss Zakhari had been found with the corpse. For that it would be necessary to walk the short distance to the end of the block and around to the back.

There was a constable on duty in the mews, and Pitt identified himself before being permitted to go through the gate beside the stables and into the leafy, damp garden. He kept to the path, although there was little to mask or spoil in the way of evidence. The wooden wheelbarrow was still there, smears of blood down the right side, from where the person pushing it would have stood, and a dark pool, almost congealed, in the bottom. The dead man must have been laid across it with his head on that side and his legs over the other.

Pitt bent and looked more closely at the ground. The wheel was sunk almost an inch deep in the loam, witnessing the weight of the load. The rut it had caused was deep for about three yards, and from that point there were tracks from where it had come, empty, been turned around and loaded. He straightened up and walked the few yards. Faint scuff marks, indistinct, showed where feet had stood and swiveled, but it was impossible even to tell how many, let alone whether they were a man's or woman's, or both. The earth was scattered with fallen leaves and twigs and occasional small pebbles, leaving only rough traces of passage.

However, when Pitt looked more closely the rusty mark of blood was clear enough. This was where Lovat had been when he fell.

He stared around him. He was about five yards into the garden, between laurel and rhododendron bushes, and in the dappled shade of birches towering a great deal higher. He was completely concealed from the mews, and obviously from the street, by the bulk of the house itself. He was a good five yards from the stone wall which concealed the back entrance to the scullery and areaway, and ahead of him across a strip of open lawn edged by flowers was a French door to the main part of the house.

What on earth had Edwin Lovat been doing here? It seemed unlikely he had arrived through the mews and was intending to enter this way, unless by prior arrangement, and she had been waiting for him inside the French doors. If she had not wished to see him, it would have been simple enough not to have answered. Servants could have dismissed him, and thrown him out if necessary.

If he were indeed arriving, it looked unpleasantly as if she had lured him here deliberately, with the intent of killing him, since she was in the garden with a loaded gun.

Or else he had been leaving, they had quarreled, and she had followed him out, again with the gun.

When had Ryerson really arrived? Before the shooting or after? Had she lifted the dead man into the wheelbarrow by herself? It would be interesting to find out his size and weight, and hers. If she had lifted him, then there would be blood, and perhaps earth, on her white dress. These were questions he needed to ask Talbot, or perhaps the constable who had actually been first on the scene.

He turned and walked back through the gate to the mews and found the constable standing fidgeting from one foot to the other in boredom. He turned as he heard the gate catch.

"Were you on duty here last night?" Pitt asked. The man looked tired enough to have been up many hours.

"Yes, sir."

"Did you see the arrest of Miss Zakhari?"

"Yes, sir." His voice lifted a little with the beginning of interest.

"Can you describe her for me?"

He looked startled for a moment, then his face puckered in concentration. "She was quite tall, sir, but very slender, like. And foreign, o' course, very foreign, like. She was . . . well, she moved very graceful, more than most ladies—not that they aren't—"

"It's all right, Constable," Pitt answered him. "I need honesty, not tact. What about the dead man? How large was he?"

"Oh, bit bigger than most, sir, broad in the chest, like. Difficult ter say 'ow tall 'cos I never saw 'im standin' up, but I reckon a bit taller 'n me, but not as tall as you."

"Did the mortuary wagon take him away?"

"Yessir."

"How many men to carry him?"

"Two, sir." His face filled with understanding. "You thinkin' as she couldn't 'ave put 'im in that barrer by 'erself?"

"Yes, I was." Pitt tightened his lips. "But it might be wiser not to express that opinion to others, at least for the time being. She was wearing white, so I'm told. Is that correct?"

"Yessir. Very sort o' close-fittin' dress it were, not exactly like most ladies wear, least wot I've seen. Very beautiful . . ." He colored faintly, considering the propriety of saying that a murderess was beautiful, and a foreign one at that. But he refused to be cowed. "Sort o' more natural, like," he went on. "No . . ." He put one hand on his other shoulder. "No puffs up 'ere. More wot a woman's really shaped like."

Pitt hid a smile. "I see. And was it stained with mud, or blood, this white dress?"

"Bit o' mud, or more like leaf dirt," the constable agreed.

"Where?"

"Around the knees, sir. Like she knelt on the ground."

"But no blood?"

"No, sir. Not that I saw." His eyes widened. "You're sayin' as she didn't put 'im in that barrer 'erself!"

"No, Constable, I think you are. But I'd be very obliged if you did not repeat that, unless you are asked to do so in a situation where not doing so would require you to lie. Don't lie to anyone."

"No, sir! I'll 'ope as I'm not asked."

"Yes, that would definitely be the best," Pitt agreed fervently. "Thank you, Constable. What is your name?"

"Cotter, sir."

"Is the manservant still in the house?"

"Yessir. No one's come out since they took 'er away."

"Then I shall go and speak to him. Do you know his name?"

"No, sir. Foreign-looking person."

Pitt thanked him again and walked across the short distance to the back door. He knocked firmly and waited several minutes before it was opened by a dark-skinned man dressed in pale, stone-colored robes. Most of his head was covered with a turban, but his beard was turning gray. His eyes were almost black.

"Yes, sir?" he said guardedly.

"Good morning," Pitt replied. "Are you Miss Zakhari's manservant?"

"Yes, sir. But Miss Zakhari is not at home." It was said with finality, as if that were the end of any possible discussion. He was obviously preparing to close the door.

"I am aware of that!" Pitt said sharply. "What is your name?"

"Tariq el Abd, sir," the man replied.

Pitt produced his card again and held it out, assuming that el Abd could read English. "I am from Special Branch. I believe the police have already spoken to you, but I need to ask you a few further questions."

"Oh, I see." He pulled the door wider open and reluctantly permitted Pitt to go through the scullery and up a step into a warm and exotically fragrant kitchen. There was no one else there. Presumably, el Abd did such cooking as was required, and other household staff who did the laundry and cleaning came in daily.

"Would you like coffee, sir?" el Abd enquired graciously, as if the kitchen were his. His voice was low and he spoke almost without accent.

"Thank you," Pitt accepted, more out of curiosity than a desire for more coffee. There was a smell of spices in the air, and of strange-shaped loaves of bread cooling on a rack near the farther window. Unfamiliar fruit lay rich and burnished in a bowl on the table.

El Abd took only a few moments to heat the coffee to the desired temperature again and bring a tiny cup of it over to present to Pitt, offering him a seat and enquiring after his comfort. He was a lean man who moved with a silent grace that made his age difficult to estimate, but the weathered skin of his hands made Pitt guess him to be well over forty, perhaps closer to fifty.

Pitt thanked him for the coffee and sipped it. It was so strong as to be almost a syrup, and he did not care for it much, but he kept all expression from his face except polite enquiry.

"What happened here last night?" he asked.

El Abd remained standing, so Pitt was forced to look up at him.

"I do not know, sir," the manservant replied. "Something awakened me, and I arose to see if Miss Zakhari had called, but I could not find her anywhere in the house." He hesitated.

"Yes?" Pitt prompted him.

El Abd looked down at the floor. "I went to the window and I saw nothing to the front, so I went to the back, and I saw movement through the bushes, the ones with the flat, shining leaves. I waited a few moments, but there was no more sound, and I knew of no reason to suppose there was anything wrong. I thought then that perhaps it was only the sound of the door that had wakened me."

"What did you do then?"

He lifted his shoulders slightly. "I was not required, sir. I went back to my bed. I do not know how long it was until I heard the people speaking, and the police called me downstairs."

"Did they show you a gun?"

"Yes, sir."

"And ask you whose it was?"

"Yes, sir. I said it was Miss Zakhari's." He looked down at the floor. "I did not know then what it had been used for. But I clean it and oil it, so of course I know it well."

"Why does Miss Zakhari have a gun?"

"It is not my place to ask such questions, sir."

"And you don't know?"

"No, sir."

"I see. But you would know if she had ever fired it before, since you clean it."

"No, sir, she has not."

"Thank you. Did you know Lovat . . . the dead man?"

"I do not think he has been here before."

That was not precisely what Pitt had asked, and he was aware of the evasion. Was it deliberate, or simply a result of the fact that the man was speaking a language other than his own?

"Have you seen him before?"

El Abd lowered his eyes. "I have not seen him at all, sir. It is my understanding that the policeman knew who he was from his clothes and the things in his pockets."

So they had not asked el Abd if he had seen Lovat before. That was an omission, but perhaps not one that would make a great deal of difference. He was Miss Zakhari's servant. Now that he knew she was accused of murdering Lovat, he would probably deny knowledge of him anyway.

Pitt finished his coffee and rose to his feet. "Thank you," he said, trying to swallow the last of the sweet, sticky liquid and clean his mouth of the taste.

"Sir." El Abd bowed very slightly, no more than a gesture.

Pitt went out of the back door, thanking Constable Cotter as he passed him. Then he walked along the mews and around the corner into Connaught Square, where he looked for a hansom to take him back to Narraway.

"WELL?" Narraway looked up from the papers he was reading. His face was a little pinched, his eyes anxious.

"The police are holding the woman, Ayesha Zakhari, and completely ignoring Ryerson," Pitt told him. "They aren't investigating it too closely because they don't want to know the answer." He walked over and sat down in the chair in front of Narraway's desk.

Narraway breathed in deeply, and then out again. "And what

are the answers?" he asked, his voice quiet and very level. There was a stillness about him, as if his attention were so vivid he dared not distract himself by even the slightest action.

Pitt found himself unconsciously copying, refraining from crossing one leg over the other.

"That Ryerson helped her, at least in attempting to dispose of the body," he replied.

"Indeed . . ." Narraway breathed out slowly, but none of the tension disappeared from him. "And what evidence told you that?"

"She is a slender woman, at the time wearing a white dress," Pitt replied. "The dead man was slightly over average height and weight. It took two mortuary attendants to lift him from the barrow into the wagon, although of course they may have been more careful with him than whoever was trying to dispose of him."

Narraway nodded, his lips tight.

"But her white dress was not stained with mud or blood," Pitt went on. "Only a little leaf mold from where she had knelt on the ground, possibly beside him where he lay."

"I see." Narraway's voice was tight. "And Ryerson?"

"I didn't ask," Pitt said. "The constable was quite aware of why I enquired, and of the obvious conclusions. Do you want me to go back and ask him? I can do so perfectly easily, but it will then—"

"I can work that out for myself, Pitt!" Narraway snapped. "No. I do not want you to do that . . . at least not yet." His eyes flickered for a moment, then he looked over at the far wall. "We'll see what happens."

Pitt sat still, aware of a curious, unfinished air in the room, as if elusive but powerful things were just beyond the edge of perception. Narraway had left something unsaid. Did it matter? Or was it just an accumulation of knowledge gathered over the years, a feeling of unease rather than a thought?

Narraway hesitated also, then the moment passed and he looked up at Pitt again. "Well, go on," he said, but with less asperity than before. "You've told me what you saw and what the constable reported. We'll save Ryerson from himself, if we can. The next move is up to the police. Go home and have breakfast. I might want you later."

Pitt stood up, still looking at Narraway, who stared back at him—his eyes bright, almost blank of emotion, but with deliberate concealment. Pitt was as certain of that as he was of the charge in the room, like electricity in the air on a sultry day.

"Yes, sir," he said quietly, and with Narraway still looking at him, he went out of the door.

WHEN HE GOT HOME, it was late morning. His children, Jemima and Daniel, were at school, and Charlotte and the maid, Gracie, were in the kitchen. He heard their laughter the moment he opened the front door. He smiled to himself as he bent and took off his boots. The sounds washed around him like a balm: women's voices, the clatter of pans, a kettle whistling shrilly. The house was warm from the kitchen stove, and there was an odor of freshly laundered cotton, still a little damp, clean wood from the scrubbed floor, and baking bread.

A marmalade-striped cat came out of the kitchen doorway and stretched luxuriously, then trotted towards him, tail up in a question mark.

"Hello, Archie," Pitt said softly, stroking the animal as it swiveled under his hand, pressing against him and purring. "I suppose you want half my breakfast?" he went on. "Well, come on then." He stood up and walked silently down to the doorway, the cat following.

In the kitchen, Charlotte was tipping bread out of its tin onto a rack to cool, and Gracie, still small and thin although she was now well over twenty, was putting clean blue-and-white china away on the Welsh dresser.

Sensing his presence rather than seeing him, Charlotte turned around, questions in her face.

"Breakfast," he replied with a smile.

Gracie did not ask anything. She was outspoken enough once she was involved. She did not regard that as impertinence, rather the role of helping and looking after him, which she had taken upon herself almost from the time she had arrived in the household, at the age of thirteen, half starved, and with all her clothes too big for her. Her hair had been scraped back off her bright little face, and although then she could neither read nor write, she had a wit as sharp as any.

Now she was far more mature, and considered herself to be an invaluable employee of the cleverest detective in England, or anywhere else, a position she would not have exchanged for one in service to the Queen herself.

"It's not the Inner Circle again, is it?" Charlotte said with an edge of fear in her voice.

Gracie stood frozen, the dishes in her hands. No one had forgotten that dreadful, secret organization which had cost Pitt his career in the Metropolitan Police—and very nearly his life also.

"No," Pitt said immediately and with certainty. "It's a simple domestic murder." He saw the disbelief in her face. "Almost certainly committed by a woman who is the mistress of a senior government minister," he added. "Equally certain he was there, if not at the time, then immediately afterwards, and helped her attempt to get rid of the body."

"Oh!" she said with instant perception. "I see. But they didn't get away with it?"

"No." He sat down on one of the straight-backed wooden chairs and stretched out his legs. "The alarm was raised by someone who heard the shots, and the police arrived in time to catch her in the back garden with the corpse in a wheelbarrow."

She stared at him in a moment's disbelief, then saw from his eyes that he was not joking.

"Must be a bleedin' idjut!" Gracie said candidly. "I 'ope 'e in't in charge o' summink wot matters in the gov'ment, or we'll all be in the muck!"

"Yes," Pitt agreed with feeling. The cat leapt up onto his knee and he stroked it absently, fingers gentle in the deep fur. "I'm afraid we will."

Gracie sighed and started to sort out the dishes he would need for breakfast, and to make him a cup of tea first. Charlotte went to the stove to begin cooking, her face eloquent of the trouble she could foresee.

CHAPTER TWO

THE EVENING NEWSPAPERS had carried a brief account of the finding of Edwin Lovat's body at Eden Lodge; however, the following morning they were full of the murder in detail.

"There you are!" Gracie said, presenting the *Times* and the *London Illustrated News* to Pitt at the breakfast table. "All over the place, it is. Says the foreign woman did it, an' the man wot's dead was real respectable, like, an' all." Charlotte had taught her to read, and it was an accomplishment of which the maid was extremely proud. A door had been opened into new worlds previously beyond even her imagination, but more important than that, she felt she could face anyone at all on an intellectually, even if not socially, equal footing. What she did not know, she would find out. She could read, therefore she could learn. "Doesn't say nothin' 'bout the gov'ment man at all!" she added.

Pitt took both papers from her and looked at them for himself, spreading the pages wide over half the table. Charlotte was still upstairs. Jemima came in looking very grown up with her hair in pigtails and her school pinafore on over her dress. She was ten years old, and very self-possessed, at least on the surface. She was growing tall, and the slight heels on her buttoned-up boots added to her height.

"Morning, Papa," she said demurely, standing in front of him and waiting for his reply.

He looked up, ignoring the newspaper, aware that she required his attention, more especially lately, since their adventure in Dartmoor, when their lives had been in danger and for the first time he had been unable to protect them himself. His sergeant, Tellman, had done an excellent job, at considerable risk to his own career. He was still at the Bow Street station, now under a new superintendent, a man named Wetron. Wetron was cold and ambitious, and with good cause; they believed him to be a senior member of the Inner Circle, possibly even with eyes on the leadership.

"Good morning," he replied gravely, looking up at her.

"Is there something important in there?" she asked, glancing for a moment at the paper spread across the table.

He hesitated only a moment. His instinct was always to protect both his children, but especially Jemima, perhaps because she was a girl. But Charlotte had told him that evasion and mystery were far more frightening than all but the very worst facts, and being excluded, even for the best of reasons, hurt. And Jemima especially nearly always understood if she were being shut out. Daniel was two years younger, and far more self-contained, happier to go about his own affairs, less reflective of Pitt's mood. He watched and listened, but not as she did.

"I don't think it will be," he said frankly.

"Is it your case?" she pressed, watching him solemnly.

"It's not a dangerous one," he assured her, smiling as he said it. "A lady seems to have shot someone, and an important man might have been there at the time. We have to do what we can to see that he doesn't get into trouble."

"Why?" she asked.

"That is a good question," he agreed. "Because he is in the government, and it would be embarrassing."

"Should he have been somewhere else?" she said, seeing the point immediately.

"Yes. He should have been at home in bed. It happened in the middle of the night."

"Why did she shoot him? Was she afraid of him?" It was the obvious thought to her. A few months ago she had known what it was like to get up in the middle of the night, pack all your belongings and run away in a pony cart along the edge of the moor in the dark.

"I don't know, sweetheart," he said, putting out his hand and touching her smooth, blemishless cheek. "She hasn't said anything yet. We still have to find out. It's just like police work, the way I used to do it a year ago, before I went to Whitechapel. There's nothing dangerous in it at all."

She looked at him steadily, deciding if he was telling her the truth or not. She concluded he was, and her face lit with satisfaction. "Good." Without waiting any longer she sat down in her own place at the table. Gracie put her porridge in front of her, with milk and sugar, and she began to eat.

Pitt returned his attention to the newspaper. The *Times* article was unequivocal. It gave a glowing obituary to Edwin Lovat, lauding him as a distinguished soldier before illness had obliged him to return to civilian life, where he had used his skills and experience in the Near East to great effect in the diplomatic service. A bright future had lain ahead of him until he was cruelly cut down by an ambitious and ruthless woman who had grown tired of his attentions and desired to seek richer and more influential patronage.

Saville Ryerson's name was not mentioned, even by implication. Exactly what patronage the murderess had sought was left to the imagination of the reader. What was spelled out very clearly was her unquestionable guilt of the crime, and the fact that she should be tried for it, and hanged without argument or delay.

Pitt found the ease of assumption behind the paper's account disquieting, even though he knew far more than the writer of the article. There was an essential absurdity in denying the story, given that the murder weapon was Ayesha Zakhari's gun and she was discovered actually trying to dispose of the body. She knew the man, and had offered no excuse at all, reasonable or otherwise, for anything that had occurred.

Perhaps it was the failure to mention Ryerson which galled him, and the fact that the writer had not even enquired into the case, but had leapt to his conclusions rather than simply reporting the evidence.

Jemima looked at Pitt solemnly, and he smiled at her. He saw the tension ease in her shoulders, and she smiled back.

He finished his breakfast and stood up as Charlotte and Daniel came into the kitchen. The conversation turned to other things—the school day, what there would be for dinner, and the question of whether they would go to watch the cricket match on Saturday afternoon, as long as it was not rained off, or to the local outdoor theater, also if the weather permitted. An argument ensued as to what one could do in the rain, and ended only when both children left for school and Pitt set out to go to Narraway's office.

HE FOUND THE ROOMS empty and closed, but Jesmond, waiting on the curb, told him that Narraway would be back within an hour and would be angry if Pitt were not there waiting for him.

Pitt masked his impatience at the time wasted. He could have been closing the case he had been working on before this tragedy happened, which as far as he could see was irrelevant to Special Branch. He paced up and down the small room at the bottom of the stairs, turning the matter over and over in his mind, to no effect at all.

Narraway arrived forty-five minutes later, looking grim. He was wearing a beautifully cut light gray suit in the latest fashion, with high lapels, and a gray silk waistcoat underneath.

"Come in," he said briskly, unlocking the door of his room and leaving Pitt to follow. He sat down behind the desk without glancing at any of the papers on it, and Pitt realized he had already read them. He had been in early, and left to go somewhere important, which he had foreseen and dressed for accordingly. It had to be to see someone high in government. Did they really care about the murder of Edwin Lovat, or that Ayesha Zakhari should be blamed? Or had something else happened?

Pitt sat down in the opposite chair.

Narraway's face was tight, his eyes wide and wary, as if even here in his own room there were something to be guarded against.

"The Egyptian ambassador went to the Foreign Office late last night," he said in carefully measured words. "They, in turn, have spoken by telephone to Mr. Gladstone, and I was sent for this morning."

Pitt waited without interrupting, the chill growing inside him.

"They were aware of the murder in Eden Lodge by yesterday afternoon," Narraway continued. "But it was in the afternoon papers, so half of London knew of it." He stopped again. Pitt noticed that Narraway's hands were stiff on the desk, his slender fingers rigid.

"And the embassy knew that Ayesha Zakhari was arrested," Pitt concluded. "Since she is an Egyptian citizen, I suppose it is natural for them to enquire after her well-being, and ensure that she was properly represented. I would expect as much of the British embassy were I arrested in a foreign country."

Narraway's mouth twisted a little. "You would expect the British ambassador to call the first minister of that country on your behalf? You overrate yourself, Pitt. A junior consul might see that you were appointed a lawyer, but not more than that."

There was no time to be embarrassed or annoyed. Obviously something had happened that worried Narraway profoundly.

"Does Miss Zakhari have some importance that we were unaware of?" Pitt asked.

"Not so far as I know," Narraway replied. "Although it does raise the question." His expression of anxiety deepened. His fingers curled and uncurled, as if he were making sure he could still feel them. "The question raised was one of justice." He took a deep breath, as though it was difficult for him to say this, even to Pitt. "The ambassador was aware that Saville Ryerson was at Eden Lodge when the police found Miss Zakhari with the body, and they want to know why he was not arrested also."

It was a perfectly reasonable question, but that was not the thought that rippled through Pitt like fire in the bones. "How did they know that?" he asked. "Surely no one allowed her to contact her embassy and say such a thing? Anyway, didn't she tell the police at the time that she was alone? Who told the ambassador?"

Narraway's mouth twisted in a bitter smile and his eyes were hard. "An excellent question, Pitt. In fact, it is the principal question, and I don't know the answer. Except that it was not the police, nor was it any lawyer of Miss Zakhari's, because she has not yet asked for one. And Inspector Talbot assures me that she has not answered any further questions or mentioned Ryerson's name to anyone."

"What about the constable who was first on the scene . . . Cotter?"

"Believe me, Talbot has had him over the coals at least twice, and Cotter swears he spoke to no one outside the station, except you." There was no accusation in his voice, not even doubt.

"Which leaves us with our anonymous informer who heard the shots and called the police," Pitt concluded. "Apparently he—or she—remained around to see what happened, and presumably saw Ryerson and recognized him."

"It was hardly the first time he'd been there," Narraway pointed out. "They may have seen him on several occasions before." He frowned, his fingers still stiff on the tabletop. "But it raises further questions, beginning with why tell the Egyptian embassy and not the newspapers, who would almost certainly pay them?"

Pitt said nothing.

Narraway stared at him. "Or Ryerson, himself," Narraway went on. "Blackmail might net them a nice profit, and on a continuing basis."

"Would Ryerson pay?" Pitt asked.

A curious expression crossed Narraway's face: uncertainty, sadness, but something which was unquestionably painful. With an effort he wiped it away, concentrating on the practicalities of the answer. "Actually I doubt it, particularly since, if Miss Zakhari has chosen to deny he was there, he would be seen to be a liar when it came to court, because the police know he was there. He is a very recognizable figure."

"Is he? I don't think I've ever seen him." Pitt tried to bring him to mind, and could not.

"He's a big man," Narraway said very quietly, his voice a little raw. "Over six feet tall, broad-shouldered, powerful. He has thick, graying hair, and strong features. He was a fine athlete as a young man." His words were full of praise, and yet he said them as if he had to make himself do it, a matter of justice rather than desire. For some inner reason of his own he was compelled to be fair.

"Do you know him, sir?" Pitt asked, then instantly wished he had not, although it was a necessary question. There was something in Narraway's face which told him he had intruded.

"I know everyone," Narraway replied. "It is my job to know them. It is your job too. I am told that Mr. Gladstone desires us to keep Mr. Ryerson's name out of the case, if it is humanly possible. He has not specified how it is to be done, and I assume he does not wish to know."

Pitt could not conceal his anger at the injustice of it, and he resented the implication that he should try to. "Good!" he retorted. "Then if we are obliged to tell him that it was impossible, he will not have the information to argue with us."

There was not even a flicker of humor in Narraway's face; even the usual dry irony in his eyes was absent. In some way this touched a wound in him not yet healed enough to be safe. "It is I who will answer to Mr. Gladstone, Pitt, not you. And I am not prepared to tell him that we failed, unless I can prove that it was already impossible before we began. Go and see Ryerson himself. If we are to save him, then we cannot work blindly. I need the truth, and immediately, not as it is unearthed a piece at a time by the police. Or, God help us, by the Egyptian ambassador."

Pitt was confused. "You said you knew him. Would it not be far better for you to see him? Your seniority would impress on . . ."

Narraway looked up, his eyes angry, his slim hand white-knuckled on top of the desk. "My seniority doesn't seem to impress you. At least not sufficiently for you to obey me without putting up an argument. I am not making suggestions, Pitt, I am telling you what to do. And I do not propose to explain myself. I am accountable to Mr. Gladstone for my success, as I will answer to him for my failure. You are accountable to me." His voice rasped. "Go and see Ryerson. I want to know everything about his relationship with Miss Zakhari in general, and that night in particular. Come back here when you can tell me, preferably tomorrow."

"Yes, sir. Do you know where I will find Mr. Ryerson at this time of day? Or should I simply make enquiries?"

"No, you will not make enquiries!" Narraway snapped, a flush in his cheeks. "You will tell no one but Ryerson himself who you are or what you want. Begin at his home in Paulton Square. I believe it is number seven."

"Yes, sir. Thank you." Pitt kept his own emotions out of his voice. He turned on his heel and went out of the room, disliking his errand but not surprised by it. The thing that confused him was that concerning a matter so important, with Gladstone involved, why Narraway did not go to see Ryerson himself. The question of being recognized by anyone did not arise. No newspaper reporters would be in Paulton Square at this hour, but even if they were, Narraway was not a public figure to be known on sight.

There must be a factor, perhaps a major one, which Narraway was not telling him, and the knowledge made him uncomfortable.

He hailed a hansom and directed it to Danvers Street, just beyond Paulton Square. He would walk the rest of the way. Since being with Special Branch he had learned a kind of carefulness in being observed. It was a precaution, no more. He disliked the secrecy of it, but he understood its worth.

By the time he had reached the first steps of number seven he had decided how to approach whoever answered Ryerson's door.

"Good morning, sir," a fair-haired footman in full livery said without interest. "How may I help you?"

"Good morning," Pitt replied, standing upright and meeting the man's eyes. "Would you be good enough to tell Mr. Ryerson that Mr. Victor Narraway sends his regards, and regrets that he is unable to call himself, but has sent me in his place? My name is Thomas Pitt." He produced his card, the plain one that stated his name only, and dropped it on the silver tray in the footman's hand.

"Certainly, sir," the footman replied, without looking at the card. "Would you care to wait in the morning room while I enquire if Mr. Ryerson is able to see you?"

Pitt smiled and accepted. That was very direct, not the usual euphemism of pretending that he did not know whether his master was at home.

The footman led the way through a magnificent hall of an opulent Italianate design, terra-cotta-colored walls and handsome marble and bronze busts displayed on plinths, paintings of canal scenes on the walls, one of which looked like a genuine Canaletto.

The morning room was also in warm colors, with an exquisite tapestry on one wall that depicted a hunting scene in the minutest detail, the grass in the foreground starred with tiny flowers. This home belonged to a man of wealth and individual taste.

Pitt had ten minutes to wait in nervous tension, trying to rehearse the scene in his mind. He was about to question a cabinet minister regarding a possibly criminal, certainly embarrassing, part of his personal life. He had come to learn the truth and he could not afford to fail.

But he had questioned important people about their lives before, probing for the wounds that had led to murder. It was his skill. He was good at it, even brilliant. He had had far more successes than failures. He should not doubt himself now.

He glanced at the books in one of the cases. He saw Shakespeare, Browning, Marlowe, and a little farther along, Henry Rider Haggard and Charles Kingsley and two volumes of Thackeray.

Then he heard the door open and he swung around.

As Narraway had said, Ryerson was a large man, probably in his late fifties, but he moved with the grace of someone trained to physical activity and who took joy in it. There was no extra flesh on him, no signs of indulgence or ease. He had the innate confidence of one whose body does as he wishes it to. Now he looked anxious, a little tired, but still very much in command of his outward emotions.

"My footman tells me you have come on behalf of Victor Narraway." He pronounced the name with a lack of emotion so complete Pitt instantly wondered if it was the result of deliberate effort. "May I ask why?"

"Yes, sir," Pitt said gravely. He had already decided that candor was the only way to achieve his goal, if it was possible at all. One trick or attempt at deviousness which failed would destroy all trust. "The Egyptian embassy is aware that you were present at Eden Lodge when Mr. Edwin Lovat was shot, and they are demanding that you also are called to be accountable for your part in those events."

Pitt expected smooth denial at first, and then perhaps bluster, anger as fear took hold. The ugliest possibility would be self-pity, and the plea to some kind of loyalty to extricate him from the embarrassment of a love affair which had turned sour. He dreaded the shame and the revulsion of it. His skin felt cold even at the thought of it. Was that why Narraway had refused to come himself? In case an old friend should become contemptible in front of him, and he would find it better for both of them if that did not happen? Then he would still be able to feign ignorance of that much at least.

But Ryerson's reaction was none of these things. There was confusion in his face—fear, but not anger, and no bluster at all.

"I was there just after," he corrected Pitt. "Although I have no idea how the Egyptian embassy would know that, unless Miss Zakhari told them."

Pitt stared at him. There was no sense of injustice in his voice or his face. He did not seem to think of it as any kind of betrayal if she had done so. And yet, according to Narraway, she had not mentioned his name at all. In fact, she had had no opportunity of speaking to anyone except the police officers who had questioned her.

"No, sir, it was not Miss Zakhari," Pitt replied. "She has spoken to no one since her arrest."

"She should have someone to represent her," Ryerson said immediately. "The embassy should do that—it would be more discreet than my doing so—but I will if necessary."

"I think it would be much better if you did not," Pitt responded, caught off balance that Ryerson should even make such a suggestion. "It might do more harm than good," he added. "Would you please tell me what happened that night, sir, as far as you know?"

Ryerson invited Pitt to sit down in one of the large, smooth, leather-covered chairs, then sat in one opposite, but not at ease, instead leaning a little forward, his face a mask of concentration. He offered no hospitality, not out of discourtesy, but it obviously had not occurred to him. His mind was consumed in the present problem. He made no attempt at dissimulation.

"I was at very late meetings that night. I had intended to be at Miss Zakhari's house by two in the morning, but I was late. It was closer to three."

"How did you come, sir?" Pitt interrupted.

"By hansom. I stopped on the Edgware Road and walked a couple of streets."

"Did you see anyone leaving Connaught Square, either on foot or in a coach or carriage?" Pitt asked.

"I don't recall seeing anyone. But I wasn't thinking of it. They could have gone in any direction."

"You arrived at Eden Lodge," Pitt prompted. "At which entrance?"

Ryerson flushed very faintly. "The mews. I have a key to the scullery door."

Pitt tried to keep his expression from reflecting any of his thoughts. Moral judgments would be unhelpful, and perhaps he had little right to make them. Curiously enough, he did not wish to. Ryerson did not fit any of the assumptions Pitt had made before meeting him, and he was obliged to start again, feeling his way through his own conflicting emotions.

"Did you go in through the scullery?" he asked.

"Yes." Ryerson's eyes were troubled by the memory. "But I was standing in the kitchen, just up the step, when I heard a noise in the garden, and I went out again. Almost immediately I ran into Miss Zakhari, who was in a state of extreme distress." He breathed in and out slowly. "She told me a man had been shot and was lying dead in the garden. I asked her who he was and if she knew what had happened. She told me he was a Lieutenant Lovat whom she had known briefly in Alexandria several years ago. He had admired her then . . ." He hesitated briefly over the choice of words, then went on, trusting Pitt to put his own interpretation on it. "And now wished to rekindle the friendship. She had refused, but he was reluctant to accept that answer."

"I see. What did you do?" Pitt kept his voice neutral.

"I asked her to show me, and followed her to where he was lying on the ground, half under the laurel bushes. I had thought perhaps he was not actually dead. I hoped she had found him knocked senseless, and perhaps leaped to a hasty conclusion. However, when I knelt down to look at him, it was quite apparent that she was correct. He had been shot at fairly close range, through the chest, and was unquestionably dead."

"Did you see the gun?"

Ryerson's eyes did not waver, but it obviously cost him an effort. "Yes. It was lying on the ground beside him. It was Ayesha's gun. I knew it immediately, because I had seen it before. I knew she owned it, for protection."

"Against whom?"

"I don't know. I had asked her, but she would not tell me."

"Could it have been this Lieutenant Lovat?" Pitt suggested. "Had he threatened her?"

Ryerson's face was tight, his eyes miserable. He hesitated before answering. "I believe not," he said at last.

"Did you ask her what had happened?"

"Of course! She said she did not know. She had heard the shot, and realized it was very close by. She had been in her upstairs sitting room, waiting for me, awake and fully dressed. She went downstairs to see what had happened, if anyone were hurt, and found Lovat lying on the ground and the gun beside him."

It was a strange story, and one Pitt found almost impossible to believe, and yet as he looked at Ryerson, he was sure that either he himself believed it or he was the most superb actor Pitt had ever seen. He was clear, calm and without any histrionics. There was a candor to him that, if it was art, then it was also genius. It confused Pitt, and he felt wrong-footed, off balance because of it.

"So you saw the dead man," he said. "And you knew from Miss Zakhari who he was. Did she have any idea what he was doing there or who had shot him?"

"No," Ryerson answered immediately. "She assumed he had come to see her, but that much was obvious. There could be no other reason for his being there at that hour. I asked her if she knew what had happened, and she said she did not." There was finality in his voice, and belief that defied sense.

"She had not invited him there, or given him reason to believe he would be welcome?" Pitt pressed, uncertain what tone to adopt. It annoyed him to be deferential, the situation was absurd, and yet his instinct was to believe him, even to feel some sympathy.

Ryerson's lips tightened. "She would hardly invite him at the same time she was expecting me, Mr. Pitt. She is a woman of high intelligence."

There was no time to afford niceties. "Women have been known to contrive that lovers should be made jealous, Mr. Ryerson," Pitt responded, and saw Ryerson wince. "It is a very old strategy, and can work well," he continued. "She would naturally deny it to you."

"Possibly," Ryerson said dryly, but there was no anger in his voice, rather a kind of patience. "But if you knew her you would not bother with such a suggestion. It is absurd, not only because of her character, but were she to have done such a thing, why in heaven's name would she then shoot him?"

Pitt had to agree that there was no sense in it, even allowing for temper, passion, or accident. If Ayesha Zakhari was convincing enough to have planned such a thing in advance, then she was far too clever to have behaved so idiotically afterwards.

"Could Lovat in some way have threatened her?" he asked aloud.

"She did not let him in, Mr. Pitt," Ryerson answered. "I don't know if there is any way of proving it, but he was never in the house."

"But she was outside," Pitt remarked. "In the garden she would have had little defense."

"You are suggesting she took her gun with her." Ryerson's lips were touched briefly with the tiniest smile. "That would seem to be excellent defense. And if she shot him because he threatened her, or even attacked her, then that is self-defense and not murder." Then the light vanished from his eyes. "But that is not what happened. She went outside only after she heard the shot, and she found him already dead."

"How do you know that?" Pitt said simply.

Ryerson sighed and his face pinched so minutely not a single feature altered, simply the vitality died inside him. "I don't know it," he said quietly. "That is what she told me, and I know her infinitely better than you do, Mr. Pitt." The words were invested with sadness and an intensity of emotion so raw Pitt was embarrassed by it. He felt intrusive, and yet he had no choice but to be there. "There is an inner kind of honesty in her like a clear light," Ryerson went on. "She would not stoop to deceive, for her own sake, for the violence it would do to her nature, not for the sake of anyone else."

Pitt stared at him. Ryerson was worried; there was even a flicker of real fear, tightly controlled, at the back of his eyes, but it was not for himself. Pitt had never seen the Egyptian woman. He had imagined someone beautiful, lush, a woman to satisfy a jaded appetite, to flatter and yield, to tease but only for her own ends. She would be the ultimate mistress for a man with both money and power, but who would marry only to suit his political or dynastic ambitions, and seek the answer to his physical needs elsewhere. Such a man would not look for love or honor; he would not even think of it. And he would expect to pay for his pleasures.

Now it occurred to Pitt with startling force that perhaps he was wrong. Was it conceivable that Ryerson loved his mistress, not merely desired her? It was a new thought, and it altered his entire perception. It made Ryerson a better man, but also perhaps a more dangerous one. Pitt's charge from Narraway, and therefore from the prime minister, was to protect Ryerson from involvement in the case. If Ryerson was behaving from love, and not self-interest, then he would be far more difficult to predict, and impossible to control. A whole ocean of danger opened up in front of Pitt's imagination.

"Yes . . ." he said quietly. It was not an agreement, he was merely acknowledging that he understood. "Miss Zakhari told you that she had heard the shots . . . Did she say how many?"

"A single shot," Ryerson corrected him.

Pitt nodded. "You went to see, and found Lovat dead on the ground near the laurel bushes. What then?"

"I asked her if she had any idea what had happened," Ryerson replied. "She told me she had no idea at all, but that Lovat had sent her letters, pressing her to rekindle an old love affair, and she had refused, fairly bluntly. He was not willing to accept that, which was presumably why he had come."

"At three in the morning?" Pitt said with disbelief. He did not add reasons for the absurdity of that.

For the first time Ryerson showed some trace of anger. "I have no idea, Mr. Pitt! I agree it is ludicrous—but he was unarguably there! And since he is dead, and no one we know spoke to him, I cannot think of any way to learn what he hoped to achieve."

Pitt had a sudden awareness of the power of the man, the inner intellectual strength and the will which had taken him to the peak of his profession and kept him there for nearly two decades. His vulnerability with regard to Ayesha Zakhari, and the fact that he was involved, in whatever way, with a murder and therefore in personal danger, had made him temporarily forget it. When Pitt spoke again it was with a new respect, even though it was unintentional. "What did you do then, sir?"

Ryerson colored. "I said that we must move the body. That was when I knew that it was her gun."

"It was your idea to move Mr. Lovat's body?"

Ryerson's face set a fraction harder, altering the planes of his cheek and jaw. "Yes, it was."

Pitt wondered if he was trying to protect the woman, but he had no doubt whatever that if it was a lie, it was one Ryerson was not going to retract. He had committed himself, and it was not in his nature to go back, whether it was pride or honor that held him, or simply the truth.

"I see. Did you fetch the wheelbarrow or did she?"

Ryerson hesitated. "She did. She knew where it was."

"And she brought it back to where the body was?"

"Yes, and the gun. I helped her lift him in. He was heavy, and extremely awkward. His body was limp. He kept sliding out of our grasp."

"Did you take the head or the feet?" Pitt already knew the answer, but he was interested to see if Ryerson would tell the exact truth.

"The head, of course," Ryerson said a trifle tartly. "It was heavier, and the wounds were in his chest, so that was where he bled. Surely you know that?"

Pitt was annoyed to find himself embarrassed, and wished he had not asked the question. "You put him in the barrow, then what did you intend to do with him?" he continued.

"Take him to Hyde Park," Ryerson answered. "It's less than a hundred yards away."

"In the barrow?" Pitt said in surprise.

Temper flashed across Ryerson's face. "No, of course not! We could hardly wheel a corpse around the streets in a garden barrow, even at three in the morning! I had gone to harness up the gig and Ayesha was going to bring him to the mews. That was when the police arrived. As soon as I heard the voices I came back. Lovat's blood didn't show on my dark suit; the constable assumed I had only just come. Ayesha immediately confirmed him in that assumption, to protect me. I was about to argue, then I saw the sense in remaining free to do whatever I could to help her."

Again, Pitt was surprised. From any other man he would have doubted that, but from Ryerson he accepted it. He had not once attempted to cover over either his presence or his involvement, and he had to know that attempting to move a body from the scene of a crime was itself an offense.

"And what are you doing to help her?" Pitt asked unblinkingly.

Suddenly desperation filled Ryerson's eyes and terror flooded up inside him for a moment beyond control. "Trying to think what the devil really happened!" he said hoarsely. "Who did kill him, and why? Why at Eden Lodge, and why in the middle of the night?" He spread his hands slightly, strong but finely sculpted for so large a man. "What was he doing there at all? Did someone follow him? Did someone meet him there? For what? That makes no sense either. You don't arrange a quarrel in someone else's back garden in the middle of the night!" He was staring at Pitt, willing him to believe. "Ayesha wouldn't have opened the door to him. Was he planning to break in? Or create a scene and waken the neighbors?" His face was now ashen pale. "I know she would not have killed him, but for the life of me I can't imagine any credible answer as to what did happen." He did not even pretend to mask his feelings.

Narraway had told Pitt to keep Ryerson out of it if it were humanly possible. Given Ryerson's emotions, perhaps the only way to do that would be to learn the truth, in the hope that it proved Ayesha Zakhari less guilty than she looked now.

"I'll try to find the answers," Pitt said aloud. "But it will require a certain cooperation from you, sir."

"As far as I am able," Ryerson replied. He was not so desperate he would play into anyone's hands with an open promise. Pitt found that faintly comforting. At least the man had some balance and judgment left. "But I will not see her blamed for my acts, nor will I swear falsely to protect my reputation. It would serve me ill anyway, and Mr. Gladstone knows it. A man who would lie to serve his own ends will eventually lie for anything."

"Yes, sir," Pitt agreed. "I had no intention of asking you to lie, rather that you tell me all the truth you know, and keep silent as to your being at Eden Lodge unless it is inescapable that you answer the police. But I think they will refrain from asking you for as long as they can."

Ryerson's smile was bittersweet. "I imagine they will," he agreed. "What will Victor Narraway ask you to do, Mr. Pitt?" There was a change in his expression so minute Pitt could not have described it, but he knew without question it reflected a darkness inside.

"Find the truth," he answered with a slight grimace, knowing both that he had set himself a huge task, perhaps an impossible one, and that even if he succeeded the truth he found would very probably be one he would hate—and might not be able to conceal without even worse pain.

Ryerson did not answer him, but rose to his feet to show him to the front door himself, ignoring the services of the waiting footman.

IT TOOK PITT the rest of the morning and into the early afternoon to find the police surgeon and obtain his attention. He was a large man with heavy shoulders and quivering chins that settled into his neck without noticeable distinction. He had an apron tied around his vast girth, and his hands were scrubbed pink, presumably to get rid of the evidence of his day's work, if not the smell of carbolic and vinegar. He greeted Pitt with indignant good humor.

"Thought I'd got rid of you when you left Bow Street," he observed in a remarkably attractive voice. It was the only physically pleasing quality about him, apart from his hair, which was thick and curling and so clean as to shine in the gaslight from the lamps above him as they stood in his office. His eyebrows rose. "What do you want now? I don't know any bombers or anarchists. My ignorance of such things is precious to me, and I intend to keep it until I die peacefully of old age, sitting in the sun on some park bench. I can't help you—but I suppose I can try, if you insist."

"Lieutenant Edwin Lovat," Pitt replied. He liked McDade and he had nothing pleasanter or more useful to do than extract information from him a piece at a time.

"Dead," McDade said simply. "Shot through the chest—heart, actually. Small handgun, close range. Very neat."

"Great skill required?" Pitt asked.

"Only for a blind man with a moving target!" McDade looked at Pitt sideways. "Haven't seen the body, have you." That was a statement, not a question.

"Not yet," Pitt agreed. "Should I?"

McDade shrugged his massive shoulders, setting his chins quivering. "Not unless you need to know what he looked like, which is much the same as any other well-built young English soldier with a comfortable style of living, plenty of good food, and not much exercise lately. He'd have run to fat in another ten years, when the muscle went soft." His expression became rueful. "Handsome, I should think, when he was alive. Good features, good head of hair, all his teeth, which in his early forties isn't bad. Mind, it's intelligence and humor that make you like a man, and it's hard to tell that when you've only seen him dead." He looked away from Pitt as he spoke those words, and there was the very faintest shred of self-consciousness in him. Was he excusing his own massive size, defending himself from critical thought even though nothing had been said?

"Exactly," Pitt agreed. He had never considered himself handsome either. He smiled suddenly.

McDade colored. "Well, what else do you want?" he demanded, swinging around. "He was shot! Through the heart. I've no idea whether that was luck or skill. Killed him on the spot—it would do!"

"Thank you. I suppose there's nothing else you can tell me?"

"Like what?" McDade's voice rose incredulously. "That he was shot by a left-handed man with a walleye and a limp? No, I can't! Shot by somebody a couple of yards away who could hold a gun steady and see what they were doing. Is that any help?"

"None at all. Thank you for your time. May I see him?"

McDade waved a short, fat arm indicating the general area beyond the door. "Help yourself. He's on the third table along. But you shouldn't have any trouble finding him. The other two are women."

Pitt forbore from remark and went out as directed.

He looked at the body of Edwin Lovat, hoping it would give him a sense of the man's reality. He stared at the waxen features, a little sunken now, and tried to imagine him alive, laughing and talking, filled with feeling. Without movement, sound, anything of the thoughts or passions that had made Lovat unique, his body told Pitt nothing more than McDade had already said. A slender woman could not possibly have lifted him. Had he suspected any violence he would presumably not have stood so close to whoever it was who shot him, which meant that either the murderer was known to him as a friend or he had not seen his assailant until the moment before the shot was fired. Either possibility answered the facts, and there was no way to tell which was the case. It was probably irrelevant anyway. The woman had killed him. Pitt's only hope to save Ryerson was to find some mitigating reason why.

He spent the remainder of the afternoon learning what he could about Ryerson: his present responsibilities, which were largely to do with trade both within the empire and beyond; and the constituency he represented, which was in Manchester, the heart of the cotton-spinning industry in England. It was the second largest city in Britain, and also the home of the prime minister, Mr. Gladstone.

He was back in Keppel Street in time for dinner.

"Can you do anything to help?" Charlotte asked, looking up from her sewing as they sat together in the parlor afterwards.

"Help whom?" Pitt asked. "Ryerson?"

"Of course." She kept on weaving the needle in and out, the light flashing on it like a streak of silver, the head of it clicking very softly against her thimble. He found it a uniquely pleasing sound; it seemed to represent everything that was gentle and domestic, and there was an infinite safety in it. He had no idea what she was mending, but it was clean cotton and the faint aroma of it drifted across the short space between them.

"Can you?" she pressed.

"I don't know," he admitted, feeling the weight of it sink on him as if the room were suddenly darker. "I'm not sure he's prepared to help himself."

She stared at him, her needle motionless in her hand, her face puzzled. "What do you mean? Are you saying he's guilty?"

"He says he's not," Pitt replied. "And I'm inclined to believe him." He pictured Ryerson's face in his mind as he had defended Ayesha Zakhari, and heard again the emotion in Ryerson's voice. "At least I think so," he added. "He's willing to admit he was there, and that he actually helped her lift Lovat's body into the barrow, intending to take it to Hyde Park."

"Then he is an accessory!" she said in amazement. "After the murder, even if not before."

"Yes, I know that," he agreed.

"And the prime minister wants you to protect him?" she asked, struggling with the idea.

He stared at her. Her expression contained too many emotions for him to be certain which was the most powerful: incredulity, anger, dismay, anxiety.

"I'm not sure," he said honestly. "I don't know which is the greatest ill."

She was confused. "What do you mean? It wouldn't bring the government down, not so soon after the election. Ryerson would have to go, that's all. And if he helped his mistress to murder a past lover, then so he should."

"The Manchester cotton workers are threatening to strike," he pointed out. "That's Ryerson's department, his constituency. He's possibly the only man who has a chance of settling the problem without ruining heaven knows how many people, workers and mill owners alike, and the shopkeepers, businesses and artisans of the nearby towns as well."

"I see," she said soberly. "What can you do? You can't conceal his involvement, can you? Would you?" She had put her sewing down now and her attention was undivided, her eyes dark and troubled.

"I don't suppose the question will arise," he answered, hoping profoundly that that was true. "The Egyptian embassy knows he was there."

Her eyebrows rose in amazement. "How do they know that? She told them?"

"Apparently not, she hasn't had the opportunity. But it's a most interesting question. She seemed to be willing to protect him when she was arrested. She behaved as if she was surprised to see him, and he'd only just arrived, although he says he had been there several minutes at least, and was the one who actually lifted the heavier part of the body into the barrow. Somebody certainly helped her. Lovat was far too heavy for her to have done it alone, and there was no blood on her dress."

"You need to know a lot more about him," she said with concern shadowing her eyes. "I mean not what everybody knows, but something personal. You need to know what to believe. Have you thought of asking Aunt Vespasia? If she doesn't know him herself, she'll know someone who does." She was referring to Lady Vespasia Cumming-Gould, actually her sister Emily's great-aunt by marriage, but both Charlotte and Pitt had grown to care for her deeply, and treated her as their own.

"I'll see her as soon as I can," Pitt agreed immediately. He glanced at the clock on the mantelpiece. "Do you think it's too late to telephone and ask her if tomorrow morning is convenient?" He was halfway to his feet already.

Charlotte smiled. "If you tell her it is to do with a crime you are investigating, with the possibility of government scandal, I imagine she will see you at dawn, if that is when you need her to," she replied.

SHE WAS ALMOST RIGHT. However, Pitt had breakfast first, and glanced at the newspapers before leaving in the morning. It was September 16, and the news headlines were taken up with Mr. Gladstone's visit to Wales, where he had apparently reached some level of agreement on the disestablishment of the Church in that country. Also written about extensively were the outbreaks of cholera in Paris and Hamburg, and on a lighter note, the fact that the recently completed bust of Queen Victoria, sculpted by Princess Louise, was to remain in Osborne House until its shipment to Chicago for exhibition there.

By nine o'clock Pitt was in Vespasia's bright, airy withdrawing room with its windows overlooking the garden. The simplicity of the furnishings, with none of the fashionable clutter of the last sixty years' taste, reminded him that she was born in another age and her memories stretched back to the time before Victoria was queen. As a child she had known the fear of invasion by the Emperor Napoleon.

Now she sat in her favorite chair and regarded him with interest. She was still a woman of remarkable beauty, and she had lost none of the wit and style that had dazzled society for three generations. She was dressed in dove gray this morning, with her favorite long rows of pearls around her neck and gleaming softly over her bosom.

"Well, Thomas," she said with slightly raised silver eyebrows. "If you wish for my assistance you had better tell me what it is you require to know. I am not acquainted with the unfortunate young Egyptian woman who appears to have shot Lieutenant Lovat. It seems an uncivilized and inefficient way to discard an unwanted lover. A firm rebuff is usually adequate, but if it is not, there are still less hysterical ways of achieving the same end. A clever woman can organize her lovers to dispose of each other, without breaking the law." She regarded him very soberly, but there was a wry humor in her silver-gray eyes, and for an instant he dared to imagine that she spoke from experience and not merely opinion.

"And how do you guarantee that your lover will remain within the law?" he asked politely.

"Ah!" she said with instant understanding. "Is that the story? Who is the lover who has behaved with such ungoverned stupidity? I assume there is no question of self-defense?" A flicker of concern crossed her face. "Is that why you are here to see me, Thomas, on the lover's behalf?"

"Yes, I am afraid it is. At least not his behalf, but in his interest."

"I see. So she was not alone, and he is a person in whom Victor Narraway has some concern. Of whom are we speaking?"

"Saville Ryerson."

She sat perfectly still, facing him with a steady, curiously sad gaze.

"Do you know him?" he asked gently.

"Of course I do," she replied. "I have known him since before his wife was killed . . . twenty years, at least. In fact, I fear it is more . . . perhaps twenty-two or twenty-three, by now."

He felt a tightening inside him. He studied her face and tried to read how much it was going to hurt her if Ryerson was guilty. Which would matter most to her—his political disgrace or the fact that he was ill-judged enough to allow what should have been a casual affair, with a woman of a different race, religion, and national loyalties, to rule his passions to the point where he colluded in murder? Sometimes one knows a person for years but sees only a surface the person wishes to show. There are vast tides underneath which are not even guessed at.

"I'm sorry," he said sincerely. He had come to her for help without thinking for a moment that perhaps the truth could be painful for her. Now he was ashamed of taking it for granted. "I need to know more of him than public opinion can tell me," he explained.

"Of course you do," she agreed with asperity. "May I ask what it is you suspect him of? Not actually murder, surely?"

"You think he would not kill, even to protect his reputation?"

"You are being evasive, Thomas!" she replied, but there was a slight tremor in her voice. "Is that your way of allowing me to understand that you do?"

"No," he said quickly, guilt biting a little deeper. "I spoke with him, and he confuses me. I want a clearer impression of him, without unintentionally placing the thoughts in your mind by telling you too much."

"I am not a servant girl to be so easily led," she said with undisguised disparagement. Then, when she saw him blush, she smiled with the charm she had used to devastate men, and occasionally women as well, all her life. "I do not believe for a moment that Saville Ryerson would kill to protect his reputation," she said with conviction. "But I do not find it impossible to accept that he would do so to defend his life, or someone else's, or for a cause that he held sufficiently important. Which I profoundly doubt would be anything to do with cotton strikes in Manchester. What other issues are there at stake?"

"None that I know of," he replied, the tightness easing out of him again at her warmth. "And I don't know of any real reason why Lovat should be a threat to Miss Zakhari."

"Might he have attacked her, or attempted an assault which she rejected?" Vespasia asked with a frown.

"At three o'clock in the morning, in her back garden?" he said dryly.

Her expression was momentarily comical.

"Oh—hardly," she agreed. "One does not meet in such circumstances unless one has some nature of assignation." Then total seriousness returned. "And one does not innocently take a gun. It was her gun, I assume?" Hope of denial was born and died in the same instant. "I admit, I read only the headlines. It seemed of no concern to me then."

"Yes," he agreed. "It was her gun, but she said she found it there. She heard the shot and that is why she went outside. He was already dead when she reached him."

"And what does Saville Ryerson say?" she asked.

"That Lovat was dead when he got there," he replied. "And he helped her lift the body into a wheelbarrow in order to take it to

Hyde Park and leave it there. The police were called by someone, we don't know who, and arrived in time to find her with the body. Ryerson had gone to the mews to harness a horse to the gig."

Vespasia sighed, her eyes troubled. "Oh, dear. I presume the evidence bears all this out." It was hardly a question.

"Yes, so far. Certainly someone lifted the body for her." He watched her face. "You don't find that hard to believe?"

She looked away. "No. Perhaps I had better tell you from the beginning."

"Please." He sat back a little in his chair, still watching her.

"The Ryersons were landed gentry," she began quietly, her voice remote in memory. "They had only the occasional link with aristocracy, but plenty of money. There were two or three sisters, I believe, but Saville was the only son. He was well educated at Eton, and then Cambridge, then the army for a spell. He served with distinction, but did not wish to make a career of it. He stood for Parliament around about 1860, and won easily." Regret touched so softly he barely saw it. "He married well," she continued. "I don't believe it was a love match, but it was certainly amiable enough, which is as much as most people expect."

Beyond the windows in the garden a bird was hopping over the grass and the late roses glowed in vivid ambers and reds.

"Then she was killed," Vespasia went on, startling Pitt so he gasped and coughed.

She glanced at him with a very slight, wry smile. "Not murdered, Thomas. It was an accident. I suppose if it happened now, you might be sent to investigate it, although I doubt you would find any more than they did then." She sat very still as she went on. "She was on holiday in Ireland. It was one of their periodic unpleasantnesses, and she was caught in the crossfire. It was criminal, of course, in that they were shooting each other. It was an ambush intended for political victims, and it was accidental that Libby Ryerson moved into the path at exactly that moment."

Pitt felt a stark sadness for Ryerson. It was a harsh way to lose someone. Had he blamed himself that he had not prevented it, somehow foreseen and guarded against it?

"Where was he?"

"In London."

"Why was she in Ireland?"

"She had many Anglo-Irish friends. She was a beautiful woman, restless for experience—adventure."

He was not sure what she meant, and hesitant to ask. It seemed intrusive not only to the dead woman but to Vespasia's implicit understanding of her as well. "Had they children?" he asked instead.

"No," she replied with a touch of sadness. "They had only been married two or three years."

"And he never married again?"

"No." Now her eyes met his candidly. "And before you ask me why, I do not know. He certainly had mistresses enough, and many women who would have accepted him." A thread of humor touched her mouth. "If you are looking for some dark secret in his personal life, I do not believe you will find it . . . not in that area, anyway. And I know of no other scandal, financial or political."

He thought carefully before asking the next question, but he realized as he formed the words in his mind that it was the one which had driven all the others and weighed most heavily on him.

"Do you know anything that connects him to Victor Narraway, professionally or personally?"

Vespasia's eyes widened very slightly. "No. Do you believe there is something?"

"I don't know." That was not strictly true. He did not know in a rational sense, but he was perfectly sure that Narraway was gripped by a hard and profound emotion when he thought of Ryerson. He had sent Pitt to see him instead of going himself for a reason so powerful it overrode judgment. He had rationalized it afterwards, not before. "I had that impression," he added aloud.

Vespasia leaned a little towards him, only the slightest yielding of the stiffness of her back. "Be careful, Thomas. Saville Ryerson is a man of intelligence and deep political judgment, but above all he is a man of feeling. He has worked hard for his beliefs and for the people he represents. He has not spared his time or his means to benefit Manchester, and much of the north of England, and he has done it alone, and quite often with too little thanks." She lifted her thin shoulders very slightly. "The Lancashire people are loyal, but they are quick-tempered and not overfond of London-made decisions. They have not always understood him. Because he is clever he has made enemies in Westminster: ambitious young men who want to topple him and take his place. Be very sure you are right before you accuse him of anything. It will ruin him, and you cannot undo that by withdrawing the charge afterwards."

"I'm trying to save him, Aunt Vespasia!" Pitt responded fervently. "I simply don't know how to!"

She turned away, staring at the gilt-edged mirror on the far wall, its beveled glass reflecting the leaves of the birch trees twisting and flickering in the slight wind outside.

"Perhaps you can't," she replied so softly he barely heard her. "He may love this Egyptian woman enough to have been complicit in her crime. Do what you have to, Thomas, but please do it as gently as you can."

"I will," he promised, wondering how on earth he would.

CHAPTER THREE

AFTER HER INDOOR DUTIES were completed, Gracie set out on her errands of the morning. It was a bright, mild day with only the slightest breeze, and she enjoyed walking, even in new boots. These were excellent ones, with black buttons, and heels that for the first time in her life made her over five feet tall.

She went briskly along Keppel Street and Store Street into the Tottenham Court Road, where she stopped at the fishmonger's and picked out some succulent-looking kippers, nice and fat, with a rich, smoky color. She did not trust the boy who brought them around on a barrow; he tended to stretch the truth a little regarding their freshness.

She had just come out onto the pavement again and was about to turn south towards the greengrocer's to get some plums, when she saw her friend Tilda Garvie, who was maid in a household a short distance away in Torrington Square. Tilda was a nice-looking girl, an inch or two taller than Gracie and a good deal plumper, which still left her becomingly slender. Usually she had a cheerfulness about her which made her agreeable company. However, today she walked past the flower girl without even a glance. Her face was set in lines of anxiety, and she seemed to be looking around her absentmindedly, as if not truly seeing what was there.

"Tilda!" Gracie called out.

Tilda stopped, swung to face Gracie and on recognizing her, her expression flooded with relief. She nearly bumped into a large woman with a shopping basket balanced on her hip and dragging an unwilling child with the other hand.

"Gracie!" Tilda gasped, just avoiding being mown down by the woman and not bothering to apologize for cutting across her path. "I'm so glad ter see you!"

"Wot's the matter?" Gracie asked, moving closer to the inside of the footpath and pulling Tilda out of the way. "Yer look like yer lost summink. D'yer drop yer purse?" It was the first and most natural thought. She had done that herself and still remembered the horror of it. That was nearly six shillings gone—a week's worth of food.

Tilda dismissed it with a shake of her head so slight it was barely a comment at all. "Can I talk to yer for a moment . . . please, Gracie? I'm that worried I dunno wot ter do. I was 'opin' I'd see yer. Ter be honest, that's why I come this way."

Gracie's concern was instant. All sorts of domestic possibilities flashed through her mind. The house in which Tilda worked was quite a large one, and there were several other servants. The first, most obvious troubles would be accusations of theft or one of the male staff's making improper demands. Gracie had never feared either of those herself, but she knew very well that it could happen. Worse still, of course, was the master of the house, making demands. Refusal and acceptance were both fraught with pitfalls. To be caught, and dismissed without a character reference, was only the lightest. One could easily be with child as well! Or accused by the mistress of all manner of wrongdoing.

Simple squabbles with other maids, lost trinkets, badly done jobs, the mistress's favorite ornament broken or dress scorched, were so simple as to be almost welcome.

"Wot's 'appened?" she said earnestly. " 'Ere, we've got time fer a cup o' tea. There's a place jus' 'round the corner. Come an' sit down an' tell me."

"I i'nt got money fer a cup o' tea right now." Tilda stood motionless on the pavement. "An' I think as it'd choke me any'ow."

Gracie began to appreciate that whatever troubled her, it was of a very serious order. "Can I 'elp?" she said simply. "Mrs. Pitt is ever so fair, an' she's clever as well."

Tilda frowned. "Well . . . it were Mr. Pitt as I were thinking of . . . if . . . I mean if . . ." She stopped, her face white, her eyes pleading.

"It's a crime?" Gracie said with a gulp.

Tears brimmed Tilda's eyes. "I dunno . . . not yet. Leastways . . . Oh, please Gawd, it ain't!"

Gracie took her by the arm and half dragged her along the pavement to be out of the way of bustling women using baskets almost like weapons. "Yer comin' with me ter get a cup o' tea," she ordered. "Summink 'ot inside yer'll 'elp. Then yer can tell me wot yer talkin' 'bout. 'Ere . . . pick yer feet up or yer'll fall flat on yer face over them cobbles, an' that won't 'elp no one."

Tilda forced herself to smile and quickened her pace to keep up. In the tea shop, Gracie informed the waitress exactly what they wanted, freezing the girl's complaints that it was too early, and sent her scurrying away to do as she was told.

"Now," she said when they were alone. "So wot's the matter then?"

"It's Martin," Tilda said huskily. "Me brother," she added before Gracie could misunderstand. " 'E's gone. 'E just in't there, an' 'e 'adn't told me nothin'. An' 'e wouldn't do that, 'cos me an' 'im is all we got. Our ma an' pa died wi' the cholera when I were six an' Martin were eight. We always looked out for each other. There in't no way as 'e'd go orff an' not tell me." She blinked rapidly, trying to control the tears, and failing. They slid more and more rapidly down the curve of her cheek, and without thinking she wiped them away with her cuff.

Gracie attempted to be practical and force herself to think clearly. "When did yer see 'im last, Tilda?"

"Three days ago," Tilda answered. "It were me day orff, an' 'is too. We 'ad 'ot pies from the man on the corner, an' walked in the park. The band were playin'. 'E said as 'e were goin' up Seven Dials. Only up an' back, like, not ter stay there!"

The waitress returned with a pot of tea and two hot scones. She glanced at Tilda's tearstained face and seemed about to say something, then changed her mind. Gracie thanked her and paid for the tea, leaving a couple of pennies for her trouble. Then she poured out both cups and waited until Tilda had sipped hers and taken a bite out of the buttered scone. She tried to collect her thoughts, and behave as she thought Pitt would have.

" 'Oo did yer speak to where 'e works?" she asked. "Where is it, anyway?"

"For Mr. Garrick," Tilda replied, putting the scone down. "Torrington Square, just off Gordon Square, it is. Not far."

" 'Oo did yer speak to?" Gracie repeated.

"Mr. Simms, the butler."

"Wot did 'e say, exact?"

"That Martin 'ad gone away an' 'e couldn't tell me where," Tilda replied, ignoring her tea now, her eyes fixed on Gracie. " 'E thought as I were walkin' out wif 'im. I said as 'e were me brother, an' it took me ages ter make 'im believe me. But me an' Martin looks like each other, so 'e understood in the end." She shook her head. "But 'e still wouldn't tell me where 'e'd gone. 'E said as no doubt Martin would let me know, but that in't right, Gracie. Yesterday was me birthday, an' Martin wouldn't never forget that unless summink was terrible wrong. 'E never 'as, not since I were little." She gulped and blinked, the tears running down her cheeks again. "Always gives me summink, even if it's only a ribbon or an 'andkerchief or like that. Reckoned it mattered more 'n Christmas, 'e said, because it were special ter me. Christmas is everyone's."

Gracie felt a sharp twist of anxiety. Maybe this was more than a domestic threat, ugly as they were. Perhaps it was something Pitt should know about. Except that he was not with the police anymore. And she did not really know what Special Branch did, except that it was secret, and she got to hear a great deal less about Pitt's work than she used to when it was the ordinary sort of crime that was written in the newspapers for anyone to read.

Whatever had happened to Martin, it was up to her to find out, at least for now. She took a sip of tea to give herself time to think.

"Did yer speak to anyone else 'ceptin' the butler?" she said finally.

Tilda nodded. "Yeah. I asked the bootboy, 'cos bootboys often gets ter see all sorts, and they're too cheeky, most of 'em, not ter tell yer. They don't get listened to much, so they got ter make up fer it when they can." The momentary humor vanished from her face. "But 'e said as Martin just disappeared sudden. One day 'e were there, just like usual, the next day 'e weren't."

"But 'e lives in, don't 'e?" Gracie said, puzzled.

"Yeah, course 'e does! 'E's Mr. Stephen Garrick's valet. Does everythin' for 'im, 'e does. Mr. Stephen swears by 'im."

Gracie took a deep breath. This was too serious for allowing kindness to overrule honesty. "Could Mr. Garrick 'ave lost his temper over summink and dismissed 'im, and Martin been too ashamed ter tell yer until 'e finds another position?" She hated suggesting such a thing, and she saw from the crumpled look in Tilda's face how much the idea hurt.

"No!" Tilda shook her head fiercely. "No! Martin wouldn't never do nothin' ter get 'isself dismissed. An' Mr. Garrick leans on 'im. I mean fer real, not jus' ter tie 'is cravats an' keep 'is clothes nice." Her hands were clenched, the buttered scones forgotten. " 'E looks after 'im when 'e drinks too much or gets sick, or does summink daft. Yer can't jus' find someone else ter do that fer yer in a moment, like. It's . . . it's loyalty." She stared at Gracie with bright, frightened eyes, pleading to be understood and believed that loyalty was too precious not to extend both ways. It deserved better than to be discarded simply because one had the power to do so.

Gracie had no such faith in the honor of employers. She had worked for the Pitts since she was thirteen and had no personal experience of anybody else, but she knew enough stories of others not to be so happily naïve.

"Did yer speak ter Mr. Garrick 'isself?" she asked.

Tilda was startled. "No, o' course I din't! Cor, Gracie, you in't half got a cheek! 'Ow'd I get speakin' ter Mr. Garrick?" Her voice rose in amazement. "It took all the nerve I got ter go an' ask Mr. Simms, an' 'e looked at me like I'd overstepped meself. 'E'd 'alf a mind ter send me packin', till 'e realized Martin were me brother. Yer gotter respec' family, like. That's only decent."

"Well, don't worry," Gracie said with determination. She had made up her mind. Pitt might be too busy with Special Branch things, but Tellman was not. He used to be Pitt's sergeant at Bow Street, and was now promoted. He had been in love with Gracie for some time, even though he was only just admitting it to himself now, and that with deep reluctance. She would tell him, and he would be able to make the proper enquiries and solve the case. And it was a case, Gracie acknowledged that. "I'll get it done for yer," she added, smiling across at Tilda with assurance. "I know someone as'll look at it proper, an' find the truth."

Tilda relaxed at last, and very tentatively smiled back. "Can yer really? I thought if there was anyone, it'd be you. Thanks ever so . . . I dunno wot ter say, 'ceptin' I really am grateful to yer."

Gracie felt embarrassed, and afraid she had promised too much. Of course Tellman would do it, but the answer might not be one that would bring Tilda any happiness. "I in't done nuffink yet!" she said, looking down and concentrating on finishing her tea. "But we'll get it sorted. Now yer'd better tell me everythin' 'bout Martin, all where 'e's worked an' things like that." She had no pencil or paper with her, but she had only just recently learned to read and write, so her memory was long trained in accuracy, as it had needed to be.

Tilda began the account, remembering details from the same

necessity. When she was finished they went outside into the busy street and parted, Tilda to continue her errands, her head higher, her step brisker than before, Gracie to return to Keppel Street and ask Charlotte if she might have the evening off in order to find Tellman.

It was granted without hesitation.

GRACIE WAS FORTUNATE at the second attempt. Tellman was not at the Bow Street station, but she found him two blocks away in a public house having a pint of ale with a constable with whom he had been working. She stood just inside the entrance, her feet on the trampled sawdust, the smell of beer in the air and the noise of men's voices and clinking glasses all around her.

She had to look for several moments before she saw Tellman tucked away in the farthest corner, his head bent, staring somberly into his glass. The young man opposite him regarded him with deference. Since Pitt's departure Tellman was a senior officer, although it still sat uneasily on him. He knew more than almost anyone else of the truth about the way Pitt had been plotted against, and who was responsible. He loathed the man who had replaced him, and more seriously than that, he also distrusted him. All his experience since Wetron's arrival had indicated that he had motives and ambitions that were far from the simple success of solving crime. It was even possible that Wetron aimed as high as taking over leadership of the terrible secret organization of the Inner Circle.

Gracie knew that both Mr. Pitt and Tellman feared that, but she had only overheard it and did not dare to speak of it openly to either of them. She looked across at Tellman now and wondered how heavily that weighed upon him. She could see in him none of the ease he had had when working with Pitt, even if he would never have admitted to it.

She made her way through the crowd towards him, elbowing her way between men all but oblivious of her, pushing and poking to make them step aside, and she was almost at Tellman's seat before he looked up and saw her. His face filled with alarm, as if she could only bring bad news.

"Gracie? What is it?" He rose to his feet automatically, but ignored his companion, not seeing any need to introduce them.

She had rather hoped to approach the subject obliquely, and that he would be pleased to see her, but she had to admit to herself that in the past she had only sought him out without invitation when she had needed his help. When it was purely personal she had waited for him to speak first. After all, to begin with she had been unwilling to offer him anything more than a rather impatient friendship. He was a dozen years older than she and firmly entrenched in his beliefs, which in most cases were contrary to hers. He passionately disapproved of being in service—it offended all his principles of social justice—whereas she saw it as an honorable way to earn a living and a very comfortable day-to-day existence. She felt no subservience and was impatient with his prickly and unrealistic pride.

She forced herself to be more polite now than she felt. She was speaking to him in front of his junior and she should treat him with respect.

"I come for yer advice," she said meekly. "If yer can spare me 'alf an hour or so."

He was startled by her unusual courtesy, and only after a moment realized it was for the constable's benefit. His lean face softened with an unusual touch of humor. "I'm sure I could do that. Is Mrs. Pitt all right?" It was not good manners that made him ask—he cared profoundly. Pitt and Charlotte were as close to him as anyone he knew. He was a stiff, proud, and lonely man, and friendship did not come easily to him. He had resented Pitt when they first met. Pitt had been promoted to a position Tellman felt was only suitable for gentlemen, or those who had served in the army or navy. The son of a gamekeeper had no qualifications for command, and for men like Tellman to be expected to call them "sir" and offer them the deference of position stuck in his throat. Pitt had won his respect only a step at a time, but once earned it was a loyalty as deep as a bond of blood.

"Well, this isn't a right place for you," Tellman said, regarding Gracie with a slight frown. "I'll walk you to the omnibus, and you can tell me what it's about." He turned to the constable. "See you in the morning, Hotchkiss."

Hotchkiss stood up obediently. "Yes, sir. Good night, sir. Good night, miss."

"Good night, Constable," Gracie replied, then turned to Tellman as he moved past her and led the way, parting the crowd for her. She followed him out of the door onto the pavement, where they were now alone. "It matters, or I wouldn't 'a bothered yer," she said gravely. "There's someone as is missing."

He offered her his arm, and impatiently she took it, then found to her surprise that it was rather pleasant. She noticed that he shortened his step to make it easier for her to match stride with him. She smiled, then realized he had seen it, and became instantly sober again. It would not do to let him know it mattered. "It's me friend, Tilda Garvie," she said in a businesslike tone. " 'Er brother Martin 'as gone from the 'ouse 'e works in. Said nothin' to 'er, nor to no one else, just gone. Three days now."

Tellman pursed his lips, his face dark, brows drawn together. He walked with his shoulders a little hunched as if his muscles were tight. It was a fine evening, but the lamps were lit and the wind gusting up from the river smelled damp. The street was quiet, just one carriage in the distance, turning the corner away from them, and in the other direction a couple of men arguing good-naturedly.

"People leave jobs," Tellman said cautiously. "More likely he was dismissed. Could be a lot of reasons, not necessarily his fault."

" 'E'd 'ave told 'er!" Gracie said quickly. "It were 'er birthday, an' 'e never sent 'er a card nor flowers nor nothin'."

"People forget birthdays," he dismissed it. "Even when there's nothing wrong, let alone if they're out of a job and a roof over their heads!" he argued, his voice impatient.

She knew he was angry with the injustice of the dependence, not with her, but it still irritated her, perhaps because she did not want it to be true, and there was a whisper of fear at the back of her mind. She was not prepared to hear a policeman's view of it.

" 'E's never forgotten 'er birthday before," she retorted, keeping up with him with an effort. He was unaware that he was walking more rapidly. "Never ever, since 'e were eight years old!" she added.

"Perhaps he'd never been thrown out of a job before," he pointed out.

"If 'e were thrown out, why didn't the butler say so?" she countered, still holding on to his arm.

"Probably because household matters like that were none of his business," he answered. "A good butler wouldn't discuss domestic unpleasantness with an outsider. Surely you know that even better than I do?" He shot a sideways glance at her, a very slight twist to his lips, as if it were a question. They had argued about the dependence of a servant upon pleasing a master or mistress, and how fragile was the safety of the warmth, the food, the roof over their heads.

"I know wot yer talkin' about!" Gracie said crossly, pulling her arm away from his. "An' I'm sick o' tellin' yer that it in't always like that! O' course there's bad 'ouses an' bad people in 'em. But there's good 'ouses too. Can yer see Mrs. Pitt ever puttin' me out inter the street 'cos I overslept or was cheeky an' answered back . . . or anythin' else, for that matter?" Her voice rang with challenge. "You daresay as yer could, an' I'll make yer wish yer'd never opened yer mouth!"

"Of course not!" he retorted, and stopping abruptly, pulled her over to the side of the pavement near the wall and away from the two men now walking towards them. "But that's different. If Martin left the Garrick house, then it was for a reason. He was obliged to or he chose to. Either way, it's not a police matter, unless the

Garricks place a charge against him. And I imagine that's the last thing Tilda wants?"

"A charge o' wot?" she said furiously. " 'E in't done nothin'! 'E's just disappeared—don't you listen ter nothin' I say? Nobody knows where 'e is!"

"No," he corrected. "Tilda doesn't know where he is."

"The butler don't know neither!" she said exasperatedly. "Nor the bootboy!"

"The butler isn't telling Tilda, and why on earth should the bootboy know?" he said reasonably.

She was beginning to feel a kind of desperation. She did not want to quarrel with Tellman but she was on the brink of it and could not help herself. They were on the corner of the main thoroughfare now and the noise in the street rumbled past them, wheels, hooves, voices. People passed back and forth, one man so close as to brush Gracie's back. Tilda's fear had caught hold of her and she was losing her ability to think without panic overtaking her.

" 'Cos bootboys see an' 'ear lots o' things!" she snapped at him. "Don't yer learn nothin' questionin' people? You bin on crimes in big 'ouses often enough! Yer've listened ter Mr. Pitt, 'aven't yer? Does 'e ever ignore people just 'cos they work in the scullery or the pantry? People notice things, yer know; they got eyes an' ears!"

He kept his patience with an effort she could see even in the lamplight, and she knew he did it only because he cared for her. Somehow that made it more annoying because it was a moral pressure, a kind of obligation to respect him when inside she was bursting to shout.

"I know that, Gracie," he said levelly. "I've questioned plenty of servants myself. And the fact that the bootboy doesn't know there is anything wrong is very good evidence that there probably isn't. Martin might have been dismissed and left, and if that is so, maybe he didn't want his sister to hear about it until he found another place." He sounded eminently reasonable. "He's trying not to worry her . . . or perhaps he's ashamed? Maybe he was dismissed for something embarrassing, some kind of mistake. It would be only natural he wouldn't want his family to know about it."

"Then why don't 'e send 'er a card or a letter for 'er birthday from somewhere else?" she challenged, pulling farther away from him and staring up into his eyes. " 'E din't do that, so she's gonna worry twice as much!"

"If he lost his position, and his bed and board at the same time," he replied, keeping his voice unnaturally calm, "then I daresay he had more pressing things on his mind, like where to sleep and what to eat! He wouldn't have remembered what day it was."

"Then if 'e's in that much trouble she's right ter be worried—in't she?" she said triumphantly.

Tellman let out his breath in a long sigh. "Worried, yes, but calling in the police, definitely not."

Gracie clenched her fists by her sides in an effort to hang on to the last shred of her temper. "She in't callin' in the police, Samuel! She told me, an' I'm askin' you. You in't police, yer me friend. Leastways, I thought yer was. I'm askin' yer 'elp, not tryin' ter start a case."

"What do you expect me to do?" His voice rose in indignation at the sheer unreasonableness of it.

She bit back her response with a mighty effort and forced herself to smile at him with the utmost sweetness. "Thank yer," she said charmingly. "I knew yer'd 'elp, when yer understood. Yer could start by askin' Mr. Garrick 'isself where Martin is. Yer don't 'ave ter say why, o' course. Mebbe 'e were a witness?"

"To what?" His eyebrows shot up in disbelief.

She ignored it. "I dunno! Think o' summink!"

"I can't use police authority to go and question someone over something I invented!" He looked offended, as if his morality had been insulted.

"Oh, don' be so . . . so . . ." She was almost lost for words. She loved him as he was, stiff, awkward, full of indignation, covering his compassion with regulations and habit, the rigidity he had been taught, but sometimes he infuriated her beyond endurance, and this was one of those times. "Can't yer see beyond the end o' yer nose?" she demanded. "Sometimes I think yer brain is shut inside yer book o' rules! Can't yer see that lives, feelin's, wot's inside people's wot matters?" She drew in breath and went on. "People are 'eart an' blood, an' . . . an' mistakes an' things. An' dreams! Tilda needs ter find wot 'appened to 'im . . . an' that's real!"

His face hardened. He clung on to what he understood. "If you break the rules, in the end they'll break you," he said stubbornly, and in that instant she knew she had lost him. He had made a statement he could not go back on. He was right as he saw it, and she understood more than she could now admit. She had been unfair, forgetting he was working for Wetron now, not Pitt, and there would be no latitude granted him for anything. He had already risked his job once to save her and Charlotte and the children, and done it without thought of himself. Another day, when she was not so angry, and when it would not look like either apology or trying to win him back, she would tell him so. Just at the moment her thoughts were centered on Tilda and what had happened to her brother.

"Well, if yer won't 'elp 'er, I'll 'ave ter do it misself!" she said at last, swinging around to move a step away from him. She could not think of anything cutting and final to say, which was very frustrating. All she could do was stand and stare for a moment, as if she were about to deliver the final blow, then let out a sigh and leave.

"No, you won't!" Tellman said abruptly. "You'll do nothing of the sort!"

She spun around to face him again. "Don't you tell me wot ter do, Samuel Tellman! I'll do wot I 'ave ter, an' you don't 'ave nothin' ter say about it!" she shouted, but she felt so much better that he had responded.

"Gracie!" He took a long stride after her as if he would reach out and grasp her arm.

She shrugged exaggeratedly and did a little skip to elude him, and then walked as quickly as she could without looking back, mostly because she wanted to think he was staring after her, perhaps even following her, and she did not want to find out that he was not.

When she reached Keppel Street and went in through the scullery to the kitchen, she was still just clinging on to anger, but unhappiness had almost drowned it out. She had not handled the encounter with Tellman well. Even if she could not have persuaded him to investigate Martin Garvie's disappearance, and just possibly he had something of an honest reason for not doing so, at least she could have behaved so that they parted friends. Now she had no idea how to retrace it so she could speak openly to him next time they met. It was amazing how sharply that hurt her. She had not expected it to matter as deeply as it did. One day quite soon she was going to have to face the fact that she cared for him very much.

Fortunately there was no one else in the kitchen, so she could blow her nose and wash her face quickly, and then try to look as if nothing were wrong. She had the kettle on when Charlotte came in.

"Would yer like a cup o' tea?" she asked almost cheerfully.

"Yes, please," Charlotte accepted, in spite of the fact that it was only half past six. She sat down at the table and made herself comfortable. "What's wrong?" she asked, waiting motionlessly as if demanding an answer.

Gracie hesitated for a moment, debating whether to say that there was nothing wrong or to tell her at least part of it—the bit about Martin Garvie. She had not realized that Charlotte could read her so well. That too was a little disconcerting. And yet they had known each other for so long that if Charlotte had not ever hurt her, it would mean she did not care, and that would have been worse.

"Saw Tilda Garvie this mornin'," she replied, banging the lid onto the tea caddy unnecessarily hard and keeping her back to the table. "She in't seen 'er brother fer days, an' she's real worried summink's wrong."

"What sort of something?" Charlotte asked.

The kettle began to whistle and Gracie put her hand around the pot holder as she lifted it off the hob. She scalded the teapot, pouring the water down the sink, then put the leaves in and filled it from the kettle. She could no longer find any excuse for not sitting down, so she did so stiffly, avoiding meeting Charlotte's eyes.

" 'E in't livin' in the 'ouse in Torrington Square where 'e worked," she answered, "an' the butler says 'e don't work there no more, but 'e din't tell 'er wot 'appened or where 'e went." She had not intended to look at Charlotte, but suddenly the reality of Martin's situation outweighed her own pride. "An' if things was all right 'e wouldn't do that, 'cos they're real close," she went on hurriedly. "They got nob'dy else. Wotever'd 'appened, 'e'd 'a told 'er, 'specially since 'e missed 'er birthday, an' 'e in't never ever done that before."

Charlotte frowned. "What did he do at the house in Torrington Square?"

"Valet ter Mr. Stephen Garrick," Gracie replied immediately. " 'E weren't just a footman or the like. An' Tilda said Mr. Garrick relied on 'im. I know people can get throwed out easy enough if they do summink daft, or even if it jus' looks like they did, but why couldn't 'e 'a said summink ter Tilda? Just ter keep 'er from worryin'."

"I don't know," Charlotte said thoughtfully. She reached over and poured the tea for both of them, then replaced the pot on the trivet. "It does sound as if he was very distressed about something, or he would surely have told her he was moving. He may even have found a better position. Can Tilda read?"

Gracie looked up, startled.

"Well, it would be harder to send her a letter if she can't," Charlotte reasoned. "Although I suppose somebody would read it for her."

Gracie felt the sinking feeling inside her grow worse. She was hollow, and yet the thought of eating was repellent. She sipped her tea, and its hot sweetness slid down her throat and made no difference.

"What else?" Charlotte asked gently.

Gracie still hesitated. There was a kind of comfort in being so well understood, but she was still embarrassed to have been so incompetent in dealing with Tellman. It was made worse by the fact that she had always done it so well before. Charlotte would expect better of her than this. She would be disappointed in her. Women were supposed to be cleverer than she had been. She sipped her tea again. It was really too hot. She should have waited.

"Did you learn something else?" Charlotte pressed.

That was easy to answer. "Not really. Even when she told the butler as she was 'is sister, 'e din't tell 'er wot 'appened, nor where 'e'd gone."

Charlotte looked down at the table. "Mr. Pitt isn't in the police anymore. Perhaps we should ask Mr. Tellman and see if he can help."

The heat burned up Gracie's cheeks. There was no escape. "I already asked 'im," she said miserably, looking down at the tabletop. " 'E says as there in't nothin' 'e can do, 'cos Martin's got a right ter come an' go without tellin' 'is sister. It in't no crime."

"Oh." Charlotte sat silently for several moments. Carefully she tried her tea and found it just cool enough to drink. "Then we'll have to do something ourselves," she said at last. "Tell me everything you know about Tilda and Martin, and about the Garrick house in Torrington Square."

Gracie felt like a lost sailor who finally sees land on the horizon. There was something they could do. Obediently she told Charlotte the facts of her acquaintance with Tilda, picking out what mattered: her honesty, her stubbornness, the memories of childhood she had spoken about, her dreams of her own family one day, and the things she had shared with her brother over the lonely years of growing up.

Charlotte listened without interrupting, and in the end nodded. "I think you are right to worry," she agreed. "We need to know where he is and if he is all right. And if he is without a position and is too embarrassed by that to have told his sister, then we must make sure she understands, and then if possible, help him to obtain something else. I suppose you have no idea if he is likely to have done something foolish?"

"I dunno," Gracie admitted. "Tilda wouldn't do nothin' daft, but that don't mean 'e's the same. She thinks 'e is—but then she would."

"It is very hard to think ill of our own," Charlotte agreed.

Gracie looked up at her, eyes wide. "What are we gonna do?"

"You are going to tell Tilda that we'll help," Charlotte answered. "I shall begin to make enquiries about the Garrick household. Stephen Garrick at least will know what happened, even if he does not know where Martin Garvie is right now."

"Thank yer," Gracie said very seriously. "Thank yer very much."

ON THE FOURTH DAY after the murder of Edwin Lovat was discovered, the newspapers openly demanded the arrest, at least for questioning, of Saville Ryerson. He was known to have been on the premises at the time, and the writer of the article did not need to do more than ask what business he would have had there to suggest the answer.

Pitt sat at the breakfast table, tight-lipped, his face pale. Charlotte did not make any comment or otherwise interrupt what was obviously a painful train of thought. The defense of Ryerson which Mr. Gladstone had commanded was becoming more and more difficult. She watched him discreetly, and wished there were some way to offer comfort. But if she were honest, she believed Ryerson was guilty, if not of the crime, then at least of attempting to conceal it. Had someone not called the police, he would have removed the body from where the murder took place and done all he could to obscure the evidence. That was a crime. No ability to solve the cotton industry problems in Manchester could justify that—in fact, there was no stretch of the imagination which could connect it at all with his keeping of a mistress in Eden Lodge. It was a private weakness, an indulgence for which he would now have to pay very heavily indeed.

She looked at the anxiety in Pitt's face and a wave of anger swept over her that he should be expected to carry the responsibility for rescuing a man from his own folly, and then blamed because he could not do what any fool could see was impossible. He was being coerced into trying to evade a truth which it was both his duty and his own moral need to expose. For years they had used him to do that; now they had forced him into the position of denying the very values which had made him honorable before.

He looked up quickly and caught her glance.

"What?" he asked.

She smiled. "Nothing. I'm going to see Emily this morning. I know Grandmama will be there, and I haven't really managed to speak to her without embarrassment ever since Mama learned about . . . what happened to her." She still found it uncomfortable to speak of . . . even to Pitt. "It is more than time I did so," she went on hastily. She had arranged the visit over the telephone the previous evening, after speaking with Gracie. Pitt had a telephone because of his professional need for it, and Emily had one because she could afford pretty well anything she cared for.

The shadow of a smile crossed Pitt's face for an instant. He was long acquainted with Charlotte's grandmother and knew her temper of old.

Charlotte said no more about it, and when Pitt left, without letting her know what he hoped to seek or to find that day, she went upstairs and changed into her best morning gown. She did not follow fashion—it was far beyond her financial means, the more so since Pitt had been demoted from being in charge of Bow Street to working for Special Branch—but a well-cut gown in a color that was flattering had a dignity no one could rob from her.

She chose a warm, autumn shade to complement her auburn-toned hair and honey-fair complexion. The gown had not the current high-shouldered sleeves, but the almost nonexistent bustle was just right.

It was not an occasion for the omnibus, so she took the price of a hansom out of the housekeeping money, and arrived at Emily's opulent town house at quarter past ten.

She was shown in by a parlor maid who knew her well and conducted her immediately to Emily's boudoir—that private sitting room wealthy ladies kept for the entertaining of close friends.

Emily was waiting for her, dressed as always with the utmost elegance, in her favorite pale green which so suited her fair coloring. She stood up as soon as Charlotte was in the room, excitement in her face, her eyes bright. She came forward and gave Charlotte a quick kiss, then stood back. "So what has happened?" she demanded. "You said it was important. It sounds terribly heartless of me to put it into words, I know, when it was a real blow to Thomas, and so unjust, but I really mind his leaving Bow Street. I've no idea what cases he has now, but they all seem to be secret." She stepped back and waved to Charlotte to be seated in one of the soft, floral-fabric-covered chairs. "I'm bored to tears with society, and even politics seems terribly tedious at the moment," she went on, sweeping her skirts tidily and sitting down herself. "There isn't even a decent scandal, except the one about the Egyptian woman." She leaned forward, her face vivid. "Did you know that the newspapers are demanding that Saville Ryerson be arrested as well? Isn't that absurd?" Her eyes searched Charlotte's face questioningly. "I suppose Thomas would have been working on that if he were still at Bow Street. Perhaps it's just as well he isn't. I wouldn't like the untangling of that affair!"

"I'm afraid my case is very pedestrian," Charlotte said, trying to keep her face comparatively expressionless. She could not afford to be sidetracked now, even by the most colorful of scandals. She sat back in the chair. The room was gold and green and there were late yellow roses and earthy-smelling chrysanthemums in a dark green vase on the table. For an instant she was taken back to the house she had grown up in, the comfort and the ignorance of the shadows and poverty in the larger world beyond.

Then the moment passed.

"So what is it?" Emily asked, folding her hands in her lap and paying complete attention. "Give me something to occupy my mind with other than trivia. I am bored to tears with talk about things that don't matter." She smiled with faint self-mockery. "I am afraid my social shallowness is passing. Isn't that alarming? The pursuit of pleasure isn't fun anymore. It is like too much chocolate soufflé, which a few years ago I wouldn't have believed possible."

"Then let me offer you something much more ordinary," Charlotte replied.

She was about to explain the situation when there was a sharp rap on the door, as with the head of a walking stick, and a moment later the door flew open and a short, fierce old woman stood on the threshold. She was dressed in plum and black, and her expression was one of undisguised outrage, although she did not seem to know whether to direct it at Emily or at Charlotte.

Perhaps it had been inevitable. Charlotte rose to her feet and with a mighty effort forced herself to smile. "Good morning, Grandmama," she said, going over to the old lady. "You look very well."

"Don't assume how I am, young woman!" the old lady snapped. "You haven't called on me in months! How could you know? You have no feelings, no sense of duty at all. Ever since you married that police person you have lost all sense of decency."

Charlotte's resolution to be polite died an instant death. "You have changed your mind, then!" she retorted.

The old lady was nonplussed. It annoyed her still more. "I don't know what you mean. Why can't you speak clearly? You used to be able to. It must be the company you keep." She glared at her other granddaughter. "Are you going to invite me to sit down, Emily? Or have you lost all your manners as well?"

"You are always welcome to sit down, Grandmama," Emily said with veiled patience. "Surely you know that?"

The old lady sat down heavily in the third chair, balancing her cane in front of her. She turned to Charlotte. "What do you mean, changed my mind? I don't change my mind!"

"You said I have lost my sense of decency," Charlotte replied.

"So you have!" the old lady said tartly. "No change in that!"

Charlotte smiled at her. "You used to say I never had any."

"Are you going to allow me to be insulted?" the old lady demanded of Emily.

"I think it is Charlotte who was insulted, Grandmama," Emily pointed out, but now there was a smile hovering around her lips and she was having trouble concealing it.

The old lady grunted. "Well, if she was insulted, no doubt she looked for it. Who insulted her? She mixes with a very low class of person. I daresay it is all she can aspire to. Comes of marrying beneath her. I always said it would lead to trouble. I told you—but would you listen to me? Of course not. Well, now you see what happens? Although what you expect Emily to do about it, I'm sure I don't know."

Charlotte started to laugh, and after a moment's hesitation Emily joined in.

The old lady had no idea what was funny, but she certainly was not going to admit it. She considered what to do for several seconds, then decided she had least to lose by joining in, which she did. It was a curious, rusty sound, one that even Emily, in whose house the old woman lived, had not heard in years.

She remained for another ten minutes or so, then in spite of the fact that she was desperately inquisitive as to why Charlotte had called, she dragged herself to her feet and stumped out. It was apparent that no one was going to tell her, and she would not sacrifice her dignity to ask.

As soon as the door was closed behind her, Emily leaned forward. "So?" she asked. "What is this more ordinary problem that has engaged you?"

"Gracie has a friend, Tilda Garvie," Charlotte began. "Her brother, Martin, is valet to Stephen Garrick, living in Torrington Square. Tilda and Martin are very close, being orphans since the ages of six and eight, respectively."

"Yes?" Emily's eyes were wide.

"Martin has not been seen for four days now, and according to Garrick's butler, is no longer in the house, but he would not tell Tilda where Martin has gone, nor why."

"A missing valet?" There was no inflection in Emily's voice to betray her emotions.

"A missing brother," Charlotte corrected. "More significant than his mere absence is the fact that it was over the time of Tilda's birthday, which he has never previously forgotten. If he had lost his position, and thus his lodging, even if the circumstances were embarrassing or disgraceful, surely he would have found a way to convey to her his whereabouts?"

"What do you suspect?" Emily frowned. "Have the Garricks reported him missing?"

"I don't know," Charlotte said impatiently. "I can hardly go to the nearest police station and ask them. But if they had, then why did they not tell Tilda so, just in case she knew where he was?"

"It would seem the intelligent thing to do," Emily agreed. "But people are not always as clever as you would suppose. The most surprising people lack ordinary sense. What other possibilities are there?" She held up her fingers. "He was dismissed for dishonesty? He ran off with a woman, one of the maids from another household? He ran off with someone's daughter, or worse, someone's wife? Or a prostitute?" She started on the other hand. "He is in debt and has to hide from his debtors? Or worst of all, he met with an accident, or was attacked on purpose, and is dead somewhere but has not been identified?"

Charlotte had already thought of most of those answers, especially the last. "Yes, I know," she said quietly. "I would like to find out which of them is the truth, for Tilda's sake . . . and Gracie's. I think she quarreled with Inspector Tellman over it because he said it wasn't a case, so he couldn't look into it."

"Inspector? Oh . . . yes." Emily's expression quickened with interest. "How is that romance going? Will she relent and marry him, do you think? What will you do without her? Look for a good maid already trained, or start again with another child? You can't! Can you?"

"I don't know whether she will or not," Charlotte said ruefully. "I rather think so . . . I hope so, because he is so much in love with her, and he is beginning to realize it slowly, and with great reluctance. And I have no idea what I shall do without her. I don't even want to think of it. I have had more changes than I wish to already."

Emily's sympathy was instant and genuine. "I know," she said softly. "I'm so sorry. It was much more fun in the old days, when we helped Thomas with his cases—our cases—wasn't it?"

Charlotte bit her lip, half to hide a smile, half so the sharpness of it would recall her to the present. "I need to find out all I can about Stephen Garrick," she said firmly. "Sufficient so I can either discover indirectly what happened to Martin Garvie or, if necessary, just ask him."

"I'll help you," Emily said without hesitation. "What do you know about the Garricks?"

"Nothing, except where they live, and even that only approximately."

Emily rose to her feet. "Then we need to begin by enquiring." She looked Charlotte up and down with more or less approval.

"You are ready to go calling, except you will need a better hat. I'll get you one of mine. I'll be ready in fifteen minutes . . ." She reconsidered. "Or perhaps half an hour."

They set off actually almost an hour later in Emily's carriage, first to call upon a friend close enough so they could be fairly open in asking questions.

"No, he's not married," Mrs. Edsel said rather seriously. She was a pleasant, rather ordinary-looking woman, distinguished only by a lively expression and an unfortunate taste in earrings. "Is someone you know considering him?"

"I rather think so," Emily lied with practiced social ease. She was used to the accommodations of good manners. "Should she not?"

"Well, there's plenty of money, I believe." Mrs. Edsel leaned forward a little, her face eager. Gossip was food and drink to her, but she also genuinely wished to be helpful. "A very good family. His father, Ferdinand Garrick, is a highly influential man. Excellent military record, so my husband says."

"So why would his son not be a good match?" Emily asked innocently.

"Perhaps for the right woman, he might be." Mrs. Edsel remembered her social aspirations and became more circumspect.

"And for the wrong woman?" Charlotte could contain herself no longer.

Mrs. Edsel regarded her with a shadow of suspicion. She knew Emily, but Charlotte was a stranger, and neither her possible use nor her danger was known.

A shadow of warning crossed Emily's face, and of criticism for having interrupted.

There was no way to take it back. Charlotte made herself smile, and it felt a bit like the baring of teeth. "I am concerned for a friend," she said with perfect honesty. Despite their differing stations, Gracie was most certainly a friend; few others were as good.

Mrs. Edsel eased a fraction. "Is your friend young?" she enquired.

"Yes." Charlotte guessed this was the correct answer.

"Then I think she would be wiser to look elsewhere—unless she is very plain."

This time Charlotte held her tongue.

"What is his fault?" Emily asked with extraordinary boldness. "Does he have disreputable friends? Who might know him?"

"Oh, really . . ." Mrs. Edsel was now torn between anxiety at committing an irretrievable indiscretion, and a burning curiosity. "He belongs to the usual clubs, I've heard," she went on. That remark was surely safe enough.

"Does he?" Emily opened her blue eyes very wide. "I cannot recall my husband mentioning him. Perhaps I simply did not notice."

"I am sure he is a member of Whites," Mrs. Edsel assured her. "And that is just about the best."

"Indeed," Emily agreed.

"Anyone who is anyone . . ." Charlotte murmured sententiously.

Mrs. Edsel gave a little gasp, and then a giggle, quickly stifled. "To be honest, I really don't know. But my husband says he drinks a good deal more than he can hold . . . rather often. It is not a gross fault, I know, but I don't care for it myself. And he is somewhat morose of temperament. I find that most difficult. I prefer a man of reliable demeanor."

"So do I." Emily nodded, avoiding Charlotte's eyes in case she should laugh, knowing what a lie that was. It sounded unutterably boring.

"And I!" Charlotte added with feeling as Mrs. Edsel looked to her for approval. "Indeed, if you are going to spend some time with a person, it is essential. One cannot be forever wondering what to expect."

"You are quite right," Mrs. Edsel said with a smile. "I hope you do not think I am forward, but I would advise your friend most decidedly to wait a few months longer. Is it her first season?"

Charlotte and Emily said yes and no at the same moment, but Mrs. Edsel was looking at Charlotte.

For the next half hour or so they spoke agreeably of the difficulty of making a suitable marriage and how glad they all were to be fortunately placed already, but not yet faced with the duty of finding husbands for their daughters. Charlotte had to work very hard, scrambling in her memory for the right things to say. It was also a balancing act worthy of a circus performer not to give away Pitt's socially unacceptable occupation. However, possibly "Special Branch" would sound better than "policeman," but she was not supposed to speak of it. It hurt her pride to pretend complete ignorance, and in these enlightened days even Mrs. Edsel was startled at such feminine simplicity.

As soon as they were back in the carriage Emily burst into such laughter she gave herself hiccups. Charlotte did not know whether to laugh back or explode with temper.

"Laugh!" Emily commanded as the driver urged the horses forward and they proceeded towards the next appointment. "You were magnificent, and totally absurd! Thomas would never let you forget it, if he knew."

"Well, he doesn't know!" Charlotte said warningly.

Emily leaned comfortably against the padded back of the carriage seat, still smiling to herself. "I think you should tell him . . . except you probably couldn't do it well. I should do it, really."

"Emily!"

"Oh, please!" That was not a request so much as a remonstration for meanness of spirit. "I am sure he would appreciate a joke—and this really is one!"

Charlotte had to admit that was true. "Well, choose your time wisely. He has a miserable case at the moment."

"Can we help?" Emily said instantly, her attention totally serious again.

"No!" Charlotte replied firmly. "At least not yet. Anyway, we need to find Martin Garvie."

"We will," Emily assured her confidently. "We are going to luncheon with just the person. I arranged it while I was dressing."

THE PERSON PROVED to be a young protégé of Emily's husband, Jack. He was confident, ambitious, and delighted to be taken to luncheon by his mentor's wife. And since her sister was present, it was as correct as could be.

To begin with, they conversed about all manner of things of general interest. It was acceptable to speak of the ugly situation in Manchester regarding the cotton workers, and from that everyone's mind moved quite naturally to the murder of Edwin Lovat, because of the connection with Ryerson, although no one actually spoke of it.

The waiter brought them the first course of their excellent luncheon, a delicate Belgian pâté for Mr. Jamieson, a clear soup for Charlotte and Emily.

Emily did not waste any more time, knowing that Jamieson would have to return to his duties soon. She could trespass only so much.

"This is an enquiry for a very secret department of the government," Emily began shamelessly, having kicked Charlotte under the table to warn her to show no surprise, and certainly not to argue. "My sister"—she glanced at Charlotte—"has made me aware of a way in which I can help, in the utmost confidence, you understand?"

"Yes, Mrs. Radley," Jamieson said gravely.

"A young man's life may depend upon it," Emily warned. "In fact, he may already be dead, but we hope profoundly that he is not." She ignored his look of alarm. "Mr. Radley tells me that you are a member of White's. Is that correct?"

"Yes, yes I am. Surely there is no—"

"No, of course not," Emily assured him hastily. "There is no question of White's being involved." She leaned a little towards him, ignoring her soup, her face intent with concentration. "I had better be candid with you, Mr. Jamieson . . ."

He leaned forward also, his eyes wide. "I promise, Mrs. Radley, that I shall hold it in the most total confidence . . . from everyone."

"Thank you."

The waiter returned to take away their dishes and serve the entrée—poached fish for the ladies, roast beef for Jamieson.

As soon as he had gone Charlotte drew in her breath, and felt Emily's foot tap her ankle. She winced very slightly.

"I believe a young man named Stephen Garrick could give us information which would help," she said.

Jamieson frowned, but he did not look as puzzled or as surprised as she would have expected. "I'm sorry to hear that," he said quietly. "We all knew there was something wrong."

"How did you know?" Charlotte urged, trying to suppress the eagerness in her voice, and the edge of fear she knew was there.

He looked at her frankly. He had wide, clear blue eyes. "He drank far too much for pleasure," he answered. "It was as if he were trying to drown out something inside himself." There was pity in his expression. "At first I thought it was just overindulgence, as anyone might, you know? Keeping up, not wanting to be the first to cry off. But then I began to realize it was more than that. It made him ill, but still he went on. And . . . he drank alone, as well as with company."

"I see," Emily acknowledged. "There is apparently something that causes him great pain. I presume from the fact that you do not mention it that you do not know what it is."

"No." He shrugged very slightly. "And honestly I don't know how I could find out. I haven't seen him for several days, and the last time I did, he was in no condition to answer anything sensibly. I . . . I'm sorry." It was not clear if his apology was for his inability, or for having spoken to them of such a distasteful subject.

"But you do know him?" Charlotte pressed. "I mean, you have his acquaintance?"

Jamieson looked doubtful, as if he sensed in advance what she would ask. "Yes," he admitted guardedly. "Er . . . not well. I'm not one of his . . ." He stopped.

"What?" Emily demanded.

Jamieson looked back at her. She sat straight-backed, like Great-Aunt Vespasia, smiling at him expectantly, her head beautifully poised.

"One of his circle," Jamieson finished unhappily.

"But you can enquire," Emily stated.

"Yes," he said reluctantly. "Yes, of course."

"Good." Emily was relentless. "There is great danger. Even a short time may be too late. Can you call upon him this evening?"

"Is it really . . . so . . ." Jamieson was not sure if he was excited or alarmed.

"Oh, yes," Emily assured him.

Jamieson swallowed a mouthful of beef and roast potato. "Very well. How shall I tell you what I learn?"

"Telephone," Emily said immediately. She pulled out a card from the tiny silver engraved case in her reticule. "My number is on it. Please do not speak to anyone but me . . . not anyone at all. Do you understand?"

"Yes, Mrs. Radley, of course."

Charlotte thanked Emily with profound sincerity and accepted the offered ride home in the carriage. At half past eight, when she and Pitt were sitting in the parlor, the telephone rang. Pitt answered it.

"It is Emily, for you," he said from the doorway.

Charlotte went into the hall and took the instrument. "Yes?"

"Stephen Garrick is not at home." Emily's voice was strange and a little tinny over the wires. "No one has seen him for several days, and the butler says he could not inform Mr. Jamieson when he would return. Charlotte . . . it looks as if he has disappeared as well. What are we going to do?"

"I don't know." Charlotte found her hand shaking. "Not yet . . ."

"But we'll do something, won't we?" Emily said after a second. "It looks serious, doesn't it? I mean . . . more serious than a valet losing his job?"

"Yes," Charlotte said a little huskily. "Yes, it does."

CHAPTER FOUR

On the day that Charlotte undertook to help Gracie, and thus Tilda, Pitt returned to Narraway's office and found him pacing the floor, five steps and then turn, another five, and back again. He spun around as Pitt opened the door. His face was pinched and tired, his eyes too bright. He stared at Pitt questioningly.

Pitt closed the door behind himself and remained standing. "Ryerson was there," he said bluntly. "He doesn't deny it. He helped her move the body and he didn't attempt to call the police. She hasn't said that, but he will if the police ask him. He'll protect her, at his own cost."

Narraway said nothing, but his body seemed to become even more rigid, as if Pitt's words had layers of meaning deeper than the facts they knew.

"Her story doesn't make sense," Pitt went on, wishing Narraway would answer, say anything at all to make the talking easier. But Narraway seemed to be so charged with emotion that he was unable to exercise his usual incisive leap of intelligence. He was waiting for Pitt to lead.

"If she had no involvement, why would she try to move the body?" Pitt continued. "Why not call the police, as anyone else would?"

Narraway glared at him, his voice cracking when he spoke. "Because she set up the situation. She wanted to be caught. She might even have been the one who called the police. Have you considered that?"

"To incriminate herself?" Pitt said with total disbelief.

Narraway's face was twisted with bitterness. "We haven't come to trial yet. Wait and see what she says then. So far, if Talbot's telling the truth, she hasn't said anything at all. What if she turns around and, with desperate reluctance, admits that Ryerson shot Lovat in a jealous rage?" His voice mimicked savagely the tone he imagined she would use. "She tried to conceal it, because she loves him and felt guilty for having provoked him—she knew he had an uncontrollable temper—but she cannot go on protecting him any longer, and will not hang for him." His look challenged Pitt to prove him wrong.

Pitt was stunned. "What for?" he asked, and as soon as the words were out of his mouth, hideous possibilities danced before him, violent, personal, political.

Narraway's stare was withering. "She's Egyptian, Pitt. Cotton comes to mind to begin with. We've got riots in Manchester over prices already. We want them down, Egypt wants them up. Ever since the American Civil War cut off our supply from the South and we've had to rely on Egypt, the balance has been different. European industry is catching up with us and we need the empire not only to buy from but to sell to."

Pitt frowned. "Don't we buy most of Egypt's cotton anyway?"

"Of course we do!" Narraway said impatiently. "But a bargain that leaves one side unhappy serves neither in the end, because it doesn't last. Ryerson is one of the few men who can both see further than a couple of years ahead and negotiate an agreement that will leave both the Egyptian growers and the British weavers feeling as if they have gained something." His face tightened. "Apart from that, there's Egyptian nationalism, and for God's sake we don't want to send the gunboats in again! We've bombarded

Alexandria once in the last twenty years." He ignored Pitt's wince. "And there's religious fervor," he went on. "I hardly need to remind you of the uprising in the Sudan?"

Pitt did not reply; everyone remembered the siege of Khartoum and the murder of General Gordon.

"Other than that," Narraway finished, "personal profit, or common or gender hatred. Do you need more?"

"Then we need to learn the truth before it comes to trial," Pitt answered. "But I don't know that it will help."

"You must make it help!" Narraway said between his teeth, his voice thick with emotion. "If Ryerson is convicted, the government will have to replace him with either Howlett or Maberley. Howlett will give in to the mill workers here and drive the prices down so far it will break the Egyptians. We'll have a few years of wealth and then disaster—poverty—Egypt will have no cotton to sell and no money to buy anything. Possibly even rebellion. Maberley will give in to the Egyptians and we'll have riots all over the Midlands here, police forced to suppress them with violence, maybe even the army out." He drew in breath to add more, then changed his mind and swung around with his back to Pitt.

"So far everything incriminates his woman, with Ryerson as a willing accomplice." He jabbed the air with his hand. "We need another answer. Find out more about Lovat. Who else might have killed him? Who was he? What was his relationship with the woman? I suppose one might hope there was some justification for her killing him?" There was no lift of hope in him, and yet Pitt had the intense feeling that, beneath the bitterness, Narraway was clinging on to a thread of belief that there could be another, better explanation.

"You know Ryerson, sir," Pitt began. "If the woman comes to trial, will he really allow himself to be implicated? If he has any kind of guilt, won't he resign first, so at least he isn't a government minister at the time?"

Narraway kept his back to him, his face hidden.

"Probably," he agreed. "But I am not yet prepared to ask the man to do that until I can see beyond doubt that he has any guilt in Lovat's death." There was dismissal in his tone and in the rigid set of his shoulders, the light from the narrow window on his dark head. "Report to me tomorrow," he said finally. He swung around just as Pitt reached the door.

"Pitt!"

"Yes, sir?"

"I accepted you into Special Branch because Cornwallis told me that you were his best detective and that you know society. You know how to tread carefully but still find the truth." It was a statement, but it was also a question, even a plea. For an instant, Pitt felt as if Narraway were asking for help in some way which he could not name or explain.

Then the impression vanished.

"Get on with it," Narraway ordered.

"Yes, sir," Pitt said again, then left, and closed the door behind him.

He went straight to the offices where Lovat had worked for the year or so before his death. Naturally the police had already been there. The information was so public it had been printed in Lovat's obituary, so when Pitt arrived he was received with weary resignation by Ragnall, an official in his early forties who had obviously already answered all the predictable questions.

Ragnall stood in the quiet, discreetly furnished office overlooking Horse Guards Parade and regarded Pitt patiently but with very little interest.

"I don't know what else I can tell you," he said, gesturing for Pitt to sit down in the armchair opposite the desk. "I can offer no explanation except the obvious one—he pestered the woman until she grew desperate and shot him . . . either in what she construed to be self-defense or more likely because he threatened to disrupt her present arrangements." A slight expression of distaste crossed his face. "And before you ask me, I have no idea what they might be."

Pitt had little hope of learning much from the interview, but he had no better place to begin. He settled into the chair and looked across at Mr. Ragnall.

"You think he may have pestered Miss Zakhari to the point that she felt a simple rebuff was not adequate to make him desist?" he asked.

Ragnall looked surprised. "Well, it seems to have been the case, doesn't it? Are you suggesting that she deliberately encouraged him, for some reason, and then killed him? Why, for heaven's sake? Why would any woman do such a thing?" He frowned. "You said you were from Special Branch . . ."

"Special Branch has no knowledge of Miss Zakhari prior to the death of Mr. Lovat," Pitt answered the implied question. "I wanted your judgment of Mr. Lovat as a man who would continue to pursue a woman who has told him that she has no desire for his attentions."

Ragnall looked very faintly uncomfortable. His smooth, rather good-looking face flushed, so slightly it could have been no more than a change of the light, except that he had not moved.

"I suppose I am saying that—yes." He made it sound like an apology. "I believe Miss Zakhari is very beautiful. At least that is what I have heard. One can become . . . obsessed." He pursed his lips, giving himself a moment to seek exactly the right words to make Pitt understand. "She is Egyptian. There are unlikely to be many other Egyptian women in London. It is not as if she were ordinary, and easily replaceable. Some men are attracted to the exotic."

"You saw Mr. Lovat regularly." Pitt too was feeling his way. "Did you gather the impression that he was 'obsessed,' as you put it?"

"Well . . ." Ragnall drew in his breath and then let it out again.

"Your protection of his reputation may condemn another man," Pitt said grimly.

Ragnall looked puzzled for a moment.

"Another man?" Then his confusion cleared. "Oh . . . this nonsense in the newspapers about Ryerson? Surely it's just . . ." He opened his palms to indicate a helplessness to describe exactly what he was thinking.

"I hope so," Pitt agreed. "Was Lovat obsessed with her?"

"I . . . I really have no idea." Ragnall was obviously uncomfortable. "I never knew of him being serious about a woman . . . at least for more than a short time. He . . ." Now there was distinct color in his face. "He seemed to find it rather easy to attract women and then . . . move on."

"He had many affairs?" Pitt concluded.

"Yes . . . yes, I'm afraid he did. He was usually reasonably discreet, of course. But one does get to know." Ragnall was acutely aware of discussing intimate subjects with a social inferior. Pitt had placed him in the position of betraying his own class, or his ethics. Either would be hard and cut across his deep convictions as to who and what he wished to be.

"With what sort of women?" Pitt asked, his voice still light and courteous.

Ragnall's eyes widened.

Pitt maintained his steady gaze. "Mr. Lovat has been murdered, sir," he reminded him. "I am afraid the reasons for such a crime are not often as simple as we should like, or as far from shame. I need to know more about Mr. Lovat and the people he knew well."

"Surely the Egyptian woman, Miss Zakhari, killed him?" Ragnall said, his composure regained. "He may have been foolish in pursuing her when his attentions would seem to have been unwelcome, but there is no need to drag anyone else into it, is there?" He regarded Pitt with a look of distaste.

"It appears as though she did," Pitt conceded. "Although she denies it. And as you say, it seems an extremely violent and unnecessary way to refuse an unwanted suitor. From what I have heard of her so far, she was a woman of more finesse. She must have had unwanted suitors before. Why was Lovat different?"

Ragnall's face tightened, and there was a dull color in his cheeks again and a stiffness in his manner. "You are right," he said grudgingly.

"If she made her living that way, and I had assumed such was the case, then she must have been better at discarding the old, in order to improve her situation, than this would suggest."

"Exactly," Pitt agreed with feeling. For the first time a point had been made in Ayesha Zakhari's favor. He was startled by how much it pleased him. "What was Lovat like? And you are not giving his obituary. Only the truth can be fair to all."

Ragnall thought for several moments. "Frankly, he was a womanizer," he said reluctantly.

"He liked women?" Pitt attempted to reach after exactly what Ragnall meant. "He fell in love? He used them? Might he have made enemies?"

Ragnall was distinctly unhappy. "I . . . I really don't know."

"What gives you the impression that he was a womanizer, sir?" Pitt said bluntly. "Men have been known to exaggerate their conquests to impress others. A lot of loose talk does not necessarily mean anything."

A flick of temper crossed Ragnall's face. "Lovat didn't talk, Mr. Pitt, at least not that I heard. It is my own observation, and that of colleagues."

"What sort of women?" Pitt repeated. "Ones like Ayesha Zakhari?"

Ragnall was slightly taken aback. "You mean foreigners? Or . . ." He did not wish to use the word *whore*. It spoke not only of the women but of the men who used them. "Not that I am aware of," he finished abruptly.

"I meant women who have no husbands or families in London," Pitt corrected. "And who are past the usual age of marrying, possibly who make their way as mistresses."

Ragnall took a deep breath, as if reaching a decision that was difficult for him.

Pitt waited. Perhaps finally he was on the brink of something that did not implicate Ryerson.

"No," Ragnall said at last. "I gathered he did not particularly care, and . . . and he had not the means to support a mistress, not in any style." He stopped, still reluctant to commit himself any further.

Pitt stared at him. "Other men's wives? Their daughters?"

Ragnall cleared his throat. "Yes . . . at times."

"Who were his friends?" Pitt asked. "What clubs did he belong to? What were his interests, sports? Did he gamble, go to the theater? What did he do in his leisure time?"

Ragnall hesitated.

"Don't tell me you don't know," Pitt warned. "The man was in the diplomatic service. You could not allow yourself to be unaware of his habits. That would be incompetent. You must know his associates, his problems, his financial status."

Ragnall looked down at his hands, spread on the desk, then up at Pitt again. "The man is dead," he said quietly. "I have no idea whether that was pure misfortune or if he contributed to it in some way himself, greatly, or very little. He was good at his job. I am unaware of him owing anyone money or, as far as I know, favors. He came from a good family, and he kept his word once he had given it. He had an honorable career in the army and he never lacked either physical or moral courage. I never caught him in a lie, nor do I know anyone who did. He was loyal to his friends, and he knew how to conduct himself as a gentleman. He had a certain charm, and there was nothing mean-spirited in him."

Pitt felt the wave of regret he always did when investigating a murder. Suddenly the truth of detail was overwhelmed by the loss of a life, the passion, the vulnerability, the virtues and the idiosyncrasies. The vitality of being was ended, not naturally in age, but without warning, and incomplete. The fault or the contributing sins of the person concerned seemed so unimportant as to be forgotten.

But emotion would cripple his analytical mind, and his job was to find the truth, easy or difficult, complicated and however painful.

"The names of his friends," he said aloud. "I may find him innocent of all blame, Mr. Ragnall, but I cannot assume. If Miss

Zakhari, or anyone else, is to be hanged for his murder, it will be because we know what happened, and why."

"Yes, of course." Ragnall pulled a piece of paper towards himself and picked up a pen, dipped it in the ink and began to write. He blotted it and pushed it towards Pitt.

"Thank you." Pitt took it, glanced at it and read the names, and the clubs at which they might be found, then took his leave.

PITT SAW ONE or two of the people Ragnall had suggested, and learned very little more. No one was comfortable discussing a colleague who was dead, and unable to defend himself. It was not a matter of affection so much as loyalty to their own ideals, perhaps in the belief that to betray was to invite a similar betrayal yourself, when your own weaknesses were questioned.

By midafternoon Pitt had given up the hope of finding anything useful this way, and decided to go and see his brother-in-law, Jack Radley, who had now been a Member of Parliament for a number of years, some of it with particular interest in the Foreign Office.

He was not in the House of Commons, and Pitt caught up with him just after four o'clock, walking in the sun across St. James's Park, a slight breeze sending a few early yellow leaves fluttering down over the grass.

Jack stopped and turned when he heard Pitt call his name. He was surprised to see him, but not displeased.

"The Eden Lodge case?" he said wryly as Pitt fell into step with him.

"Sorry," Pitt apologized. They had a genuine liking for each other, but their social circles as well as their professions kept them apart almost all the time. Jack had no money of his own, but he had always managed to live as well as his good birth invited. To begin with, it had been by liberal use of his great personal charm. Since marrying Emily, it was on the fortunes she had inherited from her first husband.

For the first year or two he had been content to continue merely enjoying himself in society. Then, with Emily's pushing, and some example of Pitt's, and possibly the respect he had observed both his wife and her sister had for achievement, he had taken up a vivid interest in politics. That did not alter the fact that he and Pitt met seldom.

"I don't know Ryerson," Jack said regretfully. "Bit above my political reach . . . for the time being." He saw Pitt's face. "I mean I intend to climb," he corrected quickly, "not that I think he is going to fall. Is he?" Now his expression was suddenly very serious.

"Too early to say," Pitt replied. "No, I'm not being discreet. I really don't know." He pushed his hands into his pockets, a dramatic contrast to Jack, who would never have dreamed of doing so. It would ruin the line of his clothes, and he was far too innately elegant to do that.

"I wish I could help," Jack said with implied apology. "It all seems ridiculous, from what I've heard."

A small black-and-white dog was charging around, wagging its tail with excitement. It did not seem to belong to the courting couple near the trees, or to the nursemaid in starched uniform, the sun shining on the fair hair escaping her white cap as she pushed a perambulator along the path.

Pitt bent and picked up a piece of stick and threw it as far as he could. The dog hared after it, barking with excitement.

"Did you know Lovat?" he asked.

Jack glanced sideways at him, unhappiness in his eyes. "Not well."

Pitt could not afford to let him escape so lightly. "He's been murdered, Jack. If it were not important I wouldn't ask."

Jack looked startled. "Special Branch?" he said with disbelief. "Why? Is there something in the Ryerson speculation? I thought it was just the newspapers."

"I don't know what it is," Pitt retorted. "And I need to know, preferably before they do. Did you know Lovat? Without the censorship of decency toward the dead."

Jack's mouth tightened and he stared into the distance.

The dog came galloping up to Pitt and dropped the stick, dancing backwards in anticipation, gazing up at him.

He bent, picked up the stick and pitched it far again. The dog hurtled after it, ears and tail flying.

"A difficult man," Jack said at last. "An ideal candidate for murder, I suppose, in a way. Actually, I'm damned sorry it happened." He turned to look at Pitt. "Tread softly, Thomas, if you can. There are a lot of people who could be hurt, and they don't deserve it. The man was a bastard where women were concerned. If he'd stayed with the sort of married women who've had their children and now play the field a bit, no one would have minded a lot, but he courted women as if he loved them, young women expecting marriage, needing it, and then once he had them, he suddenly cried off. Left everyone wondering what was the matter with them. The conclusion was usually that they had lost their virtue. Then, of course, nobody else wanted them either." He did not need to paint a further picture. They both knew what lay ahead for an unmarriageable woman.

"Why?" Pitt said miserably. "Why court a decent woman you have no intention of marrying? It's cruel . . . and dangerous. I'd—" He stopped, but in his mind he thought for a moment of Jemima, trusting, eager, so easy to hurt. If a man had done that to her, Pitt would have wanted to kill him, but not shoot him cleanly in someone else's garden in the middle of the night. He would have wanted to beat him to a pulp first, feel the crack of bone on bone, the impact of his fist on flesh, see the pain, and the understanding of why it was happening. It was probably primitive, and would be of no help at all to Jemima, except to let her know she was of infinite value to someone and that she was not alone in her pain. And it would serve the point at least that the man would be a great deal less inclined to do it again.

He looked sideways at Jack, and saw something of the same

raw anger in his face. Perhaps he was thinking of his own daughter, barely more than a baby.

"You know it for certain?" Pitt asked quietly.

"Yes. I suppose you want names?"

"No. I don't want them," Pitt replied. "I would far rather let the poor devils keep their pain secret, but I have to. If we don't get the right person, then the wrong man . . . or woman, will be hanged."

"I suppose so." Jack listed off four names, and what he knew of where they might be found.

Pitt did not need to write them down. He wished he did not even need to hear them or make enquiries; he could understand their emotions too easily. Imagination was necessary to his job, but it was also a curse.

The dog came back, quivering with excitement and delight, dropping the stick at Pitt's feet and dancing around waiting for him to throw it again. It did not often meet people so willing to play, and who obviously understood the game.

Pitt obliged and the animal went racing off again. He really would like to have a dog. He would tell Charlotte the cats would just have to accommodate it.

"You could ask Emily," Jack said suddenly, looking at Pitt and biting his lip. He looked slightly abashed to be saying it. "She notices things about people . . ." He left it hanging. They were both aware of past cases where Charlotte and Emily had interfered, sometimes dangerously, but their acute discretion and understanding of nuances of meaning had been key to the solution.

"Yes," Pitt agreed, surprised that he had not thought of it for himself. "Yes, I'll do that. Will she be at home?"

Jack smiled suddenly. "I've no idea!"

ACTUALLY, IT TOOK PITT two hours to catch up with Emily. Her butler told him that she had gone to a newly opened art exhibition, and after that she expected to return home only for the time it took her to change for the evening, and dinner at Lady Mansfield's home in Belgravia. Tomorrow morning she would be riding in the park, and then visiting her dressmaker before taking an early luncheon and making the usual afternoon calls. The evening would be spent at the opera.

Pitt thanked the butler, asked for directions to the exhibition, and took himself there immediately.

The gallery was crowded with women in beautiful gowns, and a few men escorting them, flirting a little, and passing grave and wordy comments on the paintings.

Pitt looked at them only briefly, which he regretted. He thought them not only beautiful but of great interest. The style was impressionist in a manner he had not seen before, blurred and hazy, and yet creating a feeling of light which pleased him enormously.

But he was not here for interest. He must find Emily before she left, and that would require concentration, and even considerable physical effort merely to keep on excusing himself and pushing between groups of chattering people, women with skirts which brushed up against each other and blocked the way for several feet in every direction.

He received several angry and imperious glances and heard mutters of "Well, really!" on more than one occasion, but he could not afford the time to wait until they moved on and allowed him to pass of their own accord.

He found Emily in the third room, in idle conversation with a young woman in a cornflower-blue dress and an extravagant hat which he thought was most becoming. It lent her a drama which she did not otherwise possess.

He was wondering how to attract Emily's attention without being rude when she noticed him, perhaps because he was conspicuously out of place in the rest of the crowd. Her face filled with consternation. She excused herself urgently from the woman in blue, and came straight over to Pitt.

"There is nothing wrong," he assured her.

"I had not thought there was," she said, without altering her expression in the slightest. "My fear was of being so bored I fell asleep and lost my balance. There is nothing whatever here to hold me up."

"Don't you like the pictures?" he asked.

"Thomas, don't be so pedestrian. Nobody comes to look at the paintings, not really look. They only glance at them in order to make remarks they think are fearfully deep, and hope someone will repeat. Why have you come? They're not stolen, are they?"

"No, they're not." He smiled in spite of himself. "Jack suggested that you might be able to help me."

Her face quickened with interest. "Of course!" she said eagerly. "What can I do?"

"All I want is information, and perhaps your opinion."

"About whom?" She linked her arm in his and turned towards one of the pictures as if she were studying it intently.

It was not really the situation in which to hold a hotly discreet conversation, but if he spoke softly it would probably be neither overheard nor remarked by anyone.

"About Lieutenant Edwin Lovat," he replied, also staring at the picture.

She stiffened, although not a flicker crossed her face. "Are you dealing with that case?" Her voice was sharp with excitement. She did not mention Special Branch, she was far too aware of putting even a word out of place to say that aloud, but he knew the thoughts and possibilities racing through her imagination.

"Yes, I am," he answered almost under his breath. "What do you know about him, Emily? Or what have you heard . . . and make plain the difference."

She kept her eyes fixed on the painting. It was a scene of light shining through trees onto a patch of water. It had an extraordinarily restful beauty, as of solitude on a windless, summer day. One expected to see the shimmer of dragonfly wings.

"I know that he was a dangerously unhappy man," she answered him. "He seemed to keep falling half in love, and then, the moment he had won someone's commitment, to run away as if he were terrified of allowing anyone to know him. He caused a great deal of pain, and he never regretted it enough not to go and do it again straightaway. If it was not the Egyptian woman who murdered him, then you have plenty of other possibilities to look at."

"Dangerously unhappy?" He repeated her phrase curiously.

"Well, you don't behave like that unless something is corroding inside you, do you?" she challenged, still without more than glancing up at him. "If you are merely selfish, or greedy, you might marry for money, for title, or for beauty, but what he was doing gained him nothing except enemies. And he was apparently not so stupid as to be unaware of that. Nobody could be. He was quite as intelligent as most people, and yet he behaved in a way which any fool could see would bring him nothing but grief."

He thought about it in silence for a while, turning it over in his mind. It was a concept he had not considered.

She waited.

"Do you believe he had thought as deeply as that?" he said at length.

"You didn't ask me to be logical, Thomas, you asked me what I thought of Lieutenant Lovat."

"You are quite right. Thank you. Can you give me the names of these people?"

"Naturally!" she said, raising her hand to indicate the light in the picture, as if she were remarking on it, then she reeled off half a dozen names, and he wrote them down, with at least a general idea of their addresses and a rough guide to their social pastimes. It was an ugly catalogue of hope and humiliation, embarrassment and hurt feelings, some lighter, others profound.

Pitt thanked her and left the gallery.

THAT EVENING and all the next day Pitt enquired discreetly into the whereabouts of the people whose names Emily had given him, but all of them could account for their whereabouts, or else the moral or emotional injury was too old, or too delicate, for revenge now to hurt Lovat any more than it would also hurt them. Every rational thought led Pitt back to Ryerson and Ayesha Zakhari.

The day after that he went to the records of Lovat's time in the army in Egypt, just in case they shed any new light on his character or his relationships with other soldiers, or offered an avenue to pursue another Egyptian connection that could lead back to Ayesha Zakhari and make more sense of what had happened at Eden Lodge. He realized with something of a jolt how much he wanted to discover something that would justify what he could not avoid believing . . . that Ayesha had shot Lovat, and Ryerson was so inextricably involved with her that he had been prepared to help conceal the crime.

But the records yielded nothing. Lovat seemed to have been more than adequate at his profession. He had had a natural ease with people and knew how to conduct himself in society.

His military service had been without serious blemish, and he had been honorably discharged when his health was broken after a bout of fever while stationed in Alexandria. There was no suggestion of cowardice or shirking his duty in any way. He had been a good soldier and well liked.

Was it an honest summary, or one carefully censored of any facts that would prejudice a subsequent career? It would not be the first time Pitt had come across a tacit agreement to place loyalty before truth in the concept that the highest honor lay in protecting the reputation of the service.

He had no way of knowing from the printed word, and the clerks he saw knew nothing personally and were far too well trained to speculate. They looked at him blandly and gave away nothing.

It seemed to be in Lovat's personal life that he had incurred enemies. According to those who had known him, he had been a pleasant-looking man, not traditionally handsome, but with a good physique, a fine head of hair, and a smile of great charm. He could dance well and found conversation easy. He liked music, and sang with enthusiasm, carrying a tune and remembering the words of all the sentimental ballads of the day.

"Don't know what was wrong with him," an elderly gentleman said sadly, shaking his head as he sat opposite Pitt in the Army and Navy Club in Pall Mall that evening, sipping a Napoleon brandy, his feet stretched out against the fender, scorching the soles of his boots. "Any amount of agreeable young women who would have made a decent wife. But the moment he looked as if he'd a chance of their hand, he got bored, or dissatisfied, or whatever it was . . . cold feet, I daresay . . . and went after someone else." He pushed out his lower lip in a grimace. "None too particular about who he chose either. Morals of an alley cat, sorry to say."

Pitt inched a little farther from the fire, which was burning with a brilliant glow and far more heat than was needed on a mild September day. Colonel Woodside seemed to be oblivious to it, and to the hot smell emanating from his boots.

"Did you know the Egyptian woman, Miss Zakhari?" Pitt asked, uncertain whether the colonel would consider that an improper question to a gentleman.

"Of course I didn't know her!" Woodside said testily. "And if I had, I'd not be likely to own it to the likes of you! But I saw her, certainly. Beautiful creature, quite beautiful. Never seen an Englishwoman walk with a grace like that. Moved like weeds in the water . . . sort of . . . fluid . . ." He held up his hand as if to demonstrate, then stopped abruptly and glared at Pitt. "If you want me to say Lovat pestered her . . . I can't! I've no idea. A man doesn't do that sort of thing in public."

Pitt changed direction. "Did Mr. Lovat know Mr. Ryerson?" he asked.

"No idea! Shouldn't think so. Damn!" Colonel Woodside jerked his feet off the fender, put them down on the floor, then took them up again even more quickly, and with a grimace.

Pitt kept his face perfectly straight, but with difficulty.

"Hardly frequent the same places," Woodside added, crossing his ankles gingerly to keep the soles of both feet off the floor. "Generation between them, not to mention status, money, and taste. You're thinking about the woman? For God's sake, man! Beautiful, but no better than she should be. Neither man's going to marry her. Of course she'd choose Ryerson." He looked across at Pitt with a frown. "He's got wealth, position, reputation, polish. Apart from that, he has a charm young Lovat could never achieve. And heaven knows why he never married after his wife was killed . . . bad business, that . . . but he won't do now. I daresay an heiress could pick and choose a lot better." He gave a little grunt. "Still, Egyptian women might not know that. Much wiser to play it safe."

"You don't think Ryerson would consider marrying her?" Pitt asked, more to see Woodside's reaction than because he expected a possible answer in the affirmative. He was so touched by a sense of pity for her that it was not even a real question. She was to be used, enjoyed, but never even considered as belonging. There were millions like that, for all sorts of reasons, money, appearance, things they could not change, but it still made him angry. He knew what it was like to be excluded, even if it had not happened to him very often.

Woodside stared at his feet. "Ryerson never got over the death of his wife. Don't really know why. Takes some men that way, but I hadn't thought he was one of them. Never seemed that close, but I suppose you can't tell. Pretty woman, but restless, always looking for some new taste or experience. Couldn't be bothered with her, myself. Don't mind a woman with no brains—easier sometimes—but no patience with one who's downright silly."

Pitt was surprised. He had not imagined Saville Ryerson falling in love with a woman who was markedly unintelligent. He tried to visualize her, the kind of beauty or demureness she must have possessed to capture his emotions to the degree that a quarter of a century after her death he was still mourning her too profoundly to marry again.

"Was she so very . . ." he began, then found that he did not know how he intended to finish.

"No idea," Woodside said unhelpfully. "Never understood Ryerson. Brilliant chap, at times, but devil of a temper when he was young. Only a fool would cross him, I'll tell you that!"

Again, Pitt was slightly taken aback. This was not the man he had observed a couple of days ago—calm, self-controlled, concerned only for the woman.

Had he lost all his ability to judge? Was it possible that Ryerson had shot Lovat himself, in a fit of jealousy, and the woman was shouldering the blame? Why? For love, or in some mistaken belief that he would, or even could, protect her?

"Changed, of course," Woodside went on thoughtfully, still looking at his feet as if afraid he might actually have scorched the leather of his boots. "God knows, with the government he's had enough to test any man's temper over the years. Lonely thing for a man, command, and politicians are a treacherous lot, if you ask me." He looked up suddenly. "Sorry I can't help. No idea who shot Lovat, or why."

Pitt realized it was a dismissal, and he rose to his feet. "Thank you for giving me your time, sir. I'm much obliged to you."

Woodside waved his hand and turned his feet back to the fire.

Pitt went to Ryerson's office in Westminster and requested permission to speak to him for a few minutes. He had waited rather less than half an hour when a secretary in a high wing collar and pinstriped trousers came to collect him and show him in. Pitt was surprised it had taken so short a time.

Ryerson received him in a room of somber opulence, leather-covered furniture, old wood with a polish so deep it seemed like satin beneath glass. There were shelves of morocco-bound books with gold lettering and windows looking out onto the slowly fading leaves of a lime tree.

Ryerson looked tired, dark smudges around his eyes, and his hands constantly fiddled with an unlit cigar.

"What have you found?" he said as soon as Pitt had closed the door, and even before he sat down in the chair Ryerson gestured towards, although remaining standing himself.

Pitt sat down obediently. "Only that Lovat apparently had affairs with many women and no loyalty to any," he replied. "He seems to have hurt many people, some deeply. There is a trail of unhappiness behind him." He watched Ryerson quite openly, but he saw no flicker of either anger or surprise in his face. It was as if Lovat personally did not matter to him.

"Unpleasant," he said with a frown. "But regrettably not unique. What are you suggesting? That some wronged husband could have shot him?" He bit his lip, as if to stop himself from laughing, however bitterly. "That's absurd, Pitt. I wish I could believe it, but what was this wronged man doing at Eden Lodge at three in the morning? What kind of women did Lovat pursue? Ladies? Parlor maids? Prostitutes?"

"Ladies, so far as I have heard," Pitt replied. "Young and unmarried." He did not take his eyes from Ryerson's face and saw the distaste in it. "The sort of women whom scandal would ruin," he added unnecessarily. His remark was driven by anger, not reason.

Ryerson finally threw his cigar into the fireplace, just missing and hearing it strike the brass surround with a thud. He ignored it. "And are you suggesting that the father of one of these women spent the night following Lovat until he caught up with him in the shrubbery of Eden Lodge, and then shot him? You have conducted many investigations of murder which have sooner or later led you to the withdrawing rooms of the aristocracy. You know better than to make such a preposterous suggestion." He looked closely at Pitt, as if to read some motive beyond the apparent absurdity. There was no contempt in his stare, only puzzlement and, very close beneath it, fear, real and biting deep.

Pitt realized something else also, with a sudden lurch of surprise, then instantly knew that he should have expected it.

"You have been enquiring about me!"

Ryerson shrugged very slightly. "Of course. I cannot afford less than the best. Cornwallis tells me you are the best." He did not make it a question, but there was a very slight lift in his voice as if he wanted Pitt to confirm it for him, assure him he had done everything he could.

Pitt was disconcerted to find himself embarrassed. He was angry with Cornwallis, although he knew he would have spoken only with honesty; Cornwallis had probably never lied in his life. His transparency was both his greatest virtue, along with his moral and physical courage, and at the same time his most acute disadvantage in the politics of police administration.

He was utterly unlike Victor Narraway, who was the ultimate sophisticate in subtlety, the art of deceiving without lies, and of keeping his own counsel in everything. If he had any vulnerabilities at all, Pitt had not seen them. He understood emotion in others, but Pitt had no feeling that it was other than with the brilliance of his intellect, his power of observation and deduction. He could not even guess at what Narraway felt himself, or if he felt anything at all, if he had unfilled dreams anywhere in the secret recesses of his heart, wounds unhealed or fears that drowned his solitary moments awake in the night.

Ryerson was watching Pitt now, waiting for some reply.

"Yes, I have investigated in many places," he answered aloud. "Enough to know that some things are just as simple as they appear, and some are not. It seems as if Miss Zakhari had an assignation of some kind with Mr. Lovat, or why did she go out to meet him, and why did she take the gun with her? Had she simply heard an intruder she would have sent her manservant, not gone out herself. And why would Lovat make a noise, if he was walking on grass?"

"Yes," Ryerson conceded tersely. "You have justification for your reasoning. Possibly someone followed him, and killed him at Eden Lodge in order to lay the blame on someone else. Which they seem to have done with great success."

Pitt said nothing. He was thinking of Ayesha Zakhari's gun, lying next to Lovat on the damp ground in the darkness. He looked up at Ryerson, and saw in an instant that exactly the same thought was in his mind. He knew it from the faint flush on his cheeks and the way the understanding flashed between them, and then Ryerson lowered his glance.

"Did you know Lovat?" Pitt asked.

Ryerson moved towards the window and looked out at the leaves turning in the wind. "No. I never met him. The first time I saw him was on the ground at Eden Lodge, at least as far as I know."

"Did Miss Zakhari ever mention him?"

"Not by name. She was a little upset one afternoon when we met, and she said a past acquaintance was being a nuisance. That could have been Lovat, but I suppose not necessarily." He moved his hands restlessly. He stood with his shoulders and neck stiff. "Find out the truth," he said quietly, his voice so soft it was as if he were speaking to himself, and yet the intensity in him made it obvious that he was begging Pitt, he simply did not use the words.

"Yes, sir, if I can." Pitt rose to his feet. There was a great deal more he wanted to know, but it was too ephemeral to put into words. It was ideas, emotions, things for which he had no name, and he needed to find Narraway before the end of the day.

"Thank you," Ryerson answered, and Pitt hesitated, wondering if it would be fair to warn him that the truth could be painful, and not at all what he was now forcing himself to believe. But there was no point. Time enough for that if it had to be. Instead, he simply excused himself and went out.

"WHAT HAVE YOU?" Narraway looked up from the papers he was studying and regarded Pitt with challenge. He too looked tired, his eyes red rimmed, his cheeks a little sunken.

Pitt sat down uninvited and tried to make himself comfortable, but it was impossible; the tension inside him made his back ache and his hands stiff.

"Nothing in which I can see any hope of a more satisfactory answer," Pitt replied, deliberately using words sharp enough to hurt Narraway, and himself. "Lovat was a womanizer, and careless enough to use young, unmarried and respectable women who could be ruined by his attentions, and then moving from one to another, leaving society wondering what sin he had discovered in them."

Narraway's mouth pulled tight, lips thin in disgust. "Don't be so squeamish, Pitt. You know damned well what sins society attributed to them . . . rightly or not. They don't care who or what you are, only what other people think you are. A woman's purity is worth more than her courage, warmth, pity, laughter, or honesty. Her chastity means that she belongs to you. It's a matter of ownership." There was a bitterness in his voice that was more than cynicism; Pitt would have sworn it was also pain.

Then he thought of how he would feel if Charlotte were to allow herself to be touched intimately by anyone else, let alone that she should return the passion, and any reason in the argument was overwhelmed.

"It matters." He made it a statement, too hot and sharp to be taken as debate.

Narraway smiled, but he did not meet Pitt's eyes. "Are you speaking generally, or do you know the names of any of these women, and more to the point, their fathers, brothers, or other lovers who might feel like following Lovat around London and shooting him?"

"Of course I do," Pitt responded, glad to be on safer ground, and yet feeling he had left something unsaid which mattered. Was it only his feelings, too powerful to be expressed in so few and simple words, or was there something of reason there also, a fact that momentarily escaped him?

"And from the expression in your face," Narraway observed, "it was all of no use to you."

"To us," Pitt corrected tartly. "None at all."

He was amazed and a little hurt to see the hope die out of Narraway's eyes, as if he had held it as more than a thing of the mind.

Sensing Pitt's gaze on him, Narraway turned half away, shielding something in himself. "So you have learned nothing, except that Lovat was a man courting disaster."

That was a cutting way to have worded it, but it was essentially true. "Yes."

Narraway drew in his breath to say something else, then let it out without speaking.

"I saw Ryerson," Pitt volunteered. "He's still convinced Miss Zakhari is innocent."

Narraway looked back at him, his eyebrows raised.

"Is that an oblique way of saying that he isn't going to help himself by stepping back and admitting that he arrived to find Lovat already dead?" Narraway asked.

"I don't know what he's going to say. The police know he was there, so he can't deny it."

"Too late anyway," Narraway retorted with sudden bitterness. "The Egyptian embassy knew he was there. I've moved everything I can to find out who told them, and learned nothing, except that they have no intention of telling me."

Very slowly Pitt sat up straighter. He had not even been thinking about what Narraway had been doing, but with a charge like electricity shooting through him, he realized the import of what he had said.

Narraway smiled with a downward twist of his mouth. "Exactly," he agreed. "Ryerson may be making a fool of himself, but someone is giving him some discreet and powerful assistance. What I am not yet certain of is what part Ayesha Zakhari is playing, and whether she is aware of it herself. Is she the queen or the pawn?"

"Why?" Pitt asked, leaning forward now. "Cotton?"

"It would seem the obvious answer," Narraway replied. "But obvious is not necessarily true."

Pitt stared at him, waiting for him to continue.

Narraway relaxed back into his chair, but it seemed more a resignation than a matter of ease. "Go home and sleep," he said. "Come back tomorrow morning."

"That's all?"

"What else do you want?" Narraway snapped. "Take it while you can. It won't last."

CHAPTER FIVE

CHARLOTTE GAVE A GREAT DEAL of thought to Martin Garvie and what could have happened to him. She was aware of many of the ugly or tragic things that could overtake servants, and of the misfortunes they could bring upon themselves. She also knew that Tilda was his sister, and Tilda's opinion of him was bound to be colored by her affections, and a certain innocence of the world inevitable in any girl of her lack of experience. Charlotte would not have wished it to be otherwise for Tilda's own sake. She must be of a similar age to Gracie, but she had nothing like the same spirit or the curiosity, and perhaps not the bitter experience of the streets either. Perhaps Martin had protected her from that?

They were in the kitchen, and Pitt had not been gone more than an hour.

"Wot are we gonna do?" Gracie asked with an awkward mixture of deference and determination. Nothing would persuade her to stop, and yet she knew she needed Charlotte's help. She was ashamed of having alienated Tellman, and she was confused by it, and for the first time, a little afraid of her own feelings.

Charlotte was busy removing a grease stain from Pitt's jacket. She had already made a fine powder of ground sheep's trotters. It was something she naturally kept in store, along with other ingredients for cleaning agents, such as sorrel juice, chalk, horse hoof parings—clean, of course—candle ends, and lemon or onion juice. She concentrated on what she was doing, dabbing at the stain with a cloth soaked in turpentine, and avoiding looking at Gracie so as not to give any emotional value to what she was saying.

"We should probably begin by speaking with Tilda again," she continued, reaching out and taking the powder from Gracie's hand. She shook a little onto the damp patch and looked at it critically. "A description of Martin might be helpful."

"We gonna look for 'im?" Gracie asked with surprise. "Where'd we start? 'E could be anywhere! 'E could 'a gorn . . . 'e could be . . ." She stopped.

Charlotte knew she had been going to say that he could be dead. It was the thought at the edge of her own mind too. "It's difficult to ask people questions about seeing someone if we can't say what he looks like," she replied, using a small, stiff brush to take the powder away. The stain was a lot better. One more time and it would be clean. She smiled very slightly. "It also makes it sound as if we don't know him," she added. "We don't . . . but the truth doesn't sound very believable."

"I can fetch Tilda ter tell us," Gracie said quickly. "She does 'er errands the same time most days."

"I'll come with you," Charlotte said.

Gracie's eyes widened. It was a mark of Charlotte's seriousness that she would come out into the street to wander around waiting for someone else's housemaid to pass. It was extraordinary friendship. It also made it clear that she believed he could be in very real danger. Gracie looked at Pitt's jacket, then up at Charlotte, the question in her eyes.

"I'll finish it when we get back," Charlotte said. "What time does Tilda go out?"

" 'Bout now," Gracie replied.

"Then you'd better put some more water in the stockpot and pull it to the side of the hob so it doesn't boil dry, and we'll go."

Charlotte wiped her hands on her apron, then undid it and took it off. "Fetch your coat."

It was nearly an hour before they saw Tilda coming towards them along the street, but so distracted by her thoughts that Gracie had spoken to her twice before she realized it was she who was being addressed.

"Oh, Gracie!" she said with intense relief, the furrows of anxiety ironing out of her face. "I'm so glad ter see yer. 'Ave yer 'eard anythin'? No—no, o' course yer 'aven't. I'm that stupid or I wouldn't 'ave asked. 'Ow could yer? I 'aven't 'eard a word." Her face puckered again as she said it and tears filled her eyes. It obviously cost her all the will she had to keep any composure at all.

"No," Gracie agreed, taking Tilda by the arm and pulling her a few steps sideways out of the pathway of other pedestrians. "But we're gonna do summink about it. I brought Mrs. Pitt along, an' we can 'ave a cup o' tea an' she wants ter ask yer a few things, like."

Tilda looked at Charlotte, now standing beside them. The maid's eyes were wide with alarm.

"Good morning, Tilda," Charlotte said firmly. "Can you spare half an hour without making your mistress upset with you? I should like to learn a little more about your brother so we can look for him more effectively."

Tilda was momentarily lost for words, then her fear overcame her shyness. "Yes, ma'am, I'm sure she wouldn't mind, if I tell 'er it's ter do wi' Martin. I told 'er already as 'e were missin'."

"Good," Charlotte approved. "In the circumstances I think that was very wise." She glanced up at the gray, misty sky. "Our conversation would be better held inside, over a hot cup of tea." And without waiting for agreement or otherwise, she turned and led the way to the small baker's shop where they also served refreshments, and when they were seated at a table, to Tilda's astonishment, ordered tea and hot buttered muffins.

"How old is Martin?" Charlotte began.

"Twenty-three," Tilda answered immediately.

Charlotte was impressed. That was young for a valet, which was a skilled occupation. At such an age she would have expected him to be no more than a footman. Either he had been in service since he was very young or he was unusually quick to learn.

"How long has he been in the Garrick household?" she continued.

"Since 'e were seventeen," Tilda said. " 'E went there as a footman, but Mr. Stephen took a likin' to 'im. 'E were a bootboy wi' the Furnivals afore that, but they din't need another footman, so 'e moved on, an' up, like." There was a ring of pride in her voice and she sat a little more upright, her shoulders squared as she said it.

A shred of humor flickered into Charlotte's mind. How Tellman would despise a life of such dependence upon the favor of one family, the physical comfort bought at such a price of pride. And yet, as Gracie had pointed out to him in some heat at Charlotte's kitchen table, everyone depended upon the goodwill of others, on their skills or their patronage, their friendship or their protection. It was only that some forms of dependence were more obvious than others, not any more real.

"It sounds as if he is very good at his job," she said aloud, and saw Tilda smile back. "Was he happy there, as far as you know?"

Tilda leaned forward a little. "Yes, 'e were! That's just it, 'e never said a word about not bein' suited, an' I would 'a known. We din't never tell each other lies."

Charlotte believed that was true of Tilda, the younger and far more dependent of the two, but Martin might well have kept his own counsel on some subjects. However, it would serve no purpose now to challenge Tilda's perception of his nature. "What does he look like?" she asked instead.

"Bit like me," Tilda answered very practically. "Taller, o' course, an' bigger, like, but same colored 'air an' eyes, an' same kind o' nose." She indicated her own short, neat features.

"I see. That's very helpful. Is there anything else you can tell us about him which might be of use?" Charlotte asked. "Is there any young lady he admires? Or who admires him, perhaps?"

"Yer thinkin' as someone might 'a set 'er cap at 'im, an' if 'e turned 'er down, got nasty?" Tilda said with a shiver.

The serving girl came with tea and hot buttered muffins and they waited until she was gone. Charlotte indicated that they should eat, and she herself poured the tea. "It is possible," she answered the question. "We need to know a great deal more. And since people are apparently not going to tell us willingly, we shall have to find it out for ourselves, and as soon as possible. Tilda, they already know you, and your interest in the matter. I think it will be wisest if you do not call them again, at least for the time being. I am not acquainted with the family, although I might contrive to change that. Gracie, it seems as if you will have to be the one to begin."

" 'Ow am I gonna do that?" Gracie asked, her muffin halfway to her mouth. Her voice was a mixture of determination and fear. She very carefully avoided looking at Tilda.

Charlotte had racked her brain and still had no idea. "We shall discuss that when we get home," she replied. Gracie might very well read her indecision, but she would not betray it in front of Tilda. "Would you like more tea?" she offered.

They finished the muffins, Charlotte paid for them, and as soon as they were outside on the pavement again Tilda, now acutely aware of the time she had been away on her errands, which no queuing could explain, hastily thanked them both and took her leave.

" 'Ow am I gonna get inter the Garrick 'ouse an' ask 'em questions?" Gracie said as soon as they were alone and walking back towards Keppel Street. Her slightly apologetic air, as if she knew she was causing embarrassment but could not avoid it, showed that she had no idea either.

"Well, we can't tell the truth," Charlotte replied, looking straight ahead of her. "Which is a shame, because the truth is easier to remember. So it will have to be an invention." She avoided using the word *lie*. What they must say was not really deception because it was a greater truth they were seeking.

"I don' mind bein' a bit free wi' exactness," Gracie said, creating her own euphemism. "But I can't think o' nothin' as'll get me in! An' I bin scratchin' me 'ead ter come up wi' summink. Cor, I wish as Samuel Tellman'd believe me as summink's really wrong 'ere. I knew 'e were stubborn, but 'e's worse 'n tryin' ter back a mule inter the shafts. Me granfer 'ad a mule fer 'is cart wot 'e took the coal in. Yer never saw a more awk'ard beast in all yer life. Yer'd swear as 'is feet was glued ter the floor."

Charlotte smiled at the image, but she was trying to think also. They rounded the corner from Francis Street into Torrington Square, facing the rising wind. A newsboy was grabbing at his placard as it teetered and threatened to knock him over. Gracie ran forward and helped him.

"Thank yer, miss," he said gratefully, righting the board again with difficulty. Charlotte glanced at the newspaper she had saved from being blown away as well.

"In't nuffink good, missus," the boy said, pulling his face into an expression of disgust. "The cholera's got to Vienna now too. The French is fightin' in Mada—summink, an' blamin' our missionaries fer it. Says as it's all our fault."

"Madagascar?" Charlotte suggested.

"Yeah . . . that's right," he agreed. "Twenty people killed in a train smashup in France, just when someone's gorn an' opened a new railway from Jaffa, wherever that is, ter Jerusalem. An' the Russians 'as arrested the Canadians fer nickin' seals. Or summink. D'yer want one?" he added hopefully.

Charlotte smiled and held out the money. "Thank you," she accepted, taking the top one, which was now considerably crumpled. Then she and Gracie continued on towards Keppel Street.

" 'E's right," Gracie said glumly. "There in't nothin' good in 'em." She indicated the newspaper in Charlotte's hand. "It's all 'bout fightin' an' silliness an' the like."

"It seems to be what we consider news," Charlotte agreed. "If it's good, it can wait." That part of her mind still working on how to get Gracie into the Garrick house began to clear. "Gracie . . ." she said tentatively. "If Tilda were ill, and you did not know that Martin was not there, wouldn't it be the natural thing for you to go to him and tell him about her? Maybe she is too ill to write—assuming she can?"

Gracie's eyes brightened and a tiny smile of anticipation curved her lips. "Yeah! I reckon as that's what any friend'd do—eh? She's bin took sudden, an' I gotta tell poor Martin, in case she don't get better quick. An' I know where 'e works 'cos Tilda an' I is good friends . . . which we are. I'd better go soon, 'adn't I? Give 'er time ter get 'ome, an' be took, like, an' fer me ter ask me mistress, an' 'er bein' very good, she tells me ter do it fast!" She grimaced suddenly, lighting her thin, little face with amazing vitality.

"Yes," Charlotte agreed, unconsciously increasing her pace and rounding the corner into the wind again with her skirts swirling and the newspaper flapping in her arms. "There's nothing at home that can't wait. The sooner you go, the better."

HALF AN HOUR LATER, fortified with another cup of tea, Gracie began. She was excited, and so afraid of making a mistake that her stomach was fluttering inside her and she had to breathe in and out deeply and speak her words carefully in order not to stumble. She straightened her coat one more time, swallowed hard, and knocked on the scullery door of the Garrick house in Torrington Square. There was no point in waiting any longer. Time would not improve her task. She must do this for Tilda, and for Martin, of course, unless it was too late.

She had planned what she was going to say as soon as the door opened. Nevertheless, it had stayed shut until she lifted her hand to knock again, harder this time, so that when it did swing wide she nearly fell in. She jerked herself upright, gasping, and found herself less than a foot away from the scullery maid, a fair-skinned girl several inches taller than herself, with hair falling out of its skewed pins. The maid started to speak, shaking her head. "We din't—"

"Good day," Gracie said at the same time, and carrying on when the other girl stopped. She could not afford to be refused. "I come wi' a message. I'm sorry ter disturb yer just before luncheon, like. I know as yer'll be terrible busy, but I need ter tell yer." She did not have to pretend to anxiety, and her emotion must have carried through every part of her aspect, because the girl's face filled with immediate sympathy.

"Yer'd better come in," she invited, backing inside for Gracie to pass. It was a generous gesture.

"Ta," Gracie said with appreciation. It was a good beginning—in fact, the only one that could be a beginning at all. She gave the girl a quick half smile. "Me name's Gracie Phipps. I come from Keppel Street, jus' 'round the corner, but that's not really got nuffin' ter do wif it. Me message is 'cos o' somewhere else." She glanced around the well-stocked scullery hung with ropes of onions, sacks of potatoes on the floor, and several hard, white cabbages and various other root vegetables on wooden slatted shelves. On hooks on the walls were larger cooking vessels, handles looped over the pegs, and on the floor in the corner, jars of what were presumably different kinds of vinegars, oils and perhaps cooking wines.

"I'm Dorothy," the other girl responded. "Me ma called me Dora, but they call me Dottie 'ere, an' I don't mind. 'Oo'd yer come ter see?"

Gracie blinked as if she were fighting tears. She could not afford to begin by mentioning Martin Garvie's name, or the girl might simply tell her he was not there and show her out again, and she would have learned nothing. A bit of dramatic acting might be called for. "It's 'bout me friend Tilda," she replied. "I dunno 'er that close, but she's got no one else, an' she's terrible sick. She's got no family 'cept 'er brother, an' he's gotter know afore—" She stopped. She did not actually want to say that Tilda was dying, unless it was absolutely necessary, but she was happy for it to be understood. Of course if she really had to, then she would invent anything at all that would help.

"Oh, cor!" Dottie said, her face crumpling with sympathy. " 'Ow 'orrible!"

"I gotta tell 'im," Gracie repeated. "They in't got nobody else, either of 'em. 'E'll be that upset. . . ." She allowed imagination to paint the picture.

" 'Course!" Dottie agreed, moving towards the step up to the kitchen, and the warmth and smells of cooking that drifted towards them. "Come in an' 'ave a cup o' tea. Yer look perished."

"Ta," Gracie accepted. "Ta very much." Actually she was not really cold; it was a very pleasant day and she had walked briskly, but fear had welled up inside her just as it did when one was tense with cold, and it must look the same. To be inside and form some opinion of the household was what she wanted. She followed Dottie up the wooden steps into a large kitchen with a high ceiling strung with an airing rail, presently carrying only towels for drying dishes, and several strings of dried herbs. On the walls copper pans gleamed bright and warm.

The cook, a rotund woman who obviously sampled her own skills, was muttering to herself as she beat a creamy mixture in a round bowl, rough brown on the outside, white earthenware within. She looked up as Gracie came in tentatively.

"Oh?" the cook said, fixing her with boot-button eyes. "An' what 'ave we got 'ere, then? We don' need no more maids, an' if we do, we'll get our own. Yer look like a twopenny rabbit anyway. Don' nobody feed yer?"

A thoroughly sharp rejoinder that would have put the cook in her place in a hurry rose to Gracie's lips, but she bit it back. Tilda would owe her for her forbearance.

"I in't lookin' fer work, ma'am," she said respectfully. "I got a position as suits me very well. I'm maid to a lady and gentleman in Keppel Street, wi' me own 'ouse'old, an' two children to care for."

That was a bit of an exaggeration—there was only the cleaning woman under her instruction—but it was not an outright lie either. She saw the look of disbelief in the cook's round face. "I came ter give a message," she hurried on.

"A friend of 'ers is dyin', Mrs. Culpepper," Dottie added helpfully. "Gracie's tryin' ter tell 'er family, all there is of 'em."

"Dyin'?" Mrs. Culpepper said with surprise. It was obviously not at all what she had expected, or fully believed. "Wot of?"

Gracie was prepared for that. "Rheumatical fever," she said without hesitation. "Terrible poorly, she is." She allowed her real fears for Martin, which were now gnawing deeply inside her, to invest her expression with pain.

Mrs. Culpepper must have seen it. "I'm sorry to 'ear that," she said with what looked to be a genuine pity. "Wot is it yer want 'ere? Don' stand there, Dottie! Fetch the girl a cup o' tea!" She looked back at Gracie. "Sit down." She pointed to a hard-backed kitchen chair on the other side of the table.

Dottie went to the stove and pushed the kettle over onto the heat. It began to whistle almost immediately.

Mrs. Culpepper did not miss a beat with her wooden spoon. "Now then, missy . . ." She had already forgotten Gracie's name. "Wot is it yer want 'ere? 'Oo's this message for, then?"

There was no more time for prevarication. Gracie watched Mrs. Culpepper's face intently. Expression might tell her more than words. "Martin Garvie," she replied. " 'E's 'er brother. She's got nob'dy else. Their ma an' pa died years back."

Mrs. Culpepper's face was unreadable, the slight sadness remained exactly the same, and her hand did not hesitate in the beating of the batter.

"Oh . . ." she said without looking up. "Well, that's a pity, 'cos 'e in't 'ere no more, an' I dunno where 'e's gorn."

Gracie knew there was a lie in that somewhere, or at least less than the truth, but she had the strong feeling that it was unhappiness rather than guilt which prompted it. Suddenly very real, sharp fear gripped her and the warm, sweet-smelling kitchen with its hot ovens and steaming pans swam around her. She closed her eyes to stop it swaying.

When she opened them Mrs. Culpepper was staring at her and Dottie was standing on the other side of the table with a cup of tea in her hand.

" 'Ead between yer knees," the cook said practically.

"I in't gonna faint!" Gracie was defensive, partly because she was not absolutely sure it was true. They were being kind. There was nothing to fight, and she did not know where to direct her emotions. "If 'e in't 'ere, where's 'e gorn?" She could not say that he had told no one, because Tilda was supposed to be too ill to know. She hoped fervently that when Tilda had called here asking for Martin herself, she had looked sufficiently distraught to appear on the edge of serious illness.

"We dunno," Dottie answered before Mrs. Culpepper had weighed her own reply. The cook shot her a sharp glance of warning, but whether it was to guard a secret or to keep from unnecessary hurt, there was no way to tell.

"An' why should yer know, girl!" Mrs. Culpepper found her tongue. "In't nuffink ter do wif yer where the master sends 'is staff, now is it?"

Dottie put the tea down in front of Gracie. "You drink that," she ordered. "O' course it in't, Mrs. Culpepper," she agreed obediently. "But yer'd think as Bella'd know, all the same." She turned to Gracie again. "Bella's our parlor maid, and she kinda liked Martin. Nice, 'e were, too. I liked 'im meself . . . in a friendly sort o' way," she added quickly.

"Yer got too busy a tongue in yer 'ead!" Mrs. Culpepper said critically. "If Bella knows where 'e's gorn, wot's it she should tell you, eh?"

Dottie shrugged. "I know," she said without resentment. Then her face clouded. "But I wish as I knew wot 'ad 'appened ter Martin meself."

"Don' yer go talkin' like that, you stupid girl!" Mrs. Culpepper snapped in sudden rage, her face pink. She slammed the bowl down on the table. "Anyone'd think as 'e were dead, or summink 'appened to 'im! Nothin's 'appened to 'im! 'E just in't 'ere, that's all. You button yer lip, my girl, an' go an' do summink useful. Go an' grate them ol' potatoes ready ter soak. Yer can't ne'er 'ave too much starch. Don' stand there like yer was a ruddy ornament!"

Dottie pushed her hair back with her hand, shrugged good-naturedly, and wandered off to the scullery to do as she was told.

"I'm glad nuthin' in't 'appened to 'im," Gracie said with suitable humility. "But I still gotter tell 'im about Tilda." She knew she was pressing her good fortune, but she had no choice. So far she had learned no more than Tilda had already told them. "Somebody's gotta know, in't they?"

"O' course somebody 'as," Mrs. Culpepper agreed, reaching for a baking tin and a muslin cloth with a little butter on it. She greased the tin with a single, practiced movement. "But it in't me."

Gracie took a sip of the tea. "Tilda said as 'e were Mr. Stephen's valet. 'As 'e got a new one, then?"

Mrs. Culpepper looked up sharply. "No, 'e 'asn't. Don' yer go . . ." Then her face softened. "Look, girl, I can see that yer upset, an' it's awful 'ard ter face someone real sick, as yer can't 'elp. Gawd knows, I wouldn't want a dog ter die alone, but so 'elp me, I dunno where Martin's gorn, an' that's the Gawd's truth. 'Ceptin' 'e's a good man, an' I don't believe as 'e'd ne'er give no one any trouble."

Gracie sniffed and blinked, her mind on Tilda and the fear inside her. It had been almost a week already. Why was there no letter, no message? "Wot's 'e like, Mr. Stephen? Would 'e get rid o' someone if they 'adn't done nothin' wrong?"

Mrs. Culpepper wiped her hands on her apron, abandoned the batter and poured herself a cup of tea. "Lord knows, girl," she said, shaking her head. " 'E's a poor mixed-over kind o' man. But even on 'is worst days I don't think as 'e would 'a got rid o' Martin, 'cos

Martin's the only one wot can do a thing wit 'im when 'e gets bad."

Gracie tried hard to keep her expression calm, and knew she did not entirely succeed. This was new information, and it alarmed her even though she was not sure if she understood it. She looked up at Mrs. Culpepper, blinking several times to try to disguise her thoughts. "Yer mean when 'e's sick, like?"

Mrs. Culpepper gave a start and did not reply. Her hand stayed frozen on the handle of her cup.

Gracie was afraid she had made her first serious mistake, but she knew enough not to try to mend it. She said nothing, waiting for Mrs. Culpepper to speak first.

"Yer could say that," Mrs. Culpepper conceded at last, raising the cup to her lips and sipping the hot tea. "An' I'm not 'ere ter say diff'rent." That was a warning.

Gracie understood instantly. *Sick* was a euphemism for something far worse, almost certainly *blind drunk*. Some men collapsed in a heap, or were thoroughly ill, but there were always the odd few who became belligerent and started fighting people, or took their clothes off, or otherwise were an embarrassment and a nuisance. It sounded as if Stephen Garrick was of the last sort.

" 'Course not," Gracie said demurely. "Nobody says diff'rent. In't our place."

"Not that I'm not tempted, sometimes, mind!" Mrs. Culpepper added with some heat, just as the very handsome parlor maid came into the kitchen and stopped abruptly. "You've not come for luncheon already, 'ave yer?" Mrs. Culpepper said in amazement. "I dunno where the day's gorn ter. I in't nothin' like ready."

"No, no!" Bella assured her. "Loads of time." She looked curiously at Gracie. She must have overheard the last few words of the conversation. "Not that I wouldn't fancy a cup of tea myself, if it's hot," she added.

"This is Gracie," Mrs. Culpepper said, suddenly recalling Gracie's name. "She's come 'cos Martin's sister's a friend of 'ers, an' it seems the poor girl 'as the rheumatical fever, an' she's like ter dyin', so Gracie's lookin' for Martin ter tell 'im, which is terrible 'ard."

Bella shook her head, her face grave. "I wish we could help you, but we don't know where he is," she said candidly. "Usually when Mr. Stephen goes away it's in the middle of the morning, and we all know for days beforehand, but this is different . . . He just . . . isn't here."

Gracie was not going to give up without trying every avenue. "Mrs. Culpepper's been very gracious," she said warmly. "An' she says as Mr. Garrick really depended on Martin, so 'e wouldn't a' got rid of 'im on a fancy, like."

Bella's face pinched with anger. "He behaved pretty rotten at times. My ma'd have taken a slipper to me if I'd thrown tantrums the way he does, kicking and shouting and—"

"Bella!" Mrs. Culpepper said warningly, her voice sharp.

"Well, goes on like a three-year-old, he does sometimes!" Bella protested, her cheeks flushed. "And poor Martin put up with it without a word of complaint. Cleaning up behind him, listening to him weeping and wailing about everything you could name, or just sitting there like the misery of the whole world was on his plate. You'd—"

"Yer'd best keep a still tongue in yer 'ead, my girl, or yer'll 'ave the misery o' the world on your plate, an' all!" Mrs. Culpepper warned her. "Yer might be an 'andsome piece, as speaks like a lady, but yer'll be out in the street in 'alf a trice, wi' yer bags in yer 'and an' no character if the master catches yer talkin' about Mr. Stephen ter strangers, an' that's a fact!" There was a note of urgency in her voice, and her black eyes were sharp. Gracie was sure it was not anger or dislike but affection which prompted her.

Bella sat down on the other kitchen chair, her skirts swirling around her, her white lace apron clean and starched stiff. "It's not fair!" she said fiercely. "What that man put up with is more than a soul should take. And if they've put him out . . ."

" 'Course they haven't put him out, yer daft a'p'orth!" a young footman said as he came in. His hair grew up in a quiff on his forehead; his breeches were still a fraction too large for him. Gracie guessed that he had only just graduated from bootboy within the last few weeks.

Bella rounded on him. "And how come you know so much, Clarence Smith?"

" 'Cos I see things what you don't!" he retorted. "There's nobody but Martin can do anything with him when he gets one of his black miseries. And nobody else even tries, when he flies into one of his rages. I wouldn't try for all the tea in China. Even Mr. Lyman's scared of him . . . and Mrs. Somerton. And I didn't think as Mrs. Somerton was scared of nothing. I'd have put a shilling on her against the dragon, never mind St. George, an' all."

"You get about your business, Clarence, afore I report you ter Mr. Lyman fer lip!" Mrs. Culpepper said tartly. "Yer'll be eatin' yer supper out in the scullery, an' lucky ter get bread and drippin', if 'e catches yer."

"It's true!" Clarence said indignantly.

"True in't got nothin' ter do with it, yer stupid article!" she retorted. "Sometimes I think yer in't got the wits yer was born with. Get on and carry them coals through fer Bella. On with yer."

"Yes, Mrs. Culpepper," he said obediently, perhaps recognizing in her voice anxiety rather than criticism.

Gracie thought for a moment that perhaps it would be fun to work in a large house, just for a week or two. But of course it was not nearly as important as what she was doing. She watched as Clarence went out to perform his task. She picked up her tea and finished it.

"Sorry, luv, but we can't 'elp yer," Mrs. Culpepper said to her, shaking her head and pouring out the batter into the tin at last. "Gotta get on wit the cakes fer tea. Ne'er know 'oo'll be callin'. Dottie! Dottie . . . come an' see ter 'em vegetables."

Gracie stood up to leave, carrying her empty cup over to the board beside the sink. "Thank yer," she said sincerely. "I'll just 'ave ter keep tryin', although I dunno where else ter go."

Dottie came back from the scullery, wiping her hands on the corner of her apron. "Well 'e were visitin' a Mr. Sandeman someplace down the east end," she said hopefully. "Mebbe 'e'd know summink?"

Gracie put the cup down carefully, feeling it wobble as her hands shook. "Sandeman?" she repeated. " 'Oo's 'e? D'yer know?"

Dottie looked crestfallen. "Sorry, I in't got no idea."

Gracie swallowed her disappointment. "Never mind, mebbe somebody will. Thank yer, Mrs. Culpepper."

Mrs. Culpepper shook her head. "I'm real sorry. Poor thing. Mebbe she'll get better, yer ne'er know."

"Yeah," Gracie agreed, not feeling she was lying because her thoughts were with Martin, not Tilda. "Keep 'opin', eh!"

Dottie took her to the back door, and a moment later Gracie was out on the pavement hurrying as fast as her feet could carry her towards Keppel Street.

OF COURSE SHE TOLD Charlotte all that she had learned as soon as she was back at Keppel Street, but to repeat it to Tellman was much more difficult. To begin with she had to find him, and there was nowhere to begin except the Bow Street police station, or the lodging house where he lived. It was always possible that he would go straight from whatever task he was on back to his rooms for the night, and that could be at any hour. Added to which, she had no wish to embarrass him by being seen in Bow Street, where they would know who she was, even if she did not actually ask for him at the desk. More important, they might remember that she was Pitt's maid and assume that that was why she was there to see Tellman, which could make things very awkward for him with his new superintendent.

So she ended up standing on the pavement outside his lodging house in the early evening, staring up at the windows of his room on the second floor and seeing only darkness where, were he at home, there would be slits of light between the curtains.

She stood uncertainly for several minutes, then realized that he could be an hour or more yet, or if he was on a serious case, even longer. She knew there was a pleasant tearoom only a few hundred yards away; she could spend a little time there, and return later to see if he was home yet.

She had walked fifty yards when she thought how easy it would be to return half a dozen times before she found him, or on the other hand, wait far too long. She turned and walked back, knocked on the door, and when the landlady came told her very politely that she had important information for Inspector Tellman and she would be waiting for him in the tearoom, if he could come and find her there.

The landlady looked a trifle dubious, but she agreed, and Gracie left feeling satisfied with the arrangement.

Tellman came in tired and cold almost an hour after that. He had had a long and tedious day, and he was more than ready to eat a brief supper and go to bed early. She knew as soon as she saw his face and the stiffness of his body that he remembered their quarrel and was not at all sure how to speak to her now. The fact that she had come to start the whole subject again was only going to make it worse, but she felt no choice at all. Martin Garvie's life might be at stake, and what was anyone's love or comfort worth if, when faced with unpleasantness or difference of opinion, it crumbled and fell away?

"Samuel," she began as soon as he was seated opposite her and had given his order to the waitress.

"Yes?" he said guardedly. He seemed about to add something, then bit it off.

There was nothing to it but to plunge in. The longer she sat there with either silence between them or stilted conversation, saying one thing and thinking and caring about another, the worse it would get. "I bin ter the Garrick 'ouse," she said, looking across the table at him. She saw him stiffen even more, his fingers white where his hands were clenched on the table. "I just went ter the kitchen," she hurried on. "I asked the cook an' the scullery maid, on account o' Tilda bein' ill an' Martin was the only family she got."

"Is she ill?" he said quickly.

"Only wit worry," she answered honestly. "But I said as she 'ad a bad fever." Now she was embarrassed. He would not approve of lying, and she wished she did not have to tell him that she had done so. But not to would mean lying to him, and that was something she was not prepared to do. She went on quickly to cover it. "I jus' asked where Martin were, so's I could tell 'im. They dunno, Samuel, I mean really dunno! They're worried too." She leaned forward, closer to him. "They said as Mr. Stephen drinks far too much an' 'as terrible tempers, and black moods o' misery wot are summink awful. No one can 'elp 'im, 'cept Martin, an' 'e'd never put Martin out, 'cos o' that." She stared at him, seeing the worry and the disbelief struggling in his eyes.

"You sure they told you all these things?" he said with a frown. "If they said that to anyone that came to the door, Mr. Garrick would throw them out without a character. I never met servants who would say anything about their household, unless they'd already been dismissed and were looking to make trouble."

"They didn't say it like that," she explained patiently. "I sat in the kitchen an' they gave me a cup o' tea while I told 'em 'bout Tilda, an' they was tellin' me 'ow good Martin were. It jus' sort o' come out wot sort o' good 'e were, an' why."

A tiny smile flickered over Tellman's mouth. It might have been admiration, or only amusement.

Gracie found herself blushing, something she never did as a rule, and it annoyed her, because it gave away her emotions. She had no wish at all for Samuel Tellman to get ideas that she had feelings for him.

"I'm very good at asking pert'int questions!" she said hotly. "I worked for Mr. Pitt for years and years. Longer 'n you 'ave!"

He took in his breath sharply and half smiled, then let it out again without saying whatever it was he thought. "So they are certain that Garrick wouldn't have let him go? Could he have got tired of catering to Garrick's temper and gone by himself?"

"Without tellin' Tilda, or anyone else?" she said incredulously. " 'Course not! Yer give notice, yer don' walk out." She saw the flicker of contempt in his face, reminding her again of how he viewed the whole concept of living and working in service. "Don' start that again," she warned. "We got someone in danger an' it's real, an' could be serious. We got no time ter be arguin' about the rights an' wrongs o' the way folk live." She looked at him very levelly, feeling a shiver of both excitement and familiarity as she saw the intensity with which he stared back at her. She was aware of the heat in her cheeks, and her eyes wavered. "We gotta do summink ter 'elp." She said "we" very carefully. "I can't do much without yer, Samuel. Please don' make me 'ave ter try." She had placed their relationship in the balance, and was amazed that she had taken such a risk, because it mattered far more than she had realized until this instant. "Summink's 'appened ter 'im," she added very quietly. "Mebbe Mr. Stephen's as mad as they say, an' 'as done 'im in, an' they've 'id it. But it's a crime, an' no one else is gonna 'elp, 'cos they dunno."

The waitress brought his meal and a fresh pot of tea, and Tellman thanked her. He already knew what his decision was; it was in his eyes, in the line of his mouth and the stillness of his hands. He made only a momentary gesture of resistance by hesitating, as if he were still weighing it up. It was a matter of pride to pretend, but they both knew his decision was made.

"I'll take a look," he said at last. "There's been no crime reported, so I'll have to be careful. I'll tell you what I find."

"Thank yer, Samuel," she said with perfectly genuine humility.

Perhaps he recognized that, because he suddenly smiled, and

she saw an extraordinary tenderness in it. She would never have said so to anyone else, but at that moment his face held something that she would have called beauty.

PITT LEFT THE PURSUIT of Edwin Lovat's life and the trail of pain he had created behind his various love affairs. He had followed every name, and found nothing but unhappiness and helpless anger.

A wild thought came to him as he tried looking at the case from an entirely different angle. Sometimes it was profitable to abandon even the most obvious assumptions and consider the story as if they were untrue. Lovat had been shot in a garden in the middle of the night. There seemed to be no sense in Ayesha Zakhari's having taken her gun and gone outside to see who it was lurking in the bushes. She had a perfectly capable manservant and a telephone in her home to call for assistance.

He had assumed that she had known it was Lovat, but there seemed no sane reason to have killed him. If she did not wish to see him she had merely to remain inside. If she did not know who it was, the answer was the same.

But what if she had supposed it was someone else? What if she had not recognized Lovat until after he was dead? The garden was dark. They were not in a path of light thrown from the house, even if all the lamps had been lit in the downstairs rooms, which in itself was unlikely at three in the morning.

Who might she have mistaken him for? Was it possible that a perfectly rational answer to the murder lay in the fact she had believed him to be someone else?

He began by going back to Eden Lodge. It looked curiously empty in the sharp autumn morning, the long light golden across the quiet street, and in the absolute stillness not even the leaves of the birch trees stirred. He could hear hooves in the distance, and a bird singing somewhere above him. A small black cat wove in and out through the dead lily stems waiting to be cut back.

Tariq el Abd answered the door.

"Good morning, sir," he said politely, his face expressionless. "How can I help you?"

"Good morning," Pitt replied. "I need to make some further enquiries, and you can help me."

El Abd invited him in and led the way through to the withdrawing room. He did not look entirely comfortable about having the police in this part of the house—they were hardly social acquaintances—but the kitchens and laundry rooms were his domain, and he did not wish them there either. He drew the line at offering refreshment.

"What is it you need to ask me, sir?" he said, remaining standing so Pitt should do so as well.

Pitt had little time to look around the room, but he had a sense of subtle colors and light. The lines were less cluttered than he was accustomed to; everything was simpler. There was an elaborate ornament of a dog with large ears, the whole creature perhaps a foot and a half long, crouching on one of the side tables. It was a thing of great loveliness.

El Abd must have seen his eye caught by it.

"Anubis, sir," he said. "One of the ancient gods of our country. Of course, the people who believed in him are long dead."

"The beauty of their workmanship remains," Pitt answered with feeling.

"Yes, sir. What is it you wish to ask me?" His face was still almost devoid of expression.

"Were the lights on in this room when Mr. Lovat was shot?"

"I beg your pardon, sir? I do not understand. Mr. Lovat was shot in the garden . . . outside. He never entered the house."

"You were awake?" Pitt asked in surprise.

El Abd's face showed an instant's lack of composure, then it was gone again. "No, sir, not until I heard the shot. Miss Zakhari said he did not come inside. I believe her. There had been no one in here. The lights were not on."

"Anywhere else in the house?"

"There were no lights lit anywhere downstairs, sir, except in the hall. They are never turned completely off."

"I see. And upstairs?"

"I do not understand what it is you seek, sir. The lights were on in Miss Zakhari's bedroom and her sitting room upstairs, and on the landing above the stairs, as always."

"Are there some at the front of the house, or the back?"

"The front, sir." It was natural. Master bedrooms usually faced the front.

"So there was no light from the house on the back garden where Mr. Lovat was shot?" Pitt concluded.

El Abd hesitated, as if he perceived a trap of some sort. "No, sir . . ."

"Is it possible Miss Zakhari was unaware of Mr. Lovat's identity? Might she have thought he was someone else?"

For the first time el Abd's composure cracked. He looked not merely startled but as if he was in a moment's actual danger. Then it passed, and he stared back at Pitt, blinking a little. "I never thought of that, sir. I can't say. If . . . if she thought it were a robber, surely she could have called me? She knows I would defend her . . . it is my duty."

"Of course," Pitt agreed. "I was not thinking of a robber, but of someone else she actually knew, someone who was a threat to her in some way?"

El Abd was sounding confident now, his balance found again. "I know of no such person, sir. Surely if that were so, she would have told the police that it was an accident? A mistake . . . in self-defense? Are you permitted to shoot in self-defense in England?"

"If there is no other way to protect yourself, yes you are," Pitt answered. "I was thinking of someone she knew and who was an enemy, a danger to her not physically but in another way, to her reputation, or to some interest about which she cared passionately."

"I do not know what you mean, sir." El Abd's face was back to its smooth, polite servant's mask.

"Your loyalty is commendable," Pitt said, trying to keep the sarcasm out of his voice. "But pointless. If she is found guilty of murdering Mr. Lovat, she will be hanged for it. If she mistook him for someone else, who was perhaps a threat to her, then she might be able to plead some justification."

It was marvelous how el Abd changed his expression hardly at all, and yet managed to alter from deference to contempt. "I think, sir, that it is Mr. Ryerson you are interested in seeing. And if he knew Miss Zakhari's reason for killing the man, whoever she believed him to be, then he should tell you the truth, and justify himself, and her also. If he does not know, but found only Mr. Lovat, with no excuse, then he is guilty, whatever Miss Zakhari believed. Is it not so?"

"Yes," Pitt said uneasily. "It is so. But perhaps Miss Zakhari would prefer not to accept that she shot Mr. Lovat, for no sensible reason at all, than tell us the truth of what she believed."

El Abd inclined his head with the shadow of a smile. "Then loyalty to my mistress decrees that I should abide by her decision, sir. Will there be anything else?"

"Yes, there will! I would like you to write me a list of all the people you know who have called here since Miss Zakhari moved in."

"We have a visitors' book, sir. Will that be of assistance?"

"I doubt it. But it will be a start. I require the names of the others as well."

"Very good, sir," el Abd agreed, and withdrew, his feet making no noise at all on the carpets, or on the polished wood of the hall beyond.

He returned a quarter of an hour later with a sheet of paper and a white, leather-bound book, and offered them to Pitt.

Pitt thanked him and took his leave. The book was interesting. There were more names in it than he had expected, and it would take some time to learn who they all were. The additional sheet of paper, he suspected, would be of no use at all.

He spent the rest of the day identifying various men in the city, mostly to do with the cotton trade in one way or another, but there were also others who were artists, poets, musicians and thinkers. He would be interested to know why they had called upon Ayesha Zakhari—and what Saville Ryerson would think of it, and if he knew. No times of the day were noted, simply dates.

THE NEXT MORNING Pitt received a message while he was still at breakfast telling him to report within the hour to Narraway's office. He put his knife and fork down. His kippers had lost their taste.

He still had several names both from the visitors' book and from the additional sheet to identify, and he resented being called to report when there was nothing helpful to say.

Half an hour later he told Narraway of his visit to Eden Lodge and the names he had taken from the visitors' book and from the manservant, el Abd.

Narraway sat deep in thought, his dark face pinched and smudged with weariness, but now there was something like a flicker of hope there as well, though he struggled to mask it.

"And you think she believed Lovat was one of these?" he said skeptically, leaning back in his chair and regarding Pitt through heavy, half-closed eyes, as if he had been up all night.

"It makes more sense than her knowing it was Lovat and shooting him," Pitt replied.

"No, it doesn't," Narraway said bitterly. "If Lovat was blackmailing her and he called for payment, she took the chance to shoot him and put an end to it. That makes perfect sense, and will to any jury."

"Blackmailing her over what?" Pitt asked.

"For God's sake, Pitt! Use your imagination! She's a young and beautiful woman of unknown origin. Ryerson is twenty years older than she is, highly respected, vulnerable . . ." He drew in his breath silently. "He may know perfectly well that she has had other lovers—in fact, he'd be a fool to imagine otherwise . . . It doesn't mean he can bear being told about them, perhaps in detail."

Pitt tried to put himself in Ryerson's place. He could not. If you choose a woman for her physical beauty, her exotic culture, and her willingness to be a mistress rather than a wife, surely you also accept it as a fact that you are not the first, nor will you be the last. The arrangement will survive as long as it suits you both.

But looking at Narraway he saw nothing of that understanding in his eyes, only an intense, unreadable emotion which warned Pitt that if he were to challenge Narraway now, the quarrel which resulted might not easily be overcome. He had no idea why the subject should touch a raw nerve in Narraway, only that it did.

"And you think Lovat might have blackmailed her in order to keep him silent about something in Egypt?" he said aloud.

"It is what the prosecution will assume," Narraway replied. "Wouldn't you?"

"If nothing else is suggested," Pitt agreed. "But they have to prove it—"

Narraway jerked forward, his shoulders tense, his body rigid. "No, they damned well don't!" he said between his teeth. "Unless we come up with something better, it will go by default. Use your wits, Pitt! An old lover with no money or position is found dead in her garden at three in the morning. She has the corpse in a wheelbarrow and her gun beside it. What in God's name else is anyone to think?"

Pitt felt the dark weight of the facts settle on him, almost like a physical crushing. "You mean we are merely going through the motions of looking for a defense?" he said very quietly. "Why? So Ryerson thinks he hasn't been abandoned? Does that matter so much?"

Narraway did not meet his eyes. "We are asked by men who know a different set of realities from ours," he answered. "They don't care in the slightest about Ayesha Zakhari, but they need Ryerson rescued. He's served this country long and well. A lot of the prosperity of the Manchester cotton industry, which means tens of thousands of jobs, is his doing. And if someone doesn't find an agreement on the prices they face the strong possibility of a strike. Do you have any idea how much that will cost? It won't only cost the cotton workers in the mills; it will affect all those whose businesses depend on them—shopkeepers, small traders, exporters—in the end, just about anyone from the men who sell houses to the crossing sweeper looking for a few halfpennies."

"It'll be embarrassing for the government if Ryerson is found guilty of abetting her after the fact," he agreed. "But if he is, they'll have to appoint someone else to handle trade with Egypt. And to judge from Ryerson's handling of Lovat's murder, I would rather that no national crisis were in his hands."

Temper flared up Narraway's sallow cheeks and his hand clenched on the desk, but he swallowed any outburst back with an effort so intense it was clearly visible. "You don't know what you're talking about, Pitt!" he said between his teeth.

Pitt leaned forward. "Then tell me!" he demanded. "So far I see a man in love with a highly unsuitable woman and determined to stand by her, even if she proves to be guilty of murder. He can't help her. His evidence makes it worse, not better. But either he's not aware of that and he's so incredibly arrogant he thinks his involvement will save her regardless, or else he simply doesn't care."

Narraway turned away, shifting his body around in his chair. "You're a fool, Pitt! Of course he knows what will happen. He'll be ruined. Unless we can prove some other possibility, he might even hang with her." He looked back, and when he spoke his voice was shaking. "So find out who else was involved with the woman, or hated Lovat enough to have killed him. And bring me the proof, do you understand? Tell no one else anything at all. Be discreet. In fact, be more than that—be secret. Ask your questions carefully. Use that tact you are so famous for possessing . . . at least according to Cornwallis. Learn everything and give away nothing." He swiveled back and stared levelly at Pitt as if he could read the thoughts in his head, willing or unwilling. "If you let this slip, Pitt, I will have no use for you. Remember that. I want the truth, and I want to be the only one who has it."

Pitt felt cold, but he was also angry, and curious as to why it mattered to Narraway in the fashion that it seemed to. Narraway was concealing as much from him as he was telling, perhaps more, and yet he demanded absolute loyalty in return. Who was he protecting, and why? Was it himself, or even Pitt, from some danger he was too new in the job to understand? Or was it Ryerson, out of some loyalty or other motive that Pitt did not know of? He wanted to ask for trust in return, so that he would have a better chance of succeeding, and also to protect himself if he was uncovering evidence that could endanger powerful enemies. But there was no point in asking; Narraway did not trust anyone more than he had to. Perhaps it was the way he had survived in a business that was riddled with secrets and open to a hundred different kinds of betrayal.

"I can't promise the truth," Pitt said coolly. "And you certainly won't be the only one who has it." He saw Narraway stiffen and it gave him a certain satisfaction, but it was very small, almost lost in the awareness of his own ignorance. "I doubt I'll have more than pieces of it, but whoever killed Lovat will know, and they may know that I do, depending on whether it was a clever plan or an irresponsible crime of a self-indulgent man . . . or woman."

"That is why I use you, Pitt, and not one of my men who are used to chasing anarchists and saboteurs," Narraway said dryly. "You are supposed to have a little subtlety. God knows, you can't tell a bomb from a fruitcake, but you are supposed to be a competent detective when it comes to a murder, especially if it is a crime of passion and not of politics. Get on with it! Find the rest of the people on your list. And be quick. We haven't much longer before the government is forced into giving up Ryerson."

Pitt was on his feet. "Yes, sir. I suppose there is nothing else you can tell me that would be of help?" He allowed his expression to let Narraway know he was aware of his concealment, even if not what it concerned.

Narraway's face tightened, pulling the muscles in his neck. "Cornwallis trusted you. I may come to, but I do not do so yet, and that is something for which you should be grateful. Much of what I know you are fortunate to be spared. In time you may lose that privilege, and you will wish you had it back." He leaned a little forward over the desk between them. "But believe me, Pitt, I want Ryerson saved if it is possible, and if there were anything I could tell you that would help you in that, then I would, regardless of what it cost. But if he did conspire with that damned woman to kill Lovat, or even to hide the fact that she did, and it was a simple murder, then I'll sacrifice him in a trice. There are bigger issues than you know, and they cannot be lost to save one man . . . any man."

"A cotton strike in Manchester?" Pitt said slowly.

Narraway did not reply. "Go and do your job," he said instead. "Don't stand here wasting time asking me for help I can't give you."

Pitt went out into the street and had walked only twenty yards when he passed a newspaper seller and saw the headlines, new since he had come from the opposite direction to see Narraway.

The boy noticed his hesitation. "Paper, sir?" he offered eagerly. "They're all sayin' now as Mr. Ryerson oughta be arrested wi' that foreign woman and both of 'em 'anged! Read all about it, sir?" He held out a newspaper hopefully.

Pitt forced himself to be civil. He took the paper and paid the money, walking away quickly to where he could read it without being observed. He realized with surprise at himself that he did not want his emotions seen. It might be too obvious that it mattered to him.

He took an omnibus, newspaper still folded, and got off again near one of the numerous small, leafy squares where he walked to an empty bench and sat down. He opened up the paper. It was what he would have expected. A Member of Parliament in the Opposition had demanded to know why Ayesha Zakhari was in police custody for the murder of Lovat, an honorable soldier with no stain on his character, and Ryerson, whose presence at her house at three in the morning was unexplained, and unexplainable in decent terms, had not even been questioned on the matter. He asked—in fact, he demanded in the name of justice, that the prime minister should give the House of Commons, and the British people, an answer as to why this was, and how much longer it would remain so.

By late afternoon, before dusk had done more than smudge the horizon and rob some of the color from the leaves, the government had been forced to yield. The home secretary informed the House that of course Mr. Ryerson would give full and satisfactory answers to the police.

By the time the first lamplighters were out, Ryerson was to all effect under arrest.

Pitt did not need to be sent for to return to Narraway's office. He had no further news of any worth, and he did not even bother to reveal the little he had, merely a few more acquaintances from the Eden Lodge visitors' book cleared of any involvement. There were only half a dozen or so still unaccounted for.

He stood in front of Narraway's desk, waiting for him to speak.

"Yes . . . I know," Narraway said, his jaw tight, his eyes focused on the polished desk in front of him, piled with papers, every one facedown. "I don't imagine he'll tell the police anything he hasn't already told you."

"He doesn't know me," Pitt pointed out, although he felt inexplicably as if he did know Ryerson. He could bring back to memory his face precisely, every line and shadow, the urgency and emotion in his voice, and his own sense of involvement as Ryerson had tried to explain his actions, and what he would do if Ayesha

Zakhari came to trial. "He had no reason to trust me more than the circumstances forced him to," Pitt went on. "He might say more to you." He did not add that Ryerson and Narraway were of the same social class, the same culture and understanding, because it was implicit.

Narraway ignored it. He opened his desk drawer and took out a small metal box. It appeared to have no key and he simply opened it and withdrew a handful of Treasury notes. There must have been a hundred pounds' worth at least. "I'll attend to pursuing the London evidence," he said, still not looking at Pitt. "Leave me your notes. You are going to Alexandria to find out what you can about the woman, and Lovat when he was there."

Pitt drew in his breath in amazement. It was a moment before he could find his tongue.

Narraway had apparently already counted out the money, because he took no notice of it now but simply laid it on the desk.

"But I know nothing about Egypt!" Pitt protested. "I can't speak whatever language it is they use there! I—"

"You'll get by very well with English," Narraway cut across him. "And I don't have anyone who's an expert in Egyptian affairs. You are a good detective. Find out about Lovat, but mostly learn everything you can about the woman—her background, her life, what she believes, what she wants, who she knows and cares about. See if there is anything Lovat could have blackmailed her over." His expression flickered with distaste. "Why did she come to England anyway? Who is her family? Has she lovers in Egypt, money, loyalties, religious or political ideals?"

Pitt stared at him in slowly dawning comprehension as to the magnitude of what he was being asked to do. It overwhelmed him. He had no idea how even to begin, let alone weigh any conclusion. He knew nothing about Egypt except fragments he had picked up in conversation, newspapers, and a little more recently about the cotton grown there. He did not know the city of Alexandria; he would be utterly lost. The climate would be nothing like London, or the food, the clothes, the customs.

And yet at the same moment as fear gripped him, so did a kind of excitement which grew with each second, and the words of acceptance were on his lips before he had thought clearly of how he could succeed.

"Yes, sir. What is the best way? Thomas Cook?"

The shadow of a smile touched Narraway's lips. "It was an order, Pitt, not a request. Your only alternative would have been your resignation. But I'm pleased I did not have to make that point to you." At last he turned and looked up. His eyes were cautious, softer for a few minutes. "Be careful, Pitt. Egypt is not an easy place at the moment, and you are going there to probe into delicate issues. I want the information, but I would like you back alive. Your death in some back street would not reflect well on my professional reputation." He picked the money up from the top of the desk and with it a plain white envelope. "Here are your tickets, and what I believe will be sufficient funds. If you need more, go to Mr. Trenchard at the British Consulate, but don't trust him more than you have to."

Pitt took the money and tickets. "Thank you."

"You sail from Southampton on the evening tide tomorrow," Narraway added.

Pitt turned to leave. He would have to be on the first train in the morning, and he had to pack. It had not yet even occurred to him to think what clothes he owned would be even remotely suitable.

"Pitt!" Narraway's voice recalled him sharply.

He turned. "Yes?"

"Be careful. This is probably exactly what it looks like—a man with more passion than sense. But just in case it is political, something to do with cotton or . . . or God knows what . . . listen more than you talk. Learn to watch without asking questions. You're not police in Alexandria." His face looked suddenly weary, as if he was already anticipating griefs that had not yet happened, or perhaps remembering those that had. "There'll be no one to protect you. Your white skin will be as much against you as for. For God's sake, man, take a little care!" He said it angrily, as if Pitt was in the habit of running wild risks, and it was that which touched Pitt with a coldness of fear, because he had seldom if ever really jeopardized his own life, except perhaps in Whitechapel, on his first assignment for Narraway. He was used to the safety of office, which was not a uniform but as good as one.

He found his mouth dry when he answered. "Yes, sir," he said stiffly, and went out before Narraway could say anything further, or Pitt could betray his feelings.

CHAPTER SIX

"EGYPT!" Charlotte said incredulously when Pitt told her. He had arrived home late and dinner was already served.

"I know where Egypt is," Daniel offered. "It's in the top of Africa." He said it with his mouth full, but Charlotte was too stunned to correct him. "You'll have to sail in a boat," Daniel added helpfully.

"But it will be . . ." Charlotte began, then she caught sight of Jemima's troubled face, "interesting," she finished awkwardly. "And hot . . . won't it? What will you wear?"

"I'll have to get some clothes when I get there," he replied. There were scores of things he wished to say to her, but he knew her anxiety, especially after the danger she and Gracie and the children had survived so recently, when they had had to leave Dartmoor in the middle of the night. Tellman had rescued them, arriving in the dark and packing everything they owned into a pony cart and driving them to the nearest station. They had been accosted on the way, and Tellman had actually fought the man and left him near senseless on the ground. Jemima still remembered it rather too clearly. Pitt smiled at her. "I'll bring you back something nice," he promised. "All of you," he added as Daniel was about to speak.

Charlotte was less easy to distract later when they were alone.

"What can you do in Egypt?" she demanded. "It's a British Protectorate, or something like that. Haven't we got police there? They could send a letter, and if they don't trust the postal service, a courier."

"The local police won't know what to look for, or recognize it if they find it," he answered. He had thought, as he walked quickly along Keppel Street on the way home, the wind blowing the rain in his face, the wet pavement gleaming in the lamplight and passing traffic spraying water up in sheets, that he was looking forward to the adventure of going to an ancient, sunlit city on the edge of Africa. The fact that he did not understand the language, was unfamiliar with the food, the money, and the customs, was unimportant. He could learn enough. He would do his best to find out something about Ayesha Zakhari, probably things he would rather not have known, but at least he would be as sure as he could that it was the truth. It might explain what had happened.

Now he was in the multilayered comfort of home. There was certainty of the heart here, as well as of the simple pleasures like his own chair, his own bed, knowing where everything was, homemade bread toasted crisp, with sharp, bitter marmalade and hot tea for breakfast. Above all there were the people. He would miss them, even in a few days, let alone weeks.

He told her so, over and over, in words, in touch and in silence.

PITT STOOD ON THE DECK of the ship and stared across the blue water towards a horizon which was a glittering margin between sea and sky, unbroken by even the suggestion of land. He was glad to escape from his cabin, which was in fact only half his. He was obliged to share it with a thin, unhappy man from Lancashire who made the journey regularly in the pursuit of his business. This man saw dark times ahead, and found a kind of satisfaction in saying so at every possible opportunity. The only virtue he possessed in Pitt's eyes was that he was uninterested in anyone else. Not once had he pressed Pitt as to what he did, where he came from, or why he was going to Egypt.

Narraway had given Pitt no story to explain himself, leaving it entirely up to him to invent whatever he pleased. He held that a man who created his own story was more likely to believe it and make no slips which would give him away. Pitt had spent the two-hour train journey from London to Southampton racking his brains for some excuse which did not rely on knowledge he did not possess. There was no point at all in suggesting any kind of business. Five minutes' conversation would show that he knew nothing about commerce. He was no scholar, and certainly not in the history or antiquities of Egypt, which was a subject of such interest now, and increasing all the time. His ignorance would show at the very first question.

What sort of man goes alone for a holiday to a foreign country about which he knows nothing, and where he has no friends or family? Not a married man, and he had chosen to be as close to the truth as possible, for convenience and safety, and because it gave him an anchor within himself. But if he did not go for pleasure, then it had to be some kind of necessity.

He settled on the invention of a brother who had gone for reasons of business and not been heard from in over two months. That gave him a compelling purpose and at the same time a justification for asking questions, and an explanation for his own ignorance on almost everything. So far he had answered all questions to everyone's apparent satisfaction. His cabin companion had responded only that if the brother's business was in cotton then he was doomed, and Pitt had best start looking in the alleys or even the river for what was left of him. Pitt had not replied.

Now he stared at the blue water and felt the breeze sweet and quite warm on his skin, and looked forward to the interest of a new place unlike anything he had ever imagined, let alone seen.

As soon as he landed he presented his passport, then saw to the disembarking of his luggage. With his case in his hand he stood on the quayside amid the shouting and the bustle. He heard a dozen different languages, none of which he understood, but there was something common to docksides the world over. In London it would have been bright at least, but there was always that chill in the wind up from the water. Here the heat wrapped around him like a damp, muffling blanket. The smells were at once familiar—tar, salt, fish. But there were also different smells—spices, dust, something warm, and sweat.

Some of the men worked naked to the waist. Others stood around dressed in long robes and turbans, talking to each other, inspecting a box here or a bale there.

With the captain's assistance he had already changed a little of his money into the local currency of piasters, he suspected at a highly unfavorable rate, but the convenience was worth a price.

It was late afternoon already and he must find lodgings before dark. He picked up his case and started to walk off the quay towards the busy street. Was there anyone who would at least understand English, even if they did not speak it? What sort of public transport was there?

He saw a horse and open carriage near the curb, presumably Alexandria's equivalent of a hansom. He was about to go over and ask the driver to take him to the British consulate when another man in Western clothes cut in front of him at a brisk stride, climbed up and swung into the seat, shouting his instructions in English.

Pitt determined to be quicker next time.

It took him twenty minutes to find another carriage, and a further five to persuade the driver to take him to the consulate for what he considered to be a reasonable fare. Of course he had no notion as to whether this man was taking him as he wished or not. He could have ended up in the desert, for all he was able to judge for himself, but he was too fascinated not to stare around as he was jerked and jolted along the streets. Narrow alleys opened into wide, sunlit thoroughfares.

Everything was of warm sand colors shifting into darker terracotta and the soft browns of wooden windows jutting out over the unpaved earth and stones below. Sun-bleached awnings hung motionless. Chickens and pigeons moved at will, pecking and squawking. Now and then a camel lurched with the peculiar grace of a ship bucking against the tide. Heavy-laden donkeys plodded along.

People wore pale robes, men with turbans, women with flowing scarves that also covered the lower half of their faces. Here and there was a splash of red or clear blue-green.

There seemed to be insects everywhere. Over and over again Pitt felt the needlelike sting of mosquitoes, but he could not move quickly enough to swat them.

All around him the air was pungent with the smell of spices and hot food, the sound of voices, laughter, now and then metal bells with a strange, hollow music to them.

Dusk came suddenly, and in an enamel-clear sky changing from hard blue to luminous turquoise there floated the most haunting cry, singing and yet not as he had ever heard it before. It seemed to ululate up and down without drawing breath, and floated as if from a height, penetrating the evening till it shivered from the towers and walls of every building.

No one looked startled. They seemed to have expected it exactly at the instant it came.

The carriage drew up at a marble-faced building of great beauty, its smooth stones alternating in lighter and darker shades to give it a rich appearance. Pitt thanked the driver, handed over the agreed price, and stepped out onto the baking footpath. The air around him was balmy, warm on his skin as if he were inside a room facing the sun, although the sky was darkening so rapidly he could barely see across the street for the depth of the shadows under the farther walls. There had been no twilight. The sun had disappeared and night was immediate. Already the footpaths were filling with people laughing and talking.

But it was dark already, and he had nowhere to spend the night, and the immediacy of that need should override interest. He went up the steps of the building and inside. A young Egyptian in an earth-colored robe addressed him in perfect English and asked in what way he could assist. Pitt replied that he sought advice, and repeated the name Narraway had given him.

Five minutes later he stood in Trenchard's office, the oil lamps giving a soft, muted glow to a room of antique and startlingly simple beauty. On one wall a painting of sunset over the Nile was haunting in its loveliness. On a small table a piece of Greek sculpture sat next to a rolled-up papyrus and a gold ornament that could have come from the sarcophagus of a pharaoh.

"You like them?" Trenchard asked with a smile, snapping Pitt's attention back to the present.

"Yes," Pitt said apologetically. "I'm sorry." He must be too tired, too overwhelmed by new sensation to be thinking properly.

"Not at all," Trenchard assured him. "You could never love the mystery and the splendor of Egypt more than I do. Especially Alexandria! Here the corners of the world are folded together with a vitality you will find nowhere else. Rome, Greece, Byzantium, and Egypt!" He said their names as if the words themselves captured an impressionable magic.

He was a man of instant charm and perfect diction, as if he read poetry aloud for his pleasure. He was of average height, but looked taller because he was slender, and he moved with unusual grace as he came around his desk to shake Pitt's hand. His face was patrician, with a rather large aquiline nose, and his fair brown hair waved a trifle extravagantly. Pitt had the impression of a gentleman, perhaps posted here to suit the convenience of his family rather than from any innate skill. He was no doubt well educated in the classics, possibly even with a dilettante interest in Egyptology, but he had the air of one who takes his pleasures seriously and his work with relative lightness.

"What can we do for you?" he asked warmly. "Jackson said you asked for me by name?" It was a question that politely required an explanation.

"Mr. Victor Narraway suggested you might be able to give me some advice," Pitt replied.

Trenchard's eyes flashed with understanding. "Indeed," he acknowledged. "Do sit down. You have just arrived in Egypt?"

"Off the steamer docked an hour ago," Pitt acknowledged, accepting the seat gratefully. He had not walked very far, but he had been standing on deck for a long time, too eager and too interested to wait below in his cabin.

"Have you somewhere to stay?" Trenchard asked, but his expression assumed the negative. "I would suggest Casino San Stefano. It's a very good hotel—a hundred rooms, so you'll have no trouble getting one. They are all twenty-five piasters a day, and the food is excellent. If you don't care for Egyptian, they serve French as well. Rather more important than that, you can get there by carriage down the Strada Rossa, or perhaps less expensive and more discreet is an excellent tramway, twenty-four trams a day, and both the Schatz and the Racos end at the San Stefano terminus."

"Thank you," Pitt said sincerely. It was a good beginning, but he was overwhelmed by his ignorance and the feeling of being in a city in which even the smell of the air was foreign to him. He had never felt so fumblingly blind, or so alone. Everything familiar was a thousand miles away.

Trenchard was watching him, waiting for him to continue. He could have enquired for a hotel from anyone. He must explain at least something of his purpose here. He began with what was public knowledge, at least in London. He gave Trenchard the bare facts of the murder of Lovat and the arrest of Ayesha Zakhari.

"Zakhari!" Trenchard repeated the name curiously, his face alive with interest.

"You know her family?" Pitt said quickly. Perhaps this was going to be easy after all.

"No—but it's a Coptic name, not Muslim." He saw Pitt's lack of understanding. "Christian," he explained.

Pitt was startled. He had not even considered the question of religion, but now he realized its importance.

Then the moment after, Trenchard added more, his mouth twisted in a slight, wry smile, his eyes meeting Pitt's steadily. "From what you say, she is something better than a prostitute, perhaps a rather exclusive courtesan. If she were Muslim she would be cut off from her own people for associating with a non-Muslim man in such a way, however discreetly. As a Christian, if she is extremely careful, she can maintain the fiction of acceptability."

"I don't know that she's a courtesan!" Pitt said rather hotly, then felt embarrassed at his own lack of professional detachment as he saw the laughter in Trenchard's eyes.

Trenchard forbore from comment, even though it was in his expression, not unkindly, simply as the gentle weariness of a man of the world dealing with someone of startling naïveté. Pitt felt scalded by it. He was a professional policeman with far more knowledge of the darker sides of human nature than this aristocratic diplomat. He controlled his temper with difficulty.

"The only association we know of is with Saville Ryerson," he said in a chillier tone than he had intended. "Lovat was apparently an ardent admirer when he served here in Alexandria twelve years ago, but we don't know if he was ever more than that."

Trenchard folded his hands, completely unperturbed. "And you want to know?"

"Among other things, yes."

"Presumably your brief is to clear Ryerson?" That was more an invitation to explain his precise needs than a question, but Trenchard was a man whose courtesy never failed. Pitt had the sudden, profound impression that if he were to shoot you, he would do it politely.

There was no point in being abusive; Trenchard would only consider him even more of a fool.

"If possible," he agreed.

Trenchard saw his hesitation, minute as it had been, and it was reflected in his expression.

"We need to know the truth," Pitt continued quickly. "Why would she kill Lovat? Why did she come to London in the first place? Was she seeking Ryerson or did she meet him by chance?" He realized as he said it how unlikely it was that a beautiful Egyptian woman merely happened to fall in love with the government minister in charge of cotton exports. And yet history was littered with unlikely meetings that had altered its course irrevocably.

"Yes . . ." Trenchard said, pursing his lips. "Of course. Puts a different complexion on it. Why is she supposed to have shot this Lovat?" His eyes widened very slightly. "Who is he, anyway?"

"A junior diplomat of no apparent importance," Pitt replied. He decided to say nothing yet about the possibility of blackmail. "And even if he were pestering her," he went on, "Ryerson is sufficiently in love with her that he is doing all he can to protect her from a charge of murder, even at the expense of his own reputation. She had no cause to fear that a past lover would turn his affections away from her."

"Yes, indeed," Trenchard said softly. "It seems there is something beyond the obvious, and the possibilities are numerous. Your visit here is well advised. I admit, I wondered why Narraway did not simply request someone at the consulate to look into it, but now I see that a detective is required. The answer may be complex, and it may be that there are those who would wish it to remain unknown." He smiled, a charming, candid gesture. "Are you familiar with Egypt, Mr. Pitt?"

Pitt saw behind Trenchard's easy manner a glimpse of the passion he had shown before when he spoke of the beauty and antiquity of Egypt, and the brilliance of the culture that had crossed its path, particularly here, where the Nile met the Mediterranean—in a sense, where Africa met Europe.

"Assume I know nothing," Pitt said with humility. "The little I have learned can be disregarded."

Trenchard nodded, a flash of approval in his face. "The recorded history of the country goes back not far short of five thousand years before Christ." His words were momentous, and for all his casual tone, there was awe in his expression. "But for your purposes you can disregard all of it, even the Napoleonic conquest and brief French occupation nearly a century ago. No doubt you are aware of Lord Nelson's victory at Aboukir, usually known, I believe, as the Battle of the Nile? Yes, I assumed so." There was an indefinable edge to his voice, an emotion impossible to name. "Egypt is nominally part of the Ottoman Empire, and therefore owes allegiance to the Sultan of Turkey," he continued. "But in fact for the last fifteen years it has been part of ours, although it would be extremely unwise to make any remark to that effect." He shrugged elegantly. "Or to the fact that we bombarded Alexandria ten years ago, on Mr. Gladstone's orders."

Pitt flinched, but Trenchard took no more than slight notice, just a flicker in his eyes.

"The khedive is the sultan's vassal," he continued. "There is an Egyptian prime minister, a parliament, an Egyptian army and an Egyptian flag. The finances are probably of no interest to you except regarding cotton, which is the single exported crop here, and bought entirely by Britain, a fact of no little importance."

"Yes," Pitt said grimly. "I was aware of that. And I think finances might be at the heart of the issue. But," he added hastily, "I do not require a lecture on them at present. What about police?"

Trenchard moved a little in his seat.

"I would forget the entire subject of law and courts, if I were you," Trenchard said dryly. "Egyptian jurisdiction over foreigners belongs to a whole series of courts, one for each consulate, and the circumlocutory machinations of any of them, let alone all, would confound even Theseus, trailing a thread behind him." He spread his elegant hands wide. "In effect the British run Egypt, but we do it discreetly. There are hundreds of us, and we all answer to the consul-general, Lord Cromer, who is usually referred to simply as 'the lord.' And I presume you know what they say about him?"

"I have no idea," Pitt confessed.

Trenchard raised his eyebrows very slightly, a smile on his lips. " 'It is no good having right on your side if Lord Cromer is against you,' " he quoted. "Better, I think, in this situation, if he never hears of you."

"I shall certainly work to that end," Pitt promised. "But I need to know about this woman, who she was before she came to England, and if she is really as impulsive and . . ."

"Stupid," Trenchard filled in for him, his eyes wide. "Yes, I can see the necessity. We'll start among the Copts. I'll give you a map and mark the most likely areas. I would assume that she comes from a family with a certain amount of money, since she obviously speaks English and has the means to travel."

"Thank you." Pitt stood up, finding himself stiff and making an effort to stifle a yawn. It was still extraordinarily warm, his clothes were sticking to his skin, and he was far more tired than he had expected. "Where do I catch the tram for San Stefano?"

"You have piasters?"

"Yes . . . thank you."

Trenchard rose to his feet also. "Then if you turn right and walk about a hundred yards you will find the stop on your left, immediately across the street. But I would suggest at this time of evening, while you are unfamiliar with the city, that you take a horse carriage. It should not be more than eight or nine piasters, and worth it when you have a case to carry. Good luck, Pitt." He held out his hand. "If I can be of assistance, please call me. If I know anything that might help I shall send a note to you at San Stefano."

Pitt shook his hand, thanked him again, and accepted his advice to take a carriage.

The journey was not long but the heat had not abated in the crowded streets, and once again Pitt was thoroughly bitten by mosquitoes. By the time he arrived at the hotel he was exhausted, and itching everywhere.

However, the hotel was indeed excellent and offered him a room at twenty-five piasters a night, as Trenchard had said. He was offered excellent and abundant food, but he accepted only fresh bread and fruit, and when he had eaten it he went up to his room. As soon as the door was closed he took off his shoes, walked over to the window and stared out at a brilliant black sky dotted with stars. He could smell the heat and the salt wind blowing in off the sea. He breathed in deeply and let it go in a long, aching sigh. The city was beautiful, uplifting, exciting, and so very far from home. He could hear the sound of the sea, occasional laughter, and a constant background noise like that of crickets in summer grass. It reminded him of childhood summers in the country, but he was too tired to enjoy it. He wished more than he could control and be master of that Charlotte were here, so he could say to her "Look," or bid her listen to the faraway voices speaking an utterly different language, or share with her the alien, spicy odors of the night.

He turned back to the unfamiliar room, took his clothes off and washed the dust from himself, then opened the soft drapes of the mosquito nets around the bed. He climbed in, carefully closing them again, and went to sleep almost immediately. He woke once in the darkness and for several moments could not think where he was. He missed the movement of the ship. He was oddly dizzy without it. Then realization flooded back to him, and he turned over and sank into oblivion again until late morning.

He used the first two days to learn all he could of the city. He began by purchasing suitable clothes for temperatures in the seventies at night and the eighties during the day. He made use of the excellent public transport system of trams, all newly painted, and trains, British built and oddly familiar even in the dazzling sunlight, against which he felt he was permanently squinting. Sometimes he walked the streets listening to the voices, watching the faces, noting the extraordinary mixture of languages and races. As well as Egyptians there were Greeks, Armenians, Jews, Levantines, Arabs, occasionally French, and everywhere English. He saw soldiers in tropical uniform, expatriates seeming much at ease, as if this was now home to them, the heat, the noise, the market haggling, the blistering brightness of everything. There were pale-faced tourists, tired and excited, determined to see everything. He overheard them chattering about moving on to Cairo, and then taking one of many steamers going up the Nile to Karnak and beyond.

One elderly vicar, his white mustache gleaming against his mahogany skin, spoke enthusiastically about his recent trip. He described sitting at breakfast staring across the timeless Nile as if it had been eternity itself, his *Egyptian Gazette* open in front of him, his Dundee marmalade on his fresh toast, and the burial pyramids of the pharaohs on the skyline across the sands.

"Perfectly splendid!" he said in a voice that might have been ringing across a gentleman's club in London.

It reminded Pitt sharply of the urgency of his mission, and forced him to begin asking for the Coptic family of Zakhari. Absorbing the millennia of the pharaohs; the centuries of Greece and Rome; the romance of Cleopatra; the coming of the Arabs, the Turks and Mamelukes; the conquest of Napoleon and then Nelson; would all have to wait. It was now the British who ruled, whatever the caliph in Istanbul pretended, and it was the ships of the world that sailed through the Suez Canal to India and the East beyond. It was to English cotton mills in the smoke and darkening winter of Manchester, Burnley, Salford and Blackburn that the harvest of Egypt was sold. And it was from the factories of England that the finished goods were brought back, through Suez and beyond.

There was poverty in these hot streets with the dung and the flies. There was hunger and disease. He saw beggars sitting in the partial shade of sunbaked walls, moving with the shadows, asking for alms, for the love of God. Sometimes their bodies seemed whole, some even at a glance were crippled or pitted with sores, others were blind or maimed. Some faces were scarred by the pox, or disfigured with leprosy, and he found it hard not to look away.

A few times he was spat at, and once he was caught on the elbow by a stone hurled from behind, though when he turned there was no one there.

But there was poverty in England as well, cold and wet, gutters running over, and the diseases of a different climate, the hacking coughs of tuberculosis, and there, as here, the agony of cholera and typhoid. He could not weigh one against the other.

He went back to the main suburb where the Christian Copts lived. Sitting in a small restaurant over a cup of coffee so thick and sweet he could not drink it, he began to ask questions. He used the excuse (which was the truth) that Ayesha was in trouble in London and he was seeking her family, or any friend or relative who might be able to help her. At the very least they should know of her predicament.

It took him nearly two more days before he learned anything beyond rumor and surmise. Finally he agreed to meet with a man whose sister had been a friend of Ayesha's, and by arrangement, Pitt had ordered dinner at the Casino San Stefano.

Pitt was waiting at the table when an Egyptian man of about thirty-five stopped at the entrance of the dining room. The man was dressed in the traditional robes of the country, but the cloth was rich and the colors those of the warm earth. He gazed about for a moment or two, and then, apparently identifying Pitt among the other European guests, he made his way between the tables and bowed, introducing himself formally. "Good evening, Effendi. My name is Makarios Yacoub, and you are Mr. Pitt, I think, yes?"

Pitt rose to his feet and inclined his head in a slight bow. "How do you do. Yes, I am Thomas Pitt. Thank you very much for coming." He gestured to the other chair, inviting Yacoub to be seated. "May I offer you dinner? The food is excellent, but I daresay you know that."

"Are you yourself dining?" Yacoub enquired, accepting the seat.

Pitt had already learned in his few days there to be indirect in his speech. Haste gained nothing but contempt. "It would be pleasant," he replied.

"Then by all means." Yacoub nodded. "That is most gracious of you."

Pitt made a few remarks about his interest in the city, commenting on the beauty of some of the parts he had seen, especially the causeway between the old lighthouse and the city.

"I felt as if, were I to close my eyes, then open them suddenly, I might see the Pharos as it was when it was one of the seven wonders of the ancient world," he said, then felt self-conscious for voicing aloud such a fancy.

But then he saw instantly that Yacoub understood. His face softened with a warmth and he relaxed a little in his seat. He was an Alexandrian and he loved to hear his city praised.

"The causeway is called the Heptastadion," he explained. "Built by Dinocrates. To the east is where the old harbor of the Middle Ages was. But there are so many other things you must see. If it is the past that interests you, there is the tomb of Alexander the Great. Some say it is beneath the Mosque of Nabi Daniel, others in the necropolis nearby." He smiled apologetically. "Forgive me if I say too much. I wish to share my city with everyone who looks at it with the eye of friendship. You must walk along the Mahmudiya Canal to the Antoniadis Gardens, where there is history in every handful of the earth. The poet Callinachus lived there, and taught his students, and in 640 A.D. Pompilius prevented the king of Syria from capturing the city." He shrugged a little. "And there is a Roman tomb," he finished with a smile, as the waiter presented himself.

"Are you familiar with our food?" Yacoub enquired.

"Very little," Pitt admitted, willing to allow him to help, both for practicality and courtesy.

"Then I suggest *Mulukhiz*," Yacoub replied. "It is a green soup, a great delicacy. You will enjoy it. And then *Hamam Mahshi*; that is stuffed pigeon." He looked at Pitt questioningly.

"That would be excellent, thank you," Pitt agreed.

Pitt asked him further questions about the city until the food was served. They were halfway through the soup, which was indeed delicious, when Yacoub at last raised the subject for which they were met.

"You said that Miss Zakhari was in a certain degree of difficulty," he said, laying his spoon down for a moment and looking more closely at Pitt. His voice was light, as if they were still discussing the city, but there was an intensity in his eyes.

Pitt was aware that there was an excellent telephone service in the city, more reliable at times than that in London, and it was more than possible that Yacoub already knew of her arrest, and the charges. He must not be caught in a misrepresentation, let alone an outright falsehood.

"I am afraid it is serious," he conceded. "I am not sure whether she will have had the opportunity to inform her family, or perhaps she has not wished to cause them concern. However, if she were my daughter, or sister, I should prefer to know all the details as completely as possible, so that I might know how to help."

If Yacoub knew anything he kept it from his face. "Of course," he murmured. "Naturally." But he did not betray any surprise that Ayesha Zakhari should be in difficulty or danger. Pitt would have expected surprise, even alarm, and there was none. Was that because Yacoub had already been told of her predicament through the news, or was it something not unexpected from his knowledge of Ayesha herself? Pitt remembered Narraway's warning with a sense of coldness, even here in the stifling dining room with its odors of food, and the breeze from the water drifting in through the open doors. The young man opposite him was charming, so easy of manner he could forget that his interests might be very different from Pitt's, or from the British government's.

"You are acquainted with her family?" Pitt said aloud.

Yacoub lifted his shoulders slightly, an elegant gesture that could have meant a number of things. "Her mother died many years ago, her father only three or four," he answered.

Pitt was surprised that he should feel a sense of pity. "Is there no one else? Brothers? A sister?"

"No one," Yacoub replied. "She was an only child. Perhaps that is why her father took such care that she should be educated. She was his dearest companion. She speaks French, Greek, and Italian, as well as English, of course. And Arabic is her native tongue. But it was philosophy in which she excelled, the history of thought and of ideas." He was watching Pitt, and noted his surprise. "You look at a beautiful woman and think she seeks only to please," he remarked.

Pitt opened his mouth to deny it, and realized it was true, and Yacoub knew it. He felt himself blush, and said nothing.

"She did not care much about pleasing," Yacoub went on, a faint smile in his eyes more than on his lips, and he resumed eating, breaking the bread in his fingers. "Perhaps she did not need to."

"Did her father not wish to see her married well?" Pitt knew it was a somewhat impertinent question, but he needed far more information than this, and if she had no family alive then a friend was all there was to ask.

Yacoub looked back at him. "Perhaps. But Ayesha was willful, and Mr. Zakhari was too fond of her to push her against her wish." He took several more spoonfuls of his green soup before deciding to continue. "She had sufficient means not to need to marry, and she cared nothing for convention."

"Or love?" Pitt risked asking.

Again, Yacoub gave the delicate gesture which could have meant almost anything. "I think she loved many times, but how deeply I have no idea."

Was that a euphemism? Pitt was floundering in a culture far different from his own. He still had little idea of what kind of woman Ayesha Zakhari was, except that she was unlike any other he knew.

He wished profoundly that he could have asked Charlotte. She might have been able to cut through the words and grasp reality.

"What sort of people did she love?" he asked.

Yacoub finished his green soup and the waiter removed the plates and returned with the pigeon.

Yacoub looked not at Pitt but at some point in the distance. "I knew only one personally," he answered. Then, raising his eyes suddenly to Pitt's, he demanded, "How does this help her, that you should know about Ramses Ghali? He is not in England. He can have nothing to do with her present troubles."

"Are you certain?"

There was no hesitation in Yacoub's face. "Absolutely."

Pitt was unconvinced. "Who is he?"

Yacoub's eyes were soft, but his expression was an unreadable mixture of anger and sorrow. "He is dead," he explained quietly. "He died over ten years ago."

"Oh . . ." Death again. Had she truly loved this man? Could he be the key to her behavior now? Pitt was reaching for straws, but there was nothing else. "Might she have married him, had he lived?"

Yacoub smiled. "No." Again he seemed absolutely certain.

"But you said she loved him . . ."

Yacoub looked patient, as with a child who needs endless and detailed explanations. "They loved each other as friends, Mr. Pitt. Ramses Ghali believed passionately in Egypt, as his father did." A shadow crossed his face, and an emotion Pitt could not read, but he thought there was a touch of anger in it, a darkness.

The bombardment of Alexandria had occurred ten years ago. Was that the chill Pitt saw? Or was it deeper than that, the whole matter of General Gordon and the siege of Khartoum, south from here in the Sudan? In 1882 British forces had defeated Orabi at Tel-el-Kebir, and six thousand Egyptians had been massacred by the Mahdi in Sudan. The following year an Egyptian army even larger had been similarly destroyed, and in 1884 yet a further army was defeated, and General "Chinese" Gordon had arrived. In January, Gordon had perished, and less than six months later the Mahdi himself was dead; but Khartoum was not yet retaken.

Suddenly, Pitt felt very far from home, and for all the European decoration of the hotel dining room, and its Italian name, he was acutely aware of the ancient and utterly different heritage of the young man opposite him, and of the African spice and heat of the air beyond the walls. He had to force himself to try to think clearly.

"You said Ayesha Zakhari believed in Egypt just as fiercely," he said, beginning to eat his pigeon, which he thought absentmindedly was the best he had ever had. "Is she a person to take any kind of action on her beliefs? Did she speak for a cause, seek to draw in others?"

Yacoub gave a tiny, almost smothered laugh, cut off instantly. "Has she changed so much? Or do you simply know nothing about her, Mr. Pitt?" His eyes narrowed and he ignored his food. "I have read the newspapers, and I think the English government will seek to get their own minister off, and hang Ayesha." Now there was a world of bitterness in his voice, and his smooth olive face was as close to ugly as it could be, so dark was the rage and the pain inside him. "What is it you want here? To find a witness who will tell you she is a dangerous woman, a fanatic who will kill anyone who stands in her way? That perhaps this Lieutenant Lovat knew something about her which would spoil her life of luxury in England, and he threatened to tell people?"

"No," Pitt said instantly, and perhaps the force with which he meant it carried between them.

Yacoub let out his breath slowly and seemed to listen instead of merely waiting his chance to interrupt.

"No," Pitt continued. "I would like to find the truth. I can't think of any reason why she would kill him. All she had to do was ignore him and he would have had no choice but to desist, or be dealt with, possibly unpleasantly, for making a nuisance of himself."

He saw the disbelief in Yacoub's face. "Lovat had a profession," he explained. "A career in the diplomatic service. How far would he progress if he incurred the enmity of a senior government minister like Saville Ryerson?"

"Would he exercise his influence to save her?" Yacoub asked uncertainly.

"Yes!" It was Pitt's turn to state what was so plain to him, and apparently unknown to Yacoub. "Ryerson has already committed himself to help her in Lovat's death, even at the risk of being sent to trial for it himself. He would hardly balk at warning off a young man whose attentions were unwelcome. A word to his senior in the diplomatic service and Lovat would be finished."

Yacoub still looked doubtful.

Around them in the dining room the buzz of conversation ebbed and flowed. A beautiful woman with fair hair and a porcelain complexion laughed, throwing her head back so the light caught her. Her companion gazed at her in fascination. Pitt wondered if it was a romance she would not have dared entertain at home. Was this greater freedom something Yacoub imagined to exist in British society? How could Pitt explain that it was not?

Yacoub looked down at his plate. "You don't understand," he said quietly. "You really know nothing about her."

"Then tell me!" Pitt begged. He nearly added more, then bit it back. He could see the struggle in Yacoub's face, the need to fight for some justice, to see truth destroy ignorance, and at the same time the deep need of a private person not to betray the secrets of another's passion or pain.

Again, Pitt tried to think of an argument that would win, and again he kept silent.

Yacoub pushed his plate away and reached for his glass. He sipped from it very slowly, then put it down and looked at Pitt. "Ramses's father Alexander was one of the leaders fighting to govern our own affairs when our debts ran out of control under the Khedive Ismail, before he was deposed and his son Tewfik put in his place, and Britain took over management of Egypt's financial affairs. He was a brilliant man, a philosopher and scholar. He spoke Greek and Turkish as well as Arabic. He wrote poetry in all of them. He knew our culture and our history, from the pharaohs who built the pyramids at Giza, through all the dynasties to Cleopatra, the Greco-Roman period, the coming of the Arabs and the law of Mohammed, the art and the medicine, the astronomy and the architecture. He had strength and he had charm."

Pitt did not interrupt. He had no idea if what Yacoub was saying was going to mean anything in the murder of Edwin Lovat, or if Narraway could use even a shred of it, but it fascinated him because it was part of the story of this extraordinary city.

"He could make you see the magic in the gleam of moonlight on marble shards a thousand years old," Yacoub went on, turning the goblet in his fingers. "He could bring back the life and the laughter of the past as if it had never really left, simply been overlooked for a space by people too insensitive to perceive it. With him you could see the colors of the world, hear music simply in the wind over the sand. The smell of dirt and sewage, the flies in the street, the mosquitoes, were only the breathing of life."

"And Ayesha?" Pitt asked, afraid already of the answer.

"Oh, she loved Alexander Ghali," Yacoub replied, his mouth twisted a little sideways. "She was young, and honor was dear to her. She loved her country too, and its history, its ideas, but she loved the people and hated the poverty which kept them ignorant when they could have learned to read and write, and kept them sick when they could have been well."

Pitt waited. He knew from the suppressed emotion in Yacoub's face, the shadows in his eyes, that the story was only half told, if that.

Yacoub took up the thread again. He had stopped only to regain control of his feelings so they did not show so nakedly in his face.

"He was a man of almost infinite possibilities," he said quietly. "He would even have given Egypt back her independence and financial integrity. But he was flawed. He indulged his family. He gave his sons and his brothers power, and they were greedy for themselves. He was a man who fed on the beautiful things of the heart and the mind, but he had not the inner courage to deny those around him. Leaders must be prepared to walk alone, if need be, and he was not."

He drew in a deep breath, turned his glass in his hand as if to sip it again, then ignored it after all. There was a tightness in his face, of old pain still unhealed. "Ayesha loved him, and he betrayed her, and his people. I don't know if she ever cared wholly for any man after that, unless she does for this Ryerson?" Now he raised his eyes to meet Pitt's. "Will he betray her also?"

Pitt wondered if that was why she had said nothing to the police. Was she numb inside, waiting for history to repeat itself?

"By betraying her, or betraying his own people?" he asked.

There was a flash of understanding in Yacoub's eyes. "You are thinking of the cotton? That she went to London to try to persuade him to leave us our raw cotton to weave, instead of shipping it to Manchester, for British workers to create the greater profit from it—to grow rich, instead of us? Perhaps she did. It would be like her."

"Then she was asking him to choose between Egypt and England," Pitt pointed out. "If he made a decision at all, then it had to be a betrayal of someone."

"Yes . . . of course it was." Yacoub's lips tightened. "Whether she could forgive him for that I do not know." He picked up his glass at last. "There is nothing more I can tell you. Look all you wish, you will find that what I have said is true."

"What about Lieutenant Lovat?"

Yacoub waved his hand dismissively. "Nothing of importance. He fell in love with her, and perhaps she was bruised enough to find his attention healing. It lasted a while, a few months. He was posted back to England. I think she was quite relieved by then.

Perhaps he was also. He had no intention of marrying outside his own class and station."

"Do you know anything about Lovat?"

"No. But you might find someone among the British soldiers who does. There are enough of them here."

Pitt said nothing. He was acutely aware of the British presence in all sorts of ways, not just the enormous number of soldiers, but the civilians in administration everywhere. Egypt was not a colony, and yet in many practical ways it might as well have been. If Ayesha Zakhari had wished to rid her country of foreign domination, he could understand it very easily.

Was that why she had gone to London, not out of any desire to make her own future, but to help her people? If that was so, then presumably she had sought out Ryerson specifically, as a man with the power to help her, if she could persuade him to do so.

How had she intended to do that? No matter how deeply he was in love with her, he would hardly alter government policy to please her, would he? And according to Yacoub's estimate of her character, she would have despised him if he had.

But then unless she cared for him, that would hardly matter to her. Did she? Had she unexpectedly fallen in love with him, and it was suddenly no longer simply a matter of patriotic duty?

Or had she planned to blackmail him, and Lovat's murder was part of that plan, somehow hideously gone wrong, and she herself had ended up arrested, and by now probably charged as well? What had she meant to have happen? Offer him escape from blame, and increase the pressure upon Ryerson to yield more autonomy to Egypt?

Or was her goal Ryerson's ruin, and the placement of another, more pliable minister in his place—one who would pay the Egyptian price?

But that made little sense. No minister of trade was going to yield the cotton back to Egypt unless he was forced to by circumstances far more powerful than love, or even ruin. He would simply be replaced in time by another stronger and less vulnerable man.

Pitt finished his wine and thanked Yacoub. The voices and laughter bubbled around them, but he could think of nothing further to ask, and instead they spoke again of the rich, intricate history of Alexandria.

When Pitt was at the breakfast table the following morning, a messenger brought him a note from Trenchard, asking him if all was well and if he would care for any further assistance. It also said that if Pitt cared to join him for luncheon, Trenchard would be happy to show him some of the less-well-known places of interest in the city afterwards.

Pitt requested paper and wrote back accepting, and dispatched the messenger with his reply before continuing with his excellent fresh bread, fruit, and fish. He was very rapidly growing accustomed to the exotic food, and enjoying it greatly.

He spent part of the morning in an English library reading what he could find about the Orabi uprising and looking for any reference to anyone named Ghali involved in politics at the time. The passion and the betrayal were so absorbing he was almost late for his luncheon with Trenchard, and arrived at the consulate barely by noon.

Trenchard made no comment, but rose from his chair with a smile and welcomed him in.

"Delighted you could come," he said warmly. He regarded Pitt's pale cotton shirt and trousers, and the already deepening color of his face and lower arms. "You look as if you are well settled in—apart from a few mosquito bites," he observed.

"Very well," Pitt agreed. "It is a city one could spend a year exploring, and hardly touch the surface."

Something in Trenchard's face eased. The lines of his mouth softened and there was an added reality to the warmth in his eyes.

"Egypt has you, hasn't it?" he said with evident pleasure. "And you haven't even been anywhere near Cairo yet, never mind up the Nile. I wish your detection took you to Heliopolis, or the tombs of the caliphs or the petrified forest. You could not go that far without riding out to the pyramids at Giza, and of course the Sphinx, and then sat up until you could at least see the pyramids at Aboukir and Sakhara, and the ruins of Memphis." He shook his head slightly, as if at some pleasant, well-known inner joke. "And then nothing on earth could stop you from continuing on up that greatest and oldest of all ruins till you reached Thebes, and the Temple of Karnak. That defeats even the imagination." He was watching Pitt's face as he spoke. "Believe me, no modern Western man can conceive the grandeur of it, the sheer enormity!" He did not wait for comment. He stood still in the middle of the room, oblivious of modern furniture and consulate papers around him. His vision was on the timeless sands.

Pitt did not interrupt; no answer was expected or wanted.

"Then south to Luxor," Trenchard went on. "You should cross the river at dawn. You have never seen anything in your life like first light over the desert, moving across the water's face. Then you have only about four miles to the Valley of the Kings.

"If you ride on a fast camel you will see the sunrise on the tombs of the pharaohs whose fathers ruled this land four thousand years before Christ was born. They were ancient before Abraham came out of Ur of the Chaldees. Have you any idea what that means, Inspector Pitt?" There was challenge in his eyes now. "The British Empire that circles the earth now was born in the last five minutes of time compared with them." He stopped suddenly. He took a deep breath. "But you haven't time for that . . . I know. And Narraway certainly won't pay for it. Forgive me. No doubt you are eager for your accommodation, and you are honest enough to be compelled by duty."

Pitt smiled. "Duty does not forbid me from learning something about the history of Egypt, or from wishing I needed to pursue Ayesha Zakhari's history at least as far as Cairo. I haven't found an excuse, but I haven't stopped looking."

Trenchard laughed, and led the way out through the offices to the street and a short distance along the crowded thoroughfare in a direction Pitt had not been before. He found himself staring at the beautiful buildings decorated with stone fretwork like lace in its intricacy, balconies with roofs supported by simple pillars. He saw one, shaded from the heat, where a group of elderly men sat on thick turquoise-and-gold cushions eating bread, fruit, and dates as they talked earnestly to one another. They barely glanced at the two Englishmen, contempt and dislike in their eyes for a moment, then masked, because they dared not let it be seen. Behind them, a large man with skin almost as black as his beard, dressed in loose trousers caught in below the knee, seemed to be waiting their pleasure. Pigeons fluttered around, and a tall, narrow-necked vase was stuffed full of pink roses.

Pitt thought it might have looked exactly the same a thousand years earlier.

Trenchard found the café of his choice and ordered food for both of them without consulting Pitt, and when it came it made not the slightest pretense at European form. They ate with their fingers, and it was delicious. The color, the smell, the texture—everything pleased.

"I have been making a few enquiries of my own about Ayesha Zakhari," Trenchard said when they were halfway through the meal.

Pitt stopped with a morsel of food in his hand. "Yes?"

"As we had supposed, she is Coptic Christian," Trenchard replied. "Her name tells us as much. It seems she was deeply involved with some of the leading Egyptian nationalists in the Orabi uprising, just before the bombardments of Alexandria ten years ago. I am sorry, Pitt . . ." He looked rueful. "I have asked discreetly among the friends I have here, and it seems eminently probable that she went to London with the express purpose of ensnaring Ryerson, in some foolish and highly impractical idea that he could be persuaded to alter the British financial arrangements with Egypt . . . cotton at least, perhaps more. She has always been hotheaded where her idealism is concerned. She fell in love with Alexander Ghali, Ramses's father, and even when he betrayed his cause, she was among the last to accept the truth about him." Trenchard's face was filled with profound emotion, a mixture of pity and contempt so deep even the mention of the facts which provoked it made his whole frame stiffen and his elegant hands suddenly look awkward.

Pitt felt overtaken by a feeling of emptiness also. "Disillusion is very bitter," he said quietly. "Most of us fight to deny it as long as we can."

Trenchard looked up quickly. "I'm sorry, Pitt. I am afraid you are likely to find that she is impulsive, romantic—an idealist who has been betrayed, and now acting from her own pain, and trying to make the old dreams come true, however unrealistic the means."

Pitt looked down at the food in his hand. It no longer held the exotic charm it had only a few minutes ago. That was absurd. He had never even seen Ayesha Zakhari. It should matter nothing to him except professionally that she was irresponsible, a political failure who had allowed personal hurt to spoil her judgment. Yet suddenly he felt tired, as if he too had lost a dream.

"I'll see what else I can find out about Lovat," he said aloud.

Trenchard was watching him, his face full of regret. "I'm sorry," he said again. "I knew it would have been very much pleasanter to think there was some other explanation. But possibly Lovat gained enmities in England?"

"He was shot in Miss Zakhari's garden at three in the morning!" Pitt said with a touch of bitterness. "And with her gun!"

Trenchard gave a slight gesture of resignation, graceful and sad. It had an elegance, as if he had picked up something of the innate dignity of the civilization he so admired.

They finished the meal. Trenchard insisted on paying, after

thanking the proprietor in fluent and colloquial Arabic, then he accompanied Pitt to the bazaar and helped him to bargain for a bracelet set with carnelian for Charlotte, a small statue of a hippopotamus for Daniel, some brightly colored silk ribbons for Jemima, and a woven kerchief for Gracie.

Pitt ended the afternoon with information he accepted was inevitably true, however much he would have preferred it not to be, and gifts he was delighted with, and for which he knew he had paid a very small price indeed.

He thanked Trenchard and returned on the tram to San Stefano, determined to find the army barracks where Lovat had served and spend the rest of his time in Alexandria pursuing Lovat's military and personal career and anything he could find out about him. Somewhere his path had crossed Ayesha's, and there had to be more to learn about it.

CHAPTER SEVEN

CHARLOTTE FOUND IT very difficult trying to occupy her mind with anything, knowing that Pitt was in Egypt, alone in a land of which he knew nothing. More dangerous than simply its unfamiliarity was the fact that he was there to ask questions about a woman who might well be a heroine in her people's struggle against British domination of Egyptian affairs. She tried to occupy herself with any number of other thoughts, mostly trivial, but they all fled before the enormity of his absence once she turned off the last of the gaslights downstairs and went up to her bedroom alone. Then she lay in the dark and her imagination raced.

Therefore she was pleased to see Tellman on the evening of the third day after Pitt had left. Gracie answered the back door to find him standing there looking tired and cold, his face pinched from the wind. He came in at her invitation, stamping his feet a little on the scullery floor as if to get rid of water, although it was not raining at the moment, but it had been. He took off his coat.

"Good evening, Mrs. Pitt," he said, looking at Charlotte anxiously, as if somehow it was still his concern to care for her in Pitt's absence. The old habit died hard, as did the pretense that he did not care.

"Good evening, Inspector," she replied, amusement in her smile as well as pleasure to see him. She gave him his title intentionally. She had never used his Christian name. She was not even sure if Gracie had more than the odd, highly informal time. "Come in and have a cup of tea," she invited him. "You look cold. Have you had any supper?"

"Not yet," he replied, pulling out one of the hard-backed chairs and sitting down.

"I'll get yer summink," Gracie said quickly, putting the kettle onto the hob as she spoke. "In't got nuthin' left over for yer, though, 'ceptin' cold mutton an' bubble an' squeak—'ow's that?"

"Very good, thank you," Tellman said without pleasure, glancing at Charlotte to make sure that was acceptable to her also.

"Of course," she agreed quickly. "Have you heard something about Martin Garvie?"

He looked across at her, then at Gracie, his face full of pity and a gentleness exaggerated by the gaslight's soft glow catching the angles of his high cheekbones and hollow cheeks.

"No," he admitted. "And I've looked every way I can without police authority." The urgency in his voice made it impossible to argue with him.

"Wot did yer get, then?" Gracie asked, putting the frying pan on the top of the stove and bending to riddle the ash down and allow the fire to burn hotly again. She did it almost absently, still looking mostly at Tellman.

"Martin Garvie's definitely gone," he answered unhappily. "Nobody's seen him in almost two weeks now, but nobody's seen Stephen Garrick either. None of the servants, which is what you said, so at first they supposed he was in his rooms, taken sick, in one of his tantrums—"

"Not for more than a week, without the cook at least being aware of it," Charlotte interrupted. "Whatever illness he had, she'd be sending food of some sort up to him. And in that length of time, surely they'd have the doctor in?"

"So far as I can find out, there's been no doctor," Tellman answered, shaking his head a little. "And no other caller for him either." His face tightened, his eyes black. "He's not in the house—and nor is Martin Garvie. There'd be food, bed linen, if nothing else . . ."

Gracie fetched the cold potatoes from the larder. She started to peel and chop the onions with a brief apology, fishing for a handkerchief at the same time. "Bubble an' squeak's no good without onions," she said, by way of explanation. The frying pan was already beginning to get hot.

"Were there no letters?" Charlotte asked. "Invitations? Surely they would be replied to . . . or at least forwarded?"

Tellman bit his lip. "I couldn't be that direct, but I asked around about Mr. Garrick, and it seems he doesn't have that many friends. He's not good company. At least that's what I understood."

Gracie sniffed and dabbed her eyes with her handkerchief, then slid the chopped onions into the hot fat, and the sizzle blocked out her next words. " 'E's gotta 'ave somebody!" she repeated. " 'E don't work an' 'e don't stay 'ome, so where'd 'e go? Don't nob'dy miss 'im?"

"Well, as far as I can make out, nobody sees him often enough to wonder where he's gone," Tellman replied, looking at Gracie, then turning in his chair to Charlotte. "He doesn't seem to have the same sort of life as most young men his age from a family like that. He doesn't go to a regular club, so nobody thought it odd not to see him. There's nowhere he's known, nobody he talks to, or plays any sport with, wagers with . . . nothing to make a . . . a life!" He cleared his throat. "I see the same people just about every day. If I wasn't there they'd soon miss me, an' there'd be questions asked."

Charlotte frowned. It was worrying, but there was nothing specific yet to grasp. The subject that rose to her mind was indelicate, but the matter was too serious to pay deference to such things. However, she was aware of Tellman's sensibilities, particularly in front of Gracie. "He is not married," she said, feeling her way. "And apparently not courting anyone, so far as we know. Does he have . . ." Now she was not sure what to say.

"Couldn't find anything," Tellman said hastily, cutting her off. "As far as I could learn, he was an unhappy man." He glanced at Gracie. "Much as you said. Drinks a lot and gets difficult. Lost most of his friends lately. They don't seem to see him anymore. Not that I've had time to look very deep. But nobody's seen him, and he doesn't seem to have been planning to go anywhere, so wherever it is, he went in a hurry."

"And took Martin Garvie with 'im?" Gracie said, stirring the onions without looking at them. "Then why didn't the cook know? An' Bella? Surely they'd 'ave 'eard? 'E didn't go without cases an' things. Gentlemen don't."

"No, they don't," Charlotte agreed. "And you didn't answer about his letters. Are they forwarded to him, wherever he is? Someone would decline invitations, but surely he would want his letters?"

"His father?" Tellman suggested.

"Probably," Charlotte agreed. "But does he take them to the postbox himself? Why? Most people like him have a footman to do that. Has Stephen gone somewhere so secret the household staff are not allowed to know? And why did Martin leave no message for Tilda?"

"Wasn't time," Tellman answered. "It was a sudden invitation . . . or at least a sudden decision on his part."

"To somewhere from which Martin could not send a letter, if not to Tilda, then at least to someone who could let her know?" Charlotte said dubiously.

Gracie tipped the potatoes and cabbage into the pan to let them heat through, to mix with the onions and brown nicely. "It don't sound right ter me," she said quietly. "It in't natural. I think as there's summink wrong."

"So do I." Charlotte looked unblinkingly at Tellman.

Tellman gazed back at her without shifting his eyes even momentarily. "I don't know how to take it any further, Mrs. Pitt. The police have got no reason to ask anyone. I got shown out pretty sharply more than once, as it was, and told to attend to my own affairs. I had to pretend it was to do with a robbery. Said that Mr. Garrick could have been a witness." His face pinched up, showing his loathing for having allowed himself into the position of needing to lie. Charlotte wondered if Gracie knew just what cost he had paid to please her. She looked across at Gracie's back, stiff and straight as she paid attention to the hot bubble and squeak in the frying pan, and very carefully lifted it on the slice to avoid breaking the crisp surface as she set it on the plate beside the cold mutton. Perhaps she did.

Tellman took the plate from her appreciatively. "Thank you." He began to eat after only the slightest hesitation when Charlotte nodded to indicate he was welcome to begin.

"So wot are we gonna do, then?" Gracie asked, damping the fire down and filling the teapot. "We can't jus' leave it. 'E in't gone inter thin air. If summink's 'appened ter 'im it's murder, whether it's both of 'em or just Martin." She turned to Charlotte. "D'yer reckon as Mr. Garrick 'ad one of 'is rages an' 'it Martin, mebbe real 'ard, an' 'e died? An' they're coverin' it up ter save 'im? Send 'im orff inter the country, or summink?"

Charlotte was about to say "Of course not" when she realized that she was actually considering the possibility.

Tellman drew in his breath, but his mouth was full.

"I think we need to know a great deal more about the Garrick family," Charlotte said, choosing her words carefully.

Gracie's face tightened. "Yer gonna ask Lady Vespasia?" she said hopefully. She had not only heard of Vespasia's help in other cases, she had actually met her and been spoken to on more than one occasion. Vespasia had visited Keppel Street. Gracie could not have been more impressed had it been the Queen herself. After all, the Queen was short and more than a little plump, whereas Vespasia was as regal and as beautiful as a queen should be. And more important than that, she was willing to help wholeheartedly in the solving of crimes. She might be a real lady, with all the unimaginable glamour that went with that, but she helped them detect, and that was the ultimate belonging. "She'd know," Gracie added encouragingly.

Charlotte looked at Gracie's eager face and then at Tellman, who hated aristocrats, and amateurs interfering with police business, especially women, and saw his eyes flicker, a shadow of self-mockery with the denial. She hesitated as if deferring to his opinion, then when he said nothing, she nodded.

"I can't think of anything better. As we have already acknowledged, there is no police case to pursue, but there is almost certainly something wrong," he conceded. "There's no help for it."

IT WAS FAR TOO LATE that evening to contact Aunt Vespasia, but in the morning Charlotte dressed in her best calling gown, albeit very definitely last year's cut, which she had had no reason or incentive to alter yet. Since Pitt's demotion from head of Bow Street into Special Branch, she had had absolutely no excuse, or opportunity, to attend social engagements of any importance. It was only now, looking at her overfamiliar wardrobe, that she realized it quite so forcefully.

However, there was no money to spare for unnecessary indulgences such as a fashionable gown when what she had was warm, becoming and perfectly adequate. It was not so very long ago that they had both worried as to whether there would be food and coal.

The thing that stung was that she had not had the opportunity to help Thomas, which would have been an important thing in itself, and as an added benefit would have given her the chance and the excuse to borrow something glamorous from Emily, or even from Aunt Vespasia herself, who, although two generations older, was of a more similar height.

Now she pulled out her plum-colored morning dress and changed into it, pleased that at least it still fit her very nicely. Finding the right hat was less easy, and she settled for black with a touch of soft reddish pink. She did not really like it, but she owned nothing better, and one could not call without wearing a hat of some sort. More important than her own feelings, if anyone else were calling upon Vespasia, she would not like to embarrass her. No one wishes for impecunious relatives, however distant, still less for ones with distressing taste in clothes.

Gracie saw her off with enthusiasm and last-minute advice and instruction. She would not have been so impertinent as to offer it had she thought first, but her eagerness overcame propriety.

"We gotta know wot that 'ouse'old is like," she said with a frown. "They done summink to 'im. We gotta find out wot, an' why."

"I shall tell Aunt Vespasia the truth," Charlotte answered her, standing on the front step and looking up at the sky. It was a beautiful day, bright but decidedly crisp.

"It in't gonna rain," Gracie said decisively.

"No, I can see that. I was just thinking it is the sort of day when everyone and their mothers will think to go out calling. I may be fortunate to find her alone, and it is really not the sort of conversation where I would care to be interrupted."

"Well, we gotta try," Gracie urged. "An' I can't think o' no one better than Lady Vespasia. We don't know nob'dy else, unless Mrs. Radley knows 'em?"

"Emily isn't of much help," Charlotte replied, stepping off onto the pavement. "She has not really been around long enough. I will be back when I can do no more. Good-bye." And she set off with determination, now intent upon getting a hansom rather than saving money and losing time by taking a series of omnibuses. If she did the latter she would have to get off some considerable distance from Vespasia's house. One could hardly arrive to call on Lady Vespasia Cumming-Gould having alighted from a public omnibus.

However, when she arrived, Vespasia's maid, who knew her well, told her with much regret that Lady Vespasia had decided in such clement weather to take the carriage to the park and go for a walk.

Charlotte was surprised how sharply disappointed she was. London was full of parks, but when society referred to "the Park" it only ever meant Hyde Park, so there was nothing to do but find another hansom and direct the driver to take her there.

Earlier in the year, during the season, she might have found a hundred carriages in or near the park, and looking for an individual would have been a waste of time, but now in the sharper autumn sunshine of late September, with a very decided chill in the breeze, there were not more than a dozen carriages at the nearer end of Rotten Row, and perhaps the same at the farther. Footmen and coachmen stood around gossiping with each other in the dappled shade, and keeping a weather eye open not to be caught by a returning master or mistress. Horses stood idly, moving only now and then with a clink of harness, brasses gleaming in the sun.

Charlotte was perfectly prepared to find Vespasia and join her, even if it meant interrupting almost anyone, short of the Princess of Wales. But since the Princess was seriously deaf, it was most unlikely Vespasia would be engaged in conversation with her, although they were friends, and had been so for years. If Vespasia was speaking with a duchess or countess, Charlotte would be unlikely to recognize the fact. She realized with a sharp intake of breath that she had better behave with the utmost circumspection, even if the lady in question should turn out to be of no social consequence whatever. Vespasia was perfectly capable of talking to an actress or a courtesan, if the person interested her.

It was nearly half an hour of walking at a breathless pace, moving from one group to another and wearing a blister on her left heel, before Charlotte finally caught up with Vespasia. She was actually walking alone, her head high, her steel-gray hat with its sweeping brim adorned with a magnificent silver ostrich plume. Her gown was a paler shade of gray, and there was a white ruffle at her throat of such superb lace as to look as if it were breaking foam in the sunlight.

She turned as she heard Charlotte's footsteps crunch on the grit behind her. "You look out of breath, my dear," she said, her eyebrows raised. "No doubt it is something of the utmost importance to bring you in such haste." She looked down at Charlotte's dusty hem and the slightly lopsided way she was standing, due to the blister. "Would you care to sit down for a little while?" She could already see from Charlotte's face that it was not a matter of emotional distress.

"Thank you," Charlotte accepted, suddenly feeling the blister even more profoundly. She did her best to walk more or less uprightly until they reached the next seat, then sank into it with gratitude. In a moment or two she would unbutton the boot and see what could be done to ease the pain.

Vespasia looked at her with wry amusement. "I am consumed with curiosity," she said with a smile. "What has brought you out to an unaccustomed place, alone, and in what appears to be some difficulty?"

"The need to know," Charlotte answered, wincing as she moved her foot experimentally. She smoothed her skirt and sat a little more upright, aware that passersby were looking at her, very discreetly, of course, and almost certainly because she was with Vespasia. No doubt they would be asking one another who on earth she was. Were Vespasia sensitive about her reputation, it would have embarrassed her, but she did not care in the slightest, let the world think what it wished.

"More about Saville Ryerson?" Vespasia said quietly. "I am not certain that I can help you. I wish I could."

"Actually, about Mr. Ferdinand Garrick," Charlotte corrected her.

Vespasia's eyes widened. "Ferdinand Garrick? Don't tell me that he has a connection with the Eden Lodge affair. That is absurd. So much so that it is about the only thing which could possibly redeem it from absolute tragedy. It would then become farce."

Charlotte stared at her, uncertain how serious Vespasia was. She had a sharp and highly individual sense of humor which was no respecter of persons.

"Why?" she asked.

The expression on Vespasia's face was sad, wry, and of slight distaste mixed with memory. "Ferdinand Garrick is what some people refer to as a 'muscular Christian,' my dear," she replied, and saw the answering comprehension in Charlotte's face. "A man of ebullient and officious virtue," she continued. "He eats healthily, exercises too much, enjoys being too cold, and makes everyone else in his establishment equally uncomfortable. He denies himself and everybody else, imagines himself closer to God for it. Like castor oil, he may on some occasions be right, but he is extremely difficult to like."

Charlotte hid a smile.

"Actually, it has nothing to do with Mr. Ryerson," she replied. "Thomas has gone to Alexandria to find out more about Ayesha Zakhari."

Vespasia sat absolutely motionless. A couple of gentlemen strolled past, and both of them tipped their hats to her. She appeared not even to have seen them.

"Alexandria?" she murmured. "Good heavens! I presume Victor Narraway sent him? He could not possibly have gone otherwise. No, I apologize. That was a ridiculous question." She breathed out very slowly. "So he is taking it all the way, after all. I am glad to hear it. When did he leave?"

"Four days ago," Charlotte replied, surprised how much longer it seemed. Even though he was away from the house all day, the nights were horribly empty without him, as if she had forgotten to light the fires. The warmth and the heart of the home were gone.

Did he miss her as much on the rare occasions she was away? She hoped fiercely that he did. "He should be there by now," she added.

"Indeed he should," Vespasia agreed. "He will find it extraordinarily interesting. I imagine it will not have changed a great deal, not at heart." Her mouth pulled a little twistedly. "Although I have not been there since Mr. Gladstone saw fit to bombard it. That cannot have increased their affection for us. Not that that usually worries us overmuch. But Alexandria does not bear grudges. It simply absorbs whatever is sent there, like food, and transmutes it into another part of itself. It has done so to the Arabs, the Greeks, the Romans, the Armenians, the Jews, and the French—why not the British as well? We have something to offer, and it accepts everything. Its taste is magnificently eclectic. That is its genius."

Charlotte would gladly have asked questions and listened to the answers all day, but with difficulty she forced her attention back to the only part of anything going on that she could possibly affect for good.

"I need to know something about Ferdinand Garrick because a friend of Gracie's has a brother who has gone missing," she explained.

"Gracie?" Vespasia's interest was immediate. "That little maid of yours, the one with enough spirit for two girls twice her size? From where has the young man gone missing, and why does it concern Ferdinand Garrick, of all people? If he has dismissed a servant he will believe himself to have had an excellent reason, and there will be no arguing with him. He has irredeemably absolute ideas about virtue—and justice is a great deal higher in his estimation than mercy."

"He hasn't dismissed him, as far as we know," Charlotte replied, although she felt a chill as she saw the anxiety in Vespasia's eyes. She was still speaking with a lightness in her voice, but her words about mercy were carefully chosen and Charlotte knew it. "Actually, Martin worked for Garrick's son, Stephen. He was his valet."

She shook her head in impatience with herself. "I don't know why I say was. As far as we know he still is. It is just that he has not been in touch with Tilda, who is his only relative in the world, for nearly three weeks now, and that is something that has never happened before. And when Gracie went to the Garrick house to make discreet enquiries, the staff did not appear to know where he was. And for that matter, Stephen himself does not appear to be at home. At first they assumed he was confined to his room, which apparently happens every so often. But there has been no food sent up, and no laundry came down."

"Gracie went to the house?" Vespasia said with a lift of admiration in her voice. "I should very much like to have seen that! What did she learn, other than that neither man is at home and the staff knew nothing as to where they were? Or at least will say nothing," she amended.

"That Stephen Garrick is an unhappy man with a violent temper, which he indulges freely, that he drinks too much, and that no one can manage his moods, or his times of despair, except Martin," Charlotte said succinctly. "So it would make little sense to dismiss Martin, because they would have a terrible difficulty replacing him."

Vespasia sat still for a few moments, apparently watching the occasional parade of ladies in their finest gowns on the arms of gentlemen in dark morning suits or bright military splendor.

"Unless he was unfortunate enough to witness a particularly unpleasant episode," she said at length, her voice low and sad. "And unwise enough to ask for extra remuneration as a result. Then he might be viewed as more cost than he was worth, and dismissed without a character."

"Wouldn't that be very foolish?" Charlotte questioned. "If I had a servant privy to family secrets, I would want him close by me, not looking for work elsewhere, and with a grudge . . . a justifiable one at that."

Vespasia shook her head very slightly. "My dear, a man of Ferdinand Garrick's stature does not stoop to explain himself, and prospective employers do not ask a servant they are considering what his reasons were for his actions. They would simply accept that he had threatened Garrick with loose talk of family matters. Indiscretion is the ultimate sin in a personal servant. It would have been less severe if he had taken the family silver rather than the family reputation. One can always buy more silver, or even if the worse comes to the worst, survive without it. No one survives without a reputation."

Charlotte knew Vespasia was right. "I still need to know what happened to Martin," she persisted. "If he was simply dismissed, why didn't he tell Tilda? Especially if it was unfair."

"I don't know," Vespasia admitted, nodding to an acquaintance who had seen her and doffed his hat. She looked quickly at Charlotte, so the man did not take her acknowledgment as an invitation to join them. "I think you are right to be concerned."

"What is Ferdinand Garrick like, apart from being religiously unsufferable?" Charlotte wriggled her foot, hoping the blister had eased a little. It had not.

"For goodness' sake, child, take your boot off!" Vespasia told her.

"Here?" Charlotte said in amazement.

Vespasia smiled. "You will make less of a spectacle of yourself removing a boot than you will by hobbling the length of the row back to my carriage. People will think you are intoxicated. I do not know Ferdinand Garrick well, nor do I wish to. He is a type of man I do not care for. He is devoid of humor, and I have come to believe that a sense of humor is almost the same thing as a sense of proportion." She watched with pleasure as a loose-limbed puppy capered about, throwing up gravel with its feet. "It is the absurdity of disproportion which makes us laugh," she continued. "There is something innately funny in punctured self-importance, in the positioning side by side of that which is incongruous. If everything in the world were suitable, appropriate, it would be unbearably tedious. Without laughter, something in life is lost." She smiled, but there was sudden, deep sorrow in her eyes. "Sanity, perhaps," she said quietly.

Then she lifted her chin. "But I shall find Ferdinand Garrick and see what I can discern. I have nothing more interesting to do, and certainly nothing more important. Perhaps that is the ultimate absurdity?" The puppy had disappeared across the grass, and she was regarding a man and woman who looked to be in their fifties, exquisitely dressed in the height of fashion, walking down the middle of the pathway, nodding graciously to either side of them as they saw people they knew. They acknowledged some and looked through others, now and again hesitating until they had glanced at each other and made up their minds.

"Filling your time with games," Vespasia remarked. "And imagining they matter, because you can think of nothing that does. Or you can, but do not do it."

"Aunt Vespasia," Charlotte said tentatively.

Vespasia turned to look at her, enquiry in her eyes.

"I know you would not like to think that Mr. Ryerson killed Lovat," Charlotte said. "Or even that he deliberately helped Miss Zakhari with the intention that she should get away with murdering him, but facing the worst, what do you really believe?" She saw Vespasia smile. "We cannot defend against the worst if we do not acknowledge what it is," she pointed out, but gently, aware of Vespasia's affections. "What kind of man is he, not just what the police will find, but what you know?"

Vespasia was silent for so long that Charlotte thought she was not going to answer. She stopped waiting for her to speak and bent over to finish unbuttoning her boot. She eased it off painfully. There was a hole in the heel of her stocking, which was what had caused the problem. The skin was raw, but it was not yet bleeding.

She felt a touch on her arm and looked up. Vespasia was holding out a large silk handkerchief and a tiny pair of nail scissors.

"If you cut the stocking off, and tie the silk around your foot," she said, "it will enable you to get home with a minimum of additional damage."

Charlotte thought of the appearance of the colored silk above her boot if her skirt swung wide.

"Smile," Vespasia advised. "Better to be noted for eccentric footwear than a sour expression. Besides, who are you going to encounter here that you will ever see again, and whose opinion you would care about in the slightest?"

"No one," Charlotte agreed, smiling far more broadly than the invitation had suggested. "Thank you."

"You are very delicate in your questions, my dear." Vespasia looked at the far trees, only the odd leaf here and there touched by the warm colors of autumn. "But you are quite right. Saville Ryerson is a man of deep emotions, impulsive, and . . . and physical." She bit her lip very slightly. "He lost his wife in a miserable mischance of fortune in '71, but it was more than that; there was a betrayal involved, although I do not know what, and I certainly do not know by whom." She dropped her voice even lower. "He was furiously angry, even before her death. Not only did he grieve for her, and that he had not been able to save her, but he felt a guilt that he then could never take back the things he had said, even though he believed they were true."

Charlotte finished rebuttoning her boot. "That must have been very hard. But Lovat could have had nothing to do with it, surely? It happened over twenty years ago."

"Nothing whatsoever," Vespasia agreed. "I tell you only so you may know more closely what kind of man he is. He remained alone from that time onward. He served his party and his constituents. They were hard taskmasters, capricious, demanding much and giving little—at times not even loyalty. But the best of them loved him, and he knew it. But it wearied him to the soul, and he did it alone." She made a slight, deprecatory gesture with her pale, gloved hand. "I do not mean he abstained from satisfying his desires, of course, simply that he was discreet, and he had little if any involvement of the emotions."

"Until Ayesha Zakhari . . ."

"Exactly. And a passionate man who neither gives nor receives anything for himself for over two decades, when he does fall in love, is going to do so with great violence, greater than he understands or can master. He becomes uniquely vulnerable." She said it softly, as if she had seen the reality of it herself.

"Yes . . ." Charlotte said thoughtfully, trying to picture it in her mind, imagine the waiting, the loneliness over years, and then the power of feeling when finally it came.

"What I do not understand," Vespasia countered, her voice suddenly sharp and very practical again, "is why the woman shot Lovat. Given that he was not a particularly pleasant man and that he may have been annoying her, why on earth did she not simply ignore him? If he really was a nuisance, why didn't she send for the police?"

A far uglier thought came to Charlotte's mind. "Perhaps he was blackmailing her, possibly over something that happened in Alexandria and which he threatened to tell Ryerson? Which would account for why she could not trust him with the truth."

Vespasia looked down at the grass at her feet. "Yes," she admitted reluctantly. "Yes, that would not be impossible to believe. I hope profoundly that it is not true. One would have thought she would have more sense than to do it on a night when she expected Ryerson to come. But perhaps circumstances did not allow her that choice."

"That would also explain why she still does not confide in anyone," Charlotte added, hating her thoughts, but certain it was better to say it all aloud now than let it run in her mind unanswered, but just as insistent. "Although I cannot imagine what it would be, other than some plan to compromise Ryerson . . . to do with his position in the government."

"A spy?" Vespasia said. "Or I suppose an agent provocateur would be more correct. Poor Saville—set up to be betrayed again." She drew in a very long, slow breath and let it out in a sigh. "How fragile we are." She started to rise to her feet. "How infinitely easy to hurt."

Charlotte stood up quickly and offered her arm.

"Thank you," Vespasia said dryly. "I weep inside for the pain of a man I have liked, but I am perfectly capable of standing up on my own—and I have no blisters. Perhaps you would care for my arm . . . to assist you as far as my carriage? I should be happy to take you back to Keppel Street . . . if that is where you are going?"

Charlotte bit back her smile, at least half back. "That is very good of you," she accepted, taking Vespasia's arm but leaning no weight upon it. "Yes, I am going home. Perhaps you would care for a cup of tea when we get there?"

"Thank you, I should," Vespasia accepted with barely a flicker of amusement in her gray eyes. "No doubt the excellent Gracie would make it for us, and at the same time tell me more about this missing valet?"

VESPASIA ENJOYED her tea. She insisted upon taking it in the kitchen, a room she never visited in her own house. When her cook had recovered from her astonishment, she would have been affronted. They met daily in Vespasia's morning room, where the cook came to receive her instructions, and counter with her own suggestions, and in due course a compromise was reached. The cook did not come into the withdrawing room. Vespasia did not invade the kitchen. It was a mutually agreed arrangement.

But Charlotte's kitchen was the heart of the family, where food was not only prepared but also eaten. Gas lamps reflected on the polished copper of pans, the smell of clean linen drifted from the airing rack winched up to the ceiling, and the wooden table and floor were pale from being scrubbed every day.

At first Gracie was quiet, in spite of all her good intentions to the contrary, overawed by the presence of real aristocracy in her kitchen, sitting at her table, as if she were just anyone. And of course even now, Vespasia was the most beautiful woman Gracie had ever seen, with her silver hair, hooded eyes, high fragile bones and porcelain skin.

But gradually Gracie's passion in her cause had won, and she had told Vespasia exactly what she believed, and feared, and Vespasia had eventually left with as much information on the problem as Charlotte and Gracie had themselves.

That was why at a little after half past seven that evening Vespasia stood in the foyer of the Royal Opera House, the diamonds in her tiara blazing, the lavender smoke satin of her gown a column of stillness in the rattle and rustle of pinks and golds.

She regarded the crowd as it passed her, looking for the vaguely familiar figure of Ferdinand Garrick. It had taken her most of the afternoon to discern, with the utmost discretion, where he planned to be this evening, and then to cajole a friend who owed her a favor into parting with her own tickets for the event.

Lastly had come a call to Judge Theloneus Quade, inviting him to accompany her, a request she knew he would not refuse, which caused her a sharp pang of guilt. She knew his feelings for her, and since the return of Mario Corena, honor had compelled that she did not mislead anyone, nor seem to use someone else's affections of which she was more than aware. Also the depth of that fierce love of her most vital years had come back with a tenderness now, a reality that dimmed all other possibilities, and she was not yet ready even to try to let it go. Mario was dead, but what she felt was woven into her inner self forever.

But it was the peril to Martin Garvie that must occupy her attention now, and she did believe it was real. She had not allowed Gracie, or even Charlotte, to see how much it concerned her. She knew a little of Ferdinand Garrick, and she did not care for him. She could not have explained why, it was instinctive, but because there were no conscious reasons for it, it was also impossible to argue it away.

Of course she had confided in Theloneus, not only because she owed him at the very least an explanation for such unseemly haste in attending an opera she knew he liked no better than she did, but also because she valued both his friendship and his discretion too much not to avail herself of his assistance in a cause which might prove far from easy.

She saw Garrick at the same moment that Theloneus did.

"Forward?" he said gently; it was only half a question.

"I'm afraid so," she replied, and taking his arm she started to urge her way through the crowd.

However, by the time they reached Garrick he was very obviously engaged in a conversation with an extremely conservative bishop for whom Vespasia could not even pretend to have a warmth of regard. Three times she drew breath to enter the conversation, and then found the comment dead on her tongue. There were degrees of hypocrisy she could not achieve, even in the best of causes. She felt rather than saw Theloneus's amusement beside her.

"There will be two intervals," he said in little above a whisper as Garrick and the bishop moved away and it was time to take their own seats.

The opera was a baroque masterpiece full of subtlety and light, but it had not the familiar melodies, the passion and lyricism of the Verdi she loved. She occupied her mind with plans for the first interval. She could not afford to wait until the second, in case some mischance should make visiting Garrick impossible. He might become involved in an encounter she could not decently join. Some degree of subtlety was required. He was no fonder of her than she of him.

When the curtain came down to enthusiastic applause she was on her feet as if risen spontaneously.

"I didn't know you liked it so much," Theloneus said in surprise. "You didn't look as if you did."

"I don't," she replied, disconcerted that he had been watching her and not the stage; in honesty she had nearly forgotten how deep his feeling was for her. "I wish to visit Garrick before he leaves his box," she explained. "And preferably before someone else dominates any discussion."

"If the bishop is there, I shall engage him in persuading me into one of his opinions," Theloneus offered with a wry smile, his eyes soft with laughter. He was aware of the sacrifice he was making, and that she was also.

" 'Greater love hath no man,' " she murmured. "I shall be in your debt."

"You will," he agreed fervently.

And his intervention proved necessary. Vespasia almost collided with the bishop outside Garrick's box.

"Good evening, Your Grace," she said with a freezing smile. "How pleasant to see you able to find an opera whose story does not offend your morals."

Since the tale in question was one of incest and murder, the observation was of the utmost sarcasm, and she regretted it the minute it was past her lips, even before she heard Theloneus choke off laughter and turn it into a cough, and saw the bishop's face turn a dull shade of purple.

"Good evening, Lady Vespasia," he replied coldly. "It is Lady Vespasia Cumming-Gould, is it not?" He knew perfectly well who she was, everyone did. It was intended as an insult.

She smiled charmingly at him, a look that in her prime had dazzled princes.

"It is," she replied. "May I introduce you to Mr. Justice Quade?" She waved her hand delicately. "The Bishop of Putney, I believe, or some such place, renowned for his upholding of Christian virtues, most particularly purity of mind."

"Indeed," Theloneus murmured. "How do you do." An expression of great interest filled his ascetic face, his blue eyes mild and bright. "How fortunate for me to have encountered you. I should dearly like your opinion, as an informed and, of course, enlightened source, on the choice of story for this very lovely music. Is watching such fearful behavior instructive, in that evil is punished in the end? Or do you fear that the beauty with which it is presented may corrupt the senses before the better judgment can perceive the moral behind it?"

"Well . . ." the bishop began.

Vespasia did not remain. She tapped on the door of Garrick's box, and the moment it was answered, went inside. She was dreading it. It was going to be forced, because they both knew that she would not have sought him out from friendship, and they had no interests in common.

Garrick was a widower and he had a small party with him, his sister and her husband, who was a minor banker of some sort, and a friend of theirs, a widow from one of the home counties up to London for some reason. It was she who provided Vespasia with her excuse.

"Lady Vespasia?" Garrick raised his eyebrows very slightly. It was a good deal less than an expression of welcome. "How delightful to see you." He would have used the same tone of voice had he found an apple core in his pudding.

She inclined her head. "How typical of your generosity to say so," she answered, dismissing it as if it had been a vulgarity apologized for at the table.

His face tightened. He had no choice but to continue the charade by introducing his sister, her husband, and the lady who was visiting. Vespasia's lack of reason for intruding hung heavily in the air. He did not quite ask her what she wanted, but the attitude of his body, the expectant angle of his head, demanded she explain herself.

She smiled at the widow, a Mrs. Arbuthnott. "A friend of mine, Lady Wilmslow, has mentioned you most kindly," she lied. "And she has asked me if I should encounter you to be sure to make your acquaintance."

Mrs. Arbuthnott blinked with pleasure. She had never heard

of Lady Wilmslow, who, in any event, did not exist, but she certainly had heard of Vespasia, and was enormously complimented.

Vespasia salved her guilt with generosity. "If you are in town for the rest of the month," she continued, "I shall be at home on Mondays and Wednesdays, and if you find it convenient to call, you will be most welcome." She slipped a card with her address out of its silver case in her reticule, and offered it.

Mrs. Arbuthnott took it as if it had been a jewel, and indeed in social terms it was, and one that money could not purchase. She stammered her thanks, and Garrick's sister hid her envy with difficulty. But then, if she conducted herself with any care at all, Mrs. Arbuthnott was her guest, and she could accompany her without raising any eyebrows.

Vespasia turned to Garrick. "I hope you are well, Ferdinand?" It was merely a politeness, something one would say as a matter of form. The reply was expected in the affirmative; no information was required, or wished for.

"In excellent health," he replied. "And you appear to be also, but then I have never seen you look less." He would not allow himself to be maneuvered into ill manners, especially in front of his guests.

She smiled at him as if she had heard what he had said and accepted the compliment, although she knew it was made for effect, not because he meant it.

"Thank you. You speak with such warmth one does not discard your generosity as merely the instinctive answer of courtesy." There was a dark, angry part of her enjoying this. She had forgotten how much she disliked Garrick. He reminded her of other aggressively virtuous people she had known, closer to home, obsessed with rule-keeping, self-control, and slowness to forgive, a suspicion of laughter, and an icy pleasure in being right. Perhaps her opinion was more supposed than real. She was indulging in exactly the same sin for which she blamed him. Later, when she was alone, she must try to recall what she actually knew about him.

She kept her face deliberately mild and interested. "How is Stephen? I believe I saw him in the park the other day, but he was moving at some speed, and I might have been mistaken. Would he have been riding with the Marsh girl, I cannot remember her name, the one with so much hair?"

Garrick was absolutely motionless. There was no evidence of it, but she was certain that his mind was racing for an answer.

"No," he said at last. "It must have been someone else."

She remained looking at him expectantly, as though the merest courtesy demanded some further explanation. To have stopped there would be a snub.

A flicker of annoyance crossed his face, for an instant quite unmistakable.

Vespasia considered whether to notice it or not. She was afraid he would change the subject.

"I apologize," she said quickly, just before his brother-in-law could rescue him. "I did not mean to embarrass you."

Anger washed up his cheeks, dull red, and the muscles of his body locked rigid. "Don't be absurd!" he said tartly, his eyes stabbing at her. "I was merely trying to think who it was you could have seen. Stephen has not been well. The coming winter will exacerbate his difficulty." He breathed in. "He has gone to stay in the south of France for a spell. Milder climate. Drier."

"Very wise," Vespasia acknowledged, uncertain whether she believed him or not. It was an extremely reasonable explanation in every way, and yet it did not sit well with what Gracie had heard from the kitchen staff at Torrington Square. "I hope he has someone trustworthy to care for him," she said with enough solicitude to be courteous.

"Of course," he replied. He took a breath. "He has taken his own manservant."

There was nothing she could add that would not betray an unseemly curiosity, and curiosity was a social sin of which she had never been guilty. It was vulgar, and implied that one's own life was of insufficient interest to fill one's mind. No one would care to admit to that; it was the ultimate failure.

"I daresay he will feel the benefit," she observed. "I admit I do not care for January and February very much myself. I preferred it when I spent more time in the country. A walk in the woods is a pleasure at any time of the year. London streets in the snow offer a great deal less—mostly wet skirts up to the knees, unless one is fortunate. The south of France sounds more and more appealing all the time."

He fixed her with a flintlike stare. It was not entirely her imagination that there was also enmity in it, a knowledge that she would not have come wholly as a gesture of courtesy to a woman she did not know.

"I am most pleased to have made your acquaintance, Mrs. Arbuthnott," she said graciously. "I am sure you will enjoy your stay in London." She inclined her head to the sister and brother-in-law. "Good evening, Ferdinand," she finished, and without waiting for acknowledgment she turned and went back into the passage leading from box to box. Only feet away, Theloneus was still standing with the bishop, a slightly glazed look on his face.

". . . misunderstanding of virtue," the bishop was saying intently. "It is one of the curses of modern living that . . ."

Theloneus was sorely in need of rescue.

"Bishop, would you come to join us for champagne?" Vespasia said with a dazzling smile. "Or were you going to say that we drink too much of it? I daresay you are right, and of course you are bound in honor to set us all an example. So refreshing to have seen you here. Do enjoy the evening." And she offered her hand to Theloneus, who took it immediately, trying hard to suppress his laughter.

VISITING SAVILLE RYERSON was altogether a more difficult matter to arrange, and in spite of the fact that she was genuinely concerned that Martin Garvie had met with some misfortune, regardless of Garrick's statement that he was in the south of France with Garrick's son, her fear for Ryerson was deeper. At best he was going to be disillusioned in a woman he loved, perhaps not wisely but certainly with all the power of his nature. To find yourself betrayed, not only in fact but in hope, to have your dreams stained beyond repair, was one of the hardest of all tests of the soul. And at worst he could find himself in the dock beside Ayesha Zakhari, and perhaps even on the gallows as well.

She did not bother to try the easy routes first. She could not afford the time taken by failure, nor perhaps the warning to others that she was so keenly interested she would call in old favors in order to see him.

Therefore she went straight to see the appropriate assistant commissioner of police. A long while ago, in their youth, there had been a time when he had courted her, and later, when they were both married, there had been a long weekend house party in one of the great stately homes of the duke of something-or-other. An afternoon in the yew walk sprung to mind particularly. She disliked calling on memories in such a fashion—it lacked grace—but it was extremely useful, and Ryerson's need was too profound for such delicacies to stand in her way.

He received her without keeping her waiting. Time had been kind to him, but not as it had been to her. He was standing in the center of the floor of his office when she was shown in. He looked thinner than in the past, and his hair was very gray.

"My dear . . ." he began, and then was uncertain quite how to address her. It had been many years since they were on familiar terms.

She responded quickly, to save him embarrassment. "Arthur, how generous of you to see me so quickly, especially when you must be quite certain, when I have come in such indecent haste, that I am seeking a favor." She was dressed in her customary pale colors of dove gray and ivory, pearls at her throat, gleaming to give light to her face. She had learned over the years exactly what became her best. Even the most beautiful of women, or the youngest, have colors and lines which do not flatter them.

"It is always a pleasure to see you, whatever the reason," he replied, and if he was saying only what was expected of him, he did it with an air of sincerity one could not disbelieve. "Please . . ." He indicated the chair at one side of his desk, and waited until she was seated and her skirts arranged with a single flick, to fall richly and without creasing. "What may I do for you?" he asked.

She had debated for some time whether to be direct or indirect. Arthur had been somewhat unsophisticated in the past, but time might have altered that, and he was now no longer in love with her, which fact in itself would give him a better ability to judge. There was no romantic ardor to blunt his intellect. She decided on directness. To attempt to mislead him would be insulting. But then so would simple statements of need without at least lip service to the past, and the delicacy of memory.

"I have acquired some interesting relatives since we last met," she said with ease, as if it was the most natural thing in the world to discuss. "By marriage, of course. I daresay you recall my late great-nephew, George Ashworth?"

Arthur's face fell into immediate, quite genuine regret. "I am so sorry! What a tragedy."

His words enabled her to dispense with whole paragraphs of explanation.

"There is much tragedy indeed," she agreed with a slight smile. "But through his marriage I acquired a great-niece whose sister is married to a policeman . . . of remarkable ability." She saw his start of amazement. "I have from time to time involved myself in certain issues, and learned to understand some of the causes of crime in a way I did not when I was younger. I daresay the same is true for you. . . ." She let it hang, not quite a question.

"Oh, yes, police work is . . ." He lifted his shoulders. She noticed again how much thinner he was, but it was not unbecoming.

"Exactly!" she agreed firmly. "That is why I have come to you. You are in a unique position to give me some small assistance." Before he could ask her what it was, she hurried on. "I am sure you are as puzzled and distressed as I am by this miserable business at Eden Lodge. I have known Saville Ryerson for many years—"

Arthur shook his head. "I can tell you nothing, Vespasia, for the simple reason that I know nothing."

"Of course!" She smiled. "I am not asking you for information, my dear. It would be entirely inappropriate. But I would like to be able to see Saville myself, urgently, and in private." She did not wish to offer any explanation, but she had prepared one in case he should request it.

"It would be most unpleasant for you," he said awkwardly. "And there really is nothing you can do for him. He has all the necessities, and any luxuries he is permitted. The charge is accessory to murder, Vespasia. For any man that is serious, but to one who has had the position and the trust that he has, it is devastating."

"I am aware of that, Arthur. As I said, I have had far more experience of the less-attractive sides of human nature since poor George's death. I have even been of assistance now and then. If I am placing you in a position of difficulty, where honor obliges you to refuse me, then please do me the courtesy, for old friendship's sake, of telling me so directly."

"No, it does not!" he said quickly. "I . . . I was thinking only of your sensibilities, and embarrassment if you should find him greatly . . . changed. You may not be able to avoid the conviction that he is after all guilty. I . . ."

"For heaven's sake, Arthur!" she said impatiently. "Have you confused me with someone else in the pleasant summers of your past? I fought on the barricades in Rome in '48. I am not a stranger to unpleasantness! I have seen squalor, betrayal, and death in many forms—some of them in high society! May I see Saville Ryerson—or not?"

"Of course you may, my dear. I shall see to it this afternoon.

Perhaps you will do me the honor of taking luncheon with me? And we shall talk of the parties we used to have when summers were longer—and warmer than they seem to be now."

She smiled at him with true affection, remembering the yew walk, and a certain herbaceous border with a blaze of blue delphiniums. "Thank you, Arthur. I should be delighted."

SHE WAS SHOWN into the room where her meeting with Ryerson had been arranged, and the guard withdrew and left her alone. It was a little before six in the evening, and already the gas lamps were burning inside because the single window was high and narrow.

She had not long to wait before the door opened again and Ryerson came in. Tired as he was, robbed of the immaculate shirts and cravats he normally wore, he looked pale, a little untidy. But he was still a big man, not shrunken or bowed by fear, although she saw it in his eyes as soon as the door was closed again and he turned to her.

"Good evening, Saville," she said quietly. "Please sit down. I dislike having to crane my neck to see you."

"Why have you come?" he asked, obeying her, his face sad, his shoulders a little hunched. "This is no place for you, and you hardly owe me this. All your crusading for social justice does not include visits to the guilty." His eyes did not evade hers. "And I am guilty, Vespasia. I would have helped her move the body to the park and leave it there. Indeed, I actually picked it up and placed it in the wheelbarrow . . . and the gun. I appreciate your kindness, but it is done in a misapprehension of the facts."

"For goodness' sake, Saville!" she said tartly. "I am not a fool! Of course you moved the wretched man's body. Thomas Pitt is my great-nephew . . . at least he is by virtue of several marriages. I possibly know more of the affair than you do." She was gratified to see him look genuinely startled.

"Whose marriages, in God's name?" he asked.

"His, of course, you fool!" she retorted. "It would hardly be mine."

His face relaxed in a smile, even his shoulders eased a little. "You cannot help me, Vespasia, but you certainly bring light to the gloom, and I thank you for that." He moved his hand as if to reach across the table between them and touch her, then changed his mind and withdrew it.

"I am gratified," she responded. "But it is incidental. I would like to do something far more practical, and of greater duration. Thomas has gone to Alexandria to see what he can learn of Ayesha Zakhari before she came here, and of Edwin Lovat—if there is anything to learn." She saw him tense again. "Saville, are you afraid of the truth?"

"No!" he said instantly, almost before she had let the last word drop.

"Good!" she continued. "Then let us discuss this without games of words and evasions of what is less than pleasing. Where did you meet Miss Zakhari?"

"What?" He was startled.

"Saville!" she said impatiently. "You are a senior government minister in your middle fifties; she is an Egyptian woman of what . . . thirty-five? Your worlds do not meet, let alone cross. You are a Member of Parliament for Manchester, a cotton-spinning county. She is from a cotton-growing area of Egypt. Do not pretend to be a fool!"

He sighed and ran his hand through his heavy hair. "Of course she sought me out because of the cotton," he said wearily. "And of course she tried to persuade me to scale down the industry in Manchester and invest in Egypt's spinning and weaving its own cotton. What would you expect of an Egyptian patriot?" Now his eyes were clear and challenging, as burningly dark as if he were Egyptian himself.

She smiled. "I have no quarrel with patriots, Saville, or with their arguments to be fair to their own people. Were I in her place I hope I would have the passion and the courage to do the same.

But no matter how good the cause, there are acts that may not justifiably be committed in its furtherance."

"She did not kill Lovat." He made it a simple statement.

"Do you believe that, or know it?" she asked.

He met her eyes, calm and silver-gray, and his flickered first. "But I do believe it, Vespasia. She swore it to me, and if I doubt her then I doubt everything I love and treasure, and which makes life precious to me."

She drew in her breath to say something, then realized she had nothing that would help or answer his need. He was an ardent man who had denied his nature for a long time, and now he was deeply in love. The dam gates had burst. "Then who did?" she asked instead. "And why?"

"I have no idea," he admitted quietly. "But before you suggest it was done to involve me and bring me to disgrace and loss of office, that would hardly benefit the cotton industry in Egypt. Any minister following me would be less likely than I to be of help to them. No single man has the power to change an entire industry, whether he wishes to or not. Ayesha knows that now, even if she imagined in the beginning that she could persuade me to begin such a movement for reform."

"Then why was she still here in London?" Vespasia had no alternative but to be brutal if she was to serve any purpose at all beyond comfort that would last only as long as she was in the room, if that.

"Because I wished her to be," he answered. Then he went on tentatively, as if he was half afraid she would doubt him. "And I believe she loves me as much as I do her."

To her surprise, she did not doubt him, at least not that he spoke the truth of his own feelings. Whatever Ayesha felt she was less certain of, but looking at him where he sat opposite her, there was such intensity in him, such a power of conviction, an unwavering resolve, she would not find it hard to imagine a young woman discovering that barriers of age, culture and even religion might disappear. She also found herself believing that Ryerson would go all the way to trial, even to conviction, rather than betray his mistress. He was a man of absolutes, he had been for as long as she had known him, and time had deepened his character rather than mellowed it. He was wiser, more mature in judgment and temper than in his youth, but in the last analysis his heart would always rule his head. He was the stuff of crusaders, and of martyrs.

What would Pitt find in Alexandria? Probably not a great deal. It was a city where he knew no one, where even the language was strange to him, the beliefs, the long, intertwining connections of who knew whom, of debts and hatreds, relationships and money and faith. Unless either the woman or Lovat himself had been remarkably careless, there would be little to find for a foreign policeman who was not even certain what he was looking for.

Which raised the question in her mind, why had Victor Narraway sent him at all? Was the purpose that Pitt should be in Alexandria? Or that he should not be in London?

She remained with Ryerson another quarter of an hour, but she learned nothing further that was of use. She did not lie by offering him encouragement, she merely asked if there was anything she could send to him to help his discomfort.

"No, thank you," he said instantly. "I have all I need. But . . . but I would value it above anything else if you would arrange a few comforts for Ayesha. See at least that she has clean linen . . . toiletries . . . I . . . another woman would have . . ."

"Of course," she responded before he could finish. "I doubt they will permit me to see her, but I shall arrange for such things to be delivered. I can imagine what I would wish myself, and see that it is done."

His face flooded with gratitude. "Thank you . . ." His voice caught with emotion. "I am profoundly . . ."

"Please!" she dismissed it. "It is a small thing." She was already on her feet. "I hear them returning for me." She met his eyes. She wanted to add something else, but the words died. She smiled, and turned to go.

IT TOOK HER another day and exhaustive enquiry, again a matter of discreetly seeking the return of past favors, a little flattery and a great deal of charm, before she learned where she could find Victor Narraway, and contrive to run into him. It was a reception to which she had been invited, and had declined. It was an awkwardness she loathed to have now to invent an excuse, and beg to accept instead.

Because her acceptance had been most uncomfortable she felt she had the choice either of dressing in excellent but subdued taste, something conservative in a soft color, or of being as bold and outrageous as possible, defying anyone to comment on her change of mind. She might speak with Narraway with less remark or interruption were she to choose the former, but no matter what she wore, she was not an unremarkable figure. She chose the latter, and had her maid take out a gown she had ordered in a moment of extraordinary confidence, a deep indigo silk of so fine a texture it seemed to float. The low neck and the waist were embroidered with silver thread and pearls in a rich, medieval design.

Standing in front of the glass, she was startled by the gown's drama. She usually chose the aristocracy of understatement, neutral shaded satins and laces, subtle with her silver hair and clear eyes. But this was magnificent, arresting in its simplicity of line, and the somber color was like a whisper of the night itself, elemental and mysterious.

She arrived late at the reception, causing a very considerable stir. It was not her habit to be so obvious. The lateness was her fault rather than her intention. She had left herself little time for the journey, not wanting to be early, and directed her coachman to take a route around the park, which had unfortunately been blocked by a traffic accident—a coach wheel came off, or something of the sort—and they ended arriving late.

She walked into the room alone, and there was a momentary hush. Several people, most of them men, quite openly stared. She had an instant of wondering if she had made a misjudgment, and the gown was wrong after all. She had no jewelry but pearl earrings. Maybe she was too pale, too bleached of her own color for such a depth of tone?

She saw the Prince of Wales, his blue eyes widening with amazement and then appreciation. Beside him a younger man, whom she did not know, cleared his throat, but continued staring at her.

She was greeted by her host, and within five more minutes found herself presented to the Prince. Apparently he had desired to speak to her. They had known each other for years, but it was still a highly formal occasion. One did not presume.

It was over an hour before she managed to find Victor Narraway and converse with him without being overheard.

"Good evening, Victor." She set the tone as she intended to continue it. She did not know him well, but she was quite aware of who he was, and of the regard in which he was held in the highest political circles, both his virtues and his shortcomings. But he was an intensely private man, and of his true self she knew very little. He mattered to her because of Ryerson, and she acknowledged to herself now, even more so because much of Thomas Pitt's future lay in his hands.

"Good evening, Lady Vespasia," he replied, a shadow of amusement in his dark eyes, but also a wariness. He was far too sophisticated to imagine she had found him more or less alone purely by chance.

There was no time to waste, they would be joined within minutes. "I visited Saville Ryerson yesterday," she told him, and saw no change of expression in his face. "He is going to tell you nothing, in part because I think he knows nothing. It makes no sense that the woman intended to ruin him and hope for someone in his place who would be more favorable to Egyptian financial independence. No such person exists, and she must have been as aware of that as we are."

"Of course," he agreed. If he was curious as to what she wanted of him, he was not going to allow her to see it. He remained politely interested, as a dutiful man towards an older woman of rank, but no importance.

It irritated her. "Victor, do not treat me like a fool!" she said, her voice low but her diction so crystal clear as to be cutting. "I know that you have sent Thomas to Alexandria. What on earth for? The first answer that comes to my mind is in order to keep him out of London." She was satisfied to see him stiffen so imperceptibly that she could not have told which muscle had moved, only that the tension in his body had increased.

"Lovat and the Zakhari woman knew each other in Alexandria," he replied. His words were innocent but his eyes held hers, probing, trying to feel for what she sought from him. "It would be remiss not at least to make enquiries."

"To find what?" She raised her eyebrows slightly. "That they had a love affair? One takes that for granted. Ryerson loves her, and I imagine he does not wish to know of her past admirers, but he is not naïve enough to imagine there were none."

She stopped speaking as a small, thin woman in peach-colored silk moved past them, clinging to the arm of a gentleman with receding hair.

Narraway smiled to himself, his composure perfect.

Vespasia wished she knew him better. She was aware, with amusement at herself, that were she younger she would have found him attractive. His inaccessibility was in itself a challenge. There was emotion behind the cool intelligence, of what nature she did not know. Was there moral or spiritual courage? The answer mattered, because of his power over Pitt.

"If you are considering the possibility that there was some scandal over which Lovat could have blackmailed her," she went on when they were alone again, "then you could have written a letter to the British authorities in Alexandria and asked them. They would be in a position to find out for you and advise accordingly. They will speak the language, know the city and its inhabitants, and have contacts with the kind of people who inform of such things."

He drew his breath in as if to argue with her, then looked more clearly into her eyes, and changed his mind. "Perhaps," he conceded. "But they will answer only what I ask them, whereas Pitt may find other things, answers to questions I have not thought of."

"Ah . . ." She believed him, at least as far as he had spoken. There was far more that he was not saying, but had she been able to draw from him anything he did not wish to tell her, then that would have meant that he was inadequate to his job, which thought would wake in her a real fear, deep and abiding.

He smiled very slowly. It had a charm that surprised her. For the first time she wondered if he had ever loved anyone sufficiently profound to disturb that thick layer of self-protection around him, and if so, what kind of woman she had been.

"And of course you are looking into Ryerson, and Lovat's other associates here yourself, or have someone else doing so," she stated. "One wonders whether that other person is more able to enquire into London than Thomas would be . . . or less able in Alexandria." She did not make it a question because she knew he would not answer.

His smile stayed perfectly steady, but the tension in him increased yet again, perhaps only in the totality of his stillness. "It is a delicate matter," he said so quietly that she barely heard him. "And I agree with you entirely, judging by what we know now, that it makes no sense. Lovat was nobody. Ayesha Zakhari may be vulnerable to blackmail, but I doubt profoundly that anything a man like Lovat could tell Ryerson would affect his feelings for her. It would be infinitely more likely to end in Lovat's being charged, or more simply dismissed from his position in the diplomatic service, and unable to find a new posting anywhere at all. He would probably be blackballed from his clubs as well. He had already contrived to make himself more than sufficient enemies. Also, Miss Zakhari's patriotism is easily understandable, but imagining that she could affect British policy in Egypt shows a naïveté which an intelligent woman could hardly have sustained for long, once she was here in London."

"Exactly," she agreed, watching every shadow in his face.

"Therefore . . ." he said somberly and in little more than a whisper, more like the sighing of a breath, "I am obliged to consider what profound thing it is, worth committing murder and going to the gallows for, that we have not yet considered."

Vespasia did not answer. She had been trying to avoid the thought, but now it was dark and inevitable on the horizon of her mind as it was of Victor Narraway's.

CHAPTER EIGHT

PITT WAS GAINING an increasingly clearer picture of Ayesha Zakhari and the people and political issues which had driven her. But as he stood at the window of his hotel room gazing at the wide, balmy night, the smell of spices and salt thick in the air, it was with a start of amazement that he realized he had never seen a picture of her. She would be dark, naturally, and he had assumed that she was beautiful, because he had taken it for granted that that was her stock-in-trade. But as he faced out towards the sea, the vines stirring very gently in the breeze, and stared up at the vast bowl of the sky, pale with stars, he thought of her differently. She had become a person of intelligence and strength of will, someone who fought for beliefs with which he could very easily sympathize. If it were England and not Egypt which was occupied, almost governed, by a nation foreign not only in language and look, but in faith and heritage as well, a comparatively new nation that had been civilized—building, writing, dreaming—when his own people still were savages, how would he have felt?

He heard the sound of laughter in the wind, a man's voice and then a woman's, and a stringed instrument, full of curious half tones. He took off his jacket; even at this hour the air was so warm, the cotton of his shirt was more than sufficient. He had worn it for dinner as a formality.

He gazed around, trying to imprint it all on his mind so he could tell Charlotte about it, the sounds that were so unlike England, the close, comfortable feel of the air on the skin, almost clammy, the heaviness of smell, sweet, close to stagnant at times, and of course always the flies. There was no cutting edge to the wind. It was languorous, hiding danger in ease, resentment behind smiling faces.

He thought of the wave after wave of peoples over the centuries who had come here as soldiers, religious conquerors, explorers, merchants, or settlers, each absorbed by the city, staying here and changing its nature.

Now it was the time of his own people, the English, unalterably foreign with their pale skins and Anglo-Saxon voices, their stiff backs and unshakable ideas of right and wrong. It was at once admirable and absurd. And above all it was monumentally inappropriate. This was an Egyptian city and they had no right here, except as they were invited.

He thought about Trenchard and his obvious love of the land and its people. Later, after their shopping, he had spoken a little of his life here. Apparently he had no close family in England anymore, and the woman he had loved, although not married, was Egyptian. He had spoken of her only briefly. She had been Muslim—in fact, the daughter of an imam, one of their holy men. She had died less than a year ago, in an accident that Trenchard had been unwilling to speak of, and naturally Pitt had not pressed him.

It was in some turmoil of emotions that he stood now, not yet ready to go to bed because he knew sleep would elude him. He could understand Ayesha so easily, the patriotism, the outrage at the way her people were robbed, the poverty and the unnecessary ignorance, and then in London with Ryerson, the torn loyalties.

But had it led her to murder? He still had not escaped the driving conclusion that it had. If not she, then who else?

In the morning he would continue learning what he could about Edwin Lovat. There must still be people here who had knowledge of him that would be more vibrant, more detailed and perhaps more honest than mere written records.

He turned away from the window and prepared to go to bed.

IT DID NOT take him long to discover exactly where Lovat had spent most of his time, and he was on his way there when he passed through the carpet bazaar. It was a baked-mud street perhaps forty feet wide, or more, and roofed over, three stories high, with vast wooden beams stretching from one side to the other and loosely filled over with more timber so the roof cast a barred and dappled shade on the ground. Everywhere there were awnings, over doorways, from windows, from poles like those set horizontally for flags.

Scores of people, almost entirely men, sat around with bales of cloth, rolled-up carpets, brassware, and magnificent hookah pipes emanating lazy smoke. There were many reds—scarlet, carmine, crimson, terra-cotta—and creams, warm earth shades, and black. Noise and color pressed in on every side in the heat.

Pitt was making his way down the middle of the street, trying to avoid looking as if he was there to buy, when there was a scuffle ahead of him, and voices raised in anger.

At first he thought it was merely a haggle over prices that had gotten out of hand, then he realized there were at least half a dozen men involved, and the tone was uglier than that of bystanders watching a squabble.

He stopped. If it was a real brawl he did not want to be caught up in it. He needed to make his way to the edge of the city and out to the village where the military camp was where Lovat had served. It was east, towards the nearest branch of the Nile delta, and the Mahmudiya Canal, beyond which lay Cairo and, over the sands from that, Suez. He could not afford to get caught up in a local quarrel, and if it became unpleasant, it was the job of the police here, where he had no authority, to deal with it.

He turned back. He knew there was another way around to the street beyond. It was longer, but in these circumstances, better. He started to walk more rapidly, but the noise behind him increased. He turned to look. Two men in long robes were arguing, waving their arms around and gesticulating, apparently over the price of a red-and-black rug near the feet of one of them.

Behind him a group of men pressed closer, also curious to see what the hubbub was about.

Pitt swiveled around again to continue walking, but now his way was blocked. He had to step aside not to be caught up in the heat of the crowd. Another carpet was unrolled, completely barring his way. Someone shouted out what sounded like a warning. There were voices all around him, and he understood none of it.

Overhead the dark beams gave a patchy shade, but still the heat was intense because there was no wind. The dust seemed baked under his feet, and the smell of wool, incense, spices, and sweat were heavy in the motionless air. Another mosquito bit him and he slapped at it automatically.

A young man was running, shouting. A pistol shot rang out and there was instant silence, then howls of anger. There seemed to be police of some sort, four or five of them at the far end of the bazaar, and another two only yards away from Pitt. They were European, probably British.

Someone threw a metal bowl and it hit one of the policemen on the side of the head. He staggered a little, caught by surprise.

There were cries which were unmistakably of approval and encouragement. Pitt did not need to speak the language to understand the meaning, or see the hatred in the bearded faces, most of them turbaned, dark and more African than Mediterranean.

He tried to move away from the increasing violence, and bumped into a pile of carpets, which swayed. He spun around to stop it from falling, grasping hold of it with both hands, fingers digging into the hard wool, but he could not save it. He felt himself pulled forward, losing his balance, and the next moment he was sprawled on the pile of rugs, rolling into the dust.

Men were running, robes flying. There were more shouts, the clash of steel on steel, and shots again. Pitt tried to scramble to his feet, and stumbled over an earthenware pot, sending it rolling fast until it caught another man and knocked him off balance. He fell hard on his back, swearing furiously—in English.

Pitt clambered to his feet and ran toward the man, who was still lying on the ground, apparently stunned. Pitt reached out to help him up, and was hit with great force from behind. He pitched into darkness.

He woke up lying on his back, with his head pounding. He thought it was moments since he had fallen and that he was still in the carpet bazaar, except that when he opened his eyes he saw that the ceiling was dirty white, and when he moved slightly he could see walls. There was no red anywhere, no rich colors of wool, only striped ochre and black and unbleached linen in a heap.

He sat up slowly, a little dizzy. The heat was motionless, suffocating. There were flies everywhere. He swatted at them uselessly. He was in a small room, and the heap of cloth was another man. There was a third propped up against the farthest wall, and a fourth under the high, barred window, beyond which was a square of burning blue sky.

He looked at the men again. One was bearded and wore a turban; he had a dark, heavy, swollen bruise around his left eye. It looked painful. A second was clean-shaven except for a long, black mustache. Pitt guessed him to be Greek or Armenian. The third smiled at him, shaking his head and pursing his lips. He held out a leather water bottle, offering it to Pitt.

"*L'chaim*," he said wryly. "Welcome back."

"Thank you," Pitt accepted. His mouth was dry and his throat ached. An Arab or Turk, a Greek or Armenian, a Jew, and himself, an Englishman. What was he doing here, in what was apparently a prison? He turned around slowly, looking for the door. There was no handle on the inside.

"Where are we?" he said, taking another sip of the water. He should not drink too much, it might be all they had. He passed it back.

"English," the Jew said with bewildered amusement. "What are you doing fighting the English police in a riot? You're not one of us!"

They were all looking at him curiously.

Slowly, he realized that his blundering fall must have looked like a deliberate assault. He had been arrested as part of the demonstration of feeling against the British authority in Egypt. He had sensed the resentment, the slow anger simmering beneath the surface, ever since his second or third day here. Now he began to appreciate how widespread it was, and how thin the veneer of daily life which hid it from the casual eye. Perhaps it was a fortunate chance that had put him here, if he seized it. But he must think of the right answer now.

"I've seen another side of the story," he replied. "I know an Egyptian woman in London." He must be careful not to make a mistake. If he was caught in a lie it might cost him very dearly. "Heard about the cotton industry . . ." He saw the Arab's face darken. "She gave a good argument for factories here, not in England," Pitt went on, feeling his skin prickle and smelling sweat and fear in the air. His hands were clammy.

"What's your name?" the Arab asked abruptly.

"Thomas Pitt. What's yours?"

"Musa. That's enough for you," came the reply.

Pitt turned to the Jew.

"Avram," came the answer with a smile.

"Cyril," said the Greek, also giving only his first name.

"What will they do to us next?" Pitt asked. Would it be possible for him to get a message to Trenchard? And even if he could, would Trenchard be willing to help him?

Avram shook his head. "They'll either let you go because you're

English," he replied, "or they'll throw the book at you for betraying your own. What did you attack the police for, anyway? That's hardly going to get cotton factories built here!" The smile did not fade from his lips, but his eyes were suspicious.

The other two watched, holding judgment by a thread.

Pitt smiled back. "I didn't," he admitted. "I tripped over a carpet."

There was a moment's silence, then Avram roared with laughter, and the second after the others joined in.

But judgment still hung in the balance. There was something here to learn, beyond just survival, and Pitt knew it. They might well think he had been placed with them to seek out the leaders of any potential trouble. There must be an equivalent to Special Branch in Alexandria. He must not ask questions, except about Ayesha, and perhaps Lovat, although Lovat had left Alexandria over twelve years ago. It was becoming increasingly important for him not only to learn the facts but to understand them, although he could not easily have justified it to Narraway, had he asked.

The three men were waiting for him. He must respond innocently.

"Tripped over a carpet," Avram repeated, nodding slowly, the laughter still in his eyes. "They might believe you. Just possibly. Is your family important?"

"Not in the slightest," Pitt answered. "My father was a servant on a rich man's estate, so was my mother. They're both dead now."

"And the rich man?"

Pitt shrugged, memory sharp. "He's dead too. But he was good to me. Educated me with his own son—to encourage him. Can't be beaten by a servant's boy." He added that to explain his speech. They probably knew English well enough to be able to tell the difference between one class and another.

They were all watching him, Cyril with deep skepticism, Musa with more open dislike. Somewhere outside, a dog began to bark. In the room it seemed to grow even hotter. Pitt could feel the sweat trickling down his body.

"So why are you in Alexandria?" Musa asked, his voice low and a little hoarse. "You didn't come just to see if we wanted cotton factories, and you didn't get here for nothing." That was an invitation to explain himself, and perhaps a warning.

Pitt decided to embroider the truth a little. "Of course not," he agreed. "A British diplomat, ex-soldier, was murdered. He was stationed here for a while, twelve years ago. They think an Egyptian in London killed him. I'm paid to prove she didn't."

"Police!" Musa snarled, moving very slightly, as if he would get up.

"They pay police to prove who is guilty, not who isn't!" Pitt snapped back at him. "At least they do in London. And no, I'm not police. If I were, don't you think I'd have got out of here by now?"

"You were senseless when they carried you in," Avram pointed out. "Who were you going to tell?"

"Isn't there a guard out there?" Pitt inclined his head towards the door.

Avram shrugged. "Probably, although no one imagines we're going to break out, more's the pity."

Pitt squinted up at the window.

Cyril stood up and went over to it, pulling experimentally at the central bar. He turned around and glared at Pitt, a slight sneer on his lip.

"You need brains to get out of here, not force," Musa said to him. "Or money?" He raised his eyebrows questioningly.

Pitt fished in his shoe. Would it be worth spending what he had, if he still had it, to make allies? They probably knew nothing about Ayesha or Lovat, but they might help him learn—if there was anything worth learning. And he was beginning to doubt that.

Their eyes never moved from him; they barely blinked.

He pulled out about two hundred piasters—enough to pay for his room at the hotel for eight days.

"That'll do!" Avram said instantly, and before Pitt could even consider a decision, the money was gone and Avram was banging on the door with his fists.

Musa nodded, his shoulders relaxing. "Good," he said with satisfaction. "Yes—good."

"That's two hundred piasters!" The words were out of Pitt's mouth before he thought. "I want something in return for it!"

Musa lifted his eyebrows. "Oh? And what would you like, then?"

Pitt's brain raced. "Someone to help me get some real information about Lieutenant Edwin Lovat when he served here with the British army, twelve years ago. I don't speak Arabic."

"So you want fifty piasters of my time?" Musa concluded. "Well, you can't have that if I'm in jail, now, can you?"

"I want a hundred and fifty piasters' worth of somebody's time," Pitt responded. "Or we all stay here."

Avram looked thoroughly entertained. "Are you making a bargain?" he asked with interest.

"I don't know," Pitt responded. "Am I?"

Avram looked at the window, then at the blind door. He raised his eyebrows in question to the others and said something in Arabic. There was a brief conversation. "Yes," he said finally to Pitt. "Yes, you are."

Pitt waited.

"I will take you to the village where the British soldiers spent their time off. I'll speak to the Egyptians for you." He held out his hand. "Now let's get out of here, before they come and do something unpleasant."

Pitt had very little idea of what was said to the guard, but he saw the money change hands, and half an hour later he was walking on Avram's heels along an alley back on the edge of the city, and heading east again. As always, the flies and mosquitoes were cruel, but it had become habit to swat at them without thinking. His head still ached from the blow in the bazaar.

Delicate, sweet smells mixed with the general ordure as they passed a cook sitting in the dust, leaning with one shoulder against the wall. He wore a shapeless robe of dun-colored linen and canvas shoes without heels. To one side of him was a flat, open-weave basket with dates, onions and what looked like a carrot and a pomegranate. Behind him was a large earthenware jar with a broken lip, and in front of him a brazier piled on bricks, and another earthenware pot on top of it. It was the mixture in that pot which he stirred carefully, and the steam from it which ensnared the passersby. The man's skin was as black as the dates, his beard trimmed short and his head so closely shaven as to appear bald. There was a mildness and a symmetry to his features which made him almost beautiful.

He ignored Pitt and Avram as if they had been no more interesting than the donkeys in the street or the dromedary standing patiently at the opening onto the square.

Avram was several yards ahead and Pitt hurried to catch up with him. It would be worse than a waste of time to be lost here; it could be dangerous. Since the incident in the carpet bazaar he was more aware of the underlying mood of the men who appeared to be standing around talking or haggling. At times there was a stillness in their faces he realized masked a deep anger they dared not show openly. This was their city, and he was a stranger here, a member of a foreign race who had in effect taken what was theirs. That the British used it to far greater effect, efficiency, and purpose was irrelevant.

Avram turned to make sure Pitt was there, and signaled him sharply to keep up. Thereafter they walked quickly and in silence. It was already late in the afternoon, and at this time of the year the days were shortening rapidly. They needed to reach the village near the military post before dark, and it was apparently a good distance yet.

Pitt trudged through the dust on the baked road, thinking to himself that any peddler in the market who discovered an ointment to repel mosquitoes would make his own weight in gold within a week.

They passed several men with camels, an old woman on foot, a boy with a donkey, and half a dozen people obviously returning from a celebration, singing happily and waving their arms in the air.

They reached the banks of a wide waterway as the sun sank, filling the sky with a soft, yellow light. Long-beaked wading birds stood on the banks a little distance from the reeds, half a dozen in one place, twice as many twenty yards farther off. The walls of squared stones in most buildings seemed bronze, the towering palms like absurd headdresses on stilts, feathery in the still air. The only sound was the steady slurping of water by six oxen knee-deep, heads down and great polished horns looking like golden metal in the fading sun. The shadows were already deepening into shades of mulberry and purple.

"We will stay here," Avram informed him. "We will eat, and then we can begin to ask your questions."

Pitt agreed; there was nothing else he could do. So far he had learned nothing which would help Ayesha Zakhari, let alone Ryerson. If Lovat's murder sprang from anything that had happened in Egypt, he had no idea what it could have been, and only Avram, or someone like him, could question the people who lived here.

They went into one of the smaller mud-brick buildings. Avram was greeted by a man of about twenty-five, wearing a red and dun-colored striped robe and a turban of some pale shade impossible to distinguish in the light of candles and a low fire. They exchanged a few words, and Avram introduced Pitt and gave some explanation of who he was.

Avram turned to Pitt. "This is Ishaq el Shernoubi. His father, Mohamed, was an imam, a holy man. He knew a great deal of what went on here, especially among the men of the army in the past. Ishaq used to run errands for them now and again, and he has a good memory—when he likes to. He understands a great deal more English than he pretends."

Pitt smiled. He could picture it vividly, although perhaps not with much accuracy. He could also imagine that to English soldiers a young Arab might be more or less invisible, as a servant was at home. Tongues might be equally unguarded, in the assumption that an Arab also would not repeat what he had heard his betters say.

He bowed to Ishaq.

Ishaq bowed back, his eyes so dark as to seem black in the flickering light. Already the sunset had passed from primrose to a far darker burnished gold, and the brilliance was gone. The oxen were moving in the water outside, and Pitt could hear them splashing.

Avram had warned Pitt to accept the hospitality of food and not to offer recompense for it. A gift might be given at a later date when it would not look like payment, which would have been an insult. He had also, unnecessarily, warned Pitt to eat and allow the meal to be over in peace before he approached the subject of information, even obliquely.

Pitt sat cross-legged on the floor, as he was invited, and hoped that after an hour he would still be able to stand when he got up again. As the meal wore on he began to doubt that he would. He fidgeted once or twice, and saw Avram's warning glance. Avram seemed to have entered into the spirit of the quest as if finding the truth of Lovat's service here were as important to him as it was to Pitt. Pitt wondered if Avram's interest was the result of his inveterate curiosity, the love of answers and the exercise of the skill in finding them, or if he too expected some appropriate gift at a later date. Right at the moment, sitting in acute discomfort in the balmy night a thousand miles from home and anything even remotely familiar, it mattered to him not to offend, or disappoint, this curious man, and it would require a fine judgment to succeed.

Finally the last date had been eaten and with a smile Ishaq asked why Pitt had come to Egypt. It was the signal that he was ready to be of help.

"An English soldier has been killed in London," he replied casually, trying as discreetly as possible to unfold his legs and keep the agony of cramped limbs out of his face as pain shot through him. He gasped, and turned it into a cough. "He is not so important in himself, but his death threatens to create a scandal because of who is accused of having shot him," he continued, and saw some understanding replace the bewilderment in Ishaq's face. After all, if an Egyptian is killed in London, what does that matter in Alexandria? He nodded politely.

"He served in the army here about twelve years ago," Pitt added. "In England it is harder to learn much about him. I want to know his reputation, and if he earned any enemies among his fellows." Better at this time not to mention Ayesha. He could always add that later, if it seemed a good idea. "His name was Edwin Lovat."

Ishaq waited, his eyes on Pitt's face.

Pitt named Lovat's regiment and his rank, then gave a brief description of his physical appearance, trying not to sound desperate as he saw no reaction in Ishaq's face.

Ishaq nodded. "I remember them," he said without any emotion at all.

"Them?" Pitt asked, without hope. Perhaps to Ishaq English soldiers were all much the same. He could not blame him. Pitt was trained to observe and identify, and if anyone had asked him to swear to one Egyptian in the street over another, he could not have done so.

"Those four," Ishaq replied. "Always together. Fair-haired, blue-eyed, walked like . . ." He gave up and looked at Avram. He said something in Arabic.

"Swagger," Avram supplied.

"Do you know the names of the others?" Pitt asked. If not, he could ask the present military officials. They would tell him at least that much. It was no secret which of his colleagues a man sought out in his off-duty hours.

"Yeats," Ishaq said thoughtfully. "And Garrick," he added. "I cannot think of the last one."

"That is very good. Thank you," Pitt said eagerly. "Were they good soldiers—Lovat in particular?" The moment he had said it, he thought it stupid. How could any British soldier be good in the eyes of an Egyptian?

Avram said something in Arabic and Ishaq nodded. He answered Pitt as if it were he who had asked. "He had courage and he obeyed the rules that mattered."

Suddenly, Pitt was interested. "And the other rules?" he said softly.

Ishaq grinned, white teeth in the firelight, then suddenly he was totally serious. "The others he was careful to break only when he would not be seen," he replied.

Pitt drew in his breath to ask the obvious question.

Avram interrupted. "He was brave. That is good. A coward is of use to no one. And he was obedient, yes? A soldier who cannot obey orders is a danger to his fellows, is that not true?" This time he looked at Pitt.

"Certainly," Pitt agreed, not sure why he had been cut off. Had he been too direct, or was it a question whose answer might embarrass Ishaq? Why? Illegal dealings of some sort? Immoral? "Did the soldiers spend their time off duty in the village or go into Alexandria?" he asked.

Ishaq spread his hands. "Depends how long," he replied. "There is little to do here, but the city needs money for pleasure."

"It is a beautiful city simply to walk around," Pitt said, quite sincerely. "There is much to learn of history, the cultures of many other people; not only Egypt, but Greece, Rome, Turkey, Armenia, Jerusalem—" He stopped, seeing the look in Ishaq's face. "I did not know Lovat," he finished.

"So much I see," Ishaq said dryly. "Soldiers off duty like to eat and drink, to find women, and sometimes to explore a little, look for treasures, have fun."

It sounded time-wasting if indulged to the exclusion of all else, but harmless. He had not reached the subject of broken rules, even obliquely. It looked like it was going to be a long evening, but at least Pitt was not cross-legged anymore, although the ground was hard. He had become so used to the mosquitoes that he swatted at them without thought.

"What sort of fun?" Avram asked, but with an expression of boredom, as if he was merely filling the silence.

Ishaq shrugged. "Hunting in the marshes," he replied casually. "Birds, looked for crocodiles occasionally. I think they went upriver once or twice. I arranged it for them."

"To look at the temples and ruins?" Pitt asked, trying to keep the same tone of voice as Avram.

"Think so," Ishaq agreed. "Went all the way up to Cairo once. See the pyramids at Giza, and so on." He grinned. "Got caught in a sandstorm, so they said. Mostly, though, they stayed closer."

It was not worth pursuing, but there was little else to say to keep the conversation alive. Pitt was beginning to lose hope of learning anything about Lovat that would even show his character, let alone any idea why he had been murdered. Perhaps all he would learn in Egypt was that Ayesha Zakhari was a highly educated and passionate patriot rather than a woman seeking to make use of her beauty to buy the luxuries of life.

"They usually went together, all four of them?" he asked. Perhaps he would be able to find at least one or two of these other men and learn more details of Lovat from their recollections.

"Mostly," Ishaq agreed. "Not so safe to wander around alone." He regarded Pitt closely, to see if he understood without having it spelled out to him, word for word, that the English were occupiers, an armed force in a foreign land, and as such, very naturally subjects of many emotions, some of them violent.

Pitt understood it very well. He could feel it in the air, see it in the covert glances of people when they thought themselves unobserved, both men and women. There might be gratitude for financial rescue, but no one liked to be obliged, or dependent. There would be individual affections and hatreds, like Trenchard's love for his Egyptian mistress. There would be a certain respect, possibly curiosity, and even at times a growing understanding. But always the anger was close under the surface. The memory of the bombardment of Alexandria would make it sharper now, but the same feelings would have been there then, only more deeply buried.

They sat in silence a few minutes. The sound of the oxen moving in the water was relaxing, a steady, natural noise. The night wind carried a breath of coolness, refreshing after the long, hot day.

"And of course there was the woman," Ishaq said, watching Pitt more closely than he pretended. "But if anyone were to kill him for that, they would have done it then. She was the daughter of a rich man, a learned man, but a Christian. Not as if she were a Muslim. That might have caused trouble . . . a lot of trouble. Very Christian,' Mr. Lovat." In the darkness of the hut his face was unreadable, but Pitt heard a dozen different emotions in his voice. If Ishaq had been English, Pitt might have been able to discern them, untangle one from another, but he was in an alien land, an old and infinitely complex culture, and speaking to a man whose ancestors had created this extraordinary civilization thousands of years before Christ, let alone before a British Empire. In fact, the pharaohs had ruled an empire of their own before Moses was born, or Abraham fled the destruction of Sodom and Gomorrah.

The earth under him was unyielding, the air still heavy and warm, and he could hear the beasts moving now and then outside in the starlit night, all as real as the hard ground and the whine of mosquitoes, and yet he felt an unreality of the mind as if his presence here were a dream. It was hard to remember that Saville Ryerson was actually in prison in London, and that Narraway expected Pitt to find some way to avert scandal.

"Very Christian?" he asked.

"Very." Ishaq nodded, the emotions remaining unreadable in his voice. "Used to go out to that holy place, the shrine down by the river. Loved it. He was upset because it is a very holy place indeed . . . a shrine for us as well."

"Us?" Pitt was puzzled. "For Islam?"

"Yes. Before it was—" Ishaq stopped.

Avram looked at him, his face somber.

Ishaq stared past Pitt. "It was my father who buried them all," he said so quietly Pitt barely heard the words. "I remember his face for months after that. I thought he would never get over it. Perhaps he didn't—he had dreams about it for the rest of his life. It was worst when he was dying." He took a deep, shaky breath and let it out slowly. "My sister looked after him, did what she could to make him easy, but she couldn't stop the ghosts from coming back." His face looked pinched and his voice was thick with emotion. "He used to talk to her for hours, telling her about it because he couldn't help himself. He had dreams . . . terrible dreams . . . the blood and the burst flesh, cooked like meat, faces charred until eyes could hardly tell they had once been human . . . I'd hear him crying out—" He stopped.

Pitt turned to Avram, but Avram shook his head.

They waited in silence.

"Fire," Ishaq said at last. "Thirty-four of them, as far as anyone could count, in the ashes. They were trapped inside."

"I'm sorry," Pitt said softly. He had seen fire in England; he knew the devastation, the smell of burning flesh that never left his memory.

Ishaq shook his head. "My father's dead, and my sister too now."

Avram looked startled. "I didn't know that!"

Ishaq bit his lip and swallowed hard. "In Alexandria . . . an accident."

"I'm sorry." Avram shook his head. "She was beautiful." He said it as if he was speaking of far more than merely what the eye could see.

Ishaq opened his mouth to say something, but for a moment he had not the control to master the grief within himself.

Pitt and Avram remained silent. It was dark outside now. The stars were visible through the open window, needle sharp in the velvet of the sky. The air was cooler at last.

Ishaq looked up at last. "I think Lieutenant Lovat was sickened by the fire as well," he observed, his voice quite level now. "It wasn't long after that when he got ill. Fever of some sort, they said. Seemed to be a bit of it in the camp. He was shipped home. Never saw him again."

"Did his friends stay?" Pitt asked.

"No," Ishaq replied softly. "They all went, for different reasons. Don't know what happened to them. Sent somewhere else, I expect. The British Empire is very big. Perhaps India? They can sail past Suez and down that new canal to half the earth, can't they." That was a statement, not a question. There was no lift in his voice to imply doubt.

"Yes," Pitt murmured, hoping profoundly that he would find at least one of them in London, not have to conduct questions by telegraph through some deputed official. And Ishaq was right—half the world was accessible to Britain through that genius of negotiation and engineering, the Suez Canal. Thinking of the critical importance of it to the economy and the rule of law to the entire empire, and all that meant, it was inconceivable that Britain could ever give back complete autonomy to Egypt. Cotton was only a tiny part of it. How had Ayesha Zakhari ever imagined she could succeed? The hostage of economic dependence was far too precious to yield.

Pitt felt a weight of darkness descend on him as if he were trying to untangle an impenetrable knot, and every thread he pulled only bound it tighter.

"Thank you for your hospitality," he said aloud, inclining his head to Ishaq. "Your food and your conversation have both enriched me. I am in your debt."

Ishaq was pleased; the evidence of it was something indefinable in his expression, the angle of his body, now only dimly seen in the waning candlelight.

They stayed only a few minutes longer, then left with repeated thanks.

Back on the path by the water's edge, the surface now a pale glimmer reflecting no more than the odd ripple of starlight, it was difficult to see where they were going, and Pitt realized how tired he was. His body ached not only from sitting on the ground but from the bruises gained in the incident in the carpet bazaar, and his head pounded from being hit by the police. Now, more than anything else at all, even a perfect solution to Lovat's death which would exonerate both Ryerson and Ayesha, he wanted to lie down on something soft and sink into a long, profound sleep.

He followed Avram, almost as much by sound of footfall on the dry earth as by sight, for another mile at least, before just about bumping into him when they came to a large solitary hut well away from the water. They were offered hospitality, at a price Avram paid on the promise from Pitt that he would yield up his share when they returned to Alexandria and San Stefano. At the rate he was spending, Pitt would be obliged to ask Trenchard to forward him more funds, and reclaim them from the consulate, and eventually from Narraway.

THE NEXT MORNING was cooler than before. It had a luminous, silvery clarity away from the city, and lying between the vast inland water to the south of Alexandria, and the Mahmudiya Canal leading towards the Nile itself, the reflections of light early in the day were of extraordinary beauty. The dark silhouette of camels with their silent, lurching gait was more like a dream than a reality.

Today Pitt would go to the military authorities of the post where Lovat had served. After a breakfast of fruit, dates, bread, and thick black coffee which came in a cup barely larger than a thimble, he set off. Avram accompanied him, although this time his presence was unnecessary. Pitt had the strong feeling he came largely in order not to allow Pitt the chance of escaping without fulfilling his financial obligations. Avram would not have put it so insultingly, but he was caring for his investment.

It took nearly an hour of argument and abrasive persuasion before Pitt found himself with a thin, mahogany-skinned officer of very apparent short temper and dislike of curious civilians. They stood side by side on a small shaded veranda looking onto the sun-baked drill yard. Another soldier had been left outside to wait.

"Special Branch?" Colonel Margason said with distaste. "Some kind of special police. Good God! What is the world coming to? Never thought London would stoop to that." He glared at Pitt. "Well, what do you want? I don't know any scandal about anyone, and if I did I should deal with it to a man's face, not go whispering about it behind his back."

Pitt was tired, aching, and covered with mosquito bites. There was hardly a part of him which did not hurt in one way or another.

"Then if I am unfortunate enough to be detailed to catch a spy in your command, I shall know not to expect any help from you . . . sir," he said testily, and saw Margason flush with annoyance. "However," he went on, "it is on behalf of a man murdered in London that I am enquiring. His death appears to have an Egyptian connection, and the only one we are aware of is his service at this post, some twelve years ago. It would be pleasant to be able to clear his character of any slurs that his defense in court may come up with, as soon as they are made, rather than simply denying them blindly, which too often is not believed."

Margason grunted. Dislike was set even harder between them, but Pitt's argument was undeniable, and whatever he felt about Pitt, he would defend the honor of his regiment. "What was his name?" he demanded.

"Edwin Lovat," Pitt replied, sitting down carefully on one of the chairs, as if he intended to remain as long as was necessary to get all he wanted, to the last word. Actually, the seat was hard and not particularly comfortable. It caught him in exactly the same places as the ground had yesterday evening, not to mention where he had slept on a straw palliasse through the night.

"Lovat," Margason repeated thoughtfully, and still standing. "Before my time in command, but I'll see what I can do. General Garrick was in charge then. Gone home. Find him in London, I imagine." He smiled sarcastically. "Could have saved yourself a journey. Or didn't you think of looking at any records? Heaven help Special Branch if you're typical."

"We do not take one man's opinion, unsubstantiated, Colonel Margason," Pitt said as levelly as he could. "Nor are we relying on military information alone. The man was murdered in extraordinary circumstances, and a senior minister in the government is implicated. We cannot afford to leave any possibility unexamined."

Margason grunted again, and kept his eyes on the bare, foot-pounded yard with its surrounding sand and earth-colored buildings. "Don't read that type of thing in the newspapers. Haven't got time. More to do out here." He grunted a little at the blazing sun outside. "Lot of unrest. More than they think in London, sitting in their offices. One really bad incident and it could all blow."

"I've seen it," Pitt agreed. "Nasty incident in the carpet bazaar yesterday. English officer fortunate not to be killed."

Margason's mouth pulled tight. "There's bound to be. Gordon was murdered in Khartoum, and we still haven't settled that. Damned Mahdi is dead, but that means little. Dervishes all over the place. Bloody madmen!" His voice trembled very slightly. "Kill the whole lot of us if we gave them the chance. And you come here asking about the reputation of one soldier who served in Alexandria twelve years ago and got himself killed in London. Good God, man, aren't you competent to keep a damned cabinet minister out of it without coming traipsing out here to waste my time with questions?"

"I would waste less of it if you would tell me about Lovat," Pitt replied. "Haven't you got an officer who remembers him with more detail, and more honesty, than the written records of his service? The woman accused is someone he knew when he was here."

"Really? He jilted her and she kept a grudge all those years? Remarkable. Did he rape her?" Margason sounded contemptuous, but not personally offended. Pitt was not even sure whether the man's disgust was for Lovat or his victim.

"Did your soldiers often rape the local women?" Pitt said with something close to innocence. "Perhaps you would have less difficulty keeping the ill feeling from erupting if you stopped that."

"Look, you impudent . . ." Margason snarled, whirling around with the tension and agility of an animal about to spring.

Pitt did not move. "Yes?" He raised his eyebrows.

Margason straightened up. "I was here then, but I was only a major. I don't know anything about Lovat except that he was a good soldier, not remarkable. He courted a local woman, but according to all I've heard, it was perfectly in order. Just a young man's romantic fantasy about the exotic. She certainly never had any complaint. He was invalided out."

"What with?"

"No idea," Margason replied. "Some kind of fever. No one was paying a great deal of attention then. We were all expecting trouble. It was shortly after the incident at the shrine. Over thirty people were killed in a fire. All Muslims, but the shrine was Christian as well, and feelings ran very high. We were afraid of religious battles breaking out. Colonel Garrick was very decisive. Stamped it out immediately. Arranged for burial, memorial, everything. Posted a guard on the place. Any man after that caught treating the Muslims with disrespect was confined to barracks."

"And were there further incidents?" Pitt asked, remembering what Ishaq had said.

"No," Margason replied without hesitation. "I told you, Garrick was very good. But it must have taken a great deal of skill and tight discipline. A case of fever that a man recovered from was hardly going to stay in the memory at such a time."

"Do you usually send men home for a fever?"

"If it's a recurrent sort, you might as well. Malaria, or something like that." Margason shook his head. "You can find the medical officer's report if you want to. I haven't got time to find it for you. Far as I know, Lovat was a good officer, sent home for medical reasons. Loss to the army, but plenty for him to do in England. Talk to anyone you like, just don't start rumors, and don't waste our time."

Pitt stood up. Margason would tell him nothing more, and he had no intention of wasting his own time either. He thanked him and availed himself of the permission to speak to the other men.

Pitt spent the rest of the day asking and listening, and he formed a far clearer picture of Lovat, particularly from a lean and windburned sergeant major who was finally persuaded to speak with some candor. It took a lot of recollections from Pitt of the London east end, where the sergeant major had grown up, descriptions, a trifle sentimental, of the dockside and the river stretch towards Greenwich, but eventually the man relaxed. They were walking slowly beside one of the many delta branches of one of the greatest rivers in Africa in the milk-soft, peach-colored glow of early sunset before he spoke of Lovat.

"I couldn't stand 'im meself," he said with cheerful contempt, his eye following a flight of birds, black against the luminous sky. "But 'e weren't a bad soldier."

"Why did you dislike him?" Pitt asked curiously.

"B'cause 'e was a self-righteous bastard," the sergeant major said. "I judge a man by 'ow 'e be'aves hisself when the goin's 'ard an' that, an' when 'e's drunk. See a lot o' truth about a man when 'is guard's down." He squinted sideways at Pitt to see if he understood. Apparently he was satisfied. "Got no time for a man wot wears 'is religion 'ard. Don' get me wrong, I in't no lover o' Mohammed, or anythink 'e says. An' the way they treat women is summink awful. But the way we does things sometimes in't no better. Live an' let live, I say."

"Had Lovat no respect for the religion of Islam?" Pitt asked, not sure if it made any difference. He would hardly have been killed in London for that.

"Worse 'n that," the sergeant major replied, his face puckering into a frown, dark as a bronze statue in the waning light. " 'E were angry about anythink they 'ad as 'e reckoned should 'a bin Christian. Burned the 'ell out of 'im that they ever took Jerusalem. ' 'Oly city,' 'e said. An' all places like that."

"And yet he fell in love with an Egyptian woman," Pitt pointed out.

"Oh, yeah. I know all about that. Mad about 'er, 'e were, for a time. But she were a Copt, so that made it all right." He pulled his face into an expression of disgust. "Not that 'e were ever gonna marry 'er, like. It were just one o' them things yer do when yer young, an' in a foreign place. 'Is society'd 'a had pups if 'e'd come 'ome with a foreign wife!"

"Did you know her?" Pitt asked.

"Not to say *know*," the sergeant major replied. "Beautiful, she were," he said wistfully. "Moved like them birds in the air." He gestured towards another flight of river birds gliding across the sunset.

"Did you know Lovat's friends—Garrick and Yeats?" Pitt asked.

" 'Course I did. An' Sandeman. All gone 'ome now. Invalided out at the same time. Got the same fever, I s'pose."

"Out of the army? All of them?"

The sergeant major shrugged. "Dunno. I 'eard as Yeats were dead, poor sod. Killed in some kind o' military action, so I reckon 'e must 'a stayed in, just got posted somewhere wi' a diff'rent climate. Yer wanna know about them too? Yer thinkin' as they might 'a killed 'im?" He shook his head. "Dunno wot for. Still, that's yer job, not mine, thank Gawd. I just gotta see that this lot"—he jerked his hand towards the dark silhouette of the barracks—"keeps order 'ere in Egypt."

"Do you think that's going to be difficult?" Pitt asked, more for something to say than because he expected the man to know, and then the moment after, he realized he cared. The timeless beauty of the land would remain with him long after he went back to the modern urgency of London. He would always wish he had had time, and money, to go up the river and see the Valley of the Kings, the great temples and ruins of a civilization which ruled the world it knew before Christ was born.

And he also realized how profoundly he wanted Ayesha to be innocent, and to be able to prove it. He now believed she had gone to England to try to accomplish something for the economic freedom of her people. She had been looking for a justice she was not sophisticated enough to know would never be granted as long as the cotton mills of Lancashire fed and clothed a million people, who also were poor, with all the misery and disease that poverty brought, but who had political power in London. And even larger than that, a few miles across the desert older than mankind, ochre and shadow under the first stars, lay the modern miracle of a canal cutting its way from the Mediterranean to the Indian Ocean, and the other half of the empire.

He stood beside the sergeant major and watched the very last of the light die before thanking him, and going to look for Avram, to tell him that tomorrow they would return to Alexandria, where he would find Avram a suitable reward for his help.

CHAPTER NINE

GRACIE SAT in the corner of the public house staring across the table at Tellman. He was watching her intently, more than was required for what she was telling him, and with a warm ripple of both comfort and self-consciousness, she knew he would have looked at her that way even if she had been talking complete nonsense. It was a fact she was going to have to address sooner or later. He had shown all kinds of emotions towards her, from his initial lack of interest to irritation at her acceptance of being a resident servant in someone else's house, totally dependent upon them even for the roof over her head. He had been forced into a grudging respect for her intelligence when she had assisted Pitt in certain cases, then showed more clearly than he knew, fighting for all he was worth not to admit to anyone at all, especially himself, that he was in love with her. Now he no longer pretended he was not—at least not all the time.

He had kissed her once, with a sweet, fierce honesty that she could still remember, and if she closed her eyes and blocked out the rest of the world, she could feel it again as if it were moments ago. When she had found herself doing that, standing alone in the windy street and smiling, she acknowledged it was time to admit that she loved him too.

Not that she was necessarily prepared to admit anything of the sort to him. But it was as well to know at least what she wanted, even if she did not know when.

She had been recounting to him what Lady Vespasia had learned about the Garrick household, and that Stephen Garrick was supposed to have gone to the south of France for the good of his health.

"But it's more 'n long enough for him to have written and told Tilda, in't it?" she finished. "In fact, 'e could 'ave sent 'er a message before 'e left. That in't 'ard ter do, an' surely Mr. Garrick wouldn't 'ave minded?"

He frowned. His opinion of the whole business of permission from others to attend to ordinary family commitments was a sore point they had already argued over many times.

"Shouldn't!" he said with feeling. "But you can't tell." He looked at her intently, as if no one else in the babble around them were real. "But if he went to the south of France, he must have taken cases with him, and either used a hansom or his own carriage, at least as far as the station. There'll be record of a boat across the Channel. We'll know for sure that Martin Garvie went with him. I just don't know why there was no letter back."

"Mebbe we could ask Mr. Garrick, 'oo's still 'ere in London, fer an address?" Gracie suggested. "It's fair, as 'is family should want ter know where ter write ter 'im."

Tellman pursed his lips. "It is fair," he agreed. "But we've already tried. Tilda herself tried, and then you did. I'll see what I can find out about their leaving."

She looked at him steadily. She knew every expression of his face; she could have pictured it exactly with her eyes closed. She was surprised and a little embarrassed to realize how often she had done so, not really telling herself the truth as to her reasons, or admitting the odd sense of comfort it gave her. She knew now that he was worried, and also that he was trying to hide it from her to protect her, and partly because he was uncertain.

"Yer think there's summink wrong, don't yer?" she said softly. "People don't lie fer nothin'."

He was cautious, gentle. "I don't know. Can you get the evening off the day after tomorrow?"

"If I need ter. Why?"

"I'll tell you what I've found. It may take me a while. I'll need to get witnesses, see train and ferry records and the like."

" 'Course. Mrs. Pitt'd never stand in the way of an investigation. I'll be 'ere. Yer jus' tell me wot time."

"How about early? We'll go to the music hall, see something good?" His face was eager, but the shadow in his eyes betrayed that her acceptance mattered to him, and he by no means took it for granted. This was a social engagement, something to do together for pleasure, not just as part of a case. It was the first time he had done such a thing, and they were both suddenly acutely aware of it.

She found herself blushing; the color was hot in her cheeks. She wanted to behave with lightness, as if his offer meant nothing unusual, and she was not managing it. She was awkward again.

"Yeah . . ." she said, trying to be casual, and catching her breath in a hiccup. She was going to have to make a big decision soon, and she was not ready for it. She had known for ages how he felt. She should have made up her mind by now. "Yeah. I like music." What would she wear? It must be good enough. She wanted him to think she was pretty, but she was also afraid of it. What if he got emotional, and she did not know how to handle it? Perhaps she should have said no, kept it to business.

"Good." He gave her no time to change her mind. Had he seen the indecision in her face?

"Well . . ." she began.

"Seven o'clock," he went on too quickly. "We'll have something to eat, and I'll tell you what I've found, and we can go to the music hall." He stood up, as if he felt self-conscious and wanted to escape before he did something that made him feel even more foolish.

She stood up too, knocking against the table. Thank heaven there was nothing on it to spill; the motion just rattled the glasses a little.

He waited for her to go ahead of him, and followed her out into the street. It was harder to speak there. A dray with a load of barrels was backing awkwardly around the corner into the inn yard, the driver holding the lead horse's bridle and calling out orders. Another man balanced half a dozen kegs on a trolley as he wheeled them across the cobbles, rattling at every step. Traffic clattered past in the roadway, hooves loud, harness jingling.

Gracie was glad of it, and looking quickly at Tellman's face, she thought he was too. Perhaps he would get cold feet and say nothing for ages? That would give her longer to think. About what? She would say yes. It was just how she would say it that was still to be considered. Change was frightening. She had been with the Pitts since she had been thirteen. She couldn't leave them.

Tellman was saying something, shouting above the noise.

"Yeah!" she agreed, nodding. "I'll be 'ere at seven, day arter termorrer. You find out wot 'appened ter Martin Garvie. 'Bye." And without waiting for him to say anything else she smiled brilliantly and turned on her heel.

TWO EVENINGS LATER they met at the same table in the corner of the public house. Tellman was dressed in a plain dark jacket and his white shirt looked even stiffer-collared than usual. Gracie had put on her best blue dress and bonnet, and allowed her hair to be less tightly scraped back than usual, but that was all the concession she would make to an extraordinary occasion. However, as soon as she saw Tellman's face, preoccupation with herself vanished.

"Wot?" she said urgently, as soon as they were seated and their order given. "Wot is it, Samuel?" She was not even aware of using his name.

He leaned forward. "Plenty of people saw Stephen Garrick leave his house, and they described the man who went with him—fair-haired, in his twenties, pleasant face. From what they say, he was a servant, almost certainly a valet, but there were only two small cases, no trunks or boxes. Mr. Garrick was ill. He had to be half carried out from the house and it took two men to help him into the carriage, but it was his own carriage, not an ambulance, and driven by the household coachman."

" 'Oo said?" she asked quickly.

"Lamplighter," he replied. "Just beginning."

"About six in the evening?" She was surprised. "In't that a funny time ter start on a journey ter France? Is it summink ter do wi' tides, or the like? Where'd 'e go from? London docks?"

"Morning," he replied. "Putting the lamps out, not lighting them. But that's the funny thing. I checked all sailings from the London docks that day, and they weren't on anything to France, not Mr. Garrick alone, nor with anyone else."

Their order arrived, a very good early supper of winkles and bread and butter, and there would be apple pie afterwards. Tellman thanked the serving girl and pronounced the meal excellent. Gracie picked up the long pin for digging out the flesh and held it up in her hand. "Mebbe they went from Dover? People do, don't they?"

"Yes. But I tried the station for the train, and the porter who'd been on the Dover platform said that, to the best of his recollection, there was no one with anything like that description all day. No invalid, no one that needed helping of any kind, except with heavy baggage."

She was puzzled. "So they din't go from London, an' they din't go from Dover. Where else is there?"

"Well, they could have gone anywhere else, like somewhere on the Continent that wasn't France, or anywhere in England—or Scotland, for that matter," he replied. "Except that if Stephen Garrick has poor health, and the English climate is too harsh for him, he'd hardly go to spend the winter in Scotland." He discarded his last winkle shell and finished his bread and butter.

She was even more puzzled. "But Lady Vespasia was very plain that that was wot Mr. Garrick said," she argued. "An' why would 'e lie to 'er? Rich folk often go away fer their 'ealth."

"I don't know," he admitted. "It doesn't make sense. But wherever they went, it wasn't straight to a ship and across to France." He looked intensely serious. "You were right to be worried, Gracie. When people lie and you can't see the reason, it usually means that the reason is even worse than you thought." He sat silent for a moment, his face puckered with concern.

"Wot?" she urged.

He looked up at her. "If they weren't going to catch a train, or a boat, why go at that time in the morning? They must have got up at five, when it was still dark."

A kind of heaviness settled inside her. " 'Cos they didn't wanter be seen," she replied. Suddenly matters of who loved whom and what to say or do about it had no urgency at all. She looked at him without any pretense. "Samuel, we gotta find out, 'cos if someone like old Mr. Garrick is tellin' lies, even ter 'is own 'ouse'old, an' Tilda don't know where her brother is, then the answer in't anythin' good."

He did not argue. "Trouble is, we've got no crime that we know of," he said grimly. "And Mr. Pitt's in Egypt, so we can't even ask his help."

"Then we gotta do it ourselves," she said very quietly. "I don't like that, Samuel. I wish as we din't."

He put out his hand instinctively and let it rest very gently over hers, covering it completely. "So do I, but we've got no choice. We wouldn't be happy just forgetting about it. Tomorrow we'll speak to Tilda again and get her to tell us everything Martin ever said about the Garricks. We've got to know more. As it is, we've got nothing to follow up."

"I'll fetch 'er when she does 'er errands, about 'alf past nine." She nodded. "But she never told me wot Martin said before, so mebbe 'e didn't say nothin' about the Garricks. Wot are we gonna do then?"

"Go back and talk to the parlor maid at the Garrick house, who knew him fairly well," he replied. "But that would be harder. If there is anything wrong, she won't be able to speak freely while she's there, and she'll be afraid for losing her position." He tried very hard to keep his feelings about that out of his face, and failed. "Do you want some apple pie?" he asked instead.

"Yeah . . . please." The winkles had been delicious, but they were not very filling, and there is nothing quite like really good short-crust pastry and firm, tart apples, with cream on thick enough to stand a spoon up in.

When they had finished, Tellman paid and they left. Out in the cool evening, they walked side by side along the crowded footpath half a mile or so to the entrance of the music hall. There were scores of people, much like themselves, some of them more showily dressed, but most arm in arm, men strutting a little, girls laughing and swishing skirts. They pressed close together, pushing each other in excitement to get inside.

A hurdy-gurdy man played a popular air, and one or two people joined in singing with it. Hansoms stopped and more people added to the crowd. Peddlers sold sweets, drinks, hot pies, flowers and trinkets.

Gracie had to cling to Tellman's arm not to be carried away by the press of bodies all pushing and shoving in slightly different ways. The noise of voices raised in excitement was terrific and she kept getting bumped and her feet trodden on.

Eventually they were inside. Tellman had bought tickets for seats nicely near the front of the stalls. They were going to sit down where they could see and hear properly. She had never done that before. On the few occasions she had been, she had stood at the very back, barely able to see anything at all. This was marvelous. She ought to be thinking about Martin Garvie and poor Tilda—and how on earth they were going to find out what had happened, even if they were too late to help. But the lights and the buzz of excitement, and the certainty settling warm and comfortable inside her that this was not just a single event, but the beginning of something permanent, drove everything else temporarily out of her mind.

The music started. The master of ceremonies produced wonderful tongue-twisting introductions, to oohs and aahs from the audience, and bursts of laughter. The curtain went up on an empty stage. The spotlight fell in a bright pool, and into it stepped a girl in a shining, spangled dress. She sang lilting, rather daring songs, and in spite of knowing perfectly well what they meant, Gracie found herself singing along when the audience joined in. She was happy, full of warmth.

The girl was followed by a comedian in a baggy suit, partnered by another who must have been the tallest and thinnest man alive. The audience found this hilarious, and could hardly stop laughing when the contortionist came on, and then the juggler, the acrobats, a magician, and lastly dancers.

They were all good, but Gracie liked the music best, sad songs or happy, solos or duets, and best of all when everyone sang the choruses. She barely thought of the world outside the circle of temporary enchantment right until she was at the kitchen door in Keppel Street and she turned to thank Tellman, and say good night to him.

She had intended to exercise some dignity and say it had been very nice, and not let it go to his head, as if he had taken her somewhere she had never been before. It was very foolish to let a man get above himself and think he was too clever, or that you ought to be grateful to him.

But she forgot, and all her enthusiasm was in her voice when she told him, "That was wonderful! I never seen such . . ." She stopped. It was too late to be sophisticated now. She took a deep breath. She saw in the light from the street lamp the pleasure in his face, and suddenly she was absolutely certain how very much it mattered to him. He was so vulnerable all she wanted was for him to know how happy she was. She leaned forward very quickly and kissed him on the cheek.

"Thank you, Samuel. That was the best evenin' I ever 'ad."

Before she could step back he tightened his arm around her and turned his head slightly so he could kiss her on the lips. He was very gentle, but he had no intention at all of letting her go until he was ready. She tried to pull back a little, just to see if she could, and felt a tingle of pleasure on learning that it was impossible.

Then he eased his hold on her and she straightened up, gasping. She wanted to say something clever, or mildly funny, but nothing came. It was not a time for words that meant nothing.

"Good night," she said breathlessly.

"Good night, Gracie." His voice was a little husky as well, as if he too had been taken by surprise.

She turned around and felt for the scullery doorknob, twisted it and went inside, feeling her heart beating like a hammer, and knowing that she was smiling as if she had just been told the funniest and most wonderful thing in the world.

IN THE MORNING Gracie found Tilda out shopping, and brought her back to the kitchen in Keppel Street, where Tellman was sitting across the table with Charlotte, already discussing the subject. Only for an instant, almost too small to be noticed at all, Gracie's eyes met Tellman's, and she saw a half smile on his lips, a warmth. Then it vanished and he concentrated on business.

"Sit down, Tilda," Charlotte said gently, indicating the fourth chair at the table. Gracie took the third one. There was a pot of tea there already and no need for duties of hospitality to intrude.

"Yer know somethin'?" Tilda asked anxiously. "Gracie wouldn't say nothin' to me in the street."

"We don't know where he is," Charlotte answered straightaway. She could not hold out false hope; it was crueler in the end. "But we have learned more. A friend of mine spoke to Mr. Ferdinand Garrick, and he told her that Stephen had gone to the south of France, for his health, and taken his valet with him, in order to care for him while he is away." She saw Tilda's face clear and felt an ache of guilt. "Mr. Tellman has tried to see if that is true. He found someone who saw what was almost certainly Stephen Garrick and Martin leaving the house in Torrington Square. But there is no record of their having taken any boat to France, either from London or Dover. In fact, he cannot find a train they have taken. So it seems Martin has not been dismissed, but we don't know where he is, or why he has not written to you to tell you of his circumstances."

Tilda stared at her, trying to understand what it meant. "Then where'd they go? If it in't France, why'd they go at all?"

"We don't know, but we intend to find out," Charlotte answered. "What more can you tell us about Martin, or about Mr. Stephen?" She saw the total bewilderment in Tilda's face, and wished she could be plainer. She did not know herself what she was asking. "Try to think of everything Martin ever told you about the Garrick family, and Stephen in particular. He must have spoken about his life there sometimes."

Tilda looked on the edge of tears. She was struggling hard to make her brain override her fear and the loneliness that crowded in on her. Martin was all the family she had, all the life she could remember. Her parents were beyond infant recall.

Gracie leaned forward, ignoring the cup of tea Tellman had poured for her.

"It in't the time for bein' discreet!" she said urgently. "We all tells our fam'ly. He trusted yer, din't 'e? 'E must 'a told yer summink about life in the 'ouse. Was the food good? Did the cook 'ave a bad temper? Were the butler all spit and vinegar? 'Oo were the boss—the 'ousekeeper?"

Tilda relaxed a little as a faint smile touched her mouth. "Not the 'ousekeeper," she replied. "An' the butler wouldn't say boo ter the master, but right tarter 'e were wi' everyone else . . . at least that's wot Martin said. Order everyone else around summink wicked, but not Martin, 'cos o' Mr. Stephen. Martin were the only one as could look after 'im, an' no one else wanted to any'ow, fer all their bein' so upright an' all."

"Why not?" Charlotte asked. "Was he difficult?"

"Summink terrible, when 'e 'ad the stuff in 'im," Tilda said very quietly. "But Martin'd never forgive me if 'e knew I'd told yer that. Yer don't never tell no one about wot goes on in a lady or gentleman's rooms, or yer'll never work again. Out in the gutter an' no place ter go—'cos no one else'll ever take yer in. An' worse 'n that, it's betrayin', an' there in't nothin' worse than a betrayer." Her voice was low and husky, as if even saying the words would contaminate her.

"What stuff?" Charlotte asked, keeping her tone so casual she could have been speaking of porridge.

"I dunno," Tilda answered with such openness that Charlotte had to believe her.

Tellman put his cup down. "Did Martin ever go for a holiday with Mr. Stephen before? Anywhere?"

Tilda shook her head. "Not as I know. I'd 'a told yer."

"Friends?" Tellman insisted. "What did Stephen do for pleasure? Where did he go—music, women, sports, anything?"

"I dunno!" she said desperately. " 'E were miserable. Martin said as there weren't nothing 'e really liked. 'E used ter sleep bad, 'ave terrible dreams. I think as 'e were ill summink awful." Her voice dropped so they could barely hear it. "Martin told me as 'e were going ter look for a priest fer 'im . . . one as cared special fer soldiers."

"A priest?" Tellman said with surprise. He glanced at Gracie, and at Charlotte, then back to Tilda. "Do you know if Mr. Garrick was religious?"

Tilda thought for a moment. "I . . . I s'pose 'e were," she said slowly. " 'Is pa is—Martin said that. Runs the 'ouse like 'e were a clergyman. Staff all say prayers every mornin' an' every night. An' grace at table afore every meal. Mind most do that, o' course.

"But there was other things as well, like exercise an' cold water an' bein' extra clean an' early fer everythin'. Martin said as they all lined up in the mornin' afore breakfast an' the butler led 'em in prayers for the Queen and the empire an' their duty ter God, an' again afore anyone were allowed ter go ter bed at night. So I 'spec' Mr. Stephen were religious as well. Couldn't 'ardly 'elp it."

"Then why didn't he speak with their regular minister?" Charlotte asked, not to Tilda in particular but to all of them. "They'd go to church on Sunday, wouldn't they?"

"Oh, yeah," Tilda said with certainty. "Every Sunday, sure as clockwork. The 'ole 'ouse. Cook'd leave cold cuts for luncheon, an' 'eat up vegetables quick when she come back. Mr. Garrick's very strict about it."

"So why would Martin go to find a special priest for Stephen?" Charlotte said thoughtfully.

Tilda shook her head. "Dunno, but 'e told me about it. Someone as Mr. Stephen'd known a long time ago. 'E works wi' soldiers as 'ave fallen on 'ard times, drink an' opium an' the like." She gave a little shiver. "Down Seven Dials way, where it's real rough. Sleepin' in doorways, cold an' 'ungry, an' near enough wishin' they was dead, poor souls. That in't no way for a soldier o' the Queen ter end up."

No one answered her immediately. Gracie looked at Charlotte's face and saw it filled with pity and confusion, then she turned to Tellman, and was startled to see the quickening of an idea in his eyes. "Wot is it?" she demanded.

Tellman swiveled to face Tilda. "Did Martin find this man?" he asked.

"Yeah. 'E told me. Why? D'yer think 'e'd know wot 'appened ter Martin?" The hope in her voice was needle sharp.

"He might know something." Tellman tried to be careful, without crushing her. "Did he say his name, do you remember?"

"Yeah . . ." Tilda screwed up her face in effort. "Sand—summink. Sandy . . ."

Tellman leaned forward. "Sandeman?"

Tilda's eyes opened wide. "Yeah! That's it. Yer know 'im?"

"I've heard of him." Tellman looked across at Charlotte.

"Yes," she agreed before he asked the question. "Yes, we should try to find him. Whatever Martin said to him, it might be important." She bit her lip. "Apart from that, we don't have anything better."

"It may not be so easy," Tellman warned. "It could take a while. We still haven't got proof of any crime, so—"

"I'll look," Charlotte interrupted him.

"In Seven Dials?" Tellman shook his head. "You have no idea what it's like. It's one of the worst places . . ."

"I'll go in daylight," she said quickly. "And I'll dress in my oldest clothes—believe me, they'll pass as local. There'll be plenty of women around between eight o'clock and six in the evening. And I'm looking for the priest. Other women with relatives who were soldiers must do that too."

Tellman looked at her, then at Gracie. His conflicting emotions were startlingly clear in his face.

Charlotte smiled. "I'm going," she said decisively. "If I find him I have more chance of learning something about Martin than you have, if he really went on Stephen Garrick's behalf. I'll start straightaway." She turned to Tilda. "Now you go back to your duties. You cannot afford to have your mistress dismiss you, however justified your absence." She looked at Tellman. "Thank you for all you have done. I know it took a lot of your time . . ."

He brushed it aside, but he did not have the ease with words—even to think them, let alone tell her why it had mattered to him.

She stood up, and the others accepted it as leave to go.

CHARLOTTE WALKED the streets of the Seven Dials area from midday onwards. She had dressed in a very old skirt, one she had accidentally torn and had had to stitch up rather less than successfully. Instead of a jacket over her plain blouse, she took a shawl, which was more in keeping with what other women shopping or working in that area would wear.

Even so, she was startlingly out of place. Poverty had a stench unlike anything else. She had thought she knew, but she had forgotten just how many people sat on the pavements, huddled in doorways, or stood sad-eyed and hopeless around piles of rags or boots, waiting for someone to haggle over a price, and perhaps walk away with nothing.

The open gutter ran down the center of the street, barely moving in the slight incline. Human dirt was everywhere, and human smell clogged the air because there was little clear water, even to drink, no soap, no warmth or dryness, nothing to ease the hunger and the overintimacy.

She walked among them with her head down, not merely to seem like the others, beaten by life, but because she could not look at them, and meet their eyes, knowing she would leave and they could not.

She began tentatively, asking for a soldiers' priest. It cost her considerable resolve even to approach someone and speak. Her voice would betray her as not belonging, and there was no way to disguise it. To ape their speech patterns would be to make fun of them and mark herself as dishonest before she even framed her questions, let alone received an answer.

All she achieved the first day was to eliminate certain possibilities. It was the afternoon of the second day when she succeeded suddenly and without any warning. She was in Dudley Street, trying to make her way through the piles of secondhand shoes heaped not only on the broken cobbles of the pavement but strewn across the roadway as well. Children sat untended beside them, some crying, many just watching with half-seeing eyes as people trudged by.

The man was walking towards her, moving easily as if he were accustomed to it. He looked perfectly ordinary, in his early forties, slim under his ragged coat. His head was uncovered and his brown hair was badly in need of cutting.

Charlotte stopped to allow him to pass. He had a purpose in his stride and she did not want to bar his way.

To her surprise he stopped also. "I hear you are looking for me." His voice was soft and well educated. "My name is Morgan Sandeman. I work here with anyone who wants me, but especially soldiers."

"Mr. Sandeman?" Her voice lifted more than she had meant, as if she were really some desperate wife in search of a lost husband he might know.

"Yes. How can I help you?" He stood beside her amid the piles of shoes.

There was no point in pretense, and perhaps no time to waste. "I am looking for someone who has gone missing," she replied. "And I believe he may have spoken with you shortly before the last time he was seen. May I have a little of your time . . . please?"

"Of course." He held out his hand. "If you would like to come with me, we can go to my office. I'm afraid I don't have a church, more like an old hall, but it serves."

"Yes, I'd like to," she agreed without hesitation.

He led the way with no further speech, and she followed him back up the cobbles between the silent people, around the corner and along an alley towards a tiny square. The buildings were four or five stories high, narrow and leaning together, creaking in the damp, eaves crooked, the sour-sweet smell of rotting wood clinging to everything, choking the throat. There was no distinct sound, and yet there was not silence. Rat feet scuttled over stone, water dripped, rubbish moved and fluttered in the slight wind, wood sagged and settled a little lower.

"Over there." Sandeman pointed to a doorway and walked ahead of her. It was stained with damp and swung open at his touch. Inside was a narrow vestibule and beyond a larger hall with a fire burning low in the huge open fireplace. Half a dozen people sat on the floor in front of it, leaning close to each other, but not apparently talking. It was a moment before Charlotte realized they were either insensible or asleep.

Sandeman held up his finger to request silence, and walked almost soundlessly across the stone floor towards a table in the corner to the right, at which there were two chairs.

She followed after him and sat as he invited.

"I'm sorry," he apologized. "I have nothing to offer you, and nowhere better than this." He said it with a smile, not as if he were ashamed for it. It was more an accommodation to her than to himself. His face was gaunt and the marks of hunger were plain in his thin cheeks. "Who is it you are looking for?" he asked. "If I can't tell you where he is, I can at least tell him that you asked, and perhaps he will find you. You understand that what is told me in confidence has to remain so? Sometimes when a man . . ." He hesitated, watching her intently, perhaps trying to judge something of the man she was seeking from her emotions.

She felt like a fraud, imagining the desperate women, wives, mothers or sisters who had come to him to find a man they had loved, lost to experiences he could not share with them, or whose burden he could not carry without the oblivion of drink, or opium.

She had to be honest with him. "It is not a relative of mine, it is the brother of a young woman I know. He has disappeared, and she is too distressed to look for him herself, nor has she the time. She could lose her position and not easily find another."

His expression of concern did not alter. "Who is he?"

Before she could reply the outer door swung wide open, crashing against the wall and bouncing back to catch the person coming in. It hit him so hard he lost his precarious balance and crumpled to the floor, where he remained in a heap, like a bundle of rags.

Sandeman glanced at Charlotte too briefly to speak, then stood up and went over to the door. He bent down and put his hands under the man, and with considerable effort, lifted him to his feet. The man was very obviously drunk. He looked to be in his mid-fifties, but his face sagged, his eyes were unfocused and he had several days' stubble on his cheeks. His hair was matted and the dirt on him could be smelled even from where Charlotte sat.

Sandeman looked at him with exasperation. "Come on in, Herbert. Come and sit down. You're sodden wet, man!"

"I fell," Herbert mumbled, dragging his feet as he shambled half beside, half behind Sandeman.

"In the gutter, by the look of you," Sandeman said wryly.

And the smell, Charlotte thought. She longed to move farther away, but the dignity with which Sandeman spoke to the man made her feel ashamed to.

Herbert made no reply, but allowed himself to be guided over to the bench by the low fire, and sank down onto it as if he were exhausted. None of those already there took the slightest notice of him.

Sandeman went to a cupboard against the far wall. He took a key from the ring on his belt and opened the door. He searched for a few minutes, then took out a large gray blanket, coarse and rough, but no doubt warm.

Charlotte watched him with curiosity. It was hardly enough for a bed, nor was the man sick, in the sense that rest would help him.

Sandeman closed and locked the cupboard, and went back to Herbert, carrying the blanket.

"Take off your wet clothes," he instructed. "Wrap this around you and get warm."

Herbert looked across at Charlotte.

"She'll turn her back," Sandeman promised. He said it loudly enough for her to hear and obey, swiveling the chair around so she was facing the opposite way. After that she did not see him stand up, but she heard the rustling of fabric and the slight thud as the wet cloth struck the floor.

"I'll get you some hot soup and bread," Sandeman went on. "It'll settle your stomach." He did not bother to tell the man to stop drinking the alcohol that was poisoning him. Presumably that had already all been said, and to no purpose. "I'll wash your clothes. You'll have to wait here until they're dry." Charlotte heard his feet coming towards her until he stood at her elbow.

"You can turn around now," he said quietly. "I'm afraid I have things to do, but I can talk to you as I work."

"Perhaps I can fetch him the bread and the soup?" she offered. The stench of the clothes was turning her stomach, but she tried not to allow it to show in her face.

"Thank you," he accepted. "We have a scullery through there." He pointed to a door to the left of the fireplace. "We can talk while I wash these. It will be private." He picked up the clothes again and led her into a small stone room where a huge stove kept water simmering in two kettles, a cauldron of soup near the boil, and several old pans of hot water, presumably ready to wash clothes as necessary. A tin bath on a low table served as a sink, and there were buckets of cold water from the nearest pump, perhaps one or two streets away.

She found the bread and a knife and carefully sliced off two fairly thick pieces. It was not difficult because the bread was stale. She looked around for anything to spread on it, but there was no butter. Perhaps with soup it would not matter. Anything would be good that would absorb some of the alcohol. She lifted the lid from the cauldron on the stove and saw pea soup almost as thick as porridge, bubbles breaking every now and then on the surface, like hot mud. There were bowls on a bench, and she reached for one, took the ladle and filled it.

She carried the bread on a plate in one hand, the bowl and a spoon in the other, protected by a cloth, and went back into the hall and over to Herbert. She stopped in front of him and he looked up at her. She could see in his face the instinct to rise to his feet, old discipline dying hard. He had once been a soldier, before whatever kind of pain or despair it was had destroyed him. But he was also acutely conscious of the fact that he was wearing only a blanket, and he was not sure enough of his grasp on it to maintain his decency. The nakedness of his situation was bad enough, without exposing his body as well.

"Please stay seated," she said quickly, as if he had already half risen. "You must hold the soup carefully. It is very hot. You will need both hands. Please take care not to burn yourself."

"Thank you, ma'am," he muttered, relaxing again and taking the bowl from her gingerly. He rested it on the blanket across his knee straightaway. It was too hot to hold for long, and he was aware that his fingers were clumsy.

She smiled at him, although he did not see it, then realizing that she might be embarrassing him, she turned and went back into the scullery again.

Sandeman was bending over the tin bath, rubbing at the clothes. He was using rough soap made of potash, carbolic, and lye. It was strong and would do his skin no good, but it would get rid of the worst of the dirt, and no doubt the lice, and the odor and infection that would lie with them.

"Mr. Sandeman," she said urgently, "I really do have to speak to you. This young man who has disappeared may be in some danger, and we have been told that he came looking for you. If he found you, he might have said something which could tell me where he went, and why."

He looked sideways at her, resting his thin arms on the edge of the bath and leaning his weight on them. It was a backbreaking job. "Who is it?" he asked.

"Martin Garvie . . ."

The words were barely out of her mouth when she saw him

stiffen and the color drain from his face, and then flow back in again as if the blood had rushed up in a tide. Her own heart constricted with fear. Her lips were so stiff it was difficult to form the words. "What's happened to him?" she said huskily.

"I don't know." He straightened up very slowly. He turned to face her, ignoring the wet clothes and letting them sink back into the water. "I'm sorry, I cannot tell you anything that will help you. I really cannot." He was breathing heavily, as if his chest were compressed, and yet at the same time starved for air.

"He may be in danger, Mr. Sandeman," she said quickly. "He is missing! No one has seen or heard from him for three weeks. His sister is frantic with worry. Even his master, Mr. Stephen Garrick, does not appear to have gone where he is said to have. There is no trace of him on train or ship. We need anything we can find to help us learn what has happened."

It was painfully clear that Sandeman was laboring under some intense emotion, so profound he could not control the shivering of his body or the raggedness of his breathing, but when he managed to find his voice, there was no indecision in him, no possibility of change.

"I cannot help you," he said again. "What is told me as a confession of the soul is sacred."

"But if a man's life is at stake . . ." she argued, knowing even as she did so that she was doomed to failure. She could see it in his eyes, the pallor of his face, the muscles locked tight in his jaw and neck.

"I can only trust God," he replied so softly she barely heard him. "It rests in His hands. I cannot tell you what Martin Garvie told me. If I could, I would tell you all of it. And I am still not sure it would help you find him."

"Is . . . is he alive?"

"I don't know."

She drew her breath in to try one more time, and then let it out in a sigh. She recognized the finality in his eyes, and looked away. She could not think what else to say. The emotion was too high for anything banal, and yet what else was there?

"Mrs . . ." he started, leaving it hanging because he did not know her name.

"Pitt," she answered. "Charlotte Pitt."

"Mrs. Pitt, it concerns too many other people. If it were my secret alone, and speaking would do any good . . . but it won't. It's an old story, long past helping now."

"To do with Martin Garvie?" She was puzzled. "He told you something . . ."

"I can't help you, Mrs. Pitt. I'll walk with you back as far as Dudley Street, in case you get lost." His voice was urgent, his dark eyes full of trouble. "Please go home. You don't belong here. You may get hurt, and you will do no good. Believe me. I live here, and I know this place as well as any outsider can do, but I seldom go out after dark. Come . . ." He dried his hands on a piece of torn cloth and put his jacket on again. "Do you know your way from Dudley Street?"

"Yes . . . thank you." She could only accept. There was nothing else to do with dignity, or even without it. And, she admitted, she cared what he thought of her.

WITH PITT not at home, Charlotte had no wish to light the parlor fire and sit there alone after Daniel and Jemima had gone to bed. Instead she sat in the warm, bright kitchen and told Gracie what she had discovered from Sandeman, but neither of them could think of anything further to do, unless they could find more information. In spite of the cats more or less asleep in the clothes basket beside the stove, and the soft patter of rain on the window, they shared a quiet, bitter feeling of defeat.

The evening after was no better, but at least there were domestic chores to be done, and that was more satisfying than idleness. Gracie was going through cupboards, tidying them, and Charlotte was mending pillowcases when a little after nine o'clock the doorbell rang.

Gracie was standing on a stool with her arms full of washing, so Charlotte went to answer it herself.

On the step stood a slender man, very smartly dressed in tailoring that would have astounded Pitt. He had a lean, clever face, deeply lined, and with eyes so dark they looked black in the light of the street lamp. His shock of dark hair was liberally sprinkled with gray.

"Mrs. Pitt." He said it more as an introduction than a question.

"Yes," she acknowledged cautiously. She was certainly not going to allow a stranger into the house. Nor, in fact, would it be a good idea to tell him that Pitt was away. "What may I do for you?" she added.

He smiled slightly. It was self-deprecating, and yet he was obviously full of confidence. It was a mannerism of possibly unconscious charm.

"How do you do. My name is Victor Narraway. In your husband's absence in Alexandria, where I regret I was obliged to send him, I wished to call upon you and ascertain that you are safe and well . . . and that you remain so."

"Have you some doubt, Mr. Narraway?" She was startled at his identity, and there was a flutter of fear in her that he knew something of Pitt which she did not. And for him to have come, it had to be something ugly. She had heard nothing from Pitt yet, but it was far too early. The post would take days. She tried to steady herself. "Why have you called, Mr. Narraway? Please be candid."

"Exactly as I said, Mrs. Pitt," he replied. "May I come in?"

She stood back in tacit invitation and he stepped up and past her, glancing momentarily at the delicate plasterwork on the ceiling of the hall. Then as she closed the door, he went where she indicated into the parlor.

She followed him and turned up the lamps. She hoped he was not going to be there long enough for it to matter that she had not lit the fire. She faced him almost challengingly, her heart pounding. "Have you heard something about Thomas?"

"No, Mrs. Pitt," he said immediately. "I apologize if I gave you that impression. As far as I know, he is safe and in good health. Were he not, I would have heard to the contrary. It is your safety I am concerned about."

He was very polite but she detected a shadow of condescension in his tone. Was it because Narraway was a gentleman, and Pitt was a gamekeeper's son, in spite of his perfect diction? There was always something in the manner, the bearing, which marked the confidence that was not gained but inborn.

Charlotte was not aristocracy, as Vespasia was, but she was very definitely of good family. She looked at him with a cool arrogance which Vespasia might not have disowned. Her old dress with its darned cuffs was irrelevant.

"Indeed? That is very gracious of you, Mr. Narraway, but quite unnecessary. Thomas left everything in order before he went, and all arrangements are working as they should." She was referring to the financial ones regarding his pay, but it would be crude to say so.

Narraway smiled very slightly, merely a softening of the lips. "I had not imagined otherwise," he assured her. "But then perhaps you did not tell him of your intention to investigate the apparent disappearance of one of Ferdinand Garrick's servants."

She was caught completely off guard. She scrambled for an answer that would keep him at a distance and close him out of intruding into her thoughts.

"Apparent?" she asked, her eyes very wide. "That sounds as if you know more of it than I. So you have been investigating it also? I am very pleased. Indeed, I am delighted. The case requires more resources than I can bring to it."

Now it was his turn to look startled, but he masked it so quickly she almost failed to see it.

"I don't think you understand the danger you may be in if you proceed any further," he said carefully, his dark eyes fixed on hers, as if to make certain she grasped his seriousness.

Without taking a second to think, she smiled at him dazzlingly. "Then you had better enlighten me, Mr. Narraway. What danger is it? Who is likely to hurt me, and how? Obviously you know, or you would not have taken time from your own case to come to tell me . . . at this hour."

He was disconcerted. Again it was there only for an instant, but she saw it with sharp satisfaction. He had expected her to be cowed, humbled by censure, and instead she had turned his words back on him.

He sidestepped her challenge. "You are afraid something unpleasant has happened to Martin Garvie?" he asked.

She refused to be defensive. "Yes," she said frankly. "Mr. Ferdinand Garrick says that his son and Martin have gone to the south of France, but if that is true, then why in three weeks did Martin not write to his sister and tell her so?" She was not going to let Narraway know that Tellman had also tried and failed to find any record of their having sailed, or even a witness to their taking a train. Tellman could not afford to attract the notice of his new superior, still less his criticism, and she did not trust Narraway not to use information in any way that suited his own immediate purpose.

"Do you fear an accident?" he asked.

He was playing with her, and she knew it.

"Of what sort?" She raised her eyebrows. "I cannot think of one that would cause the danger to me that you suggest."

He relaxed and smiled. "Touché," he said softly. "But I am perfectly serious, Mrs. Pitt. I am aware that you have concerned yourself with this young man's apparent disappearance, and that he is, or was, manservant to Stephen Garrick. The Garrick family is of some power in society—and in government circles. Ferdinand Garrick had a fine military career, ended with a good command—

lieutenant general, before he retired. Rigid, loyal to the empire to the last inch, God, Queen, and country."

Charlotte was perplexed. She stood in the middle of the room looking at Narraway while he relaxed a fraction more with every second. If Garrick were as upright and honorable as Narraway said, the "muscular Christian" Vespasia knew, then simply he would not be party to any abuse of a servant, let alone the kind of danger she and Gracie had come to fear.

Narraway saw her hesitation. "But he is a man of little mercy if he feels he is being criticized," he went on. "He would not like his affairs questioned, by anyone. Like many proud men, he is also intensely private."

She lifted her chin a little. "And what could he do, Mr. Narraway? Ruin my reputation in society? I do not have one. My husband is an officer in Special Branch, a man the authorities use but pretend does not exist. When he was superintendent of Bow Street, I might have entertained social aspirations, but hardly now."

He colored very faintly. "I know that, Mrs. Pitt. Many people do great things and are publicly unappreciated, possibly even unthanked. The only comfort is that if you are not praised for your successes, at least you may not be blamed for your failures." His face shadowed, fierce emotion suppressed under a tight control. "And we all have them."

There was such a heaviness in his voice, carefully as he disguised it, that she knew he was speaking of himself, and something painfully learned, not observed from others. It was not belief that moved him but knowledge.

"I am concerned for you, Mrs. Pitt," he went on. "Of course he will not change your value in the eyes of your friends, but he can wield a cruel influence on all your family, if he wishes to, or feels himself vulnerable." He was watching her closely. She found his look gripping—almost as if he physically held her.

"Do you think some harm has come to Martin Garvie?" she asked him. "Please speak honestly, whether I can do anything to help or not. Lies, however comfortable, will not improve my behavior, I promise you."

There was a quickening in his eyes, a spark of humor in spite of the other emotions crowding close. "I have no idea. I cannot think of any reason why it should. How much do you know about him?"

"Very little. But his sister, Matilda, has known him all her life, and she is the one who is afraid," she answered.

"Or hurt?" he said with very slightly raised eyebrows. "Could it be that they are growing further apart, and she finds that difficult? She is lonely, and the ties are closer for her than for him; she will believe anything, even danger from which she must rescue him, easier to accommodate than the knowledge that in fact he does not need her?"

Again she was caught by a sadness in his voice, some shadow of the gaslight that caught an old pain not usually visible . . . and by the fact that apparently he also knew at least something about Tilda as well.

"Of course it is possible," she said very gently. "But the possibility does not excuse the need to be certain that he is safe. It couldn't." She nearly added that he must know that, as she did, but she saw his understanding as the words touched her lips, and she left them unsaid.

They stood for seconds. Then he straightened. "Nevertheless, Mrs. Pitt, for your safety's sake, please do not press any further with enquiries regarding Mr. Garrick. There can be no conceivable reason for his having harmed a servant, other than possibly in reputation, and that is something you cannot undo."

"I would like to oblige you, Mr. Narraway," she replied very levelly. "But if I find myself in a position to help Tilda Garvie, then I cannot hold back from doing so. I can think of no way in which it would inconvenience Mr. Garrick, unless he has done something unjust . . . If he has, then, like anyone else, he is answerable for it."

Exasperation filled Narraway's face. "But not to you, Mrs. Pitt! Haven't you—" He stopped.

She smiled at him with great charm. "No," she said. "I haven't. May I offer you a cup of tea? It will be in the kitchen, but you are very welcome."

He stood motionless, as if the decision were a major one on which something of great importance depended, as if even from the parlor he could sense the warmth and the comfortable familiarity of scrubbed wood, clean linen, gleaming china on the dresser, and the lingering, sweet odor of food.

"No, thank you," he said at last. "I must go home." His voice held the regret he could not put into words. "Good night."

"Good night, Mr. Narraway." She accompanied him to the front door, and watched his slender, straight-backed figure walk with almost military elegance along the rain-wet footpath towards the thoroughfare.

CHAPTER TEN

PITT THANKED TRENCHARD for his help and left Alexandria with a stab of regret that surprised him. He would miss the balmy nights pale with stars, the wind blowing in off the sea, smelling clean above the spice odors and filth of the hot streets. And he would also miss the sound of music and voices he did not understand, the colors in the bazaars, the fruit. But in London there would be fewer mosquitoes, and no scorpions. Certainly in the coming winter no cloying, sticky heat to make the sweat run down his skin or light that blinded his eyes and made him permanently squint in the sun.

And there would be no more sense of being a stranger intruding in a land where his people were different and unwelcome, and the weight on the conscience of having contributed to the searing poverty. Of course there was poverty in England too. People died of hunger, cold and disease, but they were his own people; he was one of them and not to blame.

There was a sense of incompleteness in his mission as he stood on the deck of the ship, the bright water churning around him and the city already fading into the distance. What could he tell Narraway? He knew far more about Ayesha Zakhari, and she was not at all as he had assumed, which forced him to reassess the whole question of why Lovat had been killed. It seemed a pointless thing to have done, and Ayesha was not stupid.

Above all, he wanted to be home with Charlotte, his children, the comfort of his house and the familiarity of streets where he knew every corner, and understood the language.

It was another three days before he docked at Southampton, and then a train journey back to London which was in truth less than two hours but seemed to drag to the very last minute.

By seven o'clock he was on the doorstep of Narraway's office, determined to leave a note if there was no one in, but wishing intensely to say all he had to tonight, and go home to sleep as long as he wanted, luxuriously, in all that was sweet and gentle and long-loved, without the need to trouble his mind with what he must say or do in the morning.

But Narraway was in and there was no escape from reporting in person. He leaned back in his chair when Pitt was inside and the door had closed behind him. His stare was penetrating but guarded, already prepared to defend against a returning enquiry.

Pitt was too tired, both physically and emotionally, to pretend to any form of etiquette. He sat down opposite him and stretched out his legs. His feet hurt and he was cold with exhaustion and the sudden chill of English October.

Narraway simply waited for Pitt to speak.

"She is a highly intelligent, literate, and well-educated woman of Christian descent," Pitt said. "But an Egyptian patriot who cared very much for the poor in her country and for the injustice of foreign domination."

Narraway pursed his lips and made his fingers into a steeple, his elbows on the arms of his chair. "So a woman coming for a political end, not merely to make her own fortune," he said without surprise. His expression did not alter in the slightest. "Did she imagine that she could affect the cotton industry through Ryerson?"

"It seems so," Pitt answered.

Narraway sighed, his face now filled with sadness. "Naive," he murmured.

Pitt had a powerful feeling that Narraway was speaking of far more than simply Ayesha Zakhari's ignorance of political inevitability. He sat back in his chair as if at ease, and yet his body was not relaxed. There was a tension within him which was palpable in the room. "You said well educated. In what?" he demanded.

"History, languages, her own culture," Pitt replied. "Her father was a learned man, and she was his only child. Apparently he found her an excellent companion and taught her much of what he knew."

Narraway's face tightened. He seemed to understand far more from Pitt's words than the simple facts they referred to. Was he thinking that she was brought up in the intellectual company of an older man, that it was comfortable to her and she was used to both the advantages, and perhaps the disadvantages as well? Pitt wondered if it had been a training for her which enabled her to charm Ryerson without ever seeming to be too young, too unsophisticated, too impatient? Or was it the forming of a woman for whom young men were unsubtle, shallow and with whom she was ill at ease? Could she actually be as much in love with Ryerson as he believed?

Then why on earth would she have shot Lovat? Had Pitt missed something critical in Alexandria after all?

Narraway was watching him. He said abruptly, "What is it, Pitt?" He was leaning forward. His hand was shaking slightly.

Pitt was intensely aware of currents of emotion far beyond the facts he could see. He hated working with a superior who obviously trusted him so little, whatever the reason. Was it for his safety? Or someone else's? Or was Narraway protecting something in himself that Pitt could not even guess at?

"Nothing that seems to have any relevance to Lovat, or to Ryerson," he answered the question. "She was a passionate follower of one of the Orabi revolutionists, an older man. She fell in love with him, and he betrayed both her and the cause. It was a bitter hurt to bear."

Narraway drew in a long, deep breath and let it out silently. "Yes." The single word was all he said.

For seconds Pitt waited, sure Narraway would say more. There seemed to be sentences, paragraphs in his mind, just beyond reach.

But when he did speak, it was a change of subject. "What about Lovat?" he asked. "Did you find anyone who knew him? There must be something more than the written records we have here. For God's sake, what were you doing in Alexandria all that time?"

Pitt swallowed his irritation and told him briefly what he had done, his further pursuit of Edwin Lovat and his army career in Egypt, and Narraway listened, again in silence. It was unnerving. Some response would have made it easier.

"I couldn't find anything at all to suggest a motive for murder," Pitt finished. "He seemed a very ordinary soldier, competent, but not brilliant, a decent enough man who made no particular enemies."

"And his invaliding out?" Narraway asked.

"Fever," Pitt replied. "Malaria, as far as I could tell. He certainly was not the only one to get it at that time. There doesn't seem to have been anything remarkable about it. He was sent back to England, but honorably. No question over his record or his career."

"I know that much," Narraway said wearily. "His trouble seems to have begun after he got back home."

"Trouble?" Pitt prompted.

Narraway's look was sour. "I thought you looked at the man yourself?"

"I did," Pitt replied tartly. "If you remember, I told you." He was conscious of how tired he was. His eyes stung with the effort of keeping them open, and his body ached from long sitting in one position on the train. He was cold in spite of the fire in Narraway's office. Perhaps hunger and exhaustion added to it. He wanted to go home, to see Charlotte and hold her in his arms; he wanted these things so profoundly it required a deep effort to be civil to Narraway. "He's given plenty of men, and women, cause to hate him," he went on brusquely. "But we have nothing to suggest any of them were in Eden Lodge the night he was killed. Or have you discovered something?"

Narraway's face pinched tight. Pitt was startled by the sense of power in it. Narraway was not a large man, yet his mind and his emotion dominated the room, and would have, however many people had been there. For the first time Pitt realized how little he knew about a man in whose hands he placed his own future, even at times perhaps his life. He had no idea of Narraway's family or where he came from, and that did not matter. He had never known those things about Micah Drummond, or John Cornwallis, and he had not cared. He knew what they believed in, what mattered to them, and he understood them, at times better than they understood themselves. But then he was wiser, more experienced in human nature than they, who had seen only their own narrow portion of it.

Narraway was a far cleverer man, subtler. He never intentionally gave away anything of himself. Secrecy, misleading, taking knowledge without giving it, were his profession. But being obliged to trust where he could not see was a new experience for Pitt, and not a comfortable one.

"Have you?" he repeated. This time it was a challenge.

For a moment they faced each other in a silent, level stare. Pitt was not sure he could afford a confrontation, but he was too tired to be careful.

Narraway spoke very steadily, as if he had suddenly decided to take control of the exchange. "No, unfortunately not. But our job is to protect Ryerson, if possible."

"At the expense of hanging an innocent woman?" Pitt said bitterly.

"Ah!" Narraway let out his breath in a sigh, his face easing, as if he had learned something of great interest. "And are you now of the opinion that Ayesha Zakhari is innocent? If so, then there is something you found in Egypt that you have not told me. I think this would be a good time to do so. The trial begins in two days."

Pitt felt jolted as hard as if he had been slapped. Tomorrow! That was no time at all. The truth came to his tongue almost as if he had no ability to prevent it.

"I went to Egypt thinking she was a very pretty young woman of loose morals, prepared to use her charm to provide herself with the wealth and comfort she would not otherwise obtain." He saw Narraway's eyes intent upon him, and the faint curve of his lips into a smile. "And I came back knowing she was well-born, highly articulate, and probably far better educated than nine tenths of the men in London society, never mind the women. She is passionate in the cause of her country's economic independence and welfare. She has been totally betrayed once, and may find it hard to believe any man again, no matter what he professes. And yet she has said nothing in prison to implicate Ryerson."

"Which proves what?" Narraway asked.

"That there is something crucial we don't know," Pitt replied, pushing his chair back. "We haven't done very well." He stood up. "Either of us."

Narraway looked at him, tilting his head back a little to meet his eyes. "I do know that Edwin Lovat was a man of profound and corroding misery," he said very quietly. "And neither of us has uncovered the reason for it. It may have nothing to do with his murder—but it makes as much sense as anything else we have."

"Well, I have no idea what it was," Pitt replied. "According to his superiors in Alexandria, he was a man of religious conviction, well-liked, good at his job, and in love with Ayesha, but only casually. It ended before he left Egypt. He certainly wasn't heartbroken—nor was she."

"Nobody is suggesting that kind of passion, Pitt," Narraway

said with an edge to his voice; it could have been anything: pain, regret, memory, even dream. "She was beautiful, he was far from home. Since Egypt he has gone from woman to woman, but it was not for love of her. She was just one more."

"Are you sure?"

"Yes. I've spoken to those in their circle. He saw her several times in London before he bothered to pursue her at all. He was becoming more deeply involved than he wished with another woman. He wanted an escape from entanglement. Being seen to court Miss Zakhari provided it for him. He wanted to chase—he did not want to catch."

Pitt hesitated at the door. He was too tired to think clearly. "Then what was the matter with him? What happened between leaving Egypt and arriving in England?"

"I don't know yet," Narraway answered. "But I am not certain that it has nothing to do with his death."

"And Miss Zakhari?"

"As we have already said, there's something we do not know, something that may bring more than a simple, rather pointless murder with it."

Pitt opened the door and stood with his hand on it. "Good night."

Narraway smiled very slightly. "Good night, Pitt."

IT WAS DARK by the time Pitt reached Keppel Street. The lamps gleamed along the pavement like a string of endlessly reflected moons, dimming in the mist until the last he could see was no more than a suggestion, a luminescence without shape.

He opened the door with his own key and stood inside, tasting the moment, breathing in deeply the familiar odors of beeswax and lavender polish, clean linen, and the soft earthiness of chrysanthemums on the hall table. There was no light on in the parlor. The children would be upstairs; Charlotte and Gracie must be in the kitchen. He took his boots off, relishing the feel of his stocking feet on the cool linoleum. He padded down to the door and pushed it open.

For a moment Charlotte did not notice. She was alone in the room, her head bent over her needle, her face grave, heavy hair slipping out of its pins, bright in the gaslight. At that instant the sight of her was more beautiful than anything else he could imagine, more than sunset over the Nile or the desert sky white with stars.

"Hello . . ." he said quietly.

She jerked around, stared at him for an unbelieving heartbeat, then dropped the sewing on the floor and threw herself into his arms. It was long minutes later, when they heard Gracie's heels along the hall, that they broke apart and Charlotte, her face flushed, went over to put the kettle on.

"Yer 'ome!" Gracie said with exuberant delight. Then, remembering her dignity a little, and lowering her voice to something closer to normal, "Well I'm that glad ter see yer safe. I s'pose yer 'ungry?" That was hopeful. Hungry was back to normal. When he did not answer immediately she regarded him with a shadow of anxiety.

"Yes, please." He smiled at her and sat down in his usual place. "But a cold meat sandwich will be fine. Is everything well here?"

" 'Course it is," Gracie said firmly.

Charlotte turned from the stove, the kettle now on the hob. Her eyes were bright. "Very well," she confirmed, not looking at Gracie.

He caught the tension, the shadow somewhere, the communication in that neither had looked at each other, almost as if the answer was agreed before he had come in.

"What have you been doing?" he asked conversationally.

Charlotte looked at him, but after a hesitation so minute that had he not been watching her closely, he would have missed it. It was as if she had been going to turn to Gracie first, and then decided not to.

"What have you been doing?" he repeated, before she had time to say something less than the truth, which she would then be unable to withdraw.

She took in a deep breath. "Gracie has a friend whose brother seems to be missing. We have been trying to find out what happened to him."

He read her expression. "But you haven't succeeded," he said.

"No. No, and we don't know what to do next. I'll tell you about it . . . tomorrow."

"Why not tonight?" The question sprang from the nudge of anxiety that she was delaying because something in the story would displease or disturb him.

She smiled. "Because you are tired and hungry, and there are far better things to talk about. We have tried, and not achieved very much."

As if released from waiting on every word, Gracie swiveled around and darted to the pantry to slice the cold meat, and Charlotte went upstairs to wake the children.

They came racing down the stairs and threw themselves at Pitt, almost overbalancing him off his chair, hugging him, asking question after question about Egypt, Alexandria, the desert, the ship, and constantly interrupting the answers. Then he opened his case and gave them all the gifts he had brought, to everyone's intense delight.

But in the morning he raised the question again, when Gracie was out shopping and Daniel and Jemima were at school. He had slept late, and came down to find Charlotte making bread.

"Who is the missing brother?" he asked, accepting tea and toast and fishing in the marmalade pot to see if there was sufficient left to satisfy his hunger for it. Its tart pungency was one of his favorite flavors, and it seemed like months since he had enjoyed crisp toast. He thought there might be just enough. He looked up at her. "Well?"

Now her face was shadowed. She went on kneading automatically. "He was valet to Stephen Garrick, in Torrington Square. A very respectable family, although Aunt Vespasia doesn't care for the father at all—General Garrick, a—" She stopped, her hands motionless. "What is it?"

"General Garrick?" he asked.

"Yes. Do you know him?" At the moment she was no more than curious.

"He was commanding officer in Alexandria when Lovat was invalided out of the army," he replied.

Her hands stopped kneading the dough and she looked up at him. "Does that mean anything?" she said slowly, turning over the idea in her mind. "It's just coincidence . . . isn't it?" But even as she spoke, other thoughts gathered in her mind—doubts, shadows, memories of things Sandeman had said.

"What is it?" Pitt prompted, and she knew he had seen it in her face.

She wiped her hands on her apron. "I really fear something could have happened to Martin Garvie," she replied gravely. "And perhaps even Stephen Garrick as well. I found the priest that Martin went to in the Seven Dials area just before he disappeared. He works especially with soldiers who have fallen on hard times." She saw the anxiety in his face and hurried on before he could give expression to it. "I went in daylight. It was all perfectly all right! Thomas, he was very upset indeed." She remembered it with a shiver, not for the dirt or the despair, but for the pain that she had seen rack Sandeman so deeply.

Pitt was waiting, stiff, his tea forgotten and going cold in the cup.

"A priest?" he said curiously. "Why? Could he tell you anything?"

"No . . . not in words."

"What do you mean? If not in words, how? How?" he demanded.

"By his reaction," she replied. She sat down opposite him, ignoring the bread. It would come to no harm for a while. "Thomas, when I mentioned Martin's name he was filled with a horror so great that for several moments he barely recovered his composure enough to be able to speak to me." She knew her voice was thick with the emotion that came back to her in a rush—welling up inside her. "He knows something terrible," she said quietly. "But because it came to him in a confession, he cannot repeat it. Nothing I could say made any difference, even that Martin's life could be in danger." She waited, watching his face, longing for him to be able to take the burden of confusion from her, provide some other way she had not thought of in which she could still help.

"In danger from whom?" he asked.

"I don't know," she admitted. She told him very briefly what little she had been able to learn, and from it what she had deduced. "But whatever Martin said to him, Mr. Sandeman would not—" She stopped. Pitt's eyes were wide, his face pale and his body suddenly rigid as if caught in a moment of fear. "Thomas— What? What is it?"

"Did you say Sandeman?" he asked, his voice catching in his throat.

"Yes. Why? Do you know of him?" Without any clear thought, she felt his alarm as if she understood. "Who is he?" She did not want to learn something ugly of the priest. He had seemed to her a man of intense and genuine compassion, but she could not afford less than the truth, and to turn from it now would avail nothing. The fear would be just as lacerating as anything he could tell her. "Do you?" she said again.

"I don't know," he replied. "But in the army, Lovat had three friends with whom he spent most of his off-duty time: Garrick, Sandeman, and Yeats. You mentioned both Garrick and Sandeman as being in possible danger, or in distress. It is hard to believe that is coincidence."

"What about Yeats?"

"I don't know, but I think I need to find out."

"So Lovat's death did have something to do with Egypt and not necessarily with Ryerson?" she said, but surprisingly there was none of the lift of hope she would have expected only an hour ago.

"Possibly," he agreed. "But it still doesn't make any sense. Why now, years after leaving Alexandria? And what has Ayesha Zakhari to do with it? Lovat didn't want to marry her, it was just an infatuation. And from all I could learn, she wasn't in love with him either."

"Wasn't she?" she said skeptically.

He smiled. "No. She had really loved one man. He was utterly different from Lovat, a man of her own people, older, a patriot who was fatally flawed, and who betrayed her and everything they both believed in."

"I'm sorry," she said quietly, and she meant it. She had never met Ayesha Zakhari, and she knew very little about her, but she tried to imagine the bitterness of disillusion, and the magnitude of her pain. "But surely the fact that Lovat was shot in her garden can't be coincidence?" She looked at him steadily, seeing pity and reluctance in him, and a new, raw edge of feeling about the whole tragedy. She reached across and slid her hand over his.

He turned his over, palm up, and closed his fingers gently.

"I don't suppose it can," he agreed. "But I have to find Yeats, and if he is dead, then how it happened, and why."

"Ryerson's trial begins tomorrow," she said, watching his face.

"Yes, I know. I'll try to find Yeats today." He hesitated only a moment, then, letting go of her hand, pushed his chair back and stood up.

PITT STOOD on the steps in the sun, blinking, not so much at the soft, autumn sunlight as at what the stiff, sad-faced officer had told him.

Arnold Yeats was dead. It had happened less than four years after he left Egypt. He had been posted to India, his health apparently completely recovered. He was a talented officer remarkable for his extraordinary courage. He seemed to know no fear, and his men saw him as a hero they would follow anywhere.

"Brave," the officer said, looking at Pitt with pain in his eyes. "Even reckless. Took one risk too many. Decorated posthumously. Too bad . . . we can't afford to lose men like that."

"Reckless, you said?" Pitt questioned.

The officer's face tightened and something inside him closed. "Wrong word," he said tartly, and Pitt could not draw him to say anything further. He thanked him and left.

So of the four friends in Alexandria two were dead, one on the field of battle, one murdered, one was apparently missing, and the fourth was a priest in Seven Dials who had been stunned with horror at the mention of Martin Garvie's name.

He turned on his heel and walked straight to the curb, then out into the first couple of yards of the street, his arm waving to attract the next hansom that passed.

The Old Bailey was crowded with people, pressing forward, calling out to each other, complaining and jostling for a place. With difficulty, Pitt elbowed his way towards the front and finally was stopped by a constable who placed himself squarely in his path.

"Sorry, sir. Can't go in there. If you wanted a seat you should've come sooner. First come, first in, that's the rule. Fair enough?"

Pitt drew in his breath to argue, and realized it was pointless. He had no authority to show that would allow him preference. To the constable he would seem to be just another curious spectator, come to watch the fall of a powerful man and gaze at an exotic woman accused of murder. And there were certainly enough of them. He was pressed from behind, his feet trodden on, his back bumped and poked. The constable was keeping his temper with difficulty, his face overpink and gleaming with sweat.

"I'll wait out here," Pitt said.

"In't no use, sir. There isn't going to be no room in there today." The constable shook his head, indicating the courtroom.

"I need to speak to someone who is inside," Pitt replied.

The constable looked disbelieving, but he said nothing.

Pitt went past the court where Ryerson and Ayesha Zakhari were being tried, and stood impatiently in the hallway outside the next one along.

It was an hour before anyone emerged, and he had begun to wonder if he was wasting his time. Perhaps Narraway was not in there anyway. Yet the compulsion remained to wait until the adjournment and watch every person who emerged. Finally the doors opened and a small, thin man with brown hair came out. He looked left and right, then took a step forward. Pitt approached him. "Excuse me. You were in the Ryerson trial." It was more a statement than a question, but the words were out before he considered them.

"Yes," the man agreed. "But it's packed in there. You won't get in."

"What has happened so far?"

The man shrugged. "Only what you'd expect, a lot of police saying what they found. She did it, of course; the only mystery is how she thought she'd get away with it."

Pitt glanced around him at the people still waiting hopefully, as if there was yet some chance of drama in which they could share.

"It could bring the government down in time," the man said, as if in answer to the question Pitt had only thought. "Narrow majority—important minister mixed up with a woman like that. Trouble up Manchester way." He pulled his mouth into a slight sneer. "I thought it would have been more interesting. Defense lawyer's got nothing. I might come back tomorrow." And without waiting he pushed past and disappeared into the crowd.

Pitt moved closer to the door so he would have a better chance to see Narraway, if indeed he was inside.

As it was, he very nearly missed him and only caught up as Narraway moved across the hall towards the steps to leave. He looked at Pitt with momentary irritation, thinking he had been bumped into by a stranger, then he recognized him and his face sharpened with attention. "Well?" he demanded.

"What happened in there?" Pitt countered.

Narraway stopped and faced Pitt, his eyes wide. "You came here to ask me that?"

There was a dangerous edge to his voice, and Pitt saw the lines of strain etched deep into his face. He was holding control of himself with an effort. They had failed to help Ryerson, and again Pitt was reminded sharply that for some reason deeper than anything he understood, it mattered intensely to Narraway. Was it simply failure that hurt him, or was there a personal wound to do with events, feelings in the past of which Pitt was ignorant?

Narraway was waiting.

"I came to tell you that Arnold Yeats is dead," Pitt replied. "He was the fourth soldier of the group of Lovat's friends. Lovat was murdered, Garrick is missing, and Sandeman has become an obscure priest in the back alleys of Seven Dials."

Narraway stood quite stiff. "Indeed? And how do you know this?"

"I asked the War Office!" It was the obvious answer. Then he realized that Narraway was referring not to Yeats but to Garrick and Sandeman.

"Keep your wife out of it, Pitt," Narraway said in a low, careful voice, his face pinched. He ignored the flash of responding anger in Pitt's eyes. "She is the only one who has connected Lovat, Garrick, and Sandeman, so far as I know. And I still have no idea what we are dealing with." He reached out and took Pitt by the elbow, his fingers gripping hard, pulling him out of the melee towards a doorway to the side.

"It's going badly?" Pitt said. It was barely a question.

Narraway leaned against the door arch, but his body was rigid; there was no grace in it. He looked too tense to remain in any position long. "They are not here to see proof of guilt or innocence," he replied bitterly. "They take the guilt for granted, and I think the jury probably does as well. It is about whether the government can survive the scandal. It is the same instinct which makes people go stag hunting, or shooting wild animals—the spectacle of seeing something with more grace and power than themselves dragged down. They haven't the ability to create, only to destroy, and that is more intoxicating than nothing at all."

Pitt looked at the anger and helplessness in Narraway's face, and again was almost submerged in his emotion. "Are you saying it is political by accident or by design?" he asked.

Anger filled Narraway's eyes, then disappeared. "I don't know!" he said with a note of desperation.

"I don't believe Ayesha Zakhari is guilty of the stupid murder of a man she no longer knew or cared about," Pitt said miserably.

"And if her intention was to bring Ryerson down, in whatever way she could?" Narraway asked, his black eyes hard and angry.

"She came as an idealist, believing she could improve her country's economic independence," Pitt said with complete conviction. "That is not so unrealistic."

"I am as familiar with Egyptian economic history as you are!" Narraway snapped. "And it was the expansion under Said Pasha, then Khedive Ismail, and the return of American cotton after their civil war, which crippled them and forced Ismail to abdicate in '79 and opened the way for us to take the control we now have. If Ayesha Zakhari is as well-educated as you say, surely she must have known that even better than we do."

Pitt had no answer. They were caught in a morass of facts which made no coherent story, except one of impulse and stupidity, and that was not what he wanted to believe.

"You had better follow it," Narraway said quietly, already half turning away, almost as if he did not wish Pitt to see any hope in his face. "Be in my office at seven in the morning," he ordered. "Day after tomorrow." And he walked away, leaving Pitt alone.

Pitt learned all he could about Arnold Yeats, but it added nothing to his understanding of Lovat's death, or anything that had happened to him in Egypt, and there was no connection that he could see with Ayesha Zakhari. Nor was there anything in Morgan Sandeman's military record or his decision to leave the army and enter the priesthood which seemed to have any relevance. The only fact Pitt remarked with any interest was that the friendship which had been close in Alexandria appeared to have disappeared altogether after their return to Britain. But then, had they written to each other, he would not have known.

THE DAY THAT PITT left early to keep his appointment with Narraway, Charlotte also went out, but in the opposite direction. She did not tell Gracie where she was going, because she did not want to place her in the position of having to tell Pitt something less than the truth, should he return before she did.

She caught the omnibus to Oxford Street, and from there walked south as far as Dudley Street. She hesitated a moment, trying to remember exactly which way Sandeman had taken her. It was towards the circle of Seven Dials itself, but not all the way. She started off along Great White Lion Street, and turned left up the alley. It looked different in the morning light, somehow paler and bleaker, as if it were under a layer of dust.

It all seemed smaller.

How many steps had they taken? She had no idea. Anything she thought now seemed too far.

A man bent over with a misshapen body was moving towards her. There was no malice in his face, but something in his lurching gait frightened her. She made an instant decision and started away from him, towards the nearest doorway.

It proved to be a shop of some indeterminate sort. Piles of clothes lay on the floor, smelling stale and moldy. Several boxes perched awkwardly on each other.

"I'm sorry!" she said hastily and backed out, swinging around and almost bumping into a fat woman with a white face and eyebrows so sparse as to lend her expression a bald, surprised air. "I'm sorry," Charlotte repeated, and pushed past her and outside.

Now she had lost her bearings altogether. She turned all the way around, slowly, and tried another door. She was shivering, although it was not cold. Her hand was raised to knock, then she changed her mind and decided simply to open it. She realized the woman was watching her, standing so close now that if Charlotte were to step back she would bump her. She felt cut off.

She put her weight against the door and it swung open. Relief washed over her as she saw the vestibule and the long hallway beyond. Please heaven, Sandeman was there. If she was caught alone with the woman behind her, there was now no escape. That was ridiculous. The woman was probably coming for help, just as she was herself.

She went so rapidly across the stone floor to the next door she was almost running. She had closed the second door and was starting towards the big fireplace when Sandeman came out of the scullery, his face curious and welcoming, until he recognized her.

"Mrs. Pitt." He dried his hands on the rough cloth he was carrying. His skin looked red, as if the soap had burned him. "What can I do for you?" His voice had denial in it, and his face was already closed.

She had expected it, and tried to forewarn herself; even so, something inside her sank. She had intended to smile, but it died before it reached her lips. "Good morning, Mr. Sandeman," she replied quietly. "I have come back to you because circumstances have changed since we spoke before." She stopped. She knew he did not believe her. For Tilda's sake she was prepared to tell him more of the truth now, even to add a force to it she would not have before.

"Mine have not," he replied, meeting her eyes without flinching. She was struck again by the inner strength of him, as if within his mind there were an island of absolute knowledge untouched by the comings and goings of chance or other people's passions. "I am sorry," he added, to soften his refusal.

She continued only because it would be absurd to have come this far and then leave again without trying harder than this. "I did not expect you to have changed, Mr. Sandeman. But since I last saw you my husband has returned from Alexandria, and told me . . ." She stopped. The color had drained from his skin. When she glanced down at his hands, they were clenched so tightly on the rag he was holding that the folded edge of it threatened to leave marks on his flesh.

She seized the chance. "And told me a great many things he learned while he was there regarding Mr. Lovat's service in Egypt, and other things . . ." She did not wish to be specific, in case it allowed him to realize how very little she really knew. "Mr. Sandeman, I fear Martin Garvie's life is in danger. I had a very senior gentleman from Special Branch warn me that I was concerning myself with affairs of great danger and I should leave them be, but I cannot do that when I might have the key to saving someone. I fear they will allow Martin Garvie to be killed because he is of no importance to them."

Sandeman's eyes were enormous, as if staring at something that transfixed him. "Special Branch?" His lips seemed dry. "What have they to do with Martin Garvie?"

"You must be aware that Edwin Lovat has been murdered. It is in all the newspapers," she replied. "And that an Egyptian woman is on trial at the Old Bailey. Even here in Seven Dials the running patterers will be talking about it. It's a big scandal, because a major politician is involved. It could even bring the government down."

"Yes," Sandeman agreed quietly. "Of course I heard people talking about it. But it is another world from here. It's a story to us. Nothing more." He said it as if he were trying to believe it himself, pushing it away so it was not his responsibility.

Charlotte felt her brief advantage slipping out of her hands, and she did not know how to get it back. A tiny flutter of panic stirred inside her. She must try something or he would refuse her again and then it would be too late. She remembered what Pitt had said about the fourth friend. "Mr. Yeats is dead too, you know," she said abruptly.

He looked as if she had struck him. He opened his mouth and drew in his breath with difficulty. She knew she had told him something he had not known, and that it wounded him deeply. There would be time for her to be guilty about it later; now she must drag out of him whatever it was that Martin Garvie had confided in him. She was about to speak, and something in his face warned her to stop.

"How . . . how did he die?" he asked awkwardly. He was seeking information from her now, and he was aware of the irony of it.

"In battle," she replied. "In India somewhere. Apparently he was very brave . . . even reckless." She stopped, seeing the last trace of color bleach from his skin.

"Battle?" He clung to the word as if it was some kind of desperate hope. "You mean military action?"

"Yes."

He looked away.

"Please, Mr. Sandeman!" she said urgently. "My husband is clever and determined. I expect he will find out what it is you know, but it may be too late to help Martin Garvie—or Mr. Garrick, if they are together." She was not sure if that was wise, or if she had gone too far and betrayed her ignorance. She saw the indecision fighting in his face, and her heart knocked inside her in the tension as she waited.

His eyes flickered and he looked away from her, down at his hands. "I don't think there is much you can do to help," he said flatly, and there was terrible pain in his voice. "Even if I told you all that Martin said to me, I believe we are all too late."

The coldness in the room ate into her and she found she was shivering, her body tight. "You think that Martin has been murdered as well? Who next? You?" she challenged. "Are you just going to sit here and wait for whoever it is to come after you too?" Her voice was shaking with anger, and fear, and a sense that she was fighting alone, in spite of the fact that she was so close to him she could smell the carbolic in the soap he had used, even though his hands were dry. She jerked her arm out in an aimless sweep. "Don't you care enough about these people to want to save yourself? Who is going to look after them if you don't?"

He looked up at her. She had touched a nerve.

"It's your job!" she said wildly. It was not fair, and not really true. She knew nothing about him and had no business to make such a statement. If he had been angry with her she would not have blamed him.

"Martin had heard of me," he said very quietly, but as if deep in thought, not faltering as though he might stop. "I have befriended many soldiers who have fallen on hard times, drink too much because they have thoughts and memories they can't live with and can't forget. Or because they don't know how to fit back into the lives they had before they went to war." He drew in a long breath. "It may be only a few years for the people at home, whose lives are much the same every day, little dreams. For them the world stays the same."

She did not interrupt. It was irrelevant so far, but he was feeling his way toward something.

"It isn't like that in the army. It can be just a little while, but it is a lifetime," he continued.

Was he speaking about Egypt, about himself, and Stephen Garrick, and Lovat? Of all the lost and hopeless men he ministered to here in the alleys of Seven Dials?

"Martin tried to help Garrick." Sandeman stared at the floor, not meeting his eyes. "But he didn't know how to. Garrick's nightmares were getting worse, and more frequent. He drank to try and dull himself into insensibility, but it worked less and less all the time. He began to take opium as well. His health was deteriorating and he was losing control of himself." Sandeman's voice was sinking. She had to lean towards him to catch the words.

"He couldn't trust anyone," he went on. "Except Martin, because he was desperate. Martin thought perhaps I could help, if Garrick would come to me . . . or even if I went to him."

"Why didn't you go?" she asked, hearing the edge to her voice she had not meant to allow through.

He was too deep in his own thoughts to be stung.

"Just because he lives in Torrington Square instead of a doorway in Seven Dials doesn't mean he needs your help any less!" she accused him. "He was obviously in his own kind of hell."

He looked up at her, his eyes hollow. "Of course he was!" he grated. "But I can't help him. He doesn't want to hear the only thing I know how to say."

She did not understand. "If you can't help nightmares, then who can? Isn't that what you do for these men here? Why not for Stephen Garrick?"

He said nothing.

"What were his nightmares?" she prodded, knowing she was hurting him, but she could not stop now. "Did Martin tell you? Why couldn't you help him face them?"

"You say that as if it were easy." Anger lay just under the surface of his voice and in the stiff lines of his body. "You have no idea what you are talking about."

"Then tell me! From what you are saying, he is sinking into madness. What kind of a priest are you that you won't hold out a hand to him yourself, and you won't help me to?"

This time he looked up at her with rage and impotence naked in his face.

"What help have you for madness, Mrs. Pitt? Can you stop the dreams that come in the night, of blood and fire, of screaming that tears your mind to pieces and leaves the shards to cut you, even when you are awake?" His whole body was trembling. "What can you do about heat that scorches your skin, but when you open your eyes you're covered in sweat, and freezing? It is inside you, Mrs. Pitt! No one can help! Martin Garvie tried to, and it has sucked him into it. When he came to me, his fear was for Garrick, but it should have been for himself as well. Madness consumes not only those afflicted, but those who touch it as well."

"Are you saying Stephen Garrick is insane?" she demanded. "Why aren't his family treating him? Are they too ashamed of it to admit that is what is wrong with him?" It was beginning to make sense at last. Many people denied illness of the mind, as if it were a sin rather than a disease. Had it been cholera, or smallpox, no one would have hidden it. "Have they taken him to an institution?" She did not mean to have raised her voice, but it was out of control. "Is that it? But why Martin as well? Why couldn't he at least have written to his sister and told her where he was?"

His face was filled with pity so deep it seemed the pain of it wounded him as if he would carry it long after he had finished trying to make her understand it. "From Bedlam?" he said simply.

The word struck a shiver through her flesh. Everyone knew of the hospital for the insane that was like a house of hell. The name of it was an obscenity, an abbreviation of Bethlehem, the most holy town, the asylum of dreams, and this was the prison of nightmares where people were incarcerated in the torture of their own minds, screaming at the unseen.

She struggled for a moment to find her voice. "You let that happen to him?" she whispered. It was not intended as an accusation, at least not entirely. She had admired Sandeman; she had seen a compassion in him too deep to believe indifference in him now, for any reason. What she had seen was real, she had felt it in the dignity with which he had regarded the drunken man the day she had found him.

He looked at her with hurt for her judgment of him, and defiance. "How could I have prevented it? We each have to find our own salvation, Mrs. Pitt. I told Garrick what to do years ago, but I can't make him do it."

She was about to correct him, say that it was Martin Garvie she was thinking of, then she realized what he implied. "Are you saying that Stephen Garrick's madness is his own fault?" she asked incredulously.

"No . . ." He looked away, and for the first time she knew he was lying.

"Mr. Sandeman!" Then she was uncertain what she could add that would help.

He raised his head to meet her eyes. "Mrs. Pitt, I have told you more than I want to, just in case you can help Martin Garvie, who is a good man seeking to help someone in far deeper pain than he can understand—and he may suffer for it . . . terribly." There was a plea in his voice. "If you have the power to reach anyone who can get him freed, before it is too late . . . if . . . if that is where he is."

"I will!" she said with more passion than belief. "At least now I know something, somewhere to begin. Thank you, Mr. Sandeman." She hesitated. "I . . . I don't suppose you know anything about Mr. Lovat's death, do you?"

The ghost of a smile crossed his face. "No. If you ask me to guess, I should think it is exactly what it looks like—the Egyptian woman killed him, for whatever reason of her own. Perhaps it goes back to something between them in Alexandria. I thought at the time that he did her no injury, but perhaps I was mistaken."

"I see. Thank you."

This time he did not offer to walk with her as far as the street, and she left alone, determined to find Pitt as soon as possible and tell him where Martin Garvie was, and persuade him to get him freed, whatever it required to do it.

All afternoon she began and half finished tasks in the house, stopping every time she heard a footfall, hoping it was Pitt returning, so she could tell him.

When he finally did come home, as usual he walked in his stocking feet down the passage to the kitchen, so she did not hear him until he spoke. She was so startled she dropped the potato she had in her hand, and spun around to face him still holding the peeling knife.

"I know what happened to Martin Garvie," she said. "At least I think I do . . . and to Stephen Garrick. Thomas, we have to do something about it. Immediately!"

His expression darkened. "How do you know? Where have you been? Did you go back to Sandeman?"

She lifted her chin a little. If they were going to have a disagreement about it, or worse, it would have to wait. "Of course I did. He is the only one who knows anything about it."

"Charlotte—" he began.

"He's in Bedlam!" she interrupted.

It had the effect she had intended. His eyes widened and some of the color drained from his face. "Are you certain?" he said quietly.

"No," she admitted. "But it fits all the facts that we have. Stephen Garrick suffered terrible nightmares, far worse than ordinary people's, and they went on even when he was waking, delusions of blood and fire and screaming. He had uncontrollable fits of temper and weeping." Her words fell over each other. "He drank too much to try to rid himself of whatever it is that tormented him, and he took opium. Martin Garvie knew all about it, because he was the only one who could help him. But he was losing control of the situation, and he went to Sandeman to ask his advice, but there was nothing Sandeman could do either. And it was shortly after that that Stephen Garrick, and Martin, left Torrington Square early in the morning, without proper luggage, yet did not leave London in any way that we can trace. And the carriage returned to Torrington Square within a few hours, so either they traveled on by public means or they did not go far."

He stood still, turning over in his mind what she had said. She saw the gravity in his face. If he was going to criticize her for going back to Seven Dials, it was going to be long after this was dealt with.

"Can we get him out?" she said quietly. "Martin, at least, doesn't belong there. I know he may have gone originally to help Garrick, but he wouldn't have done it willingly without letting Tilda know. That proves there is something badly wrong."

"Yes, it does," he agreed, but she could see he was still deep in thought. "But we must be careful. Someone had the authority to place Garrick there. That can only have been his father."

"For Stephen Garrick, yes, but he had no right to put Martin there!" she protested. "At least not morally. I suppose he's a servant, so legally—"

"Yes . . . I know that," he interrupted. "But we must be careful."

"Get Mr. Narraway to do it!" she said urgently. "At least to be there. You need Stephen Garrick because he was in Alexandria with Lovat, and now that Yeats is dead as well . . ." She trailed off. A hideous thought was filling her mind and she could see it in his eyes also. "Do you think that's why his father put him there?" she whispered. "To protect him? Is someone from Egypt after them all? Are his nightmares actually terror?"

"I don't know," he replied. "But it is possible . . ."

She heard the unhappiness in his voice. "You don't want it to be her—do you?" she said gently.

"No . . . no, I don't. But it looks more and more like it. I heard what happened in court today." His face filled with distaste. "I don't know if it is what Ryerson wants, but his defense is doing everything they can to blacken Lovat's name. I suppose it is to cause reasonable doubt that there could be many others who wanted to kill him. I can't see it doing much good. Ayesha Zakhari was at Eden Lodge. Surely anyone else who killed Lovat out of passion would hardly follow him around at three in the morning into someone else's garden."

She realized as he said it that he was admitting a kind of defeat. He had not wanted Ryerson or Ayesha to be guilty. He had performed every contortion of reason to argue another solution, and had at last run out of the power to delude himself any further.

"I'm sorry," she said gently, putting out her hand to touch him. "But let us at least save Martin Garvie?"

"Yes . . . yes, of course. I'll go and find Narraway now. Thank you for that." He smiled bleakly, taking her hand and holding it with exquisite gentleness. "I'll deal with the issue of your going back to Seven Dials later." And he kissed her very softly before he turned to leave.

CHAPTER ELEVEN

PITT LEFT KEPPEL STREET with his mind whirling. Bedlam! If Ferdinand Garrick had committed his son to an asylum whose very name was a byword for horror, then he must have had a powerful reason to do so. Was Stephen Garrick insane? There had been no mention of any kind of mental weakness in his military record; in fact, it had been excellent. He had shown courage and initiative, physical prowess and mental agility. He was perhaps the most promising of the four.

Pitt strode down towards the Tottenham Court Road and hailed a cab, climbing in and shouting Narraway's address.

If Garrick was indeed mad now, what had driven him to it? Was it overuse of opium? Why had he taken to drinking excessively and smoking a substance that distorted the emotions and perceptions?

Or had he seen something in Egypt which had driven Yeats to the recklessness which had ended in his death, Sandeman into a kind of exile in Seven Dials, and Lovat to be the victim of murder? Had Ferdinand Garrick consigned his only son to Bedlam to protect his life?

From whom? Ayesha Zakhari? In God's name—why?

That thought was still repellent to him, but he could no longer ignore it. The evidence had to be faced.

He reached the street where Narraway lived, alighted, paid the driver, and strode across the wet footpath in the mist. There was no echo to his footsteps; everything was muffled. On the step of Narraway's house he pulled the lion-headed doorbell.

It was answered by a discreet, gray-haired manservant who recognized him immediately.

"Good evening, Mr. Pitt," he said, stepping back to allow him in. He had no need to question what Pitt was there for, or if it were urgent. He saw the answer to both in Pitt's face before he preceded him across the hall and knocked briefly on the door of the study before opening it.

"Mr. Pitt, to see you, sir," he announced.

Narraway was sitting in an armchair with his stocking feet on a stool, and a plate of sandwiches on a small table at his elbow. A cut-glass goblet of red wine sat next to the plate.

"This had better be worth it," he said with his mouth full.

The manservant retreated and closed the door behind him.

Pitt sat down in the other chair, after pulling it around a couple of feet to face Narraway.

Narraway sighed. "Pour yourself some claret." He gestured towards the bottle on the sideboard. "Glasses in the cupboard."

Pitt stood up again and obeyed, watching the dark liquid reflecting facets of silvery light as it filled the bowl. "Charlotte found Martin Garvie and Stephen Garrick," he announced.

Narraway gasped and then coughed as his sandwich went down the wrong way. He jerked forward in his chair and reached for his wine.

Pitt smiled to himself. It was exactly what he had intended.

Narraway swallowed hard, cleared his throat and sat back. "Indeed?" he said, not quite as gratingly as he would have done had he not choked. "It seems you do not have your wife under control after all. Are you going to tell me where he is, or do I have to guess?"

Pitt turned around with the claret and came back to sit down before replying.

"Actually she went to see Sandeman again." He made no comment on her lack of obedience to instructions. He crossed his legs comfortably and sipped. The claret was extraordinarily good, but he would have expected no less from Narraway. "She persuaded him to tell her the truth, or at least some of it. Garvie confided in Sandeman that Garrick was in a very bad way indeed with nightmares and delirium. Sandeman is almost certain that both he and Garvie have been taken to Bedlam." He ignored the horror in Narraway's face and continued. "Garvie perhaps unwillingly, since he apparently has had no opportunity to tell his family. It fits with all the facts we know. The question is, do Garrick's nightmares stem from his use of opium, some madness inherent in or, far more seriously, from something that happened during his service in Egypt? And—"

"All right, Pitt!" Narraway said abruptly. "You don't need to spell it out for me!" He rose to his feet in a single, smooth movement, the last of his sandwich still in his hand. "Yeats is dead, Lovat murdered, Sandeman has lost himself in Seven Dials, and now it seems Garrick is in a lunatic asylum with nightmares that have driven him mad." He picked up his glass and drained the claret. "We had better go and fetch him. See if we can get any sense out of him." He looked meaningfully at the glass in Pitt's hand.

Pitt was not going to leave a claret of that quality behind. It was a pity not to savor it, but there was no time. He drank it quickly and put the glass on Narraway's table.

Narraway ate the rest of his sandwich as they reached the door and he took his coat from the stand.

Outside, he walked briskly to the end of the street and hailed a hansom, Pitt only a stride behind him. He gave the driver a one-word command: "Bedlam!"

The hansom lurched forward and Pitt was thrown against the back of his seat. He said nothing; he would find the answers to all his questions as to how they would accomplish their task when they reached Bedlam.

It was quite a long journey, and it was not until they were rattling over Westminster Bridge, the lamps along the Embankment reflecting patchily through the mist onto the river, that Narraway at last spoke.

"Agree with anything I say, and be prepared to move quickly if necessary," he commanded. "Stay close by me; on no account allow us to be separated. Do not act arbitrarily, no matter what happens. And do not allow your emotions to distract you, however humane or commendable."

"I have been to Bedlam before," Pitt said dryly, refusing to permit the memory of it into his imagination.

Narraway glanced at him as they reached the end of the bridge and started climbing the rise on the other side, past the railway line running into Waterloo Station. At Christ's Church, they swung right into Kennington Road, where the huge mass of the Bethlehem Lunatic Hospital loomed against the night sky.

The hansom stopped, and Narraway gave the driver a sovereign and told him to wait. "There'll be four more for you if you are here when I need you," he said grimly. "And your licence canceled if you are not. Wait as long as you need to. I may be a short time, or I may be hours. If I have not come out by midnight, take this card and go to the nearest police station and fetch half a dozen uniformed constables." He passed a card over to the man, who was sitting wide-eyed and by now seriously alarmed.

Narraway strode over the path and up the steps to the front entrance of the hospital, Pitt half a pace behind him. They were met immediately by an attendant who barred the way firmly and politely. Narraway informed him that he was on a government matter to do with the security of the nation, and he had a royal warrant to pursue his business wherever it took him. One of the inmates had information urgently needed, and he must speak with him without any delay whatsoever.

Pitt's stomach sank as he realized just what a risk they were taking. He had accepted without question that Charlotte was right, and Garrick was here. If she was mistaken and he was in some other asylum, Spitalfields, or even a private institution, then Narraway was not going to forgive him for it. He was startled when he realized just how completely Narraway had trusted him, even more when he remembered that it was actually Charlotte's word he was taking.

"Yes, sir. And who would that be?" the man asked.

"He came here in the early morning in the second week of September," Narraway replied. "A young man who brought a servant with him. He could be suffering delirium, nightmares and the effects of opium. You cannot have had more than one like him that week."

"You don't know his name, sir?" The man scowled.

"Of course I know his name!" Narraway snapped. "I do not know by what name he was admitted here. Don't pretend to be a fool. I have already informed you that I am on Her Majesty's business of state. Do I need to spell out more for you?"

"No, no, sir, I . . ." The man did not know how to finish the sentence. He swiveled around and scuttled off across the hallway and then turned right, along the first wide corridor, Narraway on his heels.

Pitt's mouth was dry and he was gulping air as he followed them through empty passages with blind walls and locked doors on either side. He heard muffled moaning, laughter rising higher and higher and ending in a shriek. He wanted to drive it from his head, but he could not.

Finally they arrived at the end of the wing and the attendant hesitated, fishing for the keys on his belt, glancing nervously at Narraway.

Narraway gave him an icy stare, and the man fumbled, poking the key blindly, stabbing at the hole until Pitt could sense Narraway on the edge of snatching it from him.

The key slid in and turned the lock at last. Pitt half expected to hear screaming and braced himself for the attempted escape of a lunatic. Instead the door swung wide open to show two straw mattresses on the floor, one occupied by a figure crouched over, head half buried in a gray blanket, hair wild, and what they could see of his face unshaven.

On the other mattress a man sat up slowly and blinked at them, his eyes full of fear and a kind of despair, as if he no longer even hoped for anything except more pain. But there was still reason in him, at least at the moment.

"What is your name?" Narraway said, immediately stepping half in front of the attendant and preventing him from moving forward. He was addressing the sitting man. His voice was firm, but there was no harshness in it, only a tone that demanded answer.

"Martin Garvie," the man replied huskily. His eyes pleaded for belief, and the fear in him cut Pitt like a knife.

Narraway took a long, slow breath. When he spoke again his voice shook a little in spite of the masklike control in his face. "And I presume that is your master, Stephen Garrick?" He gestured towards the wretched creature still huddled on the other mattress.

Garvie nodded warily. "Please don't hurt him," he begged. "He doesn't mean any harm, sir. He can't help his manner. He's ill. Please . . ."

"I have no intention of harming him," Narraway said, then gulped as if he could barely catch his breath. "I've come to take you somewhere better than this . . . safer."

"You can't do that, sir!" the attendant protested. "It's more than my job's worth to let you—"

Narraway swung around on him, his eyes blazing. "It's more than your neck is worth to stand in my way!" he threatened. "I can wait for the police, if you insist, but I can promise you that you will regret it if you force me to go that way. Don't stand there like an idiot or they'll lock you up in here too!"

Perhaps it was the last suggestion, but the man dissolved in terror. "No, sir! I swear, I'm an honest citizen! I—"

"Good," Narraway cut him off. He turned to Pitt. "Lift that fellow up and assist him out." He indicated Garrick, who had not moved, as if the entire intrusion had barely penetrated his consciousness.

Pitt remembered the stricture to obey absolutely, and walked over to the recumbent man. "Let me help you to your feet, sir," he said gently, trying to sound like a servant, a familiar and unthreatening figure. "You need to stand up," he encouraged, sliding his hands under the man's shoulders and easing up what was almost deadweight. "Come on, sir," he repeated, straining his back to lift.

The man moaned as if in intense pain, and Pitt stopped abruptly.

The next moment Garvie was beside him, bending over. "He's here to help you, sir!" he said urgently. "He's taking us to a better place. Come on, now! You've got to help! We're going to be safe."

Garrick gave a choking cry, and then his body arched and he flung his arms up, covering his face as if to defend himself. Pitt was caught by surprise and lost his balance, lurching backwards into Garvie. He could feel Narraway's impatience smoldering in the air.

"Come on, Mr. Stephen!" Garvie said sharply. "We've got to get out of here. Quickly, sir!"

That seemed to have the desired effect. Whimpering with fear, Garrick rose unsteadily to his feet, lurching one way, then the other, but with Garvie and Pitt supporting him, he stumbled through the door, past Narraway and the attendant, and started off down the passage.

Pitt looked backwards once, to make sure Narraway was following them, and saw him write something on a card and give it to the attendant, then a moment later he heard his rapid footsteps behind him.

Half carrying, half dragging Garrick, who gave them only minimal assistance, Pitt and Garvie made their way back towards the entrance. More than once Pitt hesitated, uncertain whether the turn was left or right, and heard Narraway's voice directing him with a peremptory hiss. Pitt's ears were straining for every sound, and once when he heard a door close he whirled around and almost sent Garrick flying.

Narraway snarled at him, and increased his pace. Pitt grasped Garrick again, and they turned the last corner into the entrance hall. He saw two attendants standing there, and would have stopped instantly, but Garrick was oblivious to them and kept shambling on, and Garvie had no choice but to go with him or let him fall.

Pitt recovered his step and caught up with them.

The attendants jerked to attention. "Ey! Where you goin', then?" one of them called out.

"Go on!" Narraway growled behind Pitt, then turned to face the men.

Pitt grasped Garrick more firmly and, holding him hard, half pushed him at a greater pace out of the door, down the steps, and smartly right towards the waiting hansom. Please heaven Narraway managed to extricate himself from the men and get away too, because Pitt had no idea where he was to take them.

They reached the cab and Garrick stopped abruptly, his body shaking, his hands out in front of him as if to ward off an attack. Garvie put his arms around him gently, but with considerable strength, and with Pitt's assistance, they lifted him into the hansom. The driver sat facing forward, ignoring everything as though his life depended on seeing and hearing nothing.

Pitt swiveled around to see if Narraway was coming yet.

Inside the cab, Garrick began to thrash around, wailing and sobbing with terror.

Pitt swung up beside him to try to keep him from escaping, or in his delirium injuring Garvie. "It's all right, sir!" he said urgently. "You're quite safe. No one's going to harm you." He might as well have been speaking in a foreign language.

Garvie was losing control. He was white-faced in the gaslight, and there was panic and helplessness in his eyes. If Narraway did not come soon they were going to have to leave without him.

The seconds ticked by.

"Go around the hospital and back!" Pitt shouted at the driver. "Now!"

The hansom lurched forward, throwing all three of them against the back of the seat. For a few moments Garrick was too surprised to react. Please God, Narraway would be there when they reached the front again. Pitt's mind raced as to where on earth he could take Garrick if he were not? The only place he was certain of any kind of help at all, and secrecy, was his own home. And what could he and Charlotte do with a madman in delirium? For that matter, how much better was Garvie?

Narraway had spoken of the local police station, but Pitt believed that was almost certainly a bluff. And either way, Pitt had no authority he could prove to them. The very most they might do would be return them all to Bedlam and extricate Narraway, which would put them in an even worse position than that in which they had begun, because now the authorities in Bedlam would be warned.

He would have to go home, and leave Narraway to his own devices.

They were at the front of the hospital again. The footpath was deserted. Pitt's heart sank, and he could feel his stomach tighten and his whole body go cold.

"Keppel Street!" he shouted at the driver. "Slowly! Don't hurry." He felt the lurch and swing as they turned onto Brook Street, then almost immediately afterwards into Kennington Road, and back down towards the Westminster Bridge.

It was a nightmare journey. The mist had thickened and a slower speed was forced upon them. They held up no one by slackening to a walk. Stephen Garrick slumped forward, alternately weeping and groaning like a man on the way to his own death—and whatever hell he believed lay beyond. Garvie attempted now and then to comfort him, but it was a wasted effort, and the despair in his voice betrayed that he knew it.

Pitt tried desperately to think what on earth he would do if Narraway did not show up soon, and ever worse images crowded his mind as to what had happened to him. Had he been arrested for abducting an inmate? Or simply imprisoned in Bedlam as if he too were mad? Had they locked him in one of their padded rooms? Or administered some powerful sedative so he might not even be conscious to protest his sanity?

They were over the river and heading north and east. Part of Pitt wished they would hurry, so he would be home in the warmth and light of familiar surroundings, and at least Charlotte could help him. Another part wanted to spin out the journey as long as possible, to give Narraway a chance to catch up with them and take charge.

They were in a busy thoroughfare. There was plenty of other traffic, sounds of horns in the swirling mist, harness clinking, light from other coach lamps, movement reflected in bright gleams off brass.

Garrick sat up suddenly and screamed as if in terror for his life. Pitt's flesh froze. In a moment he was paralyzed, then he lunged sideways and grasped Garrick's arm and threw him back in the seat. The hansom swayed wildly and slithered around on the wet cobbles, then shot forward at increased speed. Pitt could hear the cabbie shouting as they careered along the street, but within twenty yards the ride was steadier, and within a hundred they were back to a normal trot.

Pitt tried to control his racing heart and keep hold of Garrick, who was now gibbering nonsensically, in spite of everything Garvie could say or do.

Then they pulled up and the cabbie told them loudly and with a voice trembling with fear that they were at Keppel Street and should get out immediately.

There was no alternative but to obey. With difficulty, and stiff from having sat for so long with locked muscles, Pitt alighted. He almost fell onto the pavement, and then reached to help Garrick.

Garrick stumbled after him, collapsed onto the stones, then, without any warning at all, managed to get up onto his feet and started to run, a loose, shambling gait, but covering the wet pavement with startling speed.

Garvie stared at him in silent, beaten desperation.

Pitt lurched after him, but Garrick was at the end of the block and starting across the roadway before he floundered for a moment, arms flailing, and for no reason Pitt could see, fell face forward onto the cobbles.

Pitt flung himself on top of him. Garrick whimpered like a wounded animal, but he had no strength or will to fight. Pitt hauled him up, more than a little roughly, and straightened himself, only to see a man a couple of yards away from him. He was about to try some desperate explanation when with drenching relief he recognized the neat, slender silhouette against the light—it was Narraway. For an instant Pitt was too choked with emotion to speak. He stood still, gulping air, his body shaking, his hands clinging onto Garrick—clammy with sweat.

"Good," Narraway said succinctly. "Since we are in Keppel Street, perhaps it would be more convenient to go inside and talk. I daresay Mrs. Pitt would make us a cup of tea? Garvie, at least, looks as if he could do with it."

Pitt did not even attempt to reply, but followed Narraway's elegant figure back along the footpath to the door, where Garvie was waiting for them, and led the way inside.

Charlotte and Gracie were stunned with surprise for the first moment, then pity replaced horror.

"Yer starvin' cold!" Gracie said furiously. "Wotever 'appened to yer?" She looked from Garrick to Martin Garvie, and back again. "I got blankets in the airin' cupboard. You sit there!" And whisking around, she disappeared out of the door.

Pitt eased Garrick onto one of the chairs and Martin found another for himself, sitting down hard, as if his legs had given way.

Charlotte pushed the kettle onto the hob to come to the boil, ordering Pitt to stoke up the fire. They all ignored Narraway entirely.

Gracie returned with her arms full of blankets and, after only an instant's hesitation, proceeded to wrap one around Garrick's shuddering body, then she turned to Martin with the other.

"I'll tell Tilda yer all right," she said dubiously. "Leastways, yer not actual 'urt, like."

Suddenly Garvie's eyes filled with tears. He started to speak, and changed his mind.

"S' all right!" Gracie said quickly. "I'll tell 'er. She'll be that glad! It's all 'cos of 'er we found yer." She included herself because although she assumed Narraway had no idea of her part in the search, and she was happy to leave it so, she had been the one to prompt Tellman into discovering as much as he had. She regarded Narraway discreetly, and with the same wariness one does a nameless insect which might prove to be poisonous—very interesting, but best to know precisely where it is, and stay as far away as possible.

It amused him, and Charlotte, busy making the tea, saw the flicker of it in his eyes, and was pleased to realize that he had a respect for Gracie's spirit that she would not have expected of him. She also caught his eyes on her, and absurdly, found something in them that made her self-conscious. She looked quickly back to her task, and poured out six mugs of steaming tea, sugar stirred in. One was only half full. She picked it up, tested it to see that there was sufficient milk in it that it was cool enough to sip, then went over to Garrick where he sat staring vacantly into space.

Gently she lifted the mug and tilted it to reach his lips. She waited patiently until he swallowed, and then again.

After watching her for a moment, Gracie did the same for Martin, but he was far more able to help himself.

This went on for several minutes in silence before Narraway finally spoke. He could see that learning anything from Garrick could take all night, but Martin was already burning to respond.

"How did you get to the Bethlehem Lunatic Hospital, Mr. Garvie?" he said abruptly. "Who put you there?"

Martin hesitated. His face was very white and there were dark smudges of privation and sleeplessness around his eyes. "Mr. Garrick's ill, sir. I went to look after him. Couldn't leave him on his own, sir."

Narraway's face did not change at all. "And why did you not have the kindness to tell your sister where you were going? She has been desperate with fear for you."

Martin gasped, a sheen of sweat on his face. He half turned as if to look at Garrick, then changed his mind. He stared back at Narraway, misery in his eyes. "I didn't know where I was going when they took me," he said in little more than a whisper. "I thought it were just to the country, an' I'd be able to write her. I never guessed it were . . . Bedlam." He said the word as if it were a curse that hell itself might overhear and make real again.

Narraway sat down at last, pulling the chair around to face the table. Pitt remained standing, and silent.

"Was Mr. Garrick insane when you first went to work for him?" Narraway asked Martin.

Martin winced, perhaps at the thought that Garrick would hear them.

"No, sir," he said indignantly.

Narraway smiled patiently, and Martin blushed, but he would not argue.

"What happened to him? I need to know, possibly to save his life."

Martin did not protest, and that in itself did not go unnoticed. Charlotte saw something—doubt, caution—iron out of Narraway's face. She glared at Pitt, and recognized understanding in him also.

Martin hesitated.

Pitt stepped forward. "I'll take Mr. Garrick to where he can lie down for a while."

"Stay with him!" Narraway ordered with a hard warning in his eyes.

Pitt did not bother to reply, but with considerable effort eased Garrick to his feet and, with Gracie's assistance, guided him out of the door.

"What happened to him, Mr. Garvie?" Narraway repeated.

Martin shook his head. "I don't know, sir. He always drank quite a bit, but it got worse as time passed, like something was boiling up inside him."

"Worse in what way?"

"Terrible dreams." Martin winced. "Lot of gentlemen who drink get bad dreams, but not like his—he'd lie in his bed with his eyes wide open, screaming about blood . . . and fire . . . catching at his throat like he was choking and couldn't breathe." Martin himself was trembling. "An' I'd have to shake him and shout at him to waken him up . . . Then he'd cry like a baby . . . I never heard anything like it." He stopped, his face white, his eyes imploring Narraway to let him be silent.

Charlotte sat by, hating it, knowing it had to be.

Narraway looked at her, hesitation in his face. She stared back with refusal in her eyes. She was not going to leave.

He accepted it and turned back to Martin Garvie.

"Do you know of any event that occasioned these dreams?"

"No, sir . . ."

Narraway saw the slight uncertainty. "But you know there was something." That was a statement.

Martin's voice was almost inaudible. "I think so, sir."

"Did you know Lieutenant Lovat, who was murdered at Eden Lodge? Or Miss Zakhari?"

"I didn't know the lady, sir, but I knew Mr. Garrick knew Mr. Lovat. When news came of his murder Mr. Garrick was the worst upset I've ever seen him. I . . . I think that's when he went quite mad . . ." He was embarrassed, and ashamed of putting into words what they all knew, but to say so still seemed a disloyalty.

There was a flash of pity in Narraway's face, but he conceded again almost as soon as it was there.

"Then I think it is time we spoke to Mr. Garrick and found out exactly what it is that tortures his mind—"

"No, sir!" Martin started to his feet. "Please . . . he's . . ."

The look in Narraway's eyes stopped him.

Charlotte took Martin's arm gently. "We have to know," she said. "Someone's life depends on it. You can help us."

"Thank you, Mrs. Pitt," Narraway cut across her. "But it will be distressing, and we shall not need you to endure it."

Charlotte looked back at him without moving, a faint, polite smile on her lips. "Your consideration for my feelings does you credit." She was only barely sarcastic. "But since it was I who heard the original story, it will hold no more surprises for me than for you. I shall remain."

Surprisingly, he did not argue. Together with Martin, they went through to the parlor, where Pitt and Gracie were sitting and Stephen Garrick lay half conscious on the sofa.

It took them all night to draw from the wreck of a man the terrible story. Sometimes they would prop him up and he spoke almost coherently, whole sentences at a time. At others he lay curled over like a child in the womb—silent, shivering, withdrawn into himself and beyond even Martin's reach.

It was Charlotte who took him in her arms when he wept and cradled him while the sobs racked his body.

Pitt watched her with a fierce pride, remembering the stiff, protected young woman she had been when he first fell in love with her. Now her compassion made her more beautiful than he could have dreamed she would ever be.

It seemed that the four young men had been friends almost from their initial meeting. They had much in common, both in background and interests, and had spent most of their free time together.

The tragedy was born when they learned that a shrine beside the river, sacred to Christians, was also sacred to Muslims, men who in their view denied Christ.

One night, influenced with drink, they decided to desecrate it in such a fashion that no Muslim would ever again use it. Whipped up in a frenzy of religious indignation, they stole a pig, an animal unclean to Muslims, and slaughtered it in the very heart of the shrine, scattering its blood around to make the place obscene forever after.

At this point Garrick became so hysterical even Narraway's endless patience could draw nothing further from him which made any sense. He sat slumped forward, leaning a little against Charlotte, who was beside him on the sofa. Only his open eyes, staring vacantly at some hideous sight within his own brain, indicated that he was alive.

She could remember the screams torn from him long after she had hoped to forget them.

She smiled at Narraway very slightly. "Surely you will need to know more exactly what happened?"

His eyes widened a fraction. "Sandeman?"

"You will have to, won't you?"

"Yes. I'm sorry." That apology was real; she knew it without question.

For a moment he seemed about to say more, then changed his mind, and she bent her attention on Garrick, not to speak to him, because he was obviously not hearing anything, but simply to rest her hand on his shoulder and very tentatively touch his hair. Whatever he had done, it was tormenting him beyond his ability to bear. She had no need to judge him, and nothing she or anyone else could do would inflict on him a punishment as terrible as that he put upon himself.

Narraway turned to Pitt. It was nearly four o'clock in the morning. "There is nothing more we can do for him here. There is a house where he will be safe until we can find something permanent."

"Will he be helped?" Charlotte asked when they reached the door and she held it open for them as Martin helped them pull and drag Garrick through it, talking to him softly all the time. It was rendingly clear that Garrick did not want to leave, for all Narraway's assurances that this was not a return trip to Bedlam and Martin's promises to remain with him. It was only on the footpath as Garrick turned desperately for one last look that Pitt realized it was Charlotte he clung to, not the house, and a shadow of searing pity crossed his face for an instant, and then was controlled and vanished the moment after.

She turned back and closed the door, leaning against it, almost choked for breath. She felt as if she had betrayed Garrick by allowing him to be taken, and the fact that there was no other possible answer did not take from her the memory of the anguish in his eyes, the despair as he realized she was not going with him.

"Are you gonna go an' see the priest again later?" Gracie asked very quietly when they returned to the kitchen. "Yer gotta know what's the truth of it."

"Yes," Charlotte said with hesitation. "There's a whole lot more to it, there has to be." She rubbed her hand across her eyes, exhaustion making them gritty. "You can tell Tilda that Martin's safe."

Pitt and Narraway returned to Keppel Street by half past nine, weary and aching. They stopped only long enough for breakfast, then Charlotte took them to Seven Dials, sending them through the alley and into the courtyard. This time she had no trouble remembering which door it was, and moments later they were in front of the smoldering fire while Sandeman, white-faced, stared beyond them with misery bleak and terrible in his eyes.

Charlotte felt as if she had betrayed him too, and yet surely he must have known when he told her of Garrick's nightmares that she would have to come back to him, and when she did it would be with Pitt at least. She looked across at Pitt now, and caught the pity in his face. There was no blame in him as he met her gaze. He understood the pain inside her, and exactly why.

Tears prickled her eyes and she turned away. This was not a

time to allow her own emotions to govern anything; they had no place in this.

"I need to know what happened, Mr. Sandeman," Narraway said without any leniency in his voice. "Whatever I may feel or wish, there is no room for anything but the truth."

"I know that," Sandeman replied. "I suppose I always knew that one day it would be uncovered. You can bury the dead, but you can't bury guilt."

Narraway nodded. "We know about the sacrifice of the pig and the desecration of the sanctuary. What happened after that?" he asked.

Sandeman spoke as if the pain were still with him, physically eating into his gut. "A woman returning from caring for the sick saw the torchlight and came to see what it was. She screamed." Without being aware of it, he moved his hands as if to put them over his ears and keep out the sound. "Lovat caught hold of her. She struggled." His voice was barely audible. "She went on and on screaming. It was a terrible sound . . . thick with terror. He broke her neck. I don't think he meant to."

No one interrupted him.

"But she had been heard," he whispered. "Others came . . . all sorts of people . . . They saw the dead woman lying there . . . and Lovat . . ."

The fire was burning and yet the room seemed to freeze.

"They came at us," Sandeman went on. "I don't know what they wanted . . . but we panicked. We . . . we shot them." His voice broke. He tried to add something, but the scene inside his head suffocated everything else.

Charlotte felt as if she could not breathe.

"They weren't found," Narraway stated.

"No . . . we set fire to the building." Sandeman's voice was hoarse. "We burnt them all . . . like so much rubbish. It wasn't difficult . . . with the torches. It was taken to be an accident."

Narraway hesitated only a moment.

"How many were there?" he asked.

Sandeman shivered.

"About thirty-five," he whispered. "Nobody counted, unless it was the imam who buried them."

The room was engulfed in a hideous silence. Narraway was about as ashen as Sandeman. "Imam?" he repeated huskily.

Sandeman looked up at him. "Yes. They were given a decent Muslim burial."

"God in heaven!" Narraway let out his breath in a sigh of anguish.

Charlotte felt a needle of fear inside herself, far down in the pit of her stomach. She was not even certain yet why, but something vast and unseen was terribly wrong. It was there in Narraway's face, in the stiffness of his body in its elegant suit.

"By whom?" Narraway said, his voice shaking. "Who arranged it? Who found this imam?"

"The commanding officer," Sandeman answered. "General Garrick. The place burned like an inferno, but there must have been something left." He swallowed. His face was sheened with sweat. "Anyone looking at them would know they died of gunshots, and it couldn't have been an accident."

"Who else knows about it?" Narraway asked, his voice wavering.

"No one," Sandeman replied. "General Garrick covered it up, and the imam buried the bodies. They were all wrapped up in shrouds, and he conducted all the appropriate prayers and rites."

"And that is what drove Stephen Garrick mad?" Narraway continued. "Guilt? Or fear somebody one day would come after him for vengeance?"

"Guilt," Sandeman replied without hesitation. "In his nightmares he relived it. It was the men and women we murdered who came after him."

Narraway stared back at him, unblinking. "And you, do the dead pursue you as well?"

"No," Sandeman replied, meeting his eyes, hollow and haunted by pain, but unflinching. "I let them catch me. I admitted my guilt. I can't ever undo what I did, but I shall spend whatever is left of my life trying to give back something. And if whoever killed Lovat comes after me, they will find me here. If they kill me, then so be it. If you want to arrest me, I shan't resist you. I think I am of more use here than at the end of a rope, but I shan't argue the case."

Charlotte could feel the ache in her chest tighten so hard it almost stopped her breathing.

"God is your judge, not I," Narraway said simply. "But if I need you again, you would be wise to be here."

"I shall be," Sandeman answered.

"And repeat this to no one else," Narraway added, his voice suddenly harsher than before, a note of threat in it. "I make a very bad enemy, Mr. Sandeman. And if you whisper even a word of this story to any man alive, I shall find you, and the end of the noose would seem very attractive to you in comparison with what I will do."

Sandeman's eyes widened. "Good God! Do you think it is something I repeat willingly?"

"I've known men who tell their crimes over and over, seeking absolution for them," Narraway replied. "If you repeat this, it may cost a thousand times as many lives as you have already taken. If you feel tempted to seek some kind of release by confession, remember that."

A look of irony as deep cutting as a knife to the heart covered Sandeman's face. "I believe you," he said. "I imagine that is why you do not arrest me."

An answering flash softened in Narraway, but only for a moment. "Oh . . . and mercy also," he responded. "Or perhaps it is justice? What could anyone else do to you that will equal the honesty with which you punish yourself?" He turned and walked very slowly back across the hallway towards the outside door, and Pitt took Charlotte by the arm. She tugged away from him long enough to look at Sandeman, to smile at him and know that he had seen her and understood, then she allowed herself to be led outside as well.

None of them spoke until they reached Seven Dials itself, and turned along Little Earl Street towards Shaftesbury Avenue.

It was Charlotte who broke the silence. "Surely the murder of Lovat has to be connected with this?" she said, looking at one then the other of them.

Narraway's face was blank. "For it to be otherwise would be a coincidence to beggar belief," he answered. "But that does not take away our difficulty. In fact, it adds a dimension so appalling it would be better to allow Ryerson to hang than to—" He stopped because Pitt had grasped hold of him and swung him around so sharply Charlotte almost collided with them both.

Narraway took Pitt's hand off his arm with a strength that amazed Pitt and made him wince.

"The alternative," Narraway said between his teeth, "is to allow the truth to be brought out—and see the whole of Egypt go up in revolt. After the Orabi rising, the bombardment of Alexandria, then Khartoum and the Mahdi, the place is like tinder. One spark and it could all ignite. We would lose the Suez Canal, and with it not only trade in Egypt but in the whole eastern half of the empire. Everything would have to go 'round the tip of Africa, not only tea, spice, timber and silk imports, but all our exports as well. Everything would cost half as much again. Not to mention the military and colonial traffic."

Charlotte saw the tight fear in his face, and she turned to Pitt. It was there in him also as the enormity of it hit him, as if he had seen it before but clung to the hope that it was not real, just his own personal nightmare.

"Four drunken British soldiers massacring thirty-five peaceful Muslims in their own shrine," Narraway said, barely above a whisper. Only by watching his lips could they be certain of the words. "Can you think what that will do in Egypt, Sudan, even India, if it's known?"

"You mean Ayesha killed Lovat in revenge for her own people?" Pitt said slowly. His face betrayed how deeply the thought wounded him.

Charlotte wished she could think of anything at all to comfort him, but there was nothing. Who could blame Ayesha for it? The law would do nothing to answer the massacre, but it would hang her, without doubt . . . and probably Ryerson with her. But perhaps she did not care about that. "Has Ryerson anything to do with it?" she said aloud. "Or is he just unfortunate? He fell in love with the wrong woman at the wrong time . . ."

She was startled at the pain that for a moment was naked in Narraway's face, acute and so obviously personal. Then he masked it, as if aware that she had seen. "Probably," he agreed, starting to walk again.

They turned the corner and crossed the street into Shaftesbury Avenue. Charlotte had no idea where they were going, and she had a strong belief that neither Pitt nor Narraway did either. The dread that filled their minds drowned out everything else, as it did with her. She was aware of the noise of traffic passing, but it was all a blur of meaningless movement. Alexandria was another world which she had seen only in paintings and through Pitt's descriptions he had shared with her. But it was linked with everything here as really as if it lay across some immediate border. It would be British soldiers who would be sent to fight and die there if there was an armed revolt, just as there had been in the Sudan. She could remember the newspaper accounts of that well enough. She had known and liked a woman whose only son had been killed at Khartoum.

And if Suez fell, the repercussions of it would touch every life in Britain.

But it was still wrong to sacrifice an innocent man to the rope. If he was innocent? Aunt Vespasia wanted to believe he was, but that did not make it so. Even she could be mistaken. People did things that seemed unimaginable to others when they were in love.

Narraway stopped on the footpath, facing Pitt. "Garrick is safe enough for the foreseeable future, whatever that is. I'm less happy about Sandeman, but I think if he understands the dangers he will keep silent. If he wanted to be a martyr to soothe his own conscience, he would have done it before now. Staying in Seven Dials matters to him. It is his way of answering for his soul. I believe he will die before he will sacrifice that. And Yeats and Lovat are dead."

"Is it Ayesha?" Pitt said almost hesitantly. "For vengeance?"

"Probably," Narraway replied. "And God help me, I can't blame her . . . except for drawing Ryerson in. And perhaps she couldn't help that. It was chance that brought him there that night, exactly as she was disposing of the body. She couldn't have been sure he would help rather than calling the police—as, if he had an ounce of self-preservation, he would have."

"Why did she wait for fifteen years?" Charlotte interrupted. "If some of my family had been killed like that, I wouldn't."

Narraway looked at her with curiosity turning to interest. "Neither would I," he said with feeling. "Something must have made it impossible before—a lack of knowledge? Of help? Power? Assistance from someone, their belief, money?" He looked from one to the other of them for an answer. "What would make you wait, Mrs. Pitt?"

She thought only for a moment. A brewer's dray with six gray horses rumbled past, their huge feet heavy on the cobbles, manes tossing, brasses bright. "Not knowing about it," she said first. "Either not knowing it happened, or that my family was involved, or not knowing who did it or where to find them. Some situation that I couldn't leave—"

"What situation?" Narraway interrupted.

"Illness," she said. "Someone I had to nurse, a child or a parent? Or someone I had to protect, who might be hurt if I acted? Somebody implicated, maybe? A hostage to fortune of some kind."

He nodded slowly, and turned to Pitt, his eyebrows raised.

"Only not knowing," Pitt replied, and as he said it something tingled in his memory. "I knew of the fire, but the people I spoke to believed it was an accident, at least that is what they said. How did Ayesha learn that it wasn't?"

Narraway's face set hard. "That's a very good question, Pitt, and one to which I would like the answer, but unfortunately I have no idea where to begin looking. There is a great deal about this I would like to know. For example, is Ayesha Zakhari the prime mover, or is she acting with or for someone else? Who else knows about the massacre, and why did they not expose it in Egypt? Why wait, and why in London?" His voice dropped a little and became tight and hard with emotion he barely kept in control. "And above all, is personal revenge all they want, or is this just the beginning?"

Neither Pitt nor Charlotte answered him. The question was too big, the answer too terrible.

Pitt put his arm around Charlotte's shoulders, almost without thinking, and drew her closer to him, but there was nothing to say.

CHAPTER TWELVE

VESPASIA WAS IN the withdrawing room, arranging white chrysanthemums and copper beech leaves floating in a flat Lalique dish, when she heard angry voices raised in the hall. She turned in surprise just as the door flew open and Ferdinand Garrick pushed past the maid and stood on the edge of the Aubusson carpet, his face suffused with anger and something close to despair.

"Good morning, Ferdinand," she said coolly, indicating with a slight nod that the maid might leave. She would have put an edge of ice to it sufficient to stop the Prince of Wales in his tracks but for the reality of the emotion she recognized in him. It overrode all consideration of personal manners, even the deepening dislike she felt for him. "I gather that something is seriously wrong, and you believe that I may assist you."

He was taken aback. He was quite aware of his almost unpardonable rudeness, and now that he thought of it, he had expected to meet with outraged dignity rather than any form of understanding. It robbed him momentarily of his assurance. He stood still, breathing hard. Even from across the space of the room she could see his chest rise and fall.

She broke off the last two flower stalks and floated the heads in the fan of leaves, then set the bowl on the low table. It was exquisite, as beautiful as when she did it with bloodred peonies in the summer.

"Tell me what it is that has happened," she directed. "If you would care for tea I shall send for it, but perhaps it would only be an encumbrance now?"

He jerked his hand, dismissing the idea. "My son is in desperate danger from the same people who murdered young Lovat, and now your idiot policeman has kidnapped him and removed him from the only place where he was safe!" he accused, his eyes burning. His voice shook when he went on, and he was struggling to get his breath. "For God's sake, tell them to leave it alone! They have no idea what they're meddling with! The disaster will be . . ." The enormity of it defied his ability to describe, and he stared at her in helpless fury.

She could see that there was little purpose in attempting to reason with him; he felt too much panic rising towards a breaking point to listen to anything that seemed like argument.

"If it was indeed Pitt who removed your son, then we had better inform him of the danger," she replied calmly. "At this hour in the morning I doubt if Pitt will be at home, but I may be able to find him. If I do, I shall have to tell him specifically what the danger is in order for him to guard Stephen against it."

"The man's a fool!" Garrick's voice rose, quivering near to breaking. "He's gone blundering in where he doesn't understand a damn thing, and he could set a whole continent ablaze!"

Vespasia was startled. Garrick's words were wild, but in spite of her dislike of his self-righteous, rigid beliefs, he had been an excellent soldier. He had not the imagination to be hysterical.

"Ferdinand, please calm yourself sufficiently to inform me what I must say to him," she said firmly. "I cannot give him orders, I must persuade him. Where was Stephen, and when did you learn that he had been taken, and by Pitt?"

Garrick made a tremendous effort to master the panic inside himself, but still his voice cracked with emotion.

"The people who killed Lovat will stop at nothing whatever to kill Stephen also, and Sandeman if they can find him. Stephen knew it!" His face was pink, the embarrassment painful to see, nevertheless he continued with some semblance of control. "He was . . . not well . . ."

She allowed the euphemism to pass. She knew what outward form his son's illness had taken, but it was the cause of it that mattered now, so she did not interrupt.

"He had episodes of delirium," he continued more steadily. "I had him put in a hospital . . ." He took a deep, shuddering breath. "The Bethlehem Lunatic Hospital."

Vespasia was well aware of the reputation of Bedlam; it needed no words of his to expand the horror of it. That he would place his son in such a man-made hell said more than anything else could have to show her his fear.

"And Pitt found him there and removed him?" she said with only the very slightest lift of question. "Do you not think that perhaps it was Martin Garvie he went seeking? You did send the valet as well, did you not?"

His face was slack for a moment with surprise, then the look vanished. "It seems you know even more about it than I had supposed. Yes, I imagine Garvie might be more within his circle of—" He stopped, aware suddenly that he was running a great risk of antagonizing her, and he could not afford it. "Find him!" he said desperately. "Please?"

She looked at his anguished face. "And what is it I should tell Pitt, or whoever is concerned?" she asked. "What is the danger that you fear, Ferdinand?" She moved across to the sofa as she spoke, and gestured for him to be seated, but he remained unyielding on his feet.

"Give him back to me, and I'll take care of it," he said between his teeth.

She sat down. "I think if they wanted him so little that they would be prepared to give him back simply because I asked it, then they would not have gone to the trouble of taking him in the first place," she said reasonably. "Is it not time to deal with rather more reality?"

He started to speak, and then stopped.

She waited. She would not ask again. He knew the facts. Stephen was his son.

He lowered his eyes. "He has knowledge which I believe certain people will kill him to obtain," he said.

It was an oblique answer, less than the truth. However, it served the purpose, and she knew he would not give her more unless forced to. She would leave that to Victor Narraway, and she had already made up her mind that it was he to whom she would go.

"I shall inform them of that," she promised.

Something in him eased a fraction, but now that victory was achieved, he moved from foot to foot in impatience for her to proceed.

She regarded him coldly. "I have no intention of permitting you to accompany me, Ferdinand. You have told me all I require. As you have made clear, time is of importance. Good morning."

"Thank you," he said stiffly. His expression was one of relief, gratitude, and almost disappointment, now that there was nothing more for him to do in his own cause. He hated dependence of any sort whatever, and upon a woman most of all. "Yes . . . I am obliged. Good day to you. I . . ."

"I shall inform you of the outcome," she replied coldly. "Should you not be at home, I shall leave a message with your butler."

"I shall be at home."

She inclined her head in the faintest acknowledgment.

He colored deeply, but he offered no further argument. She rose to her feet to permit him to take his leave without seeming rude.

Again, Vespasia used her telephone. It was an instrument she had been quick to adopt, and she was impatient with those who resisted its speed and convenience.

She was certain that Victor Narraway was again attending the trial of Ryerson and the Egyptian woman, and that court would adjourn for luncheon at one. That gave her an hour to be there, and convey to him that she wished to see him urgently.

As it was, they met on the steps as she was arriving. He came towards her with his customary elegance and an outward appearance of ease, but even before he spoke she saw in the shadows of his face, the tension within him, that he was profoundly worried, perhaps even afraid.

"Good afternoon, Lady Vespasia," he said quietly.

"Good afternoon, Victor. I am sorry to call you away from the business of the court, but Ferdinand Garrick came to me in profound distress this morning." She ignored his surprise. There was no time for the explanation of courtesy. "He is aware that Pitt has found Stephen Garrick in Bedlam, and removed him. I believe he would not have done that without your approval, and possibly your assistance."

He offered her his arm and she took it. Obviously he wished to move away from the steps, where they might be overheard.

"Actually, it was Garvie we were more interested in—to begin with," he told her.

"Yes, I am aware of Charlotte's concern for him; you do not need to explain that to me."

The shadow of a smile touched his lips and then disappeared. "It was Mrs. Pitt who learned where Garvie was," he said wryly. "From a priest in Seven Dials." They were walking along the footpath side by side, away from the Old Bailey down to Ludgate Hill, then east towards the vast shadow of St. Paul's, its dome dark against a bright, windy sky.

"That sounds like Charlotte," she responded.

He drew in breath as if to say something, then the thought vanished and another, far darker, took its place.

"There was an atrocity in Egypt," he said so quietly she could barely hear him. "Twelve years ago. Lovat, Garrick, Sandeman, and a man named Yeats were involved. Ferdinand Garrick concealed it then. If it is exposed now, to anyone at all, it could set Egypt ablaze, and cost us Suez. There are men who will kill to keep it silent."

"I see." She drew in a long, shaky breath. The thought did not surprise her. Money, power and passionate loyalties were involved. "Do I assume that Lovat was murdered in revenge for this?"

"It looks like it. God help them . . . who wouldn't? But I shall protect Stephen Garrick as long as it is necessary, and you may tell his father so. I have as much interest in keeping him safe from his enemies as he has. Please say no more. I don't know yet who is playing in this, or on which side. I would save Ryerson if I could, but it is beyond my ability now."

She hesitated only momentarily. "May I visit him, to offer the services of a friend?" she asked.

"I will arrange it this evening," he promised. "You should say all you wish to him then. Once the jury is in, I . . . I believe you may have no further opportunity."

She found without warning her voice was trembling. "I see. Thank you."

"Lady Vespasia!" He did not risk the impertinence of using her name without her title.

"Yes?" She had her composure again.

"I am truly sorry." The pain in his face was momentarily naked. She did not know why Ryerson's conviction should hurt him so much, or even whether he believed him guilty of more than foolishness, but she was certain beyond any hesitation at all that the emotion was deep and private, part of the man, not the calling.

She stood still, facing him on the quiet footpath in the shadow of St. Paul's. "There are some things we cannot do," she said softly. "No matter how intensely we desire it."

He was self-conscious, something she had never seen in him before.

"Come to the Newgate entrance at eight," he said, then he turned and went back into the courtroom.

EVEN NARRAWAY COULD CONTRIVE only a very brief visit for Vespasia. She had expected Ryerson to show signs of the strain he must be feeling, but in spite of her mental preparation for it, she was shocked when she saw him. She remembered him as a big man. The sense of his physical power had always been overwhelming, the most remarkable thing about him, more than the character in his face or the intelligence or the charm.

Now as he stood up at her entrance into the cell, he looked drained. His skin was pale and had a peculiar dry, papery look, and although he wore the same clothes she had seen him in last time, today they seemed too big for him.

"Vespasia . . . how good of you to come," he responded huskily, holding out one hand to greet her, then withdrawing it the moment before he touched her, as if suddenly conscious that she might not wish it.

She was stabbed by the terrible thought that the change in him was because he no longer believed in Ayesha Zakhari's innocence. He did not look like a martyr to a cause, more like a man whose dreams have been broken.

She forced herself to smile very slightly, just a warmth to her face.

"My dear Saville," she responded, "I shall owe favors to no end of people for the privilege." It was not true, but she knew that just for an instant it would make him feel better. "And I have only a few minutes before some miserable man, tied to his duty, will return to fetch me," she continued. "It occurred to me that there might be some service I could perform for you that perhaps you had not been able to ask of anyone else. If there is, then please tell me now, in case we do not have another opportunity to speak alone." It was a brutal truth, but there was no more time left for skirting around it. This was the time, here, this evening.

He controlled himself with a magnificent effort, and replied to her with total calm. Certain bequests to staff who had served him well were already attended to, but there were personal thanks he would like to have given, and an apology here or there. It was the latter which weighed upon him most heavily, and he was grateful to have her promise to do those things, should it prove necessary. He knew that she would do it graciously, with both the candor and the humility he wished.

The guard returned. She told him icily to wait, but he did so standing at the door.

"Is there anything else you need?" she asked Ryerson. "Anything personal that I may bring for you?"

The ghost of a smile flashed on his face, and vanished. "No, thank you. My valet has done that for me every day. I am so . . ."

She held up her hand to silence him. "I know," she said quickly. She looked at the guard and permitted him to hold the door open for her. "Good-bye, Saville, at least for the moment." She went out without looking back. She heard the sound of steel on steel as the door closed and the heavy tumblers of the lock fell into place.

She was crossing the entrance on her way to the outside doors when she saw a discreetly clad dark-skinned man walk almost silently past her in the opposite direction, his eyes averted. He was holding a small, soft-sided bag in his hand. Presumably, this was Ayesha Zakhari's house servant, taking her clean linen and whatever else she required. He was so self-effacing as to have mastered the art of being almost invisible, and she would not have recognized him were she to see him again in different clothes. She was forcibly reminded that he belonged to a very different culture. Then she realized with a sense of amazement that she had not actually seen Ayesha Zakhari, as far as she could recall. Surely if she had met her anywhere, she would have remembered?

And yet she was the center of this storm which was going to destroy Ryerson, and possibly Stephen Garrick as well.

Vespasia went out into the street where her carriage was waiting, and allowed her footman to assist her up the step and to be seated comfortably, her mind still absorbed in thought.

GRACIE WAS ALONE in the house when she heard the knock on the scullery door. It was late on a wet and gusty night. Charlotte and Pitt were both out briefly to visit Charlotte's mother, whom they had not seen in some time.

The knock came again, urgent and persistent.

She picked up the rolling pin, then put it down and chose the carving knife instead. Keeping it hidden in the folds of her skirt, she tiptoed to the back door and opened it sharply.

Tellman stood on the step with his hand raised to knock again. He looked cold and worried.

"You should have asked who it was before you opened," he said immediately.

The criticism stung her. "You stop telling me wot ter do, Samuel Tellman!" she retorted. "You in't got no right. This is my 'ouse, not yours." She realized as soon as the words were out that her heart was pounding with suppressed fear, and she knew he was right. It would have been so simple to ask who it was, and she had not thought of it because she had been so preoccupied with thoughts about Martin Garvie, and people taken against their will and shut up in Bedlam, and the fact that they had not been able to solve the case of a man shot to death in a woman's garden at night. What was he there for? No good, skulking in the bushes.

Tellman came inside. He was pale and his face was drawn with lines of tension.

"Somebody's got to tell you what to do," he said, closing the door hard. "You haven't got the sense you were born with. What's that?"

She put the knife down on the kitchen table. "A carvin' knife. Wot does it look like?" she snapped back.

"It looks like something a burglar would take off you and hold to your throat," he replied. "If you were lucky."

"Is that wot yer came 'ere ter tell me?" she demanded, swinging around to face him. "It in't me 'as got no wits."

"Of course I didn't come to tell you that!" He stood near the table, his whole body too tight to sit down. "But you've got to act with more sense."

If anyone else had said that, she would have brushed it aside, but from him it stung unaccountably. He was at once too far and too close. She hated that it mattered so much because it confused her, it stirred up feelings over which she had no control, and she was not used to that.

"Don't you tell me off like I belonged to yer," she said, gulping back a surge of emotion, almost a loneliness, that threatened to swamp her.

He looked startled for a moment, then he frowned very slightly. "Don't you want to belong to anyone, Gracie?" he asked.

She was stunned. It was the last thing she had expected him to say, and she had no answer for it. No, that was not true, she did have an answer, but she was not ready to admit it to him yet. She needed more time to accustom herself to the idea. She swallowed, opened her mouth to deny it, then like a wave breaking over her, she knew she could not. It would be a lie, but he might believe her and not ask again. He might even go away.

"W-well . . ." she stammered. "Well . . . I . . . s'pose I do . . ." She had said it . . . aloud!

He took a deep breath also. There was no indecision in him, only a fear that he would be rejected. "Then you'd better belong to me," he answered. "Because there isn't going to be anyone who wants you more than I do."

She stared at him. The moment had come. It was now or never. The warmth rose up inside her like sliding into delicious, hot, sweet water, almost like floating. She did not realize she was not saying anything.

"Well, you're stubborn and self-willed, and you've got the daftest ideas about people's places I ever heard," he went on in the crackling silence. "But heaven help me, there isn't anybody else I really want . . . so if you'll have me—" He stopped. "Are you waiting for me to say I love you? Maybe you haven't got the wits you were born with, but you're not so daft you don't know that!"

"Yes, I know it!" she said quickly. "An' . . . an' . . ." It was only fair that she answer him honestly, however difficult it was to say. "An' I love you too, Samuel. But jus' don' take liberties! It don' give you the right ter tell me wot I'm doin' or wot I in't."

His lantern face lit with a huge smile. "You'll do as I tell you. But I want peace in my own house, so I reckon I won't tell you anything you'd mind too much."

"Good!" She took a gulp of air. "Then we'll be all right when . . . when it's time." She took another gulp. "Would you like a cup o' tea? Yer look 'alf starved." She was using the word in the old sense of being cold.

"Yes," he accepted, pulling out a chair and sitting down at last. "Yes, I would, please." He knew better than to pursue an answer as to time now. She had accepted, that was enough.

She went past him to the stove, overwhelmed with relief. This was as far as she could go now. "Was that wot yer came for?" she asked.

"No. That's been on my mind for . . . for a while. I came to tell Mr. Pitt that the police have a new witness in the Eden Lodge case, and it looks pretty bad."

She pulled the kettle onto the hob and turned around to look at him. "Wot kind of a witness?"

"One that says he knows the Egyptian woman sent a message to Mr. Lovat, telling him to come to her," he said grimly. "They'll call him to the witness stand . . . bound to."

"Wot can we do?" she asked anxiously.

"Nothing," he answered. "But it's better to know."

She did not argue, but she worried for Pitt, and even the sense of warmth inside her, the little tingle of victory that she had faced the moment of decision and accepted it, and all the vast changes it would mean one day, did not dispel her concern for Pitt, and the case they surely could not win now.

PITT AND CHARLOTTE returned shortly after that. When Pitt had heard all that Tellman had to say, he thanked him for it, put his coat back on and went straight out again. He could not wait until tomorrow morning to inform Narraway. It was Friday night. They had two days' grace before the trial resumed, but it was a very short time to rescue anything out of this. Pitt was not used to such complete failure, and it was a cold, hollow feeling with a bitter aftertaste he believed would remain.

Of course he had had unsolved cases before, and others to which he was certain he knew the answer but could not prove it, but they had not been of this magnitude.

Narraway looked up as the manservant closed the door, leaving Pitt standing in the middle of the room. He read his face immediately. "Well?" he demanded, leaning forward as if to stand up.

"The police have a witness who says Ayesha sent Lovat a note asking him to go to her," he said simply. There was no point trying to make it sound less dreadful than it was. He was aware of all that it meant before Narraway spoke.

"So she deliberately lured him to the garden," Narraway said bitterly. "Either he destroyed the note himself or she took it from him before the police got there. It was not a crime of the moment; she always intended to kill him." His face creased in thought. "But did she intend to implicate Ryerson, or was that accidental?"

"If she did"—Pitt sat down uninvited—"then she must have been extraordinarily sure of him. How did she know that he would get there before the police, and that he would help her dispose of the body? Did she have an alternative plan if he had raised the alarm instead?"

Narraway's mouth twisted in a hard grimace. "Presumably she was the one who called the police, or had her servant do it. If it was in revenge for the massacre, then he will have been party to it."

Narraway's dark face was heavy with foreboding. He stared straight ahead at some horror he could see within his own vision. "I assume they are calling this witness on Monday?" he said without turning to Pitt.

"I should think so," Pitt replied. "It will prove intent."

"And then she will take the stand and tell the world exactly why," Narraway went on in a low, hard voice. "And the newspapers will rush to repeat it, and within hours it will be all over the country, then all over the world." His face looked bruised, almost as if he had been beaten. "Egypt will rise in revolt and make the Mahdi and the whole bloodbath of the Sudan look like a vicarage tea party. Even Gordon in Khartoum will seem a civilized difference between peoples. And inevitably we shall lose Suez." He clenched his fists, his shoulders tight. "God! What a hellish fiasco. We were damned from the start—weren't we!" It was not a question, just an exclamation of despair.

"I don't understand it," Pitt said slowly, feeling his way in a darkness of disjointed reason. "Why now? And if the purpose behind her coming to London, drawing in Ryerson, the whole business of trying to get the cotton manufacturing back into Egypt, the murder of Lovat, was in order to expose the massacre . . . then why all that trouble?" He stared at Narraway. "Why not simply make it known in Egypt? The facts are there. The bodies could be found and exhumed. With thirty-odd people shot to death, even after the burning, some of them will have bullet holes, chips in bone to show it wasn't simply an accidental fire. Why all this murder and trial? Why risk her own life at all? If they know about the massacre, surely the murder of one of the soldiers responsible is trivial, almost an irrelevance, compared with exposing it? It's ridiculously inefficient like this."

Narraway stared at him, his eyes widening. "What, exactly, are you saying, Pitt? That she is being used by someone else? Expendable?"

"I think so . . . yes," Pitt agreed. "What use is it to anyone to involve Ryerson?"

"Publicity," Narraway said instantly. "The murder of one junior diplomat is neither here nor there. It's Ryerson's involvement that has journalists from every country in Europe writing about it. If the massacre comes out in the Old Bailey, you can be sure not only will all Britain know about it, and all Egypt, but most of the rest of the world as well. We wouldn't have a chance in hell of keeping it quiet. Not only will all of the violence and horror of the event itself come out, but every stupid and ugly thing anyone has done since to conceal it."

"So she came believing she was trying to help the cotton industry, but whoever it was who sent her intended this all the time?" For Pitt it was now only half a question. At last it made sense of what he had learned of Ayesha in Alexandria. This was the woman he had discovered. And once again she had been betrayed, only this time it would cost her her life. There was only one question now. "What did they tell her to persuade her to kill Lovat?" he said aloud. "Or didn't she?"

Narraway stared at him, amazement, then comprehension, in his face. "I don't know," he said at last. "If she didn't, then who did?"

Pitt stood up. "I don't know." Anger seethed inside him for Ayesha, for Ryerson, who unquestionably had been used, for all the people who were going to be driven into the maelstrom that Egypt would become. The beauty and the warmth of Alexandria would be shattered, as would the lives of the men and women whose faces he had seen when he was there, without even knowing their names. And he hated not knowing, and having his emotions pushed and pulled, and then torn apart by pity for first one, and then another, and not knowing what to believe. "Give me the authority I need to go and see her." That was a demand, not a request.

"I can't get it until the morning," Narraway replied. "You'll need it in writing," he added as Pitt hesitated. "She's not guilty yet, and she has rights. The Egyptian embassy will still protect her. I'll have it for you by tomorrow afternoon."

Pitt accepted it because he had no choice.

THE NEXT DAY, after a restless night in which the little sleep he got was filled with dreams of violence and almost unbearable tension, he was at Narraway's house by noon. He was obliged to wait nearly two hours alone in the morning room until Narraway returned with a piece of paper in an envelope, and gave it to him without explanation.

"Thank you." Pitt took it, glanced at the few lines of writing on it and was impressed, although he had no intention of allowing Narraway to know that. "I'll go straightaway."

"Do," Narraway agreed. "Before they change their minds. And Pitt . . . be careful. The stakes could be as high as war. The people behind all this are not going to be squeamish about getting rid of one policeman more or less."

Pitt was jolted, in spite of himself. "I know that!" he said sharply, then turned and left, calling a good-bye over his shoulder so Narraway should not be aware how ugly and deep his thoughts had become. He had faced physical danger before. No one could patrol the back alleys of London as he had done without it. But this was a different venture, a conspiracy of a magnitude he had not tasted before. It was no one man's ambition but a nation's fate which could erupt in death and awful, senseless destruction.

He took the first hansom that passed and told the driver to take him as rapidly as he could to Newgate. As soon as he was there he went straight to the warden in charge and showed him the paper Narraway had given him. The man read it right through twice, and then consulted with a superior. Finally, when Pitt was about to lose his temper, he conducted him to the cell where Ayesha Zakhari was held, and unlocked the door.

Pitt stepped in and heard the steel clang behind him. The woman who turned to face him startled him so profoundly he was robbed of words. He had created a mental picture of her from his expectations, and from the Greek Alexandria he had seen. Perhaps old stories of the city had touched his imagination without his being aware of it. He had pictured someone olive-skinned with lustrous dark hair, rich and sultry, with a softly curving body, perhaps average height or less.

She was very tall, only three or four inches less than he, and slender, delicately boned. She wore a pale silk gown like those he had seen on women in Alexandria, but more graciously cut. But most extraordinary of all, her skin was almost black and her hair was no more than a dark, smooth covering for her perfectly shaped head. Her features were more than beautiful; they were so exquisite she seemed like a work of art, and yet the vitality in her made her obviously a living, breathing woman. She was not an Egyptian of the modern, sophisticated Mediterranean Islam; she was of ancient, Coptic Africa—not Cleopatra at all, but older than that, Nefertiti.

"Who are you?" Her voice jolted him back to the present. It was low and a little husky, but with hardly any accent he could place, only a slightly more precise diction than an Englishwoman would have had, other than perhaps Great-aunt Vespasia.

"I apologize," he said without thinking. "My name is Thomas Pitt. I need to speak with you, Miss Zakhari, before the court resumes on Monday morning. Certain things have transpired of which you may not be aware."

"You may tell me whatever you wish," she replied levelly. "I have nothing to tell you, beyond what I have already said. And since I cannot prove it, there is little purpose in my repeating it. You are wasting your time, Mr. Pitt, and you are wasting mine also. And I think perhaps I do not have very much of it left." It was said without self-pity, and yet he could see in her face that underneath the effort of courage there was immeasurable pain.

He remained standing because there was nowhere to sit, except the cot, and to reach that he would have had to walk past her, and then look up where she stood.

"I went to Alexandria about three weeks ago," he began, and saw the start of surprise in her, the stiffening of her body, but she did not speak. "I wanted to learn more about you," he went on. "I admit that what I found surprised me."

The ghost of a smile crossed her face, and vanished. She had a gift of stillness which was more than a mere lack of movement; it was an inner control, a peace of the spirit.

"I believe you came here to England to try to persuade Ryerson to influence the cotton industry, so more Egyptian cotton could be woven where it was grown, so that the factories could be started up again, as they were in the time of Mohammed Ali."

Again she was surprised. It was no more than a hesitation in her breathing; he felt it rather than saw it.

"So your own people could prosper from their work," he added. "It was naive. If you had understood how much money was vested in the trade, how many people's power, I think you would have realized that no one man, even with Ryerson's office, could have had any effect."

She drew in her breath as though she was going to argue, then she let it out silently and turned half away from him. The light on her smooth face shone like polished silk. Her skin was blemishless, her cheekbones high, her nose long and straight, her eyes a little slanted upwards. It was a face of passion and immense dignity, but oddly, it was not without humor. The tiny lines, visible because he was close to her, spoke of laughter, not easy as of mere good humor, but of intelligence and irony as well.

"I think that the man who sent you knew that you could not succeed," he went on. He was not certain whether it was a shadow that moved, or if her body stiffened a trifle under the silk of her dress. "I believe his purpose was different," he continued. "And that cotton was only the reason he gave you, because it is one you could serve with all your effort, whatever the cost to yourself."

"You are mistaken," she replied, without looking at him. "If I was naive, then I have paid a high price for it, but I did not kill Lieutenant Lovat."

"But you are prepared to hang for it?" he said with surprise. "And not only yourself, but Mr. Ryerson as well."

She flinched as if he had struck her, but she did not make any sound, nor move her position.

"Do you think perhaps because he is a minister in the government that they will let him off?" he asked.

She turned to face him at last, her eyes wide and almost black.

"Have you not realized yet that he has enemies?" he said more loudly than he wished to, but he could not afford gentleness. She might back away, evade the truth again. "And whoever sent you has far bigger aims than cotton, in Egypt or Manchester."

"That is not true." She stated it as a fact. There was certainty in her eyes, then, even as he was watching, it wavered before she could master it.

"If you did not kill Lovat, then who did?" he said far more quietly. He had not yet made up his mind whether to say anything of the massacre to her, or even to hint at it. He watched her, searching for anything in her expression, however fleeting, to betray the hatred that could lie behind a murder of revenge. So far he had seen nothing at all, not even a shadow.

"I don't know," she said simply. "But you said it was not to do with cotton. What, then?"

It was almost impossible to believe she knew. And if she did not, and he told her, might her love of her country, and of justice, then impel her to speak, perhaps even to make her crime seem justified? Would a judge mitigate her sentence because of such provocation? Pitt would have. "Other political reasons," he said evasively. "To expose old wrongs with a view to inciting violence, even rebellion."

"Like the dervishes in the Sudan?" she said bleakly.

"Why not? Knowing what you do now, do you really believe you ever had a chance of changing the cotton industry, before the political and financial tides have changed, no matter what Mr. Ryerson might believe or wish for?"

She thought about it for several moments before conceding. "No," she said almost under her breath.

"Then surely it is possible that whoever sent you also knew that, and had in mind another plan altogether?" he pressed.

She did not answer, but he saw that she had understood.

"And he does not care if you hang for a murder you did not commit," he went on. "Or that Ryerson should also."

That hurt her. Her body stiffened and some of the richness of color faded from her skin.

"Could he have killed Lovat?" he asked.

Her head moved fractionally, but it was an assent.

"How?" he asked.

"He . . . he poses as my servant . . ."

Of course! Tariq el Abd, silent, almost invisible. He could have taken her gun and shot Lovat, then called the police himself to make sure they came, and found Ryerson. He could easily have organized the whole thing, because she would naturally have given him any letter to deliver to Lovat. No one would question it; in fact, they would have questioned anybody else. It was perfect.

"Thank you," he said with sudden depth of feeling. It was at least a resolution of the mystery, even if it did not solve the problem. And he had not realized until this moment how much it mattered to him that she was not guilty. It was almost like a physical weight removed from him.

"What are you going to do, Mr. Pitt?" Her voice was edged with fear.

"I am going to prove that you have been used, Miss Zakhari," he replied, aware that his choice of words would remind her of that other time, years ago, when she had been used and betrayed before. "And that neither you nor Mr. Ryerson is guilty of murder. And I am going to try to do it without soaking Egypt in blood. I am afraid the second aim is going to take precedence over the first."

She did not answer, but stood motionless as an ebony statue while he smiled very slightly in parting, and knocked on the door to summon the warder.

He debated for only moments whether to go alone or to find Narraway and tell him. If Tariq el Abd was the prime mover behind the plan to expose the massacre and set Egypt alight, then he would not meekly accept arrest from Pitt or anyone else. By going to Eden Lodge alone, Pitt might do no more than warn him, and possibly precipitate the very tragedy they dreaded.

He stopped a hansom in the Strand and gave Narraway's office address. Please God, he was there.

"What is it?" Narraway said as soon as he saw Pitt's face.

"The man behind Ayesha is the house servant Tariq el Abd," he replied. He saw from Narraway's expression that no more explanation was necessary.

Narraway breathed with a sigh of comprehension, and fury with himself because he had not seen it before. "Our own bloody blindness!" he swore, rising to his feet in a single movement. "A servant and a foreigner, so we don't even see him. Damn! I should have been better than that." He yanked a drawer open and pulled a gun out of it, then slammed the drawer shut again and strode ahead of Pitt. "I hope you had the wits to keep the cab," he said critically.

"Of course I did!" Pitt retorted, striding after him out of the door and down the steps to the pavement, where the cab was standing, the horse fidgeting from one foot to the other, perhaps sensing the driver's tension.

"Eden Lodge!" Narraway said tersely, climbing in ahead of Pitt and waving the man forward as Pitt was scrambling in behind him.

Neither of them spoke all the way through the crowded streets, around squares and under fading trees until the hansom stopped outside Eden Lodge.

" 'Round the back!" Narraway ordered, moving swiftly ahead of Pitt.

But there was no one in Eden Lodge. The entire house was deserted. The stove in the kitchen was cold, the ashes in the fires gray, the food in the pantry already going stale.

Narraway swore just once, with white-hot fury, but there was nothing he or anybody else could do.

CHAPTER THIRTEEN

NO TRACE WAS FOUND of Tariq el Abd by the police, or any of the men upon whom Narraway could call. Sunday was a wretched day, cold and windy, almost as if the weather itself fretted with the same sense of impending disaster as Pitt, cooped all day at home because he had nowhere to go and nothing to do that was of use. The trial would resume in the morning, and presumably Tariq el Abd would reappear and drag out the whole violent and dreadful truth of the massacre. It would be the beginning of the end of any kind of peace in Egypt, certainly of British rule and all that Suez meant for the empire.

He had told Charlotte what he knew. There was no point in keeping it from her because the only part that was dangerous she had known before he had.

They ate Sunday dinner together. It was the most formal meal of the week, and Daniel and Jemima found it both daunting and exciting, rather like being grown-up. They very much wanted it, it was part of life, but not necessarily today.

Afterwards Pitt sat by the fire, pretending he was reading, but actually he did not turn the pages of his book. Charlotte sat and stitched, but it was a straight hem on the edge of a sheet, and required no attention at all. Gracie and the children had put on coats and gone for a walk.

"What will he do?" Charlotte asked when the silence had become more than she could bear. "Arrive as a witness for the defense and say that he killed Lovat in revenge for having lost all his family, or something of that sort? And then describe the massacre?"

He looked up at her. "Yes, I should think so," he agreed. He could see the fear in her face, and ached to be able to comfort her with some assurance that it would not be so, even a hope of something they could do to fight against it, but there was nothing. The desire to protect was deep, and yet oddly there was a sweetness for him in being able to share his thoughts with her. She understood. The gratitude inside him was almost overwhelming that she was not a woman who had to be sheltered from truth, or even who wished to be. He did not know how any man bore the loneliness of that. One shielded a child, but a wife was a companion, one who walked beside you—in the easy paths and the hard.

"I suppose Mr. Narraway will warn the defense lawyer," she said, her eyes wide in question. "Or . . . or is it the defense lawyer who will call him, do you suppose?" The ugliness of that thought was plain in her eyes. It was an alien thought in the comfort of this familiar room, with its slightly worn furniture, the cats asleep by the hearth, the firelight flickering on the walls.

But was she right? Had the lawyer who had been so ardent in defending Ryerson known this from the beginning? Pitt had no idea. The knowledge that it could be so was uniquely chilling. There was a brutality to the entire plan which had nothing of the mitigating passion of a more personal crime. If it was true, there was in it a depth of deliberate betrayal.

It was a little before three o'clock when the doorbell rang. Gracie was still out, so Pitt went to answer it. The moment he saw Narraway's face he knew something extraordinary had happened.

"He's dead," Narraway said even before Pitt could ask him.

Pitt was momentarily confused. "Who's dead?"

"Tariq el Abd!" Narraway said tartly, stepping in past Pitt and shaking himself. Although it was not raining at that moment, the wind was cold and a bank of heavy cloud was racing in from the east. He stared at Pitt, his eyes tense, filled with hard, biting fear. "The river police found his body hanging under London Bridge. It looks as if he did it himself."

Pitt was stunned. In a few words Narraway had shattered the case. Was it the solution, or did it merely make things worse?

"Suicide?" Pitt asked with disbelief. "Why? He was winning. Tomorrow morning he would have achieved everything."

"And the rope as his reward," Narraway said.

"Lost his nerve?" Pitt asked with disbelief.

Narraway looked totally blank. "God knows."

"But it makes no sense," Pitt protested. "He had manipulated everything to the exact point where he could come into court as a surprise witness and tell the world about the massacre."

Narraway frowned. "You spoke to Ayesha Zakhari yesterday. She knew that you now understood el Abd had killed Lovat—"

"Even if she told him that," Pitt interrupted him, "he would hardly have gone off and taken his own life. She couldn't have proved it. All he had to do was get into the witness stand and say that it was she who had lost relatives in the massacre—or friends, a lover, whatever you like—and that was why she shot Lovat. Even if she had denied it and claimed it was he who did, there's no proof. His death looks like an admission, and leaves the massacre a secret."

They were standing in the hall, and both turned as the parlor door opened and Charlotte stood in the entrance looking at them anxiously. She saw Narraway just as he turned, and the gaslight in the passage caught the momentary softening of his face.

"Miss Zakhari's house servant has been found dead," Pitt said to her.

She looked from him to Narraway, to see if she was being protected from some deeper meaning.

"It appears to be suicide," Narraway added. "But we can see no reason why."

She stepped back, tacitly inviting them in, and they followed her into the warmth of the parlor, Pitt closing the door behind them and poking the fire before putting more coal on. It was not that it was cold so much as the desire for the brightness of new flame.

"Then either there is something we do not know," she said, sitting down again on the sofa next to her sewing. "Or he did not take his own life, but someone else did."

Pitt looked at Narraway. "I said nothing to Ayesha about the massacre. If she didn't know about it before, then she still doesn't."

"I beg your pardon," Narraway apologized, sitting in Pitt's chair close to the fire, shivering a little. "I should not have assumed you would be so careless."

"Why would anyone kill the house servant?" Charlotte asked, looking from one to the other of them. "That kind of death couldn't be an accident, nor was it intended to look like one."

"You are right, Mrs. Pitt," Narraway agreed grimly. "Therefore it was someone who knew who he was, in relation to Lovat's murder and the entire plan to set Egypt alight." He faced Pitt. "El Abd was not the prime mover in this. There is someone else behind him, and for some reason we don't yet know, he killed el Abd." His hand clenched unconsciously. "But why? Why now? They were on the brink of victory."

Pitt stood in front of the fire, as if he too were cold.

"Perhaps el Abd lost his courage and was not going to testify?" he suggested. Then the moment the words were out of his mouth, he knew he did not believe them. "But that makes no sense either. Why would he not? He had nothing to lose. It is not as if he intended to take the blame—he was going to make her connection certain by giving her the perfect motive."

Charlotte looked at Narraway. "Will this help Ryerson? Will

you be able to show that el Abd killed Lovat, without exposing that massacre? Surely you can? He could have had any number of motives for it, dating back to Lovat's time in Alexandria . . . couldn't he?"

"Yes," Narraway said thoughtfully. "Yes . . . one result of it is that we should be able to exonerate Ryerson and Ayesha Zakhari completely . . . as long as we allow el Abd's death to be taken as suicide."

The tiny germ of an idea stunned Pitt's mind, ugly and painful, and he refused to look at it.

"Is that what you are going to do?" Charlotte asked.

Pitt did not answer.

"It is all we can do, for the meantime," Narraway replied.

They sat a little longer, warming themselves. Charlotte fetched tea. They spoke of the news for half an hour or so, even the very recent death of Lord Tennyson, and wondered who would be the next poet laureate, before Narraway rose and took his leave.

But as soon as he had gone, Pitt, restless and unhappy, also went out. He gave Charlotte no explanation because the fear inside him was too painful to give words to, even to her. It was as if, still unspoken, he could deny it a little longer.

He took an omnibus south to the Thames Embankment and the offices of the river police. There was only a sergeant on duty, but he told Pitt which morgue the hanged man had been taken to, and half an hour later Pitt was standing in the offensively clean tiled room with the familiar smell of carbolic and death filling his throat. He stared down at the swollen, purplish face of Tariq el Abd.

The mark of the rope was burned deep into his neck, crooked, high under one ear, and his head lay at an awkward angle.

Pitt touched the head to move it very slightly, searching for other marks, bruises, anything to indicate beyond doubt whether he had been struck before death.

He heard footsteps behind him and swung around more quickly

than he had meant to, as if he felt himself in danger. His heart was knocking in his chest and it was difficult to draw breath into his lungs.

McDade looked at him with wry surprise.

"Jumpy, aren't you, Pitt? What do you want to know? He died sometime during last night. Difficult to say when; the water affected the temperature of the body."

"Tides?" Pitt asked.

"I did think of that." McDade's lips thinned fractionally. "I have been aware for some time that the water in the Thames goes up and down with monotonous and predictable regularity. However, what I cannot say is whether he was caught up in the wash of a passing boat that soaked him higher than the actual water level, or even if he slipped and got wetter than he intended."

"Can you say for certain that he hanged himself?" Pitt asked. Even though it made no sense of anything they knew, he hoped intensely that McDade would tell him it was suicide.

McDade did not hesitate. "No, I can't," he said dryly. "He's been knocked around a bit, bruised under the skin, but it happened either just before death or just after. There's been no time for the blood to gather, no marks to see. Bit of a gash on his head under the hair, but that's not necessarily a blow administered by someone else. It could have happened when he dropped, or any of a dozen ways afterwards—water carried him against the arches, struck by a passing boat, or even by driftwood or flotsam." He shrugged his massive shoulders. "It could be murder, but I can't tell you anything to prove it one way or the other. Sorry."

Pitt pulled back the sheet and looked at the rest of the torso. There were other marks on it as if it had buffeted to and fro, and been caught by rough objects which had torn the skin in several places. He replaced the sheet and turned away.

"Will anyone see he gets a burial according to his faith?" he asked.

McDade's eyebrows rose. "No one to claim the body?"

"Not so far as I know. I think the court will decide by now that he was the one who shot Lieutenant Lovat."

McDade shook his head, his chins quivering. "You say that as if you are not sure it is true," he observed.

"I'm sure it's true," Pitt replied. "I'm just not sure it is all of the truth. Thank you." He closed the conversation and turned to go. McDade made him uncomfortable; he was too observant. And Pitt needed to speak once more to the river police about exactly where el Abd was found, the state of his clothes, and the precise hours of the tides last night. A time of death mattered to him; in fact, just at the moment the importance of it overrode everything else in his mind.

Two hours later, at a quarter to nine, he had the answers. He stood on the Embankment in the gusty wind, his coat flapping around his legs and his scarf whipping out sideways, staring at the racing water of the flood tide returning. Out on the river, boats churned the water, steamers, barges, a lone pleasure boat with only half a dozen people on deck.

Tariq el Abd had died between one and five in the morning. They could not be more accurate than that. It was a time when most people were at home in bed. Pitt could have proved he was there, because Charlotte always woke if he got up. A man who lived alone would have no such safety.

He realized how little he knew of Narraway's private life; he had never even wondered about it. For that matter he knew almost nothing of Narraway's past, his family or his beliefs either. He was private to the point of being secretive. The only thing Pitt was sure of was that Narraway cared passionately about his work, and the causes it served, and that there was a personal relationship between him and Ryerson which caused him deep pain and which he would not discuss, no matter what the circumstances. And it was that which ate at Pitt now with a hard, angry pain that he could no longer ignore. It must be now; there was just time before the court resumed—if Narraway was at home.

Pitt met him on the doorstep, dressed smartly in his usual perfectly tailored dark gray. Narraway stopped abruptly, his eyes wide, his face pale.

"What is it?" He caught his breath, his voice husky.

Pitt had never defied Narraway before, never even challenged him. He knew his own dependence upon Narraway too well, not only for his job in Special Branch, but for the guidance and the protection while he was feeling his way in learning a new skill. But the emotion inside him now had power to override all such careful considerations.

"Inside!" he said abruptly.

The wind was cold and there was a fine rain behind it. Narraway's face hardened. "This had better be important, Pitt," he said, now that his initial shock was controlled and the steel was back in his eyes.

"It is," Pitt answered between his teeth. Perhaps he would have been wiser to say it all out there on the doorstep. He knew it, even as he followed Narraway in and heard the door close. Narraway led the way across the hall into his study and swung around.

"Well?" he demanded. "You have ten minutes. After that I am leaving whether you are finished or not. The trial resumes at ten. I mean to be there." In the morning light through the large window, his face was ashen, the fine lines of strain and too little sleep marked harshly in the skin around his eyes and mouth.

"But the special new witness is dead," Pitt replied. "There'll be no revelations about Ayesha Zakhari's motive now. El Abd's suicide is almost as good as a confession."

"Almost," Narraway agreed tersely. "I still need to see the acquittal. What is it you want, Pitt?"

"Why do you suppose el Abd killed himself?" Pitt asked. He wished he were anywhere but here, doing anything but this. "He was on the brink of success."

"We knew he was guilty," Narraway said, but there was a fractional hesitation in his voice; perhaps no one but Pitt would have heard it.

Pitt stared at him. "And he was afraid? Suddenly? Afraid of what? That we would arrest him on the way into court and stop him from testifying?"

Narraway breathed in and out very slowly. "What are you saying, Pitt? There is no time for games."

If he did not say it now then the moment would be past, and he would live with the doubt forever.

"Convenient for us," he answered. "In fact, it has probably saved Suez." He held Narraway's gaze without blinking.

Narraway was very pale. "Probably," he agreed. Again there was the shadow across his face.

"Why would el Abd do that?" Pitt asked.

"I don't know. It makes no sense," Narraway admitted, still standing motionless in the middle of the floor.

"If I had . . ." Pitt said. "Or you . . ."

At last Narraway understood. The last vestige of blood drained from his face, leaving his skin like gray paper. "God Almighty! You think I killed el Abd!"

"Did you?"

"No," Narraway said quickly. "No, I didn't." He did not ask if Pitt had; he already knew the answer. He also knew that Pitt's question was genuine, and that it hurt him to ask. It was the doubt twisting inside him that drove him to speak. "Was he murdered?"

"Are you certain he was murdered?"

"Not beyond doubt. But I believe he was," Pitt replied. "It was done well, with great skill. Impossible to tell if the injuries were just before death or just after . . . a deliberate blow or accidental as he fell, or even from a passing ship. We'll prove nothing."

The shadow was there in Narraway's face again. "Who would kill him, and why?"

"Someone who knew of the massacre," Pitt replied. "And who

would do anything, even commit murder and allow Ryerson to hang for it, rather than see the truth exposed, and face what it will cost."

Narraway was truly astounded. "Is that what you think?" he said, his voice cracking with incredulity. "That I want Ryerson to hang?"

"No, I don't think you do," Pitt said honestly. "I think you hate it. I think the guilt tortures you, but you'll let him hang rather than expose the massacre and lose Egypt."

Narraway did not reply. The silence hung in the air like a gulf of darkness between them.

"Don't use my few minutes left for this," Pitt said, not moving from his position blocking the doorway. He did not intend a physical threat; in fact, he was not even sure if he could provide one. Narraway was lighter and shorter, but he was lean and possibly he was trained in ways that Pitt had not even thought of. He might even be armed.

Nevertheless, Pitt did not intend to move until he received an answer. It was emotion that held him, not reason. He had not thought what he would do if Narraway had confessed to having killed el Abd.

The clouds cleared and for a moment sunlight dappled the floor.

"It has nothing to do with Egypt, or Lovat's murder, or the massacre," Narraway said at last, his voice low and a little husky.

Pitt waited.

"Damn it, Pitt! It's none of your business!" Narraway exploded. "It happened years ago . . . I . . . I just . . ." He stopped again.

Pitt did not move.

"Twenty years ago," Narraway began again, "I was working on the Irish Problem. I knew there was an uprising planned—violence, assassinations . . ."

Pitt was suddenly cold.

"I needed to know what was going on," Narraway said, his eyes unflinching but hot with misery. "I had an affair with Ryerson's wife." His voice shook. "It was my fault she was shot."

So it was guilt, just not for Lovat or Ayesha or anything that was happening now. Without even thinking about it, Pitt realized that he believed him.

Narraway waited, still watching Pitt's face. He would not ask.

Very slowly Pitt nodded. He understood. More than that, he realized with amazement something that would probably never be said, never even be referred to again—Narraway cared what he thought.

"Are we going to court?" Narraway snapped. He had seen the belief in Pitt's face, and it was enough. Now the agony of tension was gone and he wanted the moment broken. He had a debt to pay and he was burning to be about it.

"Yes," Pitt agreed, turning back to the door and leading the way out again without looking to see Narraway following.

THE OLD BAILEY COURTROOM was less than full. These last few days were something of an anticlimax. The newspapers had reported the death of Tariq el Abd, but only as an unknown foreigner who had apparently committed suicide. No connection was made with the Ryerson case, the verdict of which was now taken for granted, although it was not expected until tomorrow. The defense counsel was obliged to make some attempt at explanation, reasonable doubt, anything to appear to have done his best.

Narraway and Pitt entered the courtroom just as Sir Anthony Markham, counsel for the defense, was rising to his feet to begin.

The judge looked at Narraway with annoyance at the interruption. He had no idea who he was, simply someone with the ill manners to arrive late, and conspicuously.

Pitt hesitated. Markham obviously knew Narraway, but there was no interest in his face, rather the opposite. He shook his head very slightly and turned back to the judge.

Narraway stopped. Did Markham know about el Abd or not? Surely if he did not, he would be desperate for any defense at all.

Then he realized with dismay that he was not certain whether el Abd had been a prosecution witness, to seal the case absolutely with a perfect motive, or a defense witness, to offer some mitigation for the crime?

Or was the surprise witness not el Abd, but someone else? It came back to the same question, to which they still had no answer at all—who was the prime mover behind Lovat's murder, the man who wished to bring down Suez and the eastern half of the empire? And was one of the two lawyers here in his pay?

Who had murdered el Abd, and why?

The courtroom was motionless. Pitt looked around. The public gallery was about three-quarters full. He saw Vespasia, the light on her pale face and catching the silver of her hair. She was wearing a very small, discreet hat today, possibly in consideration for those whose view she might block. In the row behind her was Ferdinand Garrick, his face rigid, eyes forward in a wide, fixed stare, almost as if he were mesmerized by what was about to play itself out on the courtroom floor below him.

The jury sat waiting, sad and no longer really interested. They listened and watched because it was their duty.

Narraway continued towards Markham and stopped at his side, Pitt a step behind him.

"The body under the bridge was Tariq el Abd," Narraway said in so low a voice that Pitt caught only every other word. "It was he who killed Lovat. Miss Zakhari admitted it, and it makes perfect sense of the evidence."

Markham stood motionless. "How convenient for Miss Zakhari . . . and of course for Mr. Ryerson," he replied with a glint of sarcasm. "Why did this Egyptian manservant kill Lieutenant Lovat? Do you know that as well?"

"No, I don't, and it doesn't matter." Narraway's voice was cold. "Perhaps Lovat misused his daughter, or his sister, or even his wife, for all I know. Just get on with it! Call the river police. Then Pitt will identify the dead man for you."

Markham glanced at Pitt.

Pitt nodded.

Markham's face was set hard. He disliked being told what to do, by anyone.

"Do you intend to proceed, Sir Anthony?" the judge enquired with a touch of irritation.

Markham looked up, as if already dismissing Narraway.

"Yes, my lord. I have just learned of some very remarkable events which shed a totally different light on Lieutenant Lovat's death. With your permission, I would like to call Thomas Pitt to the stand."

"This had better be relevant, Sir Anthony," the judge said warily. "I will not have theatrics in my court."

"The evidence will be dramatic, my lord," Markham replied coldly. "But it will not be theatrical."

"Then proceed with it!" the judge snapped.

"I call Thomas Pitt!" Markham said loudly.

Narraway looked very briefly at Pitt, then turned on his heel and walked two paces to the nearest row where there was a vacant seat, and left Pitt to go across the floor and climb up the steps to the witness stand.

Pitt swore to his name and place of residence, and waited for Markham to ask him about el Abd. He was only slightly nervous about answering. This was the first time he had not testified as a police officer. Now he was a person from the shadows, without a rank or an occupation to give him status.

"Were you acquainted with Miss Zakhari's house servant, Tariq el Abd, Mr. Pitt?" Markham enquired.

"Yes."

"In what capacity?"

"As a servant at Eden Lodge," Pitt replied. "I did not know him personally."

"But you spoke with him at some length?" Markham pressed.

"Yes, perhaps an hour altogether."

"So you would know him if you saw him again?"

"Yes."

"Have you seen him since then?"

The jurors were openly fidgeting.

The counsel for the prosecution rose to his feet. "My lord, my learned friend's idea of drama is very different from mine. I have never heard anything so unutterably tedious. Whatever relevance can it have if this . . . gentleman . . . has spent time gossiping with Miss Zakhari's house servant . . . or not?"

"I was establishing that Mr. Pitt was able to identify Tariq el Abd, my lord," Markham said with injured innocence, and without waiting for any ruling he turned back to Pitt. "Where did you see him, Mr. Pitt . . . and when?"

"In the morgue," Pitt replied steadily. "Yesterday."

There was a gasp of breath indrawn around the room.

The judge leaned forward, his face dark and angry. "Are you saying that he is dead, Mr. Pitt?"

"Yes, my lord."

"From what cause?"

The prosecution stood up. "My lord, Mr. Pitt has no established credentials in medicine. He is not qualified to give evidence as to cause of death."

The judge resented the objection, but he could not argue and he knew it. He glared at the counsel for the prosecution, then swiveled back to Pitt. "Where was this man found?"

"Hanging by his neck on a rope from under London Bridge, I was told by the river police," Pitt replied.

"Suicide?" the judge barked.

"I am not qualified to say," Pitt answered him.

There was a moment's total silence, then a nervous titter washed around the room.

The judge's face was like ice. He looked at Markham. "Can you continue with your case in view of the man's death?" he said with barely concealed anger. His face was pink. He would not forget that Pitt had made the court laugh at his expense.

"Most certainly, my lord," Markham said vigorously. "I cannot prove that Tariq el Abd's death was suicide, but I can think of no conceivable way in which a man could find himself hanging with a rope around his neck under the arches of London Bridge by accident. I believe that any jury of twelve honest men must consider his responsibility for the death of Lieutenant Edwin Lovat a more than reasonable doubt as to whether my client is guilty or not. El Abd had every access to the gun which killed Lieutenant Lovat. It was his job to clean it. And he had every opportunity to have used it at that precise time and in that place. Justice, even reason, demands that you consider his guilt. His death now, almost assuredly by his own hand, makes it absurd not to."

"It was not Tariq el Abd who was trying to dispose of the body!" The counsel for the prosecution was on his feet, his voice harsh with indignation. "If Ayesha Zakhari did not kill Lovat, why was she outside in the garden with the corpse in a wheelbarrow? That is not the action of an innocent woman."

"It is the action of a frightened woman!" Markham said instantly. "If you came upon the body of a murdered man with your gun beside him, might you not attempt to hide it?"

"I would call the police," the counsel for the prosecution retorted.

"In a foreign country?" Markham was close to jeering. "You would have such confidence in their justice, when you are of a different race, a different language, a different culture?" He did not continue. He could see in the faces of the jurors that he had made his point.

The counsel for the prosecution swung around to the judge, his arms spread wide. "Why, my lord? What reason in the world could an Egyptian house servant have for murdering an English diplomat in the middle of London?"

There was a movement in the gallery. A man rose to his feet. He was slender, elegant, beautifully dressed, his thick hair waved back from an aquiline face.

Pitt was astounded. It was Trenchard! He must have come home on leave.

"My lord," Trenchard said with the utmost respect. "My name is Alan Trenchard. I am with the British Consulate in Alexandria. I believe I may be able to answer the court's questions on that subject. I have lived and worked in Egypt for over twenty-five years, and I have been able to find a certain amount of knowledge on the issues concerned here since Mr. Pitt left Alexandria, which I was therefore unable to tell him at the time of his enquiry."

The judge frowned. "If Sir Anthony wishes to call you, then in the interest of justice, we should hear from you."

Markham had no choice. He excused Pitt, and Trenchard climbed the steps up to the witness stand and turned to face the court.

Pitt sat next to Narraway and felt him stiffen as Markham moved forward again and Trenchard swore to his name and his residence.

Markham seemed perfectly relaxed. His clients, who yesterday had faced certain conviction, now suddenly were on the brink of acquittal. It had been none of his doing, it was entirely due to circumstance he could not have foreseen or contrived, but it was still going to be an astonishing victory for him.

"Mr. Trenchard," he began, "were you acquainted with Lieutenant Lovat during his army service in Egypt?"

"Not personally," Trenchard replied. "I am in the diplomatic service; he was in the military. It is possible we may have met, but I am not aware of it."

The judge frowned.

The jury glanced around them, their interest still barely caught.

Pitt found his hands clenched, nails digging into his palms.

Markham deliberately kept his eyes on the witness stand. "Did you know the dead man, Tariq el Abd?"

"I learned a great deal about him," Trenchard replied. He was standing very stiffly with his hands on the rails, knuckles white.

Pitt felt a ripple of fear go through him, wild and unreasonable. He turned to look at the dock. Ryerson was intent, but there was no leap of emotion in him; he dared not yet hope. But Ayesha was leaning forward, her eyes wide in amazement as she gazed at Trenchard, and Pitt realized with horror that unmistakably she knew him, not by repute, as he had said, but personally, face-to-face.

Now, at last, the jury were straining to catch each word, even a look.

The courtroom was warm, but Pitt felt a deep and terrible chill inside himself. He remembered Trenchard's saying that he had loved an Egyptian woman who had died in an accident a short time ago. Suddenly, almost as if he were there sitting on the ground with his bones aching and the soft lapping of the Nile in the darkness outside, he heard Ishaq telling of his father, the imam, and his dying nightmares of slaughter and burning bodies, and the daughter who had nursed him, heard all his words, his passion of grief and guilt, and who also had died shortly afterwards.

A hideous, knife-bright possibility shone in Pitt's mind, which made perfect sense of everything. The imam's daughter and Trenchard's mistress were the same woman. That was all it needed. Trenchard, with his passionate love of Egypt, knew Ayesha's loyalties, knew of the massacre, and had pieced together the rest of it—the four British soldiers that Ferdinand Garrick had shipped out of Alexandria to protect them, and in his soul-deep and absolute devotion to his country, to protect Britain's empire in Africa and the East.

Pitt turned to Narraway. "He's going to tell them about the massacre," he whispered, hearing his own voice tremble. "Maybe he always intended to do it himself to make it complete—with no one to argue, no one to lose nerve and fail. It's not Ayesha's motive he's going to uncover—it's el Abd's. El Abd was not master to anyone—he was the perfect scapegoat. Ayesha to draw in Ryerson—so the world would be looking—el Abd to take the ultimate blame."

The blood drained from Narraway's face. "God Almighty!" he breathed. "You're right . . ."

Markham was still talking to Trenchard.

"What was it you learned about Tariq el Abd that is relevant to the death of Lieutenant Lovat?" Markham said with a lift of curiosity, his eyes wide, seeing only his own victory, so close he could already taste it.

"I learned why he killed him," Trenchard answered.

Pitt half rose to his feet. He had no clear idea what he was going to do, but he could not let this happen—the bloodshed would drown the whole of Egypt and ruin British India, Burma and beyond.

Trenchard saw him and turned toward him, and smiled.

"Tariq el Abd lost the whole of his family in a hideous—" he began.

There was a loud crack, and immediately another. Trenchard fell backwards and slid down onto the floor of the stand.

Pitt swung around just as the third crack sounded, and he saw Ferdinand Garrick's head seem to explode as he fell, the revolver still in his hand.

The judge was paralyzed.

Markham's legs folded underneath him, and he slipped down awkwardly.

Pitt walked forward, Narraway a pace behind. He went over to the witness stand where Trenchard was lying. Garrick had struck him through the head with both shots, blowing half his brain away. He had finally closed the last chapter of the massacre. Egypt and the East were safe.

Narraway looked at the body for a moment, then turned his back and stared towards the gallery, where everyone was moving away from Garrick, sprawled on the floor—except Vespasia. Oblivious of the blood on her gown, she knelt beside him and gently folded his hands. It was a pointless gesture, but it had a dignity, a peculiar respect, as if suddenly she had seen something of value in him, and a certain pity that was beyond judgments.

In the dock, Ryerson put out his hand and took Ayesha's, it was all he could reach of her, but it was enough.

"I'll see that Stephen Garrick is cared for," Narraway said quietly. "I think we owe his father that."

Pitt nodded, still looking at Vespasia. "It will be done," he said with absolute conviction. "And Martin Garvie will watch over him."

Narraway looked up at Ryerson, and something of the tension in his body softened and a burden inside him seemed to ease.

For more high-stakes murder and mystery in Victorian England, read on to sample

Treason at Lisson Grove

a Charlotte and Thomas Pitt novel from Anne Perry

CHAPTER 1

"THAT'S HIM!" GOWER YELLED above the sound of the traffic. Pitt turned on his heel just in time to see a figure dart between the rear end of a hansom and the oncoming horses of a brewer's dray. Gower disappeared after him, missing a trampling by no more than inches.

Pitt plunged into the street, swerving to avoid a brougham and stopping abruptly to let another hansom pass. By the time he reached the far pavement Gower was twenty yards ahead and Pitt could make out only his flying hair. The man he was pursuing was out of sight. Weaving between clerks in pinstripes, leisurely strollers, and the occasional early woman shopper with her long skirts getting in the way, Pitt closed the gap until he was less than a dozen yards behind Gower. He caught a glimpse of the man ahead: bright ginger hair and a green jacket. Then he was gone, and Gower turned, his right hand raised for a moment in signal, before disappearing into an alley.

Pitt followed after him into the shadows, his eyes taking a moment or two to adjust. The alley was long and narrow, bending in a dogleg a hundred yards beyond. The gloom was caused by the overhanging eaves and the water-soaked darkness of the brick, long streams of grime running down from the broken guttering. People were huddled in doorways; others made their way slowly, limping, or staggering beneath heavy bolts of cloth, barrels, and bulging sacks.

Gower was still ahead, seeming to find his way with ease. Pitt veered around a fat woman with a tray of matches to sell, and tried to catch up. Gower was at least ten years younger, even if his legs were not quite so long, and he was more used to this kind of thing. But it was Pitt's experience in the Metropolitan Police before he joined Special Branch that had led them to finding West, the man they were now chasing.

Pitt bumped into an old woman and apologized before regaining his stride. They were around the dogleg now, and he could see West's ginger head making for the opening into the wide thoroughfare forty yards away. Pitt knew that they must catch him before he was swallowed up in the crowds.

Gower was almost there. He reached out an arm to grab at West, but just then West ducked sideways and Gower tripped, hurtling into the wall and momentarily winding himself. He bent over double, gasping to catch his breath.

Pitt lengthened his stride and reached West just as he dived out into the High Street, barged his way through a knot of people, and disappeared.

Pitt went after him and a moment later saw the light on his bright hair almost at the next crossroads. He increased his pace, bumping and banging people. He had to catch him. West had information that could be vital. After all, the tide of unrest was rising fast all over Europe, and becoming more violent. Many people, in the name of reform, were actually trying to overthrow government altogether and create an anarchy in which they imagined there would be some kind of equality of justice. Some were content with blood-soaked oratory; others preferred dynamite, or even bullets.

Special Branch knew of a current plot, but not yet the leaders behind it, or—more urgently—the target of their violence. West was to provide that, at risk of his own life—if his betrayal were known.

Where the devil was Gower? Pitt swiveled around once to see if he could spot him. He was nowhere visible in the sea of bobbing heads, bowler hats, caps, and bonnets. There was no time to look longer. Surely he wasn't still in the alley? What was wrong with the man? He was not much more than thirty. Had he been more than just knocked off balance? Was he injured?

West was up ahead, seizing a break in the traffic to cross back to the other side again. Three hansoms came past almost nose-to-tail. A cart and four clattered in the opposite direction. Pitt fumed on the edge of the curb. To go out into the roadway now would only get him killed.

A horse-drawn omnibus passed, then two heavily loaded wagons. More carts and a dray went in the other direction. Pitt had lost sight of West, and Gower had vanished into the air.

There was a brief holdup in traffic and Pitt raced across the road. Weaving in and out of the way of frustrated drivers, he only just missed being caught by a long, curling carriage whip. Someone yelled at him and he took no notice. He reached the opposite side and caught sight of West for an instant as he swung around a corner and made for another alley.

Pitt raced after him, but when he got there West had disappeared.

"Did you see a man with ginger hair?" Pitt demanded of a peddler with a tray of sandwiches. "Where did he go?"

"Want a sandwich?" the man asked with eyes wide. "Very good. Made this morning. Only tuppence."

Pitt fished frantically in his pocket; found string, sealing wax, a pocketknife, a handkerchief, and several coins. He gave the man a threepenny bit and took a sandwich. It felt soft and fresh, although right now he didn't care. "Which way?" he said harshly.

"That way." The man pointed into the deeper shadows of the alley.

Pitt began to run again, weaving a path through the piles of rubbish. A rat skittered from under his feet, and he all but fell over a drunken figure lying half out of a doorway. Somebody swung a punch at him; he lurched to one side, losing his balance for a moment, glimpsing West still ahead of him.

Now West disappeared again and Pitt had no idea which way he had gone. He tried one blind courtyard and alley after another. It seemed like endless, wasted moments before Gower joined him from one of the side alleyways.

"Pitt!" Gower clutched at his arm. "This way! Quickly." His fingers dug deep into Pitt's flesh, making him gasp with the sudden pain.

Together they ran forward, Pitt along the broken pavement beside the dark walls, Gower in the gutter, his boots sending up a spray of filthy water. Pace for pace, they went around the corner into the open entrance to a brickyard and saw a man crouching over something on the ground.

Gower let out a cry of fury and darted forward, half crossing in front of Pitt and tripping him up in his eagerness. They both fell heavily. Pitt was on his feet in time to see the crouched figure swing around for an instant, then scramble up and run as if for his life.

"Oh God!" Gower said, aghast, now also on his feet. "After him! I know who it is!"

Pitt stared at the heap on the ground: West's green jacket and bright hair. Blood streamed from his throat, staining his chest and already pooling dark on the stones underneath him. There was no way he could possibly be alive.

Gower was already pursuing the assassin. Pitt raced after him and this time his long strides caught up before they reached the road. "Who is it?" he demanded, almost choking on his own breath.

"Wrexham!" Gower hissed back. "We've been watching him for weeks."

Pitt knew the man, but only by name. There was a momentary break in the stream of vehicles. They darted across the road to go after Wrexham, who thank heaven was an easy figure to see. He was taller than average, and—despite the good weather—he was wearing a long, pale-colored scarf that swung in the air as he twisted and turned.

It flashed through Pitt's mind that it might be a weapon; it would not be hard to strangle a man with it.

They were on a crowded footpath now, and Wrexham dropped his pace. He almost sauntered, walking easily, swiftly, with loping strides, but perfectly casual. Could he be arrogant enough to imagine he had lost them so quickly? He certainly knew they had seen him, because he had swiveled around at Gower's cry, and then run as if for his life.

They were now walking at a steady pace, eastward toward Stepney and Limehouse. Soon the crowds would thin as they left the broader streets behind.

"If he goes into an alley, be careful," Pitt warned, now beside Gower, as if they were two tradesmen bound on a common errand. "He has a knife. He's too comfortable. He must know we're behind him."

Gower glanced at him sideways, his eyes wide for an instant. "You think he'll try and pick us off?"

"We practically saw him cut West's throat," Pitt replied, matching Gower stride for stride. "If we get him he'll hang. He must know that."

"I reckon he'll duck and hide suddenly, when he thinks we're taking it easy," Gower answered. "We'd better stay fairly close to him. Lose sight of him for a moment and he'll be gone for good."

Pitt agreed with a nod, and they closed the distance to Wrexham, who was still strolling ahead of them. Never once did he turn or look back.

Pitt found it chilling that a man could slit another's throat and see him bleed to death, then a few moments after walk through a crowd with outward unconcern, as if he were just one more pedestrian about some trivial daily business. What passion or inhumanity drove him? In the way he moved, the fluidity—almost grace—of his stride, Pitt could not detect even fear, let alone the conscience of a brutal murderer.

Wrexham wove in and out of the thinning crowd. Twice they lost sight of him.

"That way!" Gower gasped, waving his right hand. "I'll go left." He swerved around a window cleaner with a bucket of water, almost knocking the man over.

Pitt went the other way, into the north end of an alley. The sudden shadows momentarily made him blink, half blind. He saw movement and charged forward, but it was only a beggar shuffling out of a doorway. He swore under his breath and sprinted back to the street just in time to see Gower swiveling around frantically, searching for him.

"That way!" Gower called urgently and set off, leaving Pitt behind.

The second time it was Pitt who saw him first, and Gower who had to catch up. Wrexham had crossed the road just in front of a brewer's dray and was out of sight by the time Pitt and Gower were able to follow. It took them more than ten minutes to close on him without drawing attention. There were fewer people about, and two men running would have been highly noticeable. With fifty yards' distance between them, Wrexham could have outrun them too easily.

They were in Commercial Road East, now, in Stepney. If Wrexham did not turn they would be in Limehouse, perhaps the West India Dock Road. If they went that far they could lose him among the tangle of wharves with cranes, bales of goods, warehouses, and dock laborers. If he went down to one of the ferries he could be out of sight between the ships at anchor before they could find another ferry to follow him.

Ahead of them, as if he had seen them, Wrexham increased his pace, his long legs striding out, his jacket scarf flying.

Pitt felt a flicker of nervousness. His muscles were aching, his feet sore despite his excellent boots—his one concession to sartorial taste. Even well-cut jackets never looked right on him because he weighted the pockets with too many pieces of rubbish he thought he might need. His ties never managed to stay straight; perhaps he knotted them too tightly, or too loosely. But his boots were beautiful and immaculately cared for. Even though most of his work was of the mind, out-thinking, out-guessing, remembering, and seeing significance where others didn't, he still knew the importance of a policeman's feet. Some habits do not die. Before he had been forced out of the Metropolitan Police and Victor Narraway had taken him into Special Branch, he had walked enough miles to know the price of inattention to physical stamina, and to boots.

Suddenly Wrexham ran across the narrow road and disappeared down Gun Lane.

"He's going for the Limehouse Station!" Gower shouted, leaping out of the way of a cart full of timber as he dashed after him.

Pitt was on his heels. The Limehouse Station was on the Blackwall Railway, less than a hundred yards away. Wrexham could go in at least three possible directions from there and end up anywhere in the city.

But Wrexham kept moving, rapidly, right, past the way back up to the station. Instead, he turned left onto Three Colts Street, then swerved right onto Ropemaker's Field, still loping in an easy run.

Pitt was too breathless to shout, and anyway Wrexham was no more than fifteen yards ahead. The few men and one old washerwoman on the path scattered as the three running men passed them. Wrexham was going to the river, as Pitt had feared.

At the end of Ropemaker's Field they turned right again into Narrow Street, still running. They were only yards from the river's edge. The breeze was stiff off the water, smelling of salt and mud where the tide was low. Half a dozen gulls soared lazily in circles above a string of barges.

Wrexham was still ahead of them, moving less easily now, tiring. He passed the entrance to Limehouse Cut. Pitt figured that he must be making for Kidney Stairs, the stone steps down to the river, where, if they were lucky, he would find a ferry waiting. There were two more sets of stairs before the road curved twenty yards inland to Broad Street. At the Shadwell Docks there were more stairs again. He could lose his pursuers on any of them.

Gower gestured toward the river. "Steps!" he shouted, bending a moment and gasping to catch his breath. He gestured with a wild swing of his arm. Then he straightened up and began running again, a couple of strides ahead of Pitt.

Pitt could see a ferry coming toward the shore, the boatman pulling easily at the oars. He would get to the steps a moment or two after Wrexham—in fact Pitt and Gower would corner him nicely. Perhaps they could get the ferry to take them up to the Pool of London. He ached to sit down even for that short while.

Wrexham reached the steps and ran down them, disappearing as if he had slipped into a hole. Pitt felt an upsurge of victory. The ferry was still twenty yards from the spot where the steps would meet the water.

Gower let out a yell of triumph, waving his hand high.

They reached the top of the steps just as the ferry pulled away, Wrexham sitting in the stern. They were close enough to see the smile on his face as he half swiveled on the seat to gaze at them. Then he faced forward, speaking to the ferryman and pointing to the farther shore.

Pitt raced down the steps. His feet slithered on the wet stones. He waved his arms at the other ferry, the one they had seen. "Here! Hurry!" he shouted.

Gower shouted also, his voice high and desperate.

The ferryman increased his speed, throwing his full weight behind his oars, and in a matter of seconds had swung around next to the pier.

"Get in, gents," he said cheerfully. "Where to?"

"After that boat there," Gower gasped, choking on his own breath and pointing to the other ferry. "An extra half crown in it for you if you catch up with him before he gets up Horseferry Stairs."

Pitt landed in the boat behind him and immediately sat down so they could get under way. "He's not going to Horseferry," he pointed out. "He's going straight across. Look!"

"Lavender Dock?" Gower scowled, sitting in the seat beside Pitt. "What the hell for?"

"Shortest way across," Pitt replied. "Get up to Rotherhithe Street and away."

"Where to?"

"Nearest train station, probably. Or he might double back. Best place to get lost is among other people."

They were pulling well away from the dock now and slowly catching up with the other ferry.

There were fewer ships moored here, and they could make their way almost straight across. A string of barges was still fifty yards downstream, moving slowly against the tide. The wind off the water was colder. Without thinking what he was doing, Pitt hunched up and pulled his collar higher around his neck. It seemed like hours since he and Gower had burst into the brickyard and seen Wrexham crouched over West's blood-soaked body, but it was probably little more than ninety minutes. Their source of information about whatever plot West had known of was gone with his death.

He thought back to his last interview with Narraway, sitting in the office with the hot sunlight streaming through the window onto the piles of books and papers on the desk. Narraway's face had been intensely serious under its graying mane of hair, his eyes almost black. He had spoken of the gravity of the situation, the rise of the passion to reform Europe's old imperialism, violently if necessary. It was no longer a matter of a few sticks of dynamite, an assassination here and there. Rather, there were whispers of full governments overthrown by force.

"Some things need changing," Narraway had said with a wry bitterness. "No one but a fool would deny that there is injustice. But this would result in anarchy. God alone knows how wide this spreads, at least as far as France, Germany, and Italy, and by the sounds of it here in England as well."

Pitt had stared at him, seeing a sadness in the man he had never before imagined.

"This is a different breed, Pitt, and the tide of victory is with them now. But the violence . . ." Narraway had shaken his head, as if awakening himself. "We don't change that way in Britain, we evolve slowly. We'll get there, but not with murder, and not by force."

The wind was fading, the water smoother.

They were nearly at the south bank of the river. It was time to make a decision. Gower was looking at him, waiting.

Wrexham's ferry was almost at the Lavender Dock.

"He's going somewhere," Gower said urgently. "Do we want to get him now, sir—or see where he leads us? If we take him we won't know who's behind this. He won't talk, he's no reason to. We practically saw him kill West. He'll hang for sure." He waited, frowning.

"Do you think we can keep him in sight?" Pitt asked.

"Yes, sir." Gower did not hesitate.

"Right." The decision was clear in Pitt's mind. "Stay back then. We'll split up if we have to."

The ferry hung back until Wrexham had climbed up the narrow steps and all but disappeared. Then, scrambling to keep up, Pitt and Gower went after him.

They were careful to follow from more of a distance, sometimes together but more often with a sufficient space between them.

Yet Wrexham now seemed to be so absorbed in his own concerns that he never looked behind. He must have assumed he had lost them when he crossed the river. Indeed, they were very lucky that he had not. With the amount of waterborne traffic, he must have failed to realize that one ferry was dogging his path.

At the railway station there were at least a couple of dozen other people at the ticket counter.

"Better get tickets all the way, sir," Gower urged. "We don't want to draw attention to ourselves from not paying the fare."

Pitt gave him a sharp look, but stopped himself from making the remark on the edge of his tongue.

"Sorry," Gower murmured with a slight smile.

Once on the platform they remained close to a knot of other people waiting. Neither of them spoke, as if they were strangers to each other. The precaution seemed unnecessary. Wrexham barely glanced at either of them, nor at anyone else.

The first train was going north. It drew in and stopped. Most of the waiting passengers got on. Pitt wished he had a newspaper to hide his face and appear to take his attention. He should have thought of it before.

"I think I can hear the train . . . ," Gower said almost under his breath. "It should be to Southampton—eventually. We might have to change . . ." The rest of what he said was cut off by the noise of the engine as the train pulled in, belching steam. The doors flew open and passengers poured out.

Pitt struggled to keep Wrexham in sight. He waited until the last moment in case he should get out again and lose them, and, when he didn't, he and Gower boarded a carriage behind him.

"He could be going anywhere," Gower said grimly. His fair face was set in hard lines, his hair poking up where he had run his fingers through it. "One of us better get out at every station to see that he doesn't get off at the last moment."

"Of course," Pitt agreed.

"Do you think West really had something for us?" Gower went on. "He could have been killed for some other reason. A quarrel? Those revolutionaries are pretty volatile. Could have been a betrayal within the group? Even a rivalry for leadership?" He was watching Pitt intently, as if trying to read his mind.

"I know that," Pitt said quietly. He was by far the senior, and it was his decision to make. Gower would never question him on that. It was little comfort now, in fact rather a lonely thought. He remembered Narraway's certainty that there was something planned that would make the recent random bombings seem trivial. In February of last year, 1894, a French anarchist had tried to destroy the Royal Observatory at Greenwich with a bomb. Thank heaven he had failed. In June, President Carnot of France had been assassinated. In August, a man named Caserio had been executed for the crime. Everywhere there was anger and uncertainty in the air.

It was a risk to follow Wrexham, but to seize on an empty certainty was a kind of surrender. "We'll follow him," Pitt replied. "Do you have enough money for another fare, if we have to separate?"

Gower fished in his pocket, counted what he had. "As long as it isn't all the way to Scotland, yes, sir. Please God it isn't Scotland." He smiled with a twisted kind of misery. "You know in February they had the coldest temperature ever recorded in Britain? Nearly fifty degrees of frost! If the poor bastard let off a bomb to start a fire you could hardly blame him!"

"That was February, this is April already," Pitt reminded him. "Here, we're pulling into a station. I'll watch for Wrexham this time. You take the next."

"Yes, sir."

Pitt opened the door and was only just on the ground when he saw Wrexham getting out and hurrying across the platform to change trains for Southampton. Pitt turned to signal Gower and found him already out and at his elbow. Together they followed, trying not to be conspicuous by hurrying. They found seats, but separately for a while, to make sure Wrexham didn't double back and elude them, disappearing into London again.

But Wrexham seemed to be oblivious, as if he no longer even considered the possibility of being followed. He appeared completely carefree, and Pitt had to remind himself that Wrexham had followed a man in the East End only hours ago, then quite deliberately cut his throat and watched him bleed to death on the stones of a deserted brickyard.

"God, he's a cold-blooded bastard!" he said with sudden fury.

A man in pin-striped trousers on the seat opposite put down his newspaper and stared at Pitt with distaste, then rattled his paper loudly and resumed reading.

Gower smiled. "Quite," he said quietly. "We had best be extremely careful."

One or the other of them got out briefly at every stop, just to make certain Wrexham did not leave this train, but he stayed until they finally pulled in at Southampton.

Gower looked at Pitt, puzzled. "What can he do in Southampton?" he said. They hurried along the platform to keep pace with Wrexham, then past the ticket collector and out into the street.

The answer was not long in coming. Wrexham took an omnibus directly toward the docks, and Pitt and Gower had to race to jump onto the step just as it pulled away. Pitt almost bumped into Wrexham, who was still standing. Deliberately he looked away from Gower. They must be more careful. Neither of them was particularly noticeable alone. Gower was fairly tall, lean, his hair long and fair, but his features were a trifle bony, stronger than average. An observant person would remember him. Pitt was taller, perhaps less than graceful, and yet he moved easily, comfortable with himself. His hair was dark and permanently untidy. One front tooth was a little chipped, but visible only when he smiled. It was his steady, very clear gray eyes that people did not forget.

Wrexham would have to be extraordinarily preoccupied not to be aware of seeing them in London, and now again here in Southampton, especially if they were together. Accordingly, Pitt moved on down the inside of the bus to stand well away from Gower, and pretended to be watching the streets as they passed, as if he were taking careful note of his surroundings.

As he had at least half expected, Wrexham went all the way to the dockside. Without speaking to Gower, Pitt followed well behind their quarry. He trusted that Gower was off to the side, as far out of view as possible.

Wrexham bought a ticket on a ferry to St. Malo, across the channel on the coast of France. Pitt bought one as well. He hoped fervently that Gower had sufficient money to get one too, but the only thing worse than ending up alone in France, trying to follow Wrexham without help, would be to lose the man altogether.

He boarded the ferry, a smallish steamship called the *Laura*, and remained within sight of the gangplank. He needed to see if Gower came aboard, but more important to make sure that Wrexham did not get off again. If Wrexham were aware of Pitt and Gower it would be a simple thing to go ashore and hop the next train back to London.

Pitt was leaning on the railing with the sharp salt wind in his face when he heard footsteps behind him. He swung around, then was annoyed with himself for betraying such obvious alarm.

Gower was a yard away, smiling. "Did you think I was going to push you over?" he said amusedly.

Pitt swallowed back his temper. "Not this close to the shore," he replied. "I'll watch you more closely out in mid-channel!"

Gower laughed. "Looks like a good decision, sir. Following him this far could get us a real idea of who his contacts are in Europe. We might even find a clue as to what they're planning."

Pitt doubted it, but it was all they had left now. "Perhaps. But we mustn't be seen together. We're lucky he hasn't recognized us so far. He would have if he weren't so abominably arrogant."

Gower was suddenly very serious, his fair face grim. "I think whatever he has planned is so important his mind is completely absorbed in it. He thought he lost us in Ropemaker's Field. Don't forget we were in a totally separate carriage on the train."

"I know. But he must have seen us when we were chasing him. He ran," Pitt pointed out. "I wish at least one of us had a jacket to change. But in April, at sea, without them we'd be even more conspicuous." He looked at Gower's coat. They were not markedly different in size. Even if they did no more than exchange coats, it would alter both their appearances slightly.

As if reading this thought, Gower began to slip off his coat. He passed it over, and took Pitt's from his outstretched hand.

Pitt put on Gower's jacket. It was a little tight across the chest.

With a rueful smile Gower emptied the pockets of Pitt's jacket, which now sat a little loosely on his shoulders. He passed over the notebook, handkerchief, pencil, loose change, half a dozen other bits and pieces, then the wallet with Pitt's papers of identity and money.

Pitt similarly passed over all Gower's belongings.

Gower gave a little salute. "See you in St. Malo," he said, turning on his heel and walking away without looking back, a slight swagger in his step. Then he stopped and turned half toward Pitt, smiling. "I'd keep away from the railing if I were you, sir."

Pitt raised his hand in a salute, and resumed watching the gangway.

PHOTO: © JONATHAN HULME

ANNE PERRY is the bestselling author of two acclaimed series set in Victorian England: the Charlotte and Thomas Pitt novels, including *Treachery at Lancaster Gate* and *The Angel Court Affair*, and the William Monk novels, including *Revenge in a Cold River* and *Corridors of the Night*. She is also the author of a series of five World War I novels, as well as fifteen holiday novels, most recently *A Christmas Return*, and a historical novel *The Sheen on the Silk*, set in the Ottoman Empire. Anne Perry lives in Los Angeles and Scotland.

anneperry.co.uk

To inquire about booking Anne Perry for a speaking engagement, please contact the Penguin Random House Speakers Bureau at speakers@penguinrandomhouse.com

Printed in the United States
by Baker & Taylor Publisher Services